Suzanne Wright lives in England with her husband and two children. When she's not spending time with her family, she's writing, reading or doing her version of housework – sweeping the house with a look.

She's worked in a pharmaceutical company, at a Disney store, at a primary school as a voluntary teaching assistant, at the RSCPA, and has a First Class Honours degree in Psychology and Identity Studies.

As to her interests, she enjoys reading, writing, reading, writing (sort of eat, sleep, write, repeat), spending time with her family, movie nights with her sisters and playing with her two Bengal kittens.

To connect with Suzanne online:

Website: www.suzannewright.co.uk
Facebook: www.facebook.com/-
suzannewrightfanpage
Twitter: www.twitter.com/suz_wright
Blog: www.suzannewrightsblog.blogspot.co.uk

THE DARK IN YOU SERIES

SUZANNE WRIGHT
OMENS

PIATKUS

PIATKUS

First published in Great Britain in 2020 by Piatkus

3 5 7 9 10 8 6 4 2

A CIP catalogue record for this book
is available from the British Library.

ISBN 978-0-349-41633-5

Printed and bound in Great Britain by
Clays Ltd, Elcograf S.p.A.

Papers used by Piatkus are from well-managed forests
and other responsible sources.

Piatkus
An imprint of
Little, Brown Book Group
Carmelite House
50 Victoria Embankment
London EC4Y 0DZ

An Hachette UK Company
www.hachette.co.uk

www.littlebrown.co.uk

For everyone who was so understanding about the release date being set back—thank you for being so awesome.

CHAPTER ONE

Khloé Wallis downed her shot and then slammed her glass on the table. "All I'm saying is, Jack and Jill's parents were plain mean to send the kids *up a hill* to get a tub of water."

"A pail," said Raini, her amber eyes a little glassy.

Khloé frowned at the succubus. "What?"

"A *pail* of water."

"What's a pail?"

"Duh. A pan."

Awkwardly adjusting her impressive cleavage, Devon shook her head. "No, it's a bucket. I think. Could be a vase. I like vases. They're pretty. Sometimes."

Khloé lazily flicked her hand at the hellcat. "Whatever. The point is . . . if Jack's parents had gotten up off their lazy asses, he wouldn't have broken his leg."

"Crown," said Raini.

Khloé blinked. "What?"

"Jack broke his crown, not his leg."

"Semantics, dude, semantics." Khloé bopped her head to the music, feeling all warm and fuzzy and tingly. Maybe some wouldn't go on a girls' night out if they had to work the next morning, but demons didn't require much sleep. In fact, they could go days without it. Which was super, because she *loved* hitting the Xpress bar with her girls. They always had a blast.

It was an upscale hotspot within the Las Vegas Underground, which was a subterranean, demonic playground of sorts. It had *everything*—bars, clubs, rodeo, casinos, racing stadiums, the whole shebang. And as her cousin, Harper, was mated to the billionaire who owned it, they all had VIP access to their favorite spots—including the Xpress bar.

Happy freaking days.

Having grown up in the same lair, the four women had been close friends since they were kids. That was probably why they worked so well together. Their tattoo studio had become even more popular since they'd relocated to the Underground.

Of course, part of the studio's appeal was Harper. People wanted to say they'd been tattooed by the powerful Prime. She and Knox were the only mated Primes in the world—demons didn't like to share power.

Khloé wasn't artistic like her girls, so she left the tattoos and piercings to them. She was happy working as their receptionist, and she was damn good at her position, even if she did say so herself.

It wasn't a typical job for a demon, considering they tended to seek out positions that provided them with control, power, challenges, and respect. Many were lawyers, entrepreneurs, stockbrokers, politicians, bankers, police officers, surgeons, people in the media, or CE-fucking-Os.

Khloé liked power as much as the next demon, but she didn't crave it. She liked "the smaller things in life." The strange.

The quirky. The fun. Which was why . . . "God, I badly want a bullshit."

Harper slanted her head, making her sleek dark hair tumble over her shoulder. "What?"

"A dog that's half bulldog, half Shih Tzu. I'd call it Winnie."

"Why Winnie?"

"Because then I could sing 'Winnie the Bullshit' to him."

Devon's face went all soft and she put a hand to her chest. "Aw, that would be so cute. I can just imagine little Winnie, barking and running and giving us his paw, like a good little bullshit. I think Tanner would *love* one," she added, referring to her mate.

Weaving slightly in her seat, Harper snickered at Khloé. "You're too OCD to cope with a dog peeing and shitting and shedding hairs all over your house."

"We've been over this," said Khloé. "I'm not OCD. I just value order and precipitation."

"*Precision.*"

"That, too." Khloé frowned at her glass. "Who the hell drank my drink?"

"You did, dufus," said Devon.

Khloé felt her nose wrinkle. "You sure? My mind says no."

Raini leaned forward, making her striking blonde hair fall around her face like a curtain; the dusky pink highlights glimmered under the lighting. "Hey, want to know a secret?"

Devon's cat-green eyes gleamed. "Always."

"You didn't hear this from me," began Raini, "but I think we're smashed."

"Really? Damn. I just wanted to get buzzed," said Devon. "I like being buzzed. But I don't like buzzing sounds. Makes me think of bees. Bees sting you. That's just mean and— hey, Raini, you're not listening to me. You gotta listen, because I don't know sign language. Ooh, we should all learn sign language!"

Harper's eyes widened. "I'm totally up for that."

"*And* we should get more shots," said Khloé. "I want shots. Anyone else want shots? Okay, shots it is." She went to stand, but Harper grabbed her arm.

"No more shots for you, missy," said the sphinx. "You're already blitzed. No, don't tell me you're not. You're so gone, you didn't even notice that Keenan's been glaring at you for the past half hour—he's standing at the other end of the VIP section with Knox, Tanner, and Levi."

Oh, Khloé had noticed. She *always* noticed Keenan Ripley. It was hard to miss over six feet of sculpted muscle, sinful hotness, and uber-masculinity. Especially when it was usually glowering at you. What fun.

As an incubus, sex appeal was literally encoded in his freaking DNA. His compelling, hooded eyes were a striking shade of blue that made Khloé think of shimmering steel. They *commanded* your attention. Snared your focus. Made all your senses zing to life. And, for most people, they sent a powerful need rushing through your body with the force of a storm.

Hypersexual beings with insatiable appetites, incubi radiated a preternatural allure that enchanted humans and demons alike. That allure drew their "prey" closer. It assailed their bodies with molten lust, muddied their thoughts, and subtly lifted their inhibitions.

She'd always been resistant to preternatural allure, so his mojo didn't work on her. But that wasn't to say that he didn't make all her feminine parts do a mighty cheer. *Everything* about him was inviting—his perfectly symmetrical face, his carnal mouth, and his short blond hair that glistened like flecks of gold. His smooth, sleepy, post-orgasm voice felt like fingertips teasingly trailing over her skin.

His crooked, boyish "you can trust me" smile could loosen any girl's panty-elastic, but it didn't give him an approachable vibe. Not when he had "bad boy" stamped all over him. Yeah, Keenan was by no means harmless. He was a cunning, ruthless, cynical motherfucker who had an *incredibly* short fuse.

He was also packing some *serious* heat in his jeans. She'd gotten a glimpse of his disproportionately large Johnson during one of her drunken mishaps.

She wanted to dislike him. Wanted to dislike that cocky "I know who I am and where I fit in the world" swagger. Wanted to find that blatant danger he oozed a complete turn-off. Wanted to be immune to the alpha-male confidence that seemed ingrained in his very being.

There was no such luck, apparently.

Her demon liked him. Liked that he was a guy who never gave ground, never sought anyone's approval, or ever showed weakness—that kind of strength and personal power was an aphrodisiac for her demon. It wanted to get *all* up in his business.

Every breed of demon had a dualism to the soul. There was nothing easy about sharing your soul with a psychopathic predator that felt no empathy, remorse, guilt, or love. Especially when said predator could take control of your body whenever it pleased, making your eyes bleed to black. Thankfully, for the most part, Khloé was pretty in sync with her demon.

Feeling the weight of Keenan's gaze, she flicked him a haughty look that made his eyes blaze. Ha. She did like to prick at that volatile temper of his. Well, if she couldn't fuck him, she could certainly fuck *with* him.

"Oh yeah, Keenan's throwing you glowers from hell, all right," said Devon, gathering her long, ultraviolet curls in one hand so she could fan her nape.

"In my humble opinion, Khlo," Raini began, "the dude likes

you. And I mean, *likes* you likes you. But I don't think he likes that he *likes* you likes you. And I don't like that he doesn't like that he *likes* you likes you."

Devon raised her glass to Raini. "Couldn't have said it better myself."

"Seriously, what do you think his deal is?" asked Raini. "It'd better not be that he looks down on your family, Khloé."

"He wouldn't be the only one," Khloé pointed out. Her family was notorious for being what her grandmother and Prime, Jolene, liked to call "multi-talented." Which, roughly translated, meant they were masters at all kinds of illegal shit—particularly forgery, embezzlement, and hacking into bank accounts. And they were utterly unashamed about it.

"I don't think it's that," said Harper. "I mean, I was a Wallis before I mated Knox. Keenan never made any shitty remarks about our family to me."

"Doesn't matter either way," said Khloé. He might be a decadent, drool-worthy enticement, but . . . "I already have one alcoholic in my life—I don't need another." .

Demons were predisposed to developing addictions, so Khloé knew plenty of compulsive gamblers, drug addicts, adrenaline junkies, and alcoholics. Sadly, her mother was one of the latter.

Penelope drank to cope, to destress, to relax, to sleep, to calm down, to perk up, to pretty much *anything*. She hadn't always been that way. It wasn't until Khloé and her twin brother, Ciaran, were teenagers that it all went to shit.

Harper nudged her with her elbow. "Knox says he's sure that Keenan could easily give up drinking if he really wanted."

Khloé sighed. "Yeah, yeah, so you've said before. But no one carries around a flask of vodka if they're not dependent on alcohol, so I ain't buying his denials. I will, however, buy us shots.

Seriously, *we need shots*. I'll go get— Oh, I love this song! Girls, this is our jam! We gotta dance."

"*Not on the table, Khloé, not on the table!*"

*

"You're sure you don't want to hear what Thea has to say?" Knox asked Keenan, watching him with that piercing gaze. "Not that I believe you *should*. I was glad when you cut all ties with her, you know that. She's not a bad person, but she's never been a healthy presence in your life. I just want to be sure that you won't second-guess your decision later. I don't want this playing on your conscience."

Keenan almost snorted. "My conscience isn't that well developed," he pointed out. "I don't know why she'd suddenly reach out to me via you, and I can honestly say I'm not the least bit curious about it. That won't change. She's walked in and out of my life too many times, always giving me the same spiel, never meaning a fucking word of it. I'm done listening to it. I told her that the last time she came knocking at my door." That had been six years ago, and the memory made his demon clench its fists.

Keenan had first met Thea after he'd been dumped at Ramsbrook House, a home for orphaned demonic children. Knox and the other sentinels had also resided there throughout most of their childhood.

Keenan had grown to care for her and, looking back, he could see that he'd felt challenged by her sky-high mental walls; he'd wanted to smash through them. When they'd all left Ramsbrook as adults, Keenan had asked her to come with him. But scarred from her own experiences with lairs, Thea had refused, intent on flitting from place to place, irrespective of the dangers that came with being a stray demon.

She'd reappeared in his life every now and then, but she

never stuck around for longer than a few weeks, despite whatever promises she made. She also never told him when she was leaving. She'd quite simply disappear, like he wasn't even worthy of a goodbye.

"She evidently heard you loud and clear when you said you were done, because she didn't try to contact you directly this time," said Levi, a reaper who was not only a sentinel but Knox's bodyguard.

"Smart move on her part."

"I don't think she ever *wanted* to hurt you, Keenan," added Levi. "I think she was just too messed up by her past to put down roots. She needed to feel free—especially after being stuck in the orphanage for so long."

It was true that such an upbringing could leave a person with plenty of issues. Keenan couldn't say he'd walked out of Ramsbrook a well-adjusted person. The militant, tyrannical staff there had thoroughly enjoyed throwing their weight around. They'd punished the slightest indiscretion, and those punishments had been harsh.

They'd been so domineering in their efforts to control the children that they'd pushed for mental submission—something Keenan had refused to give them, so his time there hadn't been plain sailing.

He didn't allow his past to massively affect his present, though. Nor did he dwell on his childhood much—after all, his life would be very different now if he hadn't met Knox and the other sentinels.

"It's sad that she didn't get her shit together until it was too late," said Tanner, a hellhound and fellow sentinel.

"Things turned out well for her in the end," Keenan reminded him. "She has a mate and son now."

"I poked into her life when I heard she wanted to speak with you," said Levi. "She recently split with her mate. He cheated on her. I'd feel bad for her if she hadn't betrayed your trust countless times. Karma comes for us all, I guess."

"In that case, each of us is fucked," quipped Keenan.

Tanner let out a soft snicker. "You're not wrong there."

"You're *certain* you don't wish to speak with her, Keenan?" Knox asked.

"I'm certain," replied Keenan. "She has nothing to say that I could want to hear." She was part of his past, and he intended for her to remain there.

"All right," said Knox. "I'll be sure to communicate that to her."

Satisfied, Keenan nodded.

Knox's gaze flitted to the table at which his mate sat. His lips thinned. "I think it's safe to say that Harper's going to crash pretty heavily when she gets home."

Keenan glanced her way, but his eyes unerringly slid to the female imp on her left. His body tightened. His hands fisted. His cock stirred—it always did around Khloé Wallis.

She wasn't conventionally beautiful, but there was something very bewitching about her. It was in the way she spoke, laughed, walked, and embraced life so fully. As sparkly and bubbly as a chute of champagne, Khloé was her very own party.

Her eyes were as gray and mysterious as smoke, and there was an ever-present glint of mischief in their depths. She was small and slender and had the smoothest-looking olive skin. He often found his gaze dropping to those perky breasts that made him think of apples, just as he often found himself watching that tight little ass as she walked.

His gut clenched whenever her bow-shaped mouth curled into a lazy, devilish, "I know something you don't" smile. It made you want to be in on the secret; made you want to smile back. Made you want to feast on that mouth while tangling your fingers in the sleek, midnight-black hair she often tied in a high, unruly swirl.

If anyone could write a handbook on not giving a single rat's ass, it would be Khloé. She had her own special brand of logic, was a magnet for trouble, had no sense of self-preservation, and could stir shit in an empty room.

Technically, she should annoy the fuck out of him. Particularly since she seemed to have made it her life's mission to be a pain in his ass. She teased him, prodded him, riled him—all of which she seemed to take delight in doing.

And yet, he liked the fucking nutcase. More, he wanted her. He'd wanted her for years. He'd told himself over and over that it was best to keep his distance; that she wasn't for him; that it would make him an asshole to run the risk of hurting her. All the while, he could feel himself weakening.

He never would have thought he could be so drawn to someone like her. But she fascinated him. Beckoned him. Made him laugh when little else did anymore.

"You gonna glare at Khloé all night?" asked Levi, his voice laced with amusement.

"I'm not glaring at her, I'm watching her . . . because it's only a matter of time before she does something stupid, and then I'll have to wade in."

"What's wrong with her having a good time?"

"Nothing, if she didn't always do crazy shit when smashed. The last time I gave her drunken ass a ride home, she wanted to go skinny dipping. I said no. Then she wanted to go to church. I said no. Then she wanted to break into the zoo to 'see some fucking penguins.' Again, I said no. What else would I say?"

Tanner chuckled. "In case you've forgotten, she's an imp. They specialize in irritating people. But I don't think you'd get half so frustrated with Khloé if you weren't fighting how much you want her. All that pent-up sexual need must be messing with your head."

It was messing with *everything*—his concentration, his dreams, his resolve to not give into it. Still, he said, "I don't get involved with women who mean something to the people in my life—you know that. Khloé is the cousin of one of my Primes. It's not wise to shit where you eat." Which was why Keenan also never got involved with women from his lair.

"You think we can't sense how close you are to breaking that rule for her?" asked Tanner. "What's holding you back? Does your demon dislike her?"

Keenan snorted inwardly. The dark entity within him was cold to the bone and had time for very few people, but it wanted to outright own Khloé Wallis. It wanted to collect this bold, vibrant creature—there was simply no one like her. Who didn't like to collect the unusual?

"My demon likes her just fine," said Keenan.

"If you're worried that things might be awkward between you afterward, there's no need," Knox cut in. "As my mate says, Khloé doesn't do 'awkward.' And she's not likely to want more than sex. She doesn't seem to be looking for a relationship any more than you are. In fact, she seems to quickly tire of any guy she dates."

Yeah, Keenan had noticed that. He couldn't deny that it pleased him. He could be a selfish, possessive fucker when it came to her.

"Seriously, what's really holding you back?" pushed Tanner.

Keenan rubbed a hand over his jaw. "You know what powers I have as an incubus, right?"

The hellhound nodded. "You can infuse lust into people, implant thoughts and images into their minds, and incite sexual desires that only you can satisfy. You're in total control of their lust and pleasure, which means you can heighten and prolong orgasms while feeding on their sexual energy."

"Right," said Keenan. "I'm also in complete control of my own lust and arousal, so I don't get hard unless I want to . . . or, at least, I didn't until *she* came along."

Tanner's brows shot up, and Levi let out a low whistle.

"You're saying you can't control how your body reacts to her?" asked Knox.

"That's exactly what I'm saying." Keenan had heard of such a thing happening to other incubi, but it was a rare phenomenon—one he hadn't thought he'd experience. "It's like she's living, breathing Viagra to me."

Not once in all Keenan's centuries of existence had he ever felt so . . . aware of another person. Whenever Khloé's attention settled over him, it was like an electric shock to his senses. The sexual chemistry that pulsed between them was as dizzying as it was intoxicating, and it never failed to make his dick jerk to life.

"Surely it's refreshing to naturally experience a normal bodily reaction," said Levi.

Yes, it was, but . . . "I don't trust it. Not even a little bit."

"And you don't like that she makes your infamous self-discipline go right out the window," Knox guessed.

"No, I don't," Keenan admitted. He liked to be in control of his world. Liked consistency, certainty, and predictability—things he'd lacked as a young child when he'd lived on the streets with his mother; things he'd continued to lack during the years he'd spent in Ramsbrook House.

On leaving the shithole, he'd sworn that no one would have that level of control over him again. He obeyed his Primes, but he didn't follow them blindly. He was very much his own man. But Khloé . . . yeah, she had power over him.

It felt alien. Wrong. Uncomfortable. It felt as if she'd turned his own body against him; as if she'd stripped aspects of his gift from him. "At first, I thought she was doing it on purpose. I thought she had an ability that allowed her to overpower mine. But it's clear that she has no idea she's doing . . . whatever it is she's doing."

"Maybe she's not *doing* anything," suggested Levi. "Maybe this is just as much out of her control as it is yours."

Possibly. Although it spooked the absolute shit out of Keenan on a number of levels that he couldn't control his body around her, he could admit that he was beyond curious to know what it would be like to have sex while *not* in complete control of his body. He'd never had that. But tumbling Khloé into bed would be no easy thing anyway. She was attracted to him, but she was also convinced he was an alcoholic and, as such, wanted nothing to do with him.

"Let's not pretend you won't pursue her sooner or later," said Tanner. "It's going to happen. Just go with it. Enjoy it. There's no need to overthink—"

"*Not on the table, Khloé, not on the table!*"

Hearing Harper's shout, Keenan looked to see the little imp jump onto the table with a whoop of sheer joy. Then she was all sexual confidence and erotic power—fluidly swaying, dipping, and working her hips like a fucking lap dancer. And his dick went hard.

Where the hell had she learned to move like that?

A group of men circled the table, cheering her on and whistling—much like Devon and Raini were doing. Keenan was pretty sure his blood pressure *soared*.

"Let me ask you one question," said Knox. "If Khloé crossed the 'casual' line with a guy, how would you feel about it?"

Anger flared through him so hot and fast, Keenan ground his teeth. "It would be her business."

"Yeah, it would. But can you be sure you'd let that guy live?"

Keenan didn't speak. The honest to God's truth? No, he couldn't be sure. Which must have been apparent on his face, because Knox gave him a knowing look.

"Then maybe you should shove all your reservations aside and act before you miss your chance," suggested Knox. "I'm not saying you should dive into a relationship. Take it slow, if that's what you think both of you need. If you go too fast, you'll spook her anyway."

Hearing more loud whistles, Keenan looked back at the table on which she was dancing. Oh, she'd gathered quite a crowd. And now he needed to end this shit fast.

Keenan made his way across the large space, never once moving his eyes from her. He *couldn't* move his eyes from her. Every captivating twitch of her hips and delightful jiggle of her breasts was like a stroke to his cock. And probably to the dick of every man watching her – the very thought made a vein in his temple throb.

He shouldered his way through the catcalling crowd and moved to stand in front of her table. It took her a few moments to notice him. Did she stop dancing? No. She flashed him a sultry, wicked smile that he felt in his balls.

"Don Juan, how's it going?"

Don Juan? Keenan sighed. "Come on, time for you to go home."

"But I'm getting jiggy with— Hey!" Khloé pouted when he lifted and set her on the floor. "Dude, you are *such* a Debbie Downer. I was—"

"Seconds away from stripping off your clothes," he finished. "No, don't even deny it."

"Why? You deny you're an alcoholic with a gargantuan dick."

He briefly closed his eyes. He wouldn't lose it. He wouldn't.

"Just get your purse so we can leave."

It should have been simple for him, Knox, and the other sentinels to move along four drunk women. It wasn't. Harper and Khloé fled to the restroom, saying they were desperate to pee. Devon started frantically searching for her jacket, despite Tanner's insistence that she hadn't brought one. Raini asked them to leave her to sleep in the booth, claiming she'd only "slow them down."

Finally, they all got the fuck out of the bar and headed down the "strip." Most of the bars, clubs, casinos, and restaurants had no front wall, allowing people to see what was going on inside the venues. There was mostly a lot of drinking, dancing, eating, and brawling.

A quick upward elevator ride later, they'd ascended to the basement of a popular nightclub that Knox had built to disguise the entrance of the Underground from humans.

Outside, Levi escorted Knox and Harper to their Bentley while Tanner took Devon—who was barely awake—straight to his Audi.

Keenan ushered Khloé and Raini toward his car. The women lived reasonably close to each other, so it made sense for him to give them both a ride. Taking a drunk Khloé *anywhere* was never an easy feat, but he liked to be sure she got home safely.

Having ushered the two females into the vehicle, he closed the rear passenger door, hopped into the front seat, and drove to north Las Vegas. That was when Khloé's idea of "fun" began.

She drew satanic-looking symbols on Raini's face with red lipstick. She sang Afroman's "Because I Got High" in a Smurf-like voice. She asked Keenan to take her to an Amish community so she could "see some Amish dudes—they might be cute." When he refused, she proclaimed him an Amish cockblocker.

He growled. "Have you lost your mind?"

"Long ago." Khloé tilted her head. "I miss it sometimes."

Certifiable. The woman was a certifiable nutcase.

Finally, they arrived at Raini's house. Only when the succubus was safely inside with the front door locked behind her did Keenan then drive Khloé home.

As he steered her up the path with his hand on her back, he sighed. "Could you stop singing 'Amish Paradise'?"

"You gotta love Weird Al Yankovic," she said. "Hey, why do you think humans sterilize lethal injections?"

"I don't know." He plucked her keys out of her clutch, unlocked the front door, and then shepherded her inside.

"Farewell, Don Juan." She mule-kicked the door, almost slamming it in his face. He whipped up his hand, caught it before it could close, and shoved it open.

"You forgot this." Returning her keys to her clutch, he tossed it at her feet just as she sat on the hallway bench. "Lock up behind me."

She didn't respond, preoccupied with trying to remove her shoes. Honestly, it hurt to watch her awkwardly fumble with the ankle straps. Sighing, Keenan stepped inside and closed the door. He crouched in front of her and gently batted her hands away. "I'll do it."

This close, he had no choice but to breathe in her scent. She smelled like marshmallows and honeysuckle, edible and far too fucking tempting.

He carefully worked to undo the left shoe-strap. His fingers grazed her warm, petal-soft skin, and he almost pulled back as a shot of static electricity surged through him. It was sudden. Irrepressible. Jarring.

Being so near to her was a sweet agony. His palms itched to stroke and explore and bite her smooth skin. His demon urged him to spread both her legs wide and taste—

Keenan cursed silently. Refusing to be a slave to the sexual connection that seemed determined to bind them, he forced his mind back to the task at hand. He removed her shoe, set it aside, and moved on to the next.

"Your schlong went hard when you saw me dancing, didn't it?"

And his fingers slipped right off the strap.

She laughed, low and smoky, not in the least bit daunted by the glare he shot her. "Oh, come on, I'm just messing with ya, Keenan. I know incubi only get a hard-on if they want to."

He could only shake his head. She had no idea what she did to him. No idea that she seemed to have more control over his body than he did. He slipped off her second shoe, tossed it aside, and then stood.

"On a serious note, though," she began, rising to her feet, "does it hurt to walk when you're hard? Because that monster in your jeans has to weigh a few pounds."

His patience gone, Keenan went nose to nose with her. "Swear to Christ, Khloé, if you mention my cock one more time, I'm going to thrust it inside you and fuck you so hard you'll be screaming."

*

Goosebumps swept across Khloé's skin as the atmosphere snapped taut. She stared at him, at a loss for words – a rare occurrence in her world.

Her body, well, it just lit up. Tingled and buzzed and hummed. Her mouth went dry. Her pulse skittered. Need pooled low in her stomach, raw and wicked.

Yeah, the gorgeous bastard rang every sexual bell she had.

The eyes boldly holding her own smoldered with something dark and hot. It was a stare that said, "I could pound into you all night and ruin you for other men."

Hell, she didn't doubt it. If he could reduce her brain to mush with just the heat and intensity of his stare, he'd most definitely be a goddamn rock star in bed.

Finally, his eyes released hers. They dropped to her mouth, and he swallowed hard. Then that broody gaze drifted lower and lower, peeling off her clothing, tracing every line and curve, stripping her of her defenses, making pure heat ripple through her body.

Hell, she'd just gotten laid *by his eyes*. It was a rush and a tease.

He needed to say something. Or she did. The tension just kept on building and building . . . until she wanted to scream, and her nerves were on the verge of exploding.

Seriously, *someone* needed to say *something*.

The only thing that eased the sensual torture was the comforting knowledge that she wasn't the only one suffering. His breathing was no steadier than her own.

There was a possessive glint in his gaze that pleased her demon. But unlike the entity, Khloé knew better than to think he'd ever act on any possessiveness he might feel. If he had any intention of doing so, he'd have done it by now.

Digging deep for some element of calm, she went for blasé. "Sorry, alcoholics aren't my type."

A muscle in his cheek flexed. "I'm not addicted to alcohol. I drink because I want to. And, you know, you're pretty judgmental about drinking for someone who gets blitzed almost every weekend."

"Ah, but I don't do it to escape or function. I do it to have fun with my friends – that's different."

"I could give up drinking any time."

She snickered. "For maybe a day, sure. But for longer? Nu-uh."

Cunning flashed in his eyes. "Yeah? How about we test your little theory?" He folded his arms. "I'll go one full week without alcohol – I won't have so much as a sip of it."

"Sure," she drawled, openly skeptical.

"I'm serious."

"You truly think you can do that?"

"Yes. And if I'm right . . ." His gaze darkened, focusing on her so intensely it made her scalp prickle. "I get to feed from you."

Khloé's heartbeat stuttered. "Feed from me?"

"I won't touch you, but I *will* use my powers to make you come for me. Hard."

Well, hell. Sexual energy was like an aphrodisiac to incubi. They built up their prey's need without even physically touching them, blanketing them with pleasure-inducing pheromones, and then they fed off that energy.

She'd seen it happen once at a club. An incubus had done nothing more than pin a woman close to his body, breathing in every breath that left her lungs as she writhed and moaned in his arms.

"Not willing to take the risk that you're wrong?" asked Keenan.

Her smile dripped with pity. "Sweetie, did you hit your head? You'd *never* manage to abstain from drinking for a week." It was laughable that he'd think differently.

"With the right motivation, a man can do anything."

She didn't see how he'd find the idea of feeding from her *that* motivational. He might be attracted to her, but that would never be enough to fight his craving for a drink. There was no *way* he'd win this little bet, and she saw no reason why she couldn't capitalize on that—she was an imp, after all.

"Okay. But if you *do* cave like a loser—which you will, my friend—you have to be my slave for the day," she said. "That means cooking, cleaning, doing my laundry, chauffeuring me around, and doing pretty much whatever else I want you to do." She thought he'd balk at that. He didn't.

"All right," he *far* too easily agreed. Like a dumbass.

If he was anyone else, she would have asked how she could be sure he'd stick to his part of the deal, but Keenan had way too much integrity to go back on his word—something her relatives would never understand.

"So the bet is on?" There was a definite dare in his tone.

Khloé lifted her chin. "It's on, but only because I know you'll cave and reach for the bottle—or, in your case, the flask in your jacket."

His eyes bled to black as his demon rose to the fore, and the air temperature dropped a few degrees. The entity stared at her, its black gaze cold, unblinking, and . . . assessing.

Her own demon stirred, curious about the entity in front of them. It was much older than Khloé would have guessed, but she couldn't sense just how old. What she could sense was that it was super fucking dangerous.

"Be sure you can stick to the terms of the wager," it said, its tone flat and utterly without emotion, "because you will lose."

The amount of confidence in that statement was a little unnerving. "You can't even be sure your incubus powers will work on me." She was resistant to the incubi mojo, so there was a possibility that she was also immune to—

A delicious, spicy, aphrodisiac scent surrounded her. The air turned warm and muggy, like sultry summer heat. She sucked in a breath as that heat swept through her entire body.

Lust twisted her insides. Her nipples pebbled. Her breasts began to ache. Her clit started to throb.

The corner of the demon's mouth kicked up. "They'll work."

"Stop," she clipped. To her surprise, it did. The spicy scent dissipated, the air cooled, and the heat within her dwindled.

The demon's black eyes flicked to the hallway clock. "It is 1:05am. The countdown begins now. This time next Monday, I

will come for you. And I will take what you owe me. Be ready."
It then subsided, and she found herself staring into familiar
blue eyes.

Khloé inhaled deeply. "Your power sure does pack a punch."
He could make her come like a freight train without even laying
a finger on her, but he didn't have a *prayer* of winning their little
wager. His demon might be arrogant enough to think it could
hold out, but the entities often were so supremely self-assured.

Keenan skimmed the tip of his finger down the side of her
face, leaving a trail of fire in his wake. "That was only a tiny
demonstration of what I can do to you."

He called that *tiny*? For the first time, unease slithered through
her. She swallowed, her eyes flickering.

A smile tugged at one corner of his mouth. "Ah, so you're
finally coming to see what you've gotten yourself into. Good.
But it's a little late now."

His gaze dropped to her lips again, glittering with a dark
need that answered her own. She thought he might kiss her. He
didn't. He took a single step back, blanking his expression with
an enviable ease.

"A week, Khloé." It was a warning and a promise. And then
he was gone.

She blew out a breath. "Well fuckadoodledo."

CHAPTER TWO

"Hey, wake up."

Lying on her stomach, Khloé grunted. "Fuck off." There was an awful draft as the covers were dragged off her body.

"*Wake up*," urged Ciaran. "Grams needs your help. Like *now*."

Just like that, tension zipped through her. Khloé lifted her head. "Help? Why?"

"I don't have time to explain. Come on, we need to go."

She edged out of bed and began pulling on clothes. "Give me the bare bones of the situation."

Facing the wall to give her some privacy, he replied, "Some shit's gone down with Enoch. It's just . . . fucked up."

Enoch had been a member of their lair since before they were born. She didn't know him well—he mostly kept to himself. That suited her fine, because something indefinable about him rubbed her demon up the wrong way. "I'm ready. What do you mean by fucked up?"

Ciaran turned to face her and grabbed her hand. "Brace

yourself. You're not gonna like what you see."

A slight breeze swept over her skin, the world around her flashed white, and then Khloé found herself stood in—ah, hell—a basement. She *hated* basements. They were dark and creepy and dank. And, God, the stench in this one was *foul*. Like rot, decay, and old blood.

Hearing two voices behind her, she spun. Her mouth fell open in horror, and she almost jerked back a step. Her inner demon recoiled, just as disgusted.

Oh God, this was wrong. So very, very wrong. *Twisted*, even.

"Ah, your grandchildren have come to join you, Jolene," Enoch said, a bitter twist to his mouth. "Isn't that sweet?"

Jolene didn't glance their way. Like the two sentinels at her back, Orrin and Mitch, she kept her attention locked on Enoch.

He cut his gaze back to the Prime. "You won't take my daughter from me," he told her, his jaw set, his chin high, his chest thrust out—clearly aiming to look as intimidating as possible as he stood between her and the twisted sight behind him.

"You think this is good for Molly?" Jolene challenged, clearly not in the least bit rattled. The woman might be crazy, but she was also a strong, shrewd Prime who could blow shit up with a mere thought, so she had every right to be confident in the face of a threat. "You think it's fair to her?"

His nostrils flared. "It's better than her being six feet under the goddamn ground."

She sighed. "Enoch—"

"*Leave*," he bit out. "This isn't your business."

Jolene lifted her chin a notch. "Oh, this is very much my business. When you first joined my lair, you made me a promise that you wouldn't use your main gift without consulting me. You broke that promise."

Oh, he'd broken it in a *spectacular* fashion, thought Khloé, as she and her brother flanked Jolene. She could already guess why her grandmother had sent for her, and she wanted to be ready to make her move.

"I haven't done anyone any harm," he insisted.

"If the parents of those poor children behind you knew what you'd done, they'd be devastated," said Jolene. "That means nothing to you?"

"I brought their children back from the dead—they'd be pleased. *Grateful.*"

Grateful? This guy was warped for sure. The decomposing kids breathed, moved, and sluggishly shuffled around on their little feet within the translucent forcefield that surrounded them. But there was nothing of those kids there. No personality or spirit or *life*.

With the exception of little Molly, Khloé didn't recognize any of them, so she could only assume he'd exhumed them from human cemeteries. None appeared to have been dead more than a few years, but there was no way their parents could look at them and fool themselves into believing their kids were "back" from the dead. They were just empty shells.

Although he'd clearly cleaned and redressed them—even going as far as to brush and style their hair, which she couldn't help but find seriously freaking weird—the sight was still nauseating. Especially with their rotting, pale, sagging flesh and their vacant soulless eyes. And he treated them like they were dolls or something.

"You didn't resurrect their souls, Enoch," said Jolene. "You merely took control of their corpses; you use them as puppets. You desecrated their graves and disturbed their rest."

His mouth tightened. "Molly needed friends."

"Molly is dead. It's tragic, but it's true. That isn't your child over there. It's her body. It's no more than a suit she no longer needs. Her soul has moved on."

"She talked to me. She knew me—"

"At first, yes, she probably did. But I'll bet it wasn't long before she lost whatever echoes of herself were left in that body. It's an 'it' now, not a 'she.' Not a living person. Not Molly."

"Just because she's not *your* definition of alive doesn't make her *gone*. What she is now . . . it's just another state of being. There's nothing wrong with it."

Jolene sighed. "I understand you must feel very alone right now, especially since your mate walked out on you a few years back. But no amount of pain or loneliness gives you the right to do what you've done. You need to return all those bodies to their graves—"

"I won't lose Molly," he gritted out.

"You already lost her, Enoch. Let her rest in peace."

His jaw hardened. "She stays with me."

"Don't make me take this matter into my own hands. I've been gentle with you because I know you're in great pain, but that can change in a heartbeat."

He smirked. "There's nothing you can do. Any living thing that touches that forcefield will die. You have no way of getting past it. Of course, you could kill me, but you'd fail to make it a permanent death—not even you could destroy a Lazarus demon. My body would turn to ash, but I wouldn't *psychically* be dead, so the forcefield would remain intact. And when my body regenerated, I'd come back for my girls. You can't get to them."

"Last chance, Enoch," said Jolene. "Agree to return the children to their graves."

His mouth twitched into an ugly smirk. "Or what? Oh, I get it, you intend to sic your granddaughter on me." He chuckled and cut his gaze to Khloé. "My kind is resistant to mind control, so you can't force me to do your bidding, no matter how strong you are."

Well of course he'd assume that was why she was there.

He didn't know of Khloé's other ability—many didn't. "Jolene didn't call me here to hijack your mind," she said, flexing her fingers as the potent force humming in her belly pushed for freedom.

Sliding her gaze to the forcefield, Khloé lifted her hand, palm-out, and sent out a blast of electric fire. A beautiful mix of blue and amber, it crackled and flickered as it rippled through the air. The power enveloped the forcefield like a net, buzzing and sizzling. She snapped her fist closed, and the electric net sliced through the forcefield.

"No!" yelled Enoch, his eyes wide. A smoky, black sphere appeared in his hand. *The fuck?* He tossed three in quick succession.

Her grandmother slammed up a hand, causing a protective shield to pop up in front of her, Khloé, Ciaran, and the sentinels. The shield absorbed two of the orbs, but it didn't pop up fast enough to block all three.

The other sphere crashed into Khloé's head and . . . God, it was like having someone pour noxious gas up her nose and into her mouth. It seemed to burn her insides as it dived down her lungs and consumed the oxygen there.

Dropping to her knees, she coughed and gagged and tried sucking in fresh air, but it was like the dark force blocked her airways. She couldn't breathe. Couldn't fight it.

She was distantly aware of the mayhem around her—of the sentinels surrounding her, of hellfire orbs being tossed, of Enoch screaming in agony, of the corpses collapsing to the floor, of a cluster of ashes zooming out of the basement window like a swarm of bees. But she was mentally caught up in the fact that *she was choking.*

Spots filled her vision. Her burning chest *screamed* for air. A feeling of weightless fluttered through her.

Her demon went apeshit, knowing they were both going to die—

A hand slapped against her back, and power punched inside her like a cold breeze. It drew her own power like a magnet. The two forces clashed and melded into one. Then it exploded.

Wave upon wave of power rushed through her, clearing the darkness that clogged her lungs. Khloé sucked in a sharp breath. And another. And another. And another. God, fresh air had never tasted so good.

"Stop, or you're going to hyperventilate," said Ciaran, his hand still on her back. "Breathe slowly. Come on, deep breath in, deep breath out."

Struggling to fight the reflexive urge to suck in mounds of air, she concentrated on trying to calm her breathing. Soon enough, the dark tinge to the edges of her vision cleared, but panic remained a living thing inside her. And, Jesus, what was that godawful taste on her tongue?

Looking up at her twin, she gave him a nod of thanks. They'd always been able to join their collective power that way, but they didn't do it too often as it left them both *wiped*.

Ciaran rubbed her back. "You okay?"

"Never better," croaked Khloé. She coughed to clear her throat. "What the fuck did he hit me with?" She coughed again as Orrin and Ciaran helped her stand.

"I'm not entirely sure," said Jolene. "I'm assuming it was a poisonous gas of some kind, considering you almost choked to death. Mitch, go get her some water."

The sentinel promptly disappeared up the basement's staircase.

Jolene rested a hand on her shoulder. "I'd apologize for bringing you into this, but I had to send for you. You're the only one in our lair who could have collapsed that forcefield. I had no other way of freeing those children."

Rubbing her aching chest, Khloé said, "It's fine." She looked at the spot where Enoch had stood. "Shame you didn't kill him for good."

Jolene sighed. "I had hoped to make him see reason, but that didn't work so well."

Just then, Mitch reappeared with a tall glass of water. "Here, drink this."

"Thanks," said Khloé. She took the glass and practically inhaled the water.

"Feeling better?" asked Orrin.

She nodded. In truth, she felt like utter shit.

"How long do you think it'll be before Enoch's body regenerates?" asked Ciaran.

"Probably a few days." Jolene smoothed a hand down her blouse and swatted at the material of her sleek pencil skirt, as if she felt stained by the whole encounter. The veneer of elegance she oozed was an innate quality that Khloé couldn't help but envy.

"If he has any sense, he'll disappear," Jolene went on. "I might not be able to kill a Lazarus demon, but I can certainly make him suffer a terrible death, over and over." She looked down at the corpses. "Since bodies can't be resurrected more than once, these poor little ones will be safe from him in the future."

"Jolene," said Mitch, who'd wandered over to the other side of the basement and was staring into a large wooden trunk. "There's something you need to see."

Khloé and the others followed her grandmother, who sidled up to Mitch. Peering into the trunk, Khloé felt her stomach lurch. She jerked back. "Holy fuck."

"Lolita," said Jolene with a sigh, staring at the dead body. Much like the children, its clothes were clean, and its hair had been styled into a tidy braid. But it was mighty clear by the state of decomposition that the corpse had been dead for a number of years.

"Either he lied that Lolita walked out on him *or* he caught up to her," said Mitch. "Whatever the case, it seems highly likely that he killed her."

"If she threatened to leave him, it's possible he killed and then reanimated her to keep her with him," mused Orrin. "Why wouldn't he have kept her body with Molly's?"

"He sees them all as living beings of a sort," said Jolene. "To him, they're truly not dead. If he's angry with Lolita, he wouldn't reunite her with their daughter."

Khloé nodded. "Keeping her trapped in a trunk seems something of a punishment to me."

Ciaran shoved a hand through his hair. "This is all so unbelievably fucked up."

Orrin turned to the Prime. "Me, Mitch, and the other sentinels will take care of moving the bodies. You, Khloé, and Ciaran should go breathe in some air that isn't filled with death."

Jolene put a hand to her throat. "It just devastates me that we'll have to cremate the human children's corpses if we can't locate their resting places. They don't deserve that."

"Enoch probably would have taken them from local cemeteries," said Ciaran. "Want me to make some calls and find out if there's been reports of bodies being exhumed?"

"Yes," said Jolene. "He must have taken them at some point in the last month, since they were supposed to be 'friends' for Molly. She died four weeks ago tomorrow. I can't say for sure how soon after that he reanimated the other corpses. If one of our lair members hadn't noticed that Molly's grave had been desecrated, I might never have learned what he'd done."

"He could come back for her body," said Orrin. "It would be pointless, I know, since he can't resurrect her again. But he's not ready to let her go yet. It might be best to have someone watch over her grave."

Mitch nodded. "Then we can grab him if he reappears."

"Once she's back in the cemetery, arrange for some of our Force to stand watch but to stay out of sight," Jolene ordered. "The rest of us need to work on tracking him. He doesn't have many living family members. Those that are alive belong to another lair. I'll pay them each a visit and see if he's contacted any of them. They could even give him sanctuary."

"I want to be there," said Khloé.

"Yes, I thought you might," Jolene groused. "I'll allow it, since he may well pop up a shield to protect himself. And while it vexes me that you'd make such a request to come along yet refuse to accept my offer for you to join our Force's ranks, I won't comment on it."

"You just did."

"Then I won't comment on it again."

"I'll go make those calls and see if I can find out where he took the human kids from," announced Ciaran.

Khloé put a hand to her stomach. "I say we both go throw up first."

Her brother pursed his lips. "Sound idea."

*

Slurping her mango smoothie, Khloé glanced out the window that overlooked the Underground. The place was busy twenty-four/seven, and this part of the strip got a lot of foot-traffic due to it being close to the mall and the most popular eateries and bars. "No sign of Harper and Devon yet," she told Raini.

It had become their ritual for all four women to meet at the coffeehouse before work, since their tattoo studio was located next door. Whoever arrived first at the coffeehouse often bought drinks for the others to save them having to wait in the long-ass queue.

Around them, voices murmured, machines hummed, and dishware clattered. The delicious scents of fresh pastries, coffee beans, and vanilla filled the air.

"They'll be here soon," said Raini. "I hope they bring Asher. I haven't seen him in over a week. I miss my little dude. Is he or is he not the most adorable thing ever?"

"Totally. And he cracks me up."

Demonic children were more advanced than humans, so the eighteen-month-old could talk a little and had excellent balance. He also had a very firm grip on his abilities—some of which were seriously impressive. But if he were her kid, it would make her a little nervous that such a high concentration of power lived within him. There was a current rumor going around that he could conjure the flames of hell, though she had no idea where it came from.

"God, my head is killing me. I don't get why they call it a hangover," said Raini, rubbing her temple. "Shouldn't it be called, like, a drunk-over? I don't see where the 'hang' part comes in."

Bracing her elbows on the bistro table, Khloé slanted her head. "You know, I'm annoyed that that didn't occur to me before now."

"I feel bad for humans. Demons rarely get hangovers; ours never last long. But humans, well, that's a whole other story." Raini sipped at her coffee. "From now on, we should call this circle-of-hell state either a drunk-over or a blitzed-over."

"I vote for the latter."

"Then it is done."

Khloé gave a curt nod. Spotting a familiar figure walk by, she frowned. "On another note . . . I can't help but notice that members of Maddox's lair seem to pass by us a lot these days."

Raini turned stiff as a board. "They do, don't they?" she clipped.

Maddox Quentin was not only a local Prime, he was Raini's anchor. All demons had predestined psychic mates that were often referred to as anchors. When they fused their psyches together, they created an unbreakable link that gave each other the strength, stability, and power to maintain dominance over their inner entity—meaning they would never turn rogue.

Although the anchor bond wasn't emotional, anchors were *exceedingly* loyal to one another and often became close friends. They also supported and protected each other. They trusted each other more than they trusted their Primes, partners, and friends. Sometimes anchors were a little *too* protective, not to mention notoriously possessive—even if the latter was only on a platonic level.

Raini and Maddox had first met at his club, the Damned, when her lair was searching for information on who'd tried to have Devon kidnapped. In fact, Devon had originally thought *he* might have brokered the deal—he was known for doing such things.

Given that Maddox was also rumored to be a somewhat pitiless, unremorseful demon who possessed very few ethics, it was little wonder that Raini was disappointed to have him as an anchor. He was a "descendant," a breed of demon that came into being after The Fallen mated with demons and created something darker than dark. They were a secretive, inclusive bunch who never permitted anyone outside of their own breed to join their lairs.

Raini and Maddox hadn't formed the anchor bond, and it didn't seem as if either party wanted to. But he didn't seem inclined to leave her alone. He telepathed her often, even though she never responded to him. But she hadn't been clear to anyone on just what he said when he contacted her.

"Do you think he has people subtly watching over you?" Khloé asked.

Raini gave a haughty shrug. "Don't know, don't care."

Yes, she did. Anyone who knew the succubus well could sense that it was getting to her. "Has he said anything to indicate he wants the anchor bond?"

"No. He mostly just telepathically checks-in to see if I'm fine, even though I never answer." Raini sighed. "He was supposed to get bored and leave me alone."

Khloé could recall the moment that Maddox and Raini discovered they were anchors; could remember how his shock had quickly been replaced by a dark, proprietary look. "I know from experience that the pull of the anchor bond is seriously strong. He's probably having a hard time fighting it. Aren't *you*?"

Raini looked down into her mug. "My demon keeps pushing me to seek him out; it wants the bond. But I don't want an anchor I can't trust, Khloé. Maddox Quentin is not a demon who can be trusted."

"That doesn't mean he wouldn't be someone *you* could trust. Demons are often different with their anchors."

"I don't see that it matters much. He's never claimed to want the bond."

"He probably doesn't want it. Tanner said he's a control freak. A control freak won't react well to something being completely outside of his control. But that doesn't mean Maddox won't eventually lose the fight. And if he does, he'll come for you. You need to be ready for that."

It wouldn't be easy to deal with him. The guy hummed with a dark power that had both intrigued and unnerved Khloé's demon. "We'll all be here for you. And we'll burn his dick with hellfire if he upsets you."

A weak chuckle bubbled out of Raini. "That should be fun to watch."

On hearing the bell above the door chime, Khloé looked to see Harper, Tanner, Devon, and Keenan breeze into the coffeehouse. She felt her eyebrows dip. Given that Tanner was Harper's bodyguard and Devon's mate, the three often rode to the Underground together. Keenan, however, didn't usually accompany them unless Asher was present. Today, he wasn't.

As Keenan's blue eyes locked on her, remnants of last night's raw need stirred in her belly. Unbidden, his words whispered into her mind . . .

I swear to Christ, Khloé, if you mention my cock one more time, I'm going to thrust it inside you and fuck you so hard you'll be screaming.

Khloé shoved the memory in a mental box and wrapped it in parcel tape. She would not think about it. Or about their wager. Or about their hot little eye-fuck. Nope.

Taking in the hard set of his jaw and the dark glitter in his eyes, it was clear he had a bug up his ass about something. How delightful.

Raini waved a hand at the table. "Morning, people. Your drinks await you. Except for yours, Keenan. Didn't realize you'd be gracing us with your big, bad presence."

The newcomers said their hellos as they claimed seats.

His eyes boring into Khloé, Keenan took the chair beside hers, making her hormones do a little cheer. "Were you hurt last night?"

Khloé frowned. "Last night?"

"During that whole clusterfuck with Enoch," he elaborated.

She looked at her cousin. "I take it Grams told you a little about Enoch and you blabbed to Keenan." Jolene wouldn't have told her *everything*—not now that Harper no longer belonged to their lair. Demons were secretive that way.

Cradling her mug of caramel latte between her hands, Harper replied, "She mentioned it earlier over the phone when I called her. Just hearing about it was disturbing. I can't imagine how horrible it must have been to actually *be* there."

It was a memory that would stick with Khloé, that was for sure.

"Were you hurt?" Keenan repeated, his tone clipped. She'd bet the reason he was so pissed was that he'd heard about the incident second-hand instead of directly from her. He had a habit of poking his big, fat nose into her business. Which baffled her, because it wasn't like said habit got him anywhere.

"No," Khloé replied.

His eyes narrowing, he tilted his head. "Why don't I believe you?"

"I don't know. Why don't you?"

His lips thinned. "Are you aware that you look like shit?"

"Smooth, Keenan," mumbled Tanner.

"Well, she does," said Keenan.

Khloé couldn't even deny it. Worse, she *felt* like shit. She was so tired and drained that she could easily nap right there. Her throat felt all scratchy and sore, and her chest still ached from last night's near-choking incident.

As she had no wish to share that with Keenan, she turned back to Harper. "I don't know how Enoch couldn't have found what he did *wrong*," she said, using the straw to stir her smoothie, "but he'd fully justified it in his head."

Devon blew over rim of her steaming mug. "A part of me feels bad for the guy—no parent should have to bury their own kid. But there are lines you don't cross."

Tanner nodded. "Reanimating the body of his daughter was bad enough. Resurrecting the others so she'd have friends to play with . . . that's just fucked up, no matter what way you look at it."

Oh, Khloé couldn't agree more.

Keenan's knee knocked hers beneath the table—such a small thing, but it was enough to make her pulse jump. "You need to be careful. Jolene didn't say exactly what you did last night, only that you helped her defeat Enoch. That means you played a part in him losing his daughter all over again—that's how he's likely to see it. I doubt he'll thank you for it."

"He's not dumb, he'll lay low," said Khloé.

"He doesn't seem to be operating on all cylinders right now, so there's no knowing what he'll do."

"Keenan's right, Khloé," Harper cut in. "And I'm annoyed that I didn't think of it myself. The guy may confront you or Grams. Maybe even both of you. You could probably kick his ass on your worst day, but he's a *Lazarus* demon—they're practically impossible to permanently kill. Just be careful."

"I always am," said Khloé.

Keenan snorted. "No, you're not."

"Well, we can pretend I am."

His eyes narrowed again. "Why did Jolene need your help with Enoch? You're not one of her sentinels or a member of her Force. Why call on you?"

Khloé shrugged one shoulder, nonchalant. "You'll have to ask her."

"I'm asking you."

"I know. I heard you."

He muttered a curse. "Do you have any idea how exasperating you can be?"

"Where'd you learn that big word?"

He ground his teeth so hard she almost snickered. Oh, he was just too easy.

"I feel all warm and squishy inside when you get this way." She lifted her cell phone from the table and aimed it at him, as if she'd snap a picture.

"Don't you dare," he all but barked.

She rolled her eyes. He positively despised having his picture taken. She'd asked him about it once, and he'd said, "You take photos to record memories. People take them of me because they like what they see—that's all. After centuries of that shit, it gets fucking old."

She'd have branded him dramatic if she hadn't seen how many people—humans and demons alike—covertly took photos of him in passing, just as they might any incredibly hot guy. It seemed harmless enough, but Khloé had to admit that she wouldn't whatsoever like perfect strangers snapping pictures of her.

"You're no fun, Keenan." She looked away, dismissing him. "I really should have stolen a donut."

Watching as the imp closed her mouth around her straw and then sucked in her cheeks, Keenan felt his dick twitch. Jesus, the woman could make him hard without even trying.

After hearing from Harper what went down with Enoch, he'd wanted to see for himself that Khloé was fine. He also wanted to understand why Jolene would call on her for aid, but it was clear that Khloé had no intention of telling him shit.

No surprise there. Nothing could ever be that simple with Khloé Wallis.

He'd seen her fight in the Underground's combat ring a few times, so he knew she was strong. But he'd seen nothing to suggest she was a power in her own right. The fact that she wasn't part of Jolene's ranks only supported that idea.

Many demons, including himself, kept some of their abilities quiet just to keep others guessing. He knew she had wings, could control most minds, was wicked fast, and possessed the standard ability to conjure hellfire. He wondered what other gifts his little imp possessed.

His demon studied her carefully, trying to sense just where she sat on the power spectrum. It wasn't easy to gauge a person's strength, but his demon had always been good at that. With Khloé, however, it was stumped.

It was also pissed that she hadn't called Keenan about the Enoch matter. But then, why would she? She might be under his protection, but she didn't accept said protection. And she'd never share lair business with outsiders unless cleared by Jolene to do so. His inner demon understood that, but it didn't care for rationality. As far as it was concerned, she should have called them.

The entity hadn't wanted to leave her last night. It constantly bugged him to seek Khloé out, to take what they both craved, to make her theirs. It considered the whole thing a done deal, and it wanted Keenan to get with the program.

Her bracelets jangled as she lifted her hand and curled stray strands of hair around her ear. The rest of her hair was gathered in a messy bun. Khloé kept her home and workspace freakishly tidy, but you'd never know it to look at her. When it came to her appearance, she was nowhere near as attentive, always combining ill-fitting clothes from different eras.

Her tees often featured quotes or pictures, and her skin-tight jeans were often ripped or bejeweled. Then there were the headbands, random bracelets, and dangly earrings.

Sometimes she wore dark pieces. Other days she was one big pop of color, just as she was right then. She always looked cute and quirky and, some-fucking-how, stylish. He honestly didn't know how she did it, but he strongly suspected she didn't work it so well on purpose.

Maybe it was a mistake to have made their little wager, considering it would be utter torture to stop at only feeding from her, but he didn't intend to back out. If he couldn't have her, he could at least have one taste of her; he could see her come just once.

His demon wasn't the most patient of creatures, but it didn't mind that it would need to wait seven days before taking what it wanted. The anticipation would only heighten the pleasure.

Keenan knew she doubted that he'd win the wager. She was wrong to doubt him. He'd meant what he told her; he wasn't an alcoholic, and it wasn't a struggle for him to not overindulge. He had more self-discipline than most. It was only Khloé who'd ever shot that self-discipline to shit.

A female mind touched his. *You can stop glaring at my cousin any minute now,* said Harper, a smile in her telepathic voice.

He cut his gaze to the sphinx. *I'll stop glaring when she starts taking the issue of her safety more seriously.*

Teague will be back from his trip next week. He'll look out for her.

Keenan fought the urge to snap his teeth. He was not a fan of Khloé's anchor at all. Not only because Teague tried keeping her away from Keenan, but because . . . *As anchors go, he's fucking useless. He doesn't try to keep her out of trouble or watch out for her.*

I'll admit he's not always the most attentive anchor, but he has saved her from herself a number of times. I think it's just that, being as crazy as she is, he sees most of her behavior as normal.

"Would the two of you like to share whatever you're telepathically talking about with the rest of the class?" Devon asked, a playful haughty note to her voice.

The sphinx pursed her lips. "No, not really."

Devon pouted. "But I wanna know. I'm feeling left out here."

Khloé drank the last of her smoothie. "Curiosity poisoned the cat, you know."

Devon frowned. "I thought it killed the cat."

"Not in my version."

"Where did you get your version?"

"My Aunt Mildred."

"You don't *have* an Aunt Mildred."

"You don't remember her? Brown hair. Pointy nose. Crooked

front teeth. Huge mole on her chin. Hazel eye."

Tanner's brow creased. "Eye? Not Eyes?"

"She lost the other eye," Khloé told him. "Snake bite."

You do not have an aunt named Mildred, Devon insisted.

"I do! Seriously, why would I lie about it?"

"No idea. But then, I have no idea why you do *half* the things you do."

"And I have no idea how you could forget Mildred."

Keenan felt his mouth twitch. Even for an imp, she was especially good at fucking with people.

Devon pushed out of her chair. "It's too early in the day for this shit, Wallis. Let's just get to work."

Khloé huffed and stood. "Fine. But I can't *believe* you don't remember Aunt Mildred."

"Oh my god, stop!"

As they all walked out of the coffeehouse, Keenan telepathically reached out to Khloé. *I look forward to collecting on my wager.*

Aw, you really think you'll win it? she asked without sparing him a glance. *I can't help but feel sorry for you.*

His mouth twitched. *I'll win. And then I'll have my taste of you.*

She flicked him a look full of pity, and his demon smiled. It liked that she was so over-confident—it would make the win all the sweeter for the entity. In effect, it had cornered and captured its prey. She just didn't know it yet.

CHAPTER THREE

Later that day, Keenan knocked on the door to Knox's main office within the Underground. Hearing the Prime's bid to enter, Keenan walked inside and then closed the door behind him.

Knox sat at the executive desk, shuffling papers. The printer on his left whirred as it fired up. A glass of what looked like gin and tonic sat next to the hi-tech computer, along with stationery and a block of memo notes.

The Prime wasn't alone in the office.

Sitting on the sofa near the large window that overlooked the combat ring, Larkin briefly peered up from her laptop and said, "Hey, Keenan."

"Hey," he returned, watching as the harpy's fingers deftly ran across the keyboard. When Knox needed access to private information of any kind, he set the female sentinel on it. She was a whizz with computers.

Standing in the corner of the sleek, modern space while

talking into his cell phone, Levi merely tipped his chin at Keenan in greeting.

Keenan gave the reaper a short nod and then strolled toward the desk. He flicked a brief glance at the wall-mounted security monitors that provided CCTV footage of the goings-on within the Underground. There was never any real peace there—it was full of demons, after all. They had to be watched carefully.

"You investigated the complaint?" asked Knox, leaning back in his seat.

Keenan sank into the chair opposite him. Like the rest of the ample seating, it was cushioned with rich Italian leather and comfy as fuck. "Yes. It was legit."

The Prime was as merciless as they came, but there were always demons who rebelled and earned themselves a punishment. Knox's Force handled the smaller matters, but there were times when the sentinels needed to step in. Like when someone from their lair complained that a member of the Force had not only roughly detained them without due cause but had also physically assaulted them—something that would not be tolerated.

Only Knox and the sentinels dished out physical punishments. No one else had that right. To take such a liberty came close to challenging Knox's authority—another thing that wouldn't be tolerated.

"I locked the asshole in the Chamber so you can deal with him at your leisure," said Keenan, referring to the basement beneath Knox's prison filled with dozens of torturous implements.

People who wronged Knox—whether they be members of their lair or outsiders—were taken there to endure punishment. Depending on the severity of the felony, some were then released; others were incarcerated.

"Good," said Knox. "This is the second time he's crossed a

line. I warned him that he'd lose his position on the Force if he abused his authority again. Replace him."

"It'll be done." Keenan twisted his mouth. "I wanted to pick your brain about something. How long does a Lazarus demon take to fully regenerate?"

Knox pursed his lips. "Three or four days, depending on how powerful they are." He narrowed his eyes. "You think Enoch might make a reappearance?"

"Maybe. He wasn't ready to accept that his daughter's gone. In doing whatever they did, Jolene and Khloé *forced* him to accept it."

"And you're worried for Khloé."

"She doesn't have any sense of self-preservation. Nor does she have an anchor who watches out for her well enough."

"Khloé won't accept you acting as a bodyguard, Keenan, if that's what you're hoping."

"Tanner guarded Devon when she had people looking to kidnap her."

"That was different. Jolene's lair was up against outsiders, so our lairs banded together to deal with it; we were presenting a united front to others. This problem exists *within* Jolene's lair. She has to deal with this herself. If she doesn't, she'll look weak to her lair members and then someone might challenge her for her position."

Keenan snorted. "I can't see anyone being stupid enough to try to steal Jolene's position from her."

"Perhaps not. But Harper already tried to convince Jolene to involve us; she refused. She did, however, promise to keep us in the loop and to ask for aid if she felt she truly needed it. Of course, Harper and I will quietly do what we can to locate Enoch, much as Jolene often quietly tries to contribute to our lair issues. But that's all we can do. Anyway, you could be wrong. Enoch might not have any intention of seeking revenge on them."

Keenan wished he could agree with that, but his gut told him different. Or maybe his concern for Khloé clouded his judgement—he couldn't be sure. "What would it take to permanently kill a Lazarus demon?"

"The flames of hell could destroy them. Nothing is impervious to them."

Keenan had witnessed their destructive nature for himself. The rumors that Knox possessed the exceedingly rare ability to conjure them was in fact true, which only very few people knew. The Prime kept a lot of secrets, including the dark truth of just what type of demon he was.

"But, unlike you, Khloé can't call on the flames," said Keenan. "What *can* she do to kill him?"

Idly tapping his pen on the papers in front of him, Knox replied, "Steel forged in the pit of hell is fatal to any demon. If she can get her hands on a blade made of such steel, she could certainly kill Enoch. But weapons like that aren't easy to come by."

"Where would she find one?"

"The black market would be her best bet," Larkin cut in. "You can get pretty much anything there. Leave it with me. If there's such a blade for sale, I'll find one."

Keenan gave her a nod of thanks, confident that Larkin would come through for him. He pushed out of his chair. "I'll let Khloé know about the blade. She'll no doubt pass the info on to Jolene."

"All right. But it probably won't be anything Jolene hasn't already learned for herself—she has many, many sources."

Keenan turned and headed for the door just as Knox's office phone began to ring.

"Yes?" Knox answered. "Gavril, it's a surprise to hear from you."

Keenan halted in his tracks. Another US Prime, Gavril was a complete prick who Knox had butted heads with more than once. He was also Thea's Prime.

Keenan slowly turned just as Knox pressed a button that put the call on speakerphone.

"It has been many years since we last spoke," said Gavril. "It's regrettable that our alliance crumbled the way it did."

Knox leaned back in his chair. "Is it?"

Gavril chuckled. "I suppose you'd think not."

"What is it you want?"

"I'm sure you remember Thea Whitman well enough."

Knox's eyes flicked to Keenan. "I remember."

"She killed her ex-mate last night."

Keenan stilled. *The fuck?*

"Killed her ex-mate?" echoed Knox.

"Killed him and then fled with their son. I have my demons tracking her, of course. It won't be easy, since she can use glamor to change the appearance of herself and others, but she can't evade us for long."

Keenan exchanged a look with Levi. *Well, shit.*

"It struck me that if she were to seek help or sanctuary from anyone, it would be you, given that you have known her since childhood," said Gavril. "If not you, she'll certainly contact your sentinel, Ripley—they were reasonably close at one time, I believe. As incubi are able to see through glamor, he'll see through her disguise and know if she's nearby. If he sees or hears anything from her, I would appreciate it if you contacted me. She needs to be brought back to the lair to face punishment for what she's done. And we don't want anything happening to her son."

"I'll tell Keenan to inform me if she attempts to reach out to him."

Keenan noted that Knox hadn't agreed to then pass on such information to Gavril.

"Your aid is appreciated." Gavril said his goodbyes and rang off.

"So, Thea killed her ex to avenge what he'd done to her." Levi looked at Keenan. "Think the reason she's been trying to contact you lately is that she'd hoped to ask you to do it for her?"

"No idea," replied Keenan. But if so, he'd have turned down said request. He wasn't a hitman for hire.

"You didn't tell Gavril she's been in touch with you," Larkin said to Knox.

"I wouldn't do him even a hint of a favor—he's never cooperated with me in the past." Knox slid his gaze to Keenan. "When I conveyed your message to Thea yesterday, she wasn't pleased, to say the least. She seemed desperate to speak with you, but she wouldn't tell me why."

"Do you think she'll contact you?" Larkin asked Keenan.

He considered it for a moment. "Now that she's on the run, no. She'll be well-aware that Gavril will expect her to come to us. She'll want to stay off his radar, and that means not doing what he would expect of her. Her best bet would be to leave the country. If she used glamor, she could wear different faces as she moved from city to city on her way out of the US."

Larkin gave a slow nod. "I feel sorry for her kid. His world has been turned upside down. Hopefully she manages to keep him safe—the demon world is brutal toward strays."

Yeah, Keenan knew that from personal experience.

*

"Back off, pooch, I'm trying to clean up here." Devon shoved Tanner hard, making him plop onto the sofa. "Sit. Stay. Good dog."

The hellhound grinned. "Ooh, you'll pay for that, kitten."

"Sounds promising. Now just watch TV and look pretty."

Khloé snickered and went back to adding new pieces of jewelry to the glass display case beneath her desk.

Tanner always turned up at Urban Ink near closing time, ready to take both Harper and Devon home. While the other females tidied their stations, Khloé took responsibility for the reception area. It was the first thing people saw when they walked in—if it was messy and dirty, that would reflect on the studio itself.

She'd already swept the floor, cleaned the coffee table, and tidied the portfolios. She didn't need to neaten her desk. Every object—the computer, the phone, the appointment book, the pen holder, the cashier's till, and the stapler—had its own proper place, so the surface was *always* perfectly organized . . . until people started moving her shit. She *hated* that.

Khloé locked the jewelry case and stood. Her nose wrinkled. The scents of disinfectant and citrus cleaner laced the air, almost completely drowning out the scents of ink and paint.

She turned to Raini, who was almost done tidying her station. All the tattoo stations featured a recliner, checkered glass partitions, a large wall mirror, and framed licenses. Each of the women had also tacked photographs and sketches of tattoos near their mirror.

"Are you looking forward to your birthday?" Khloé asked the succubus.

"I'll be spending it on Harper and Knox's yacht with all my girls there, what's not to like?" replied Raini, wiping down the black leather recliner.

The weekend-long booze cruise had been Khloé's idea. They didn't plan to spend the entire time plastered, especially since they'd have Asher with them. They'd indulge in watersports, and they'd make use of the yacht's pool, cinema room, and stuff. But they'd certainly spend their evenings tossing back some shots.

"Speaking of my birthday, we haven't yet gone on our trip to the mall to buy new clothes for the weekend," added Raini.

"How about Wednesday after work?" suggested Devon, polishing a piece of metal art that adorned the white wall. There were several such pieces, including flames, Chinese dragons, a wolf head, and a guitar—all of which were also enlarged copies of tattoos. They added to the studio's artsy/biker/rock theme.

"Works for me," said Khloé. "Harper, can we count you in?"

"I'd give it a miss, but you'll only whine like babies," grumbled the sphinx, who preferred online shopping. She used the remote control to switch off the TV. "Almost done here. Just got to grab something from my office." She set the remote control on the coffee table and then headed to the rear of the studio.

Done for the day, Khloé picked up her purse. "You ready to go, Raini?" They often carpooled to work, since they lived so close to one another.

"More than ready," replied Raini.

Both of them crossed to the coat rack near the vending machine and grabbed their jackets. Khloé had just finished slipping hers on when the front door opened and none other than Keenan stepped inside.

His eyes immediately found her. "Going somewhere?"

"Slowly insane."

He grunted. "That I can agree with." He folded his arms. "I have some news you need to hear."

She listened as he relayed what Knox had told him. Her nose wrinkled. "A steel blade forged in the pit of hell? The best hope I have of killing Enoch is to stab him with one of those?"

"Yes. Unfortunately, not many such blades exist."

Khloé blew out a breath. "Well that sucks balls."

"Larkin is currently searching the black market to see if any are for sale. With any luck, there'll be at least one."

Khloé's relatives were also highly familiar with the black market, so she'd pass on the information to Jolene and have the imps search for one, too. Although he hadn't given Khloé any info that her grandmother wouldn't have unearthed for herself at some point, she nonetheless said, "Thanks for letting me know. I appreciate you looking into it."

He inclined his head. "Anything to keep Harper's panic level to a minimum; she's worried about you."

Khloé almost laughed at the "don't read anything into it" message. Oh, she wasn't. He considered her under his protection, sure, but he also considered Raini and Devon under his protection—*all* because they were important to one of his Primes. The only people who held any importance to Keenan were the other sentinels, Knox, Harper, and Asher.

Khloé wondered if he'd told any of them about their wager. Probably not.

She gave him a quick head-to-toe scan. He wasn't sweating, tremoring, or showing any other signs of withdrawal. He would soon, though. It was inevitable.

"I gotta get home. Farewell, muchachos," Khloé loudly called out as she and Raini breezed out of the studio.

She dropped Raini off at her house and then drove straight home. She'd no sooner walked through the door than her parents showed up, wanting to check on her after the Enoch business. It was no surprise. She'd called Penelope and Richie early that morning to tell them what had happened, not wanting them to hear about it via the lair's grapevine.

While Penelope, Richie, and his mate, Meredith, settled themselves on the cream upholstered sofa, Khloé made coffees.

Penelope and Meredith luckily got along like a house on fire. But then, Richie's mate was easy to like. The stunning redhead also seemed to take it in her stride that Richie had several kids with numerous women.

Maybe Penelope might have felt a twinge of jealousy if she and Richie had loved each other once upon a time, but they'd had nothing more than a shallow fling that had resulted in a multiple pregnancy that shocked the hell out of them both.

It was still a little weird for Khloé to see him all loved-up. Until Meredith, Richie hadn't stayed with one woman for more than a few years. Khloé had begun to wonder if he'd ever take a mate. It was good to see him happy and settled. She just wished her mother would find that same happiness.

Despite her addiction, Penelope was still a giving and sensitive person who supported, encouraged, and loved her children. But she wasn't so caring toward herself—she had a self-destructive streak that had been born a decade ago, after she gave birth to a stillborn baby girl. It had broken something in Penelope.

Khloé didn't judge her mother for looking to numb her pain in some way. But she *did* judge that her mother insisted on bringing asshole-men into her life—fellow addicts who treated her like shit, spent every cent of her money, and liked to smack her around.

Penelope had occasionally tried overcoming her addiction, but she'd always veered off the path at some point. And the years of denials, lies, broken promises, and useless interventions had taken a toll on their mother-daughter relationship.

Joining her visitors in the living area a few minutes later, Khloé set a tray on her trunk-slash-coffee table. They descended on it, claiming cups and a cookie or two. She sank into her overstuffed armchair and turned her gaze to the partially open window as she sipped at her coffee. Sounds filtered through it—car engines purring, pedestrians murmuring, wind chimes jingling.

"Enoch always seemed like a normal enough guy to me," said Meredith, adjusting the throw pillow behind her. "A little odd and withdrawn, maybe. I never would have imagined he'd . . . It's just *horrible* to even think of those children's bodies being used like puppets."

Penelope nodded. "Losing a child is a pain like no other," she said, her voice cracking, her sad eyes arrowed on the wall-mounted TV, unseeing—she was stuck in the past. "You'd do anything to hold them again. Anything to bring them back. But reanimate their corpse? No. That's not bringing them back to life. There's no life in them."

Thanks to the layers of makeup and her attempt at contouring, Penelope's face didn't look as bloated as usual, the dark smudges under her eyes were hidden, and the red blush-like patches on her cheeks were covered. She always cleaned up before leaving her house, as if she could somehow fool people—particularly Khloé and Ciaran—into thinking she had her shit together and that her alcoholism wasn't really affecting her body.

"Enoch truly didn't view them as 'dead,'" said Khloé. "Or he just didn't want to—one or the other."

"Heidi heard what happened," Richie told Khloé, referring to her youngest half-sibling. "Molly was her friend. She misses her. This shit has brought back all the grief and pain she'd worked through. I'd like to kick Enoch's ass for that alone. I'd also happily rip out his guts for hitting you with that toxic gas."

She knew her father wasn't kidding. Though Richie was often described as a "fixer," he was no innocent. When he wasn't producing and selling counterfeit paintings, he was doing "odd jobs" for Jolene—most of which involved violence of some kind. Since he could break a person's bones with the will of his mind alone, he was good at it.

"Jolene told me you intend to accompany her when she visits Enoch's relatives," Richie went on. "You're strong, Khloé, but you don't have Force-training."

Khloé lifted her mug toward her mouth. Steam fanned her face, filling her senses with the scent of fresh coffee. "But I *can* cut through forcefields—something none of the others can do. Enoch's likely to raise one to protect himself if any of us get near him."

"True enough," Richie grumbled.

Penelope bit her lip. "I don't like it, Khloé."

"Neither do I," said Meredith. "But I can't blame you for wanting to help track him. Just be careful. And maybe take your brother with you—he's officially a member of the Force now, and he can teleport all of you out of danger in a blink."

"It's thanks to him that we know what cemeteries the other bodies were taken from." Richie placed his mug on the glass coaster on her coffee table. "According to Jolene, Orrin and some of the Force will return the bodies tonight."

Khloé gave a curt nod. "Good. I'm guessing Molly's been returned to her grave."

"She has," Richie confirmed. "Jolene has people watching it, just in case Enoch turns up. It would be best for him if he disappears."

"But he hasn't been showing good judgement lately, so we can't be sure what he'll do," said Khloé, paraphrasing the point that Keenan had earlier made.

Her father's expression was grave. "That's what worries me."

CHAPTER FOUR

With Ciaran and Orrin hot on her heels, Khloé followed Jolene into the bakery the next day. Enoch's sister apparently owned and lived above the shop, which was located in San Antonio. As they couldn't simply *appear* in the middle of the bakery, Ciaran had teleported them to a local alleyway.

Two women stood behind the counter. One was cleaning a coffee machine while the other was adding more baked goods to the shelves in the glass case. The latter woman was a ringer for Enoch, so it was easy to guess which of the females was his sister.

Jolene smiled at her. "Abiela Cohen?"

The woman's gaze took all four of the newcomers in. "Yes."

"I'm Jolene Wallis. We spoke on the phone earlier."

"Oh, of course. Come through." Abiela led them into an empty breakroom. "You said you were looking for my brother? That he fled from your lair?" She didn't sound terribly concerned for him.

"Yes. This is my sentinel, Orrin, and these are my

grandchildren, Khloé and Ciaran. All have had . . . shall we say a close encounter with Enoch recently."

A close encounter Khloé's body hadn't yet recovered from. Her throat and chest still hurt, her appetite had gone to shit, and she still felt drained a lot of the time.

"I'm not sure how much contact you have with him," Jolene added.

"We're not in contact at all," said Abiela, not looking or sounding the slightest bit regretful about it. "As far as I'm aware, neither of my other siblings speak with him either. That may seem harsh to you, considering he's our brother, but the things he's done . . . they're hard to forgive."

"May I ask you what he did?" Jolene gently enquired.

Abiela folded her arms across her chest. "After our parents died, he resurrected their bodies. We were all devastated. He'd *promised* us that he wouldn't do it. Promised that he'd let them rest in peace. But he didn't. God, he treated them like playthings. Washed them, dressed them, forced them to sit at a table at meal-times or on the sofa to watch TV with him. It was just . . . *wrong*."

Khloé exchanged a look with Ciaran. Apparently, Enoch was more fucked up than they'd thought.

"When we confronted him about it, he refused to undo what he'd done. He even forced our parents' bodies to attack us." Abiela closed her eyes and took a steadying breath. "You can't imagine the pain of fighting people you love, even if those people are technically dead."

"I'm sorry," said Jolene. "I can see this is difficult for you to speak of."

Opening her eyes, Abiela licked her lips. "We had to find another demon with the power of necrokinesis to intervene for us. Enoch almost killed him in retaliation. In Enoch's view, we forced him to relive the loss of our parents."

"Did your Prime banish him?" asked Khloé.

"No," replied Abiela, her mouth tightening. "But he threatened to do so if Enoch ever used his gift again without the Prime's consent." She inhaled deeply. "Enoch swore revenge on me and our other two siblings, and he had it."

Khloé tilted her head. "In what way?"

"He killed people we cared for—my boyfriend, my sister's best friend, and my brother's roommate. We couldn't prove Enoch had done it, but we know he did. Worse, he resurrected their bodies and sent them after us. He didn't succeed in killing us, obviously, but he killed every bit of our love for him. Our Prime then banished him, and I haven't heard or seen anything of him since."

Well, fuck. Khloé had originally thought he'd only reanimated Molly because he was lost in grief. But, yeah, it would appear that Enoch had been riding the crazy train for *years*. He'd done a good job of hiding it from their lair. But then, people like that often *were* good at pretense. She supposed they had to be.

Jolene's lips thinned. "I contacted your Prime when Enoch first applied to join my lair—I like to make enquiries about the demons who come knocking at my door. Your Prime failed to tell me about your brother's crimes. He never even mentioned that Enoch was banished."

"It wouldn't surprise me to learn that he promised Enoch he'd keep it all quiet so long as my brother left quietly," said Abiela. "Our Prime's done such things before."

Jolene's eyelid twitched, and Khloé knew her grandmother wouldn't let this shit slide.

"If you haven't spoken to Enoch in some time, you probably weren't aware that he had a mate and child," Jolene said to Abiela. "I'm sorry to tell you this but, unfortunately, both are dead. We suspect he killed his mate, but his daughter—Molly—died in a car accident quite recently. It was a terrible blow for him, and he wasn't ready to accept that she was gone."

"He resurrected her body, didn't he?" Abiela guessed.

"Among other things, yes," confirmed Jolene. "We were able to break the psychic connection he had with Molly, so her body has been returned to its grave, but he is nowhere to be found. I fear that he's not in his right mind at the moment."

"I don't think he's been in his right mind for a long time, if ever." Abiela patted her tight bun. "It's likely that he'll seek revenge on you. Ensure that all those you love are protected."

"Do you have any idea where he could be?" Khloé asked her.

"No, I'm sorry. You could speak to my siblings, of course, but I don't foresee him seeking their aid. They'd tell him to go fuck himself. Do you have their contact details?"

Jolene nodded. "Yes. I do. Here are mine." She handed the other woman a card. "I would appreciate if you'd call me if he does reach out to you. I won't lie, he'll be punished for the things he did."

Abiela took the card from Jolene. "Oh, I certainly hope he is. Enoch's not a person who can be helped."

"Do you know of any friends he had in your lair?" Khloé asked.

Abiela slanted her head. "His closest friend was David Shore. Well, I wouldn't say they were truly friends. Enoch used him. Manipulated him. Even bullied him, in some ways. Like an alpha might toy with a weak omega."

God, Enoch was *such* a piece of shit. "What breed of demon is David?"

"A familiar," Abiela replied. "I always felt bad for him, because he's pretty low on the power spectrum—he doesn't even have the ability to telepath others. I think it was why he put up with Enoch's bullshit. My brother was powerful enough to protect him from others. David left our lair some time ago, and I have no idea where he went. I'm sorry."

"It's fine, we'll hopefully find that out for ourselves." Jolene gave her a slow nod. "Thank you for your time, Abiela."

Outside the bakery, Ciaran turned to Jolene and puffed out a breath. "Well, it's safe to say that Enoch's a *whole* other level of 'twisted.' I always found him kind of odd, but there's no crime against odd, so I never thought to look deeper. I'm pissed I didn't."

"Same here," said Jolene, her face hard. "His old Prime described Enoch as 'a little weird but harmless.' *Harmless.* It didn't occur to me that the Prime might have lied."

"You had no reason to think he would," Orrin pointed out. "There's no point in us getting upset with ourselves for not seeing the real Enoch. He was very good at pretending to be someone he wasn't. Maybe if he'd mingled more with the lair, we'd have seen that it was an act, but he mostly kept to himself."

Khloé nodded. "He socialized *just enough* to come across as an introvert instead of someone who may have something to hide. He only really let Lolita and Molly close."

"Neither of them said anything about him that would have concerned me," said Jolene. "I wonder how much of the real him they saw."

"Probably not all of him until the end." Ciaran glanced at the bakery. "Do you think she'll really contact us if he reaches out to her?"

"Yes, I do," replied Jolene. "She fears him. If he reappears in her life, she'll panic and want him gone."

"*Especially* since she has a mate to protect," added Khloé. "Enoch would kill and sic the guy on her."

"Is there any point in speaking with his other siblings?" Orrin asked. "I'm doubting he'll have gone to any of them for sanctuary."

The Prime pursed her lips. "Perhaps not, but it is best to check."

So they checked, teleporting from location to location. The others said pretty much the same as Abiela—their brother was cruel, beyond help, and they wanted nothing to do with him. They also had no idea where he could be.

Back in her grandmother's kitchen later that day, Khloé suggested, "We should speak to this David Shore guy."

"I agree," said Jolene. "I'll have some of the Force find out his location. In the meantime, we keep an eye out for signs of Enoch. A Lazarus demon with revenge on its mind is always a dangerous thing."

Hear, fucking hear.

*

A few days later, Khloé sharply thumped the side of the coin machine, expertly extracting a blue plastic bubble. With a smile, she promptly picked it up.

"Why does that never work for me?" whined Devon.

"You're not special enough."

"Hey!"

"What? It's not my fault." Khloé opened the bubble, and the corners of her mouth turned down. "Not so keen on apricot flavor. Anyone else want it?"

Devon snatched the gum. "I'll have it."

Harper cast a pained look around the mall and rolled back her shoulders. "Does it really have to be so busy?"

Khloé almost smiled. Unlike the sphinx, she wasn't bothered by crowds and enjoyed ambling through the Underground's mall. Usually, anyway. Today, the over-bright lighting irritated her dry eyes, and the sounds echoing throughout the large building made the strange pulsating pain in her head worsen—voices talking, shoes clicking on the floor, cell phones chiming, the splashing of the water fountain, music playing low.

She'd had the headache since she'd woken that morning, and it hadn't eased in the slightest. It was like a hangover—well, drunk-over—headache on steroids, and she'd just love to go home and shut herself in a dark room. But she wasn't willing to miss the mall trip with her girls.

The place sold just about everything—clothes, bags, shoes, cosmetics, books, toys, electronics. The list went on and on. Some places were trendy and sold designer stuff. Others offered lesser quality items and seemed to always have some sort of sale going on.

Tanner grimaced as a bunch of shrieking kids skipped by them. "What exactly is it you're all hoping to buy? Just a dress each, right?"

"One or two," replied Raini. "Plus a few bikinis. Shoes. Sandals. Don't worry, it won't take long."

Tanner snorted, knowing full well that was a damn lie.

"The food court is calling my name," said Harper. "Seriously, the smell of spicy foods is tugging at my stomach like a magnet."

"We'll go there when we're done," promised Raini. "First, we shop and—"

Khloé frowned when the succubus stared at something to their far right. "What's wrong?" She tracked her friend's gaze and winced. "Oh." She didn't know the burly guy or his female companion personally, but she recognized them as members of Maddox Quentin's lair.

The two demons gave Raini a blank look before disappearing out of the automatic doors and onto the Underground strip.

"Has Maddox eased up on telepathically bugging you?" Harper asked Raini.

"No," replied the succubus. "And he's not put off by my not responding."

Devon sidled closer to her. "What exactly does he say?"

Raini shrugged. "Stuff."

No one pushed her to talk further, knowing it wouldn't get them anywhere. She was always vague when speaking of the things he said to her.

Khloé *hated* how stressed the whole thing was making her friend. That was partly why she'd proposed the booze cruise—she wanted to take Raini somewhere where there was no chance of the succubus bumping into him or one of his lair members on her birthday. She wanted Raini to have a break from all that bullshit.

She also wanted to stomp on the fucker's windpipe a few times. A girl had to get her kicks where she could.

The succubus forced a smile. "Well, shall we get moving?"

Using the escalators, they went from floor to floor, breezing past shoppers who were carrying bags, pushing baby strollers, or chatting on their cell phones.

Raini led the way, as usual, which suited everyone else just fine. She might be an avid shopper, but she never overspent. Raini was *a master* at sniffing out bargains. She was one of those people who could buy bags of stuff yet never go over her allotted budget.

They browsed many stores, purchasing various items with Raini's advice, since she had a talent for sensing just what clothes would best suit a person. Really, she could make a living as a personal shopper.

Hours later, as they were walking along the top floor, Khloé tapped Raini on the shoulder and said, "Just so you know, Harper looks near the point of slapping random people just for jostling her." The sphinx never lasted long at the mall.

"I smell coffee." Devon turned as if to follow the scent trail, but Raini tugged her back.

"Not yet," said the succubus.

"But my feet hurt." The hellcat pouted. "And the bag handles are digging into my hands."

Raini sighed. "You're carrying *two small bags*, since you're using your mate as a mule. One more store, and then we're done, I promise."

Harper stared longingly at the lounge area near the jewelry kiosk. "I could just wait there."

"But then you wouldn't be finished shopping, and we'd have to come back another day," Raini pointed out.

Harper's mouth tightened. "Fine, fine, let's get this over with."

Raini dragged them over to a store that featured a window display with mannequins in various poses. As always, Tanner stood outside the shop, on guard, while the females browsed the rails and shelves.

Checking the price tag on a trendy leather purse, Devon said, "Hey, Khlo, I've been meaning to ask you . . . Why does Keenan keep giving you looks?"

Khloé paused in sliding the metal hangers on a rack and, going for clueless, asked, "Looks? What kind of looks?"

"I don't know how to describe them, but they're full of heat and promise."

Raini hummed, fingering the fabric of a royal blue dress. "I've noticed them. They make me all tingly, and they're not even directed at me."

They made Khloé a little tingly too. He'd telepathed her several times over the last few days—sometimes they were in the same room, sometimes they were far apart. Always he'd make some teasing comment about how much time she had left before he'd have his taste of her.

Honestly, she was surprised he'd lasted this long without

reaching for his flask. Her mother couldn't go ten hours without a drink, let alone a few days. Was it possible that he wasn't truly an addict? Or could it be that he had some sort of power that enabled him to hold out or something?

Devon nodded. "He's been tossing you those looks for *days* now."

"Know what else?" asked Harper. "I haven't seen him take a swig from his flask for days either. Knox told me that Keenan hasn't been drinking lately."

Khloé went back to skimming through the clothes. "Hmm. Odd."

"Ooh, she's feigning obliviousness, girls," said Devon, her eyes bright. "That means she's hiding something."

"Fess up, Khloé." Harper folded her arms. "Are you two sleeping together?"

Khloé sighed. "No."

"Then what are we missing? Come on, cousin, start talking."

Knowing they wouldn't drop this, Khloé shrugged and said, "He and I have a little wager going on."

Raini's brows lowered. "A wager? What kind of wager?"

"He bet me that he could go a week without drinking," Khloé replied. "If he caves, he has to be my slave for the day."

"And if he doesn't cave?" prodded Devon.

Khloé licked her front teeth. "Hegetstofeedfromme."

Raini put a hand to her forehead. "Oh, Lord."

Harper sighed. "*Khloé.*"

"What's the big deal? There isn't a hope in hell that he'll abstain from drinking for an entire week," Khloé scoffed.

"Keenan would *never* have made such a bet unless he was sure he'd win it," said Harper. "He's done this so that he can taste you, not to prove he isn't an alcoholic—he doesn't care what people think of him."

"Tricky bastard," Devon muttered.

Khloé shook her head. "He'll never hold out." But even as she said that, unease knotted her stomach. Her demon wasn't so anxious—it had no issues with the thought of him feeding from it.

"All's not lost," Raini cut in. "He doesn't need to be an addict to lose the bet, he just needs to have a drink, right? Khloé could drive anyone to drink."

Harper's brows hiked up. "That's true."

"Is he still coming on the mini booze cruise?" asked Raini.

Harper nodded. "Asher's coming with us, and Keenan's his bodyguard, so . . ."

Raini turned to Khloé. "You should use that opportunity to push all his buttons. If you're at your best, he'll snap sooner or later."

"And you should go on a date at some point," Harper added. "He positively *hates* it when you do that."

"I don't have time to go on a date. I'll be packing tomorrow so that we can leave Friday morning for the booze cruise," said Khloé.

"Then we'll just say that you went on a date." Harper waved a hand. "He won't know any different."

Khloé felt her face scrunch up. "Lying that I went on a date feels kind of juvenile."

"When have you ever cared about acting juvenile?" asked the sphinx.

"Never."

"Then why start now?"

"You make a good point."

"Seriously, he hates hearing about you going on dates. It always seems to take him a step closer to asking you out, but he never does." Harper pursed her lips. "I can only assume he has commitment issues or something."

"He's not the only one." Devon threw a meaningful look at Khloé.

"I don't have commitment issues, I just avoid relationships," said Khloé. "And for good reason."

Raini looked upward. "Oh, don't start with that whole 'my family is cursed' thing again."

"It's true," Khloé insisted. "My maternal line is cursed to live alone. It's the only thing that makes sense."

Raini folded her arms. "*That* makes sense to you? Really?"

Khloé tapped her foot. "I looked up my family's history. My great-great-great-great grandmother Irene once pissed off a female incantor by fucking the woman's mate. It's only been since then that every female member of my mother's line has grown old alone. None of them have taken mates; none have even found themselves in a long-term relationship. There must be a curse at work. And so, like my other maternal female relatives, I am doomed to grow old and die alone."

"Or maybe there is no curse, and you're just wacked," said Devon.

Khloé scowled. "I can't believe you'd even suggest that."

Harper put a hand on her back. "I think you just have no faith in relationships. Why would you? Neither of your parents know a thing about healthy, functional relationships."

"My dad and Meredith are doing okay," Khloé pointed out.

"Yeah, he got there *eventually*." The sphinx shrugged. "Maybe you will too, one day."

"No, I'm too busy paying for Irene's fuck-up, like the rest of my maternal relatives."

"Is that what your fictional Aunt Mildred told you?" asked Devon.

"I can't *believe* you don't remember her." Khloé planted her hands on her hips. "Come on, think back. She had a limp.

Carried a cane everywhere. Always wore black. And she had that rash on her hands that—"

"Stop," the hellcat burst out. "Just stop."

"Fine." Khloé pulled a dress of the rack. "Where's the fitting room?"

CHAPTER FIVE

Friday morning, Keenan shoved open the door of his apartment building and strode outside, heading for the parking lot. He needed to collect Khloé and Raini and drive them to the airport, where his Primes' private jet was waiting to fly them to the yacht.

He wasn't looking forward to the trip. And yet he was.

Being in close proximity to Khloé for three whole days wouldn't be easy—she could push his buttons like no one else, and he was sure she'd give him a stomach ulcer sooner or later. But she also made him feel more alive than anyone had in a very long time. Their verbal spars sometimes felt like foreplay.

He wondered if she'd yet begun to realize that she'd made a mistake in ignoring his insistence that he wasn't an alcoholic. He could honestly say that he hadn't once been tempted to reach for his flask. Especially since his reward would be a taste of what he'd been craving for years. A reward he could claim in just three days if he managed to hold out.

Feeding from her just once could be enough to weaken the

chemistry that pulsed between them. He'd spent so long imagining how she tasted that he'd built it up in his head. The reality couldn't possibly match the fantasy, could it? He'd for sure feel disappointed to some degree, and that would—

"Keenan?"

He froze. He knew that voice far too well. It brought back so many memories—some good, some bad. And it made his demon bare his teeth.

He slowly turned. A tall brunette stood a few feet away from him, her hand clasped around that of a small boy. *Thea.* He knew by the slight glow to their faces that they were currently wearing "glamor masks." He couldn't see the masks, due to his ability to see through glamor, so he couldn't be sure what she'd look like to those who didn't possess that ability.

She offered Keenan a shaky, tentative smile, clearly unsure of her welcome. She shouldn't be unsure. He'd made it clear through Knox that he had no wish to talk to her. It wasn't a complicated concept.

He didn't hate Thea, though he'd tried to. He just didn't want his past to invade his present. Nor did he like being reminded of his mistakes. Placing his trust in her had definitely been a mistake.

Her tongue darted out and nervously swiped over her lower lip. He'd kissed that mouth more times than he could count. She was still beautiful. But she didn't hold the same appeal for him that she once had. Maybe because she'd stomped on his trust. Or maybe because another female occupied his thoughts these days.

His demon sniffed, unaffected by her beauty. It had slammed a mental door on her long ago, and it had no time or patience for her.

Rubbing her hand on her jean-clad thigh, Thea gestured at the little boy. "This is Lane. Lane, this is a friend of mine, Keenan Ripley. Say hello, Lane."

Clutching a tablet tight to his chest with one arm, the boy looked at him, his eyes startlingly blank. "Hello."

Keenan ground his teeth. She hadn't just brought the boy along for sympathy, she'd done it because she knew Keenan wouldn't cause a scene in front of him. "Good to meet you, Lane," he said, unable to drum up a false smile.

"I left my lair," Thea blurted out. "Lane and I are strays now." She tilted her head. "You're not asking why I left, so I'm guessing you know—" She cut herself off, her eyes darting to her son. "Some things," she finished lamely.

Bending to Lane, she said, "Baby, put your earphones in; play on your tablet for a while."

"Okay." Obligingly, the kid switched on the tablet.

Only once Thea had put earbuds in his ears and seemed satisfied that he wouldn't overhear her did she turn back to Keenan. "Gavril contacted Knox?"

Keenan nodded.

She licked her lower lip. "I didn't kill my ex-mate. I swear, I didn't. I was mad at him, yes, but he was Lane's *father*. I wouldn't have taken my son's father from him. Gavril's setting me up."

Keenan felt his brows rise. "Why would he set you up?"

She bit her lip. "I can't tell you. It's not that I don't want to, I just can't."

Well of course she couldn't. Because there was nothing to tell—she was feeding him bullshit, just as she'd done many times before. "Why are you here?"

She flinched at his curt tone. "Look, Keenan, I can understand if I'm not your favorite person. I let you down so many times, I know that, and I'm so sorry for it."

She meant it. He could see that. Her apology might have

meant something to his demon once, but not now. Too much time had passed. "What do you want, Thea?"

"I need your help. I've been trying to contact you for days, because I knew Gavril was going to do something bad, and I didn't know who else to turn to. The last thing I expected was for him to kill Lee-Roy and then make it look like I did it."

Keenan squinted. "Gavril killed him?"

"Yes."

"Why?"

She closed her eyes. "I can't tell you that either. I know how that sounds. I know you have no reason to trust that I'm telling you the truth, but I am. I didn't kill anyone, and I won't be punished for something I didn't do. I can't go back there, and I have nowhere to go."

"You want a place in my lair," Keenan realized. At one time, that would have delighted him—he'd tried to convince her to join it for years. Now, it infuriated him, because she had some fucking nerve to request anything of him.

"Gavril won't fight Knox for me," she said, her words coming fast. "He fears him too much. But anyone else? He'd take them on, and what Prime would go to war with another to protect an accused killer? They'd just hand me and Lane over. I don't deserve your help, but I'm asking for it anyway. For Lane's sake, if nothing else."

Keenan felt his nostrils flare. "I can't grant you a place in my lair—I don't have that kind of authority. Only Knox and his mate do. And if you're not going to be straight with them about everything, they won't even consider taking you in."

Her eyes slid to the side. "Could you not ask them to give me and Lane a place as a personal favor to you?"

"It *wouldn't* be a personal favor to me. I don't want you in my lair."

She flinched. "Keenan, I'm so sorry that you're still hurting after I—"

"Hurting?" he echoed. His demon laughed. "I'm not hurting, I'm just plain pissed. Mostly at myself for choosing to buy your lies and excuses over and over. I meant it when I said I was done, Thea."

His gaze flicked to Lane. He was a cute kid. And he looked about as sober as Keenan had no doubt looked as a small child, when his mother had dragged him to the homes of "old friends," looking for their help. They'd never helped Katherine, just as her parents hadn't helped her. She'd been viewed as lower than dirt for having a child while unmarried—it was unthinkable in those days.

Keenan looked back at Thea. "But I won't turn away a kid who needs protection—something you know perfectly well. And I don't fucking appreciate that you'd use my past against me."

"I'm not trying to manipulate you—"

"Yes, you are."

"Okay, fine, maybe I am. But not to be cruel. I want my son safe, and I'll do anything to make that happen. Lie. Cheat. Manipulate. Anything." She closed her eyes. "*Please*, Keenan. Please help us."

"I'll relay your story to Knox and Harper. I can't say whether they'll choose to grant you a place in my lair. You'll be contacted either way." That was truly the best he could do. Had she been Keenan's mate or anchor, his Primes would have granted her a place without question. But Thea was none of those things to him, so she'd be assessed in the same way anyone else would.

"I'm sorry for everything, Keenan. Really. Whatever you might think, I do care about you—I always have. And I-I missed you. A lot."

Keenan laughed, and there was a bitter edge to it. "You

took a mate, Thea. You had a child with him. You couldn't have missed me that much."

Annoyance in every stride, he crossed to his car, unlocked it with his key remote, and then yanked open the driver's door. He honestly wasn't sure what pissed him off more: that Thea would think it acceptable to ask a favor of him, or that she really thought he'd *want* to do her a favor.

It was like she had no self-awareness; no ability to look back on her actions and realize that, hey, she'd fucked up in a major way. It was one thing to know you'd done wrong. It was another to fully grasp the *weight* of said wrongdoing. She didn't seem able to do that. Never had.

Although his peripheral vision told him she hadn't moved an inch from where she stood near the building, he didn't look at her as he smoothly reversed out of the parking space. Nor did he glance back at her as he drove through the parking lot and out onto the main road.

He wasn't sure if he believed her story that Gavril had set her up to take the fall. Purely because she'd given him no reason to believe it was true. Why she thought Keenan would have taken her at her word when she'd proven in the past that her word meant shit, he had no clue.

Would Gavril frame someone for murder? Maybe. He didn't seem to have a lot of scruples, from what Keenan had observed. But that wasn't to say that he'd framed Thea, was it? What motive would he have to possibly do it? And why would she withhold said motive when it could prove her innocence?

Her story just didn't make any sense.

Keenan couldn't have turned her kid away, though. It would have made him no better than the many people who'd turned Keenan and his mother away all those centuries ago. Shit, he needed to shut down that line of thinking fast. Ruminating on his childhood only ever pissed him off. He hated that Thea had dredged it all back up again.

By the time he arrived at Raini's address, he'd found some inner calm. After sticking her luggage in the trunk of his car, he ushered her into the rear seat and then drove to Khloé's home. He beeped the horn and then slid out of the car.

Looking as high on life as always, the imp walked out of the house, swinging her travel bag. His gut clenched, and his dick twitched. Fuck if she didn't work that outfit, especially those fuck-me heels.

Her tight white vest and skinny jeans clung to her like a second skin. The black lace shrug she wore trailed all the way down to her thighs, and he could just imagine her wearing that and nothing else. On second thought, she could keep the high heels as well.

Smoky-gray eyes took him in. "'Sup, Don Juan? You've missed me, I can tell."

He wouldn't smile. Nope. Sighing, he grabbed her bag. "Get in the car. I'll put this in the trunk."

"Works for me."

Although she was sexy as hell, she was also pale and had dark smudges under her eyes. His demon didn't like it *at all*. "You look like shit again."

She tilted her head. "Brown and turd-shaped?"

He felt like pinching the bridge of his nose. "Just get in the car."

Minutes later, they were driving en route to the airport. While the two women discussed their plans for the weekend, Keenan telepathically reached out to Knox and said, *Thea was waiting for me outside my complex this morning.*

The Prime's mind touched his. *I was clear that you had no wish to see her,* he said, his voice hard.

Well, she didn't let it sway her. Keenan quickly brought him up to speed. *If it hadn't been for the kid, I'd have turned her away.*

Which she no doubt knew, so that's probably why she took him along.

That would be my guess. I don't have a clue how much of what she said was true. Hell, it could all have been lies. But I said you might agree to hear her out.

I'll be honest with you, Keenan. Although I sympathize with her son, I don't want her in our lair. Harper wouldn't want her around either, given your history with Thea. If Thea gives me the full—and truthful—story of what happened with her ex-mate and I'm satisfied that she deserves sanctuary, I can talk to another Prime and see if they'd be willing to take in her and Lane.

Keenan slowed the car as he reached a red light. *She said she believes our lair is the best choice because Gavril wouldn't dare fuck with you.*

There are other Primes he wouldn't think to challenge, particularly Raul. On another note, how far are you from the airport?

Not far. Which is good, because Khloé is currently acting deranged, convinced there's a bee in the car and that it's going to sting her.

A vibe of amusement brushed the edges of Keenan's mind. *Well, bees do sting.*

Keenan's mouth tightened. *There's no bee, just like there's no Aunt Mildred.*

Who?

Nothing; forget it. Seeing that the light had turned green, he drove onward. *We'll be at the airport soon.*

"Lower the windows so it can fly out!" Khloé urged, cowering against Raini.

God, the woman drove him insane. Humoring her just so the craziness would stop, Keenan lowered the electronic windows. "There," he snapped. "Happy now?"

She breathed a sigh of relief and straightened. "Yes. It's

gone. Phew. That was a close call. I don't know why bees hate me so much."

He frowned, closing the windows. "Bees do not hate you."

"Really? Then why do they always come at me like I fucked their mother or something?" she challenged.

The woman was honestly sent to test him. "What is *wrong* with you?"

"I'm sexually repressed," she replied, deadpan.

He flexed his hands around the steering wheel. "Do you ever wonder how different things would be if you weren't fucking demented?"

"Ooh, who shit on your Pop Tarts, Mr. 'I'm an alcoholic in denial'?"

He ground his teeth, not sure what would bring him more pleasure—gripping her by the throat or fucking her within an inch of her life. "Personally, I think you should be heavily medicated for the safety of you and everyone around you," he sniped.

She slapped a hand to her chest, as if hurt. "Scarred for life over here."

"Just . . . be quiet. All right?"

"All right." The "quiet" lasted all of six seconds. "Keenan, pull my finger."

"No."

It wasn't until much later that he realized she'd taken his mind completely off Thea and his childhood so effortlessly.

*

The ride on the swanky private jet had been fun enough for Khloé. But being on the sleek, white, four-decked mega-yacht had her doing happy dances in her head. Its level of luxuriousness blew her mind.

Everything seemed to glimmer and shine. The spacious

interior was as bright and stylish as the yacht itself. It had everything from a gym to a home theater. Sunlight shone through the large windows, brightening the rooms and casting faint shadows here and there.

After giving them a quick tour and introducing them to the uniformed crew, Harper had shown Khloé and Raini to the guest cabins on the lower deck. Khloé couldn't help but note that hers wasn't too far from Keenan's room. Devon, of course, was sleeping in Tanner's cabin, which was on the same floor. Harper, Knox, and Asher, however, slept on the upper deck in their "stately room," which was one heck of a bedroom suite.

Once they'd all changed into swimwear, they'd headed to the awesome sun deck. Sun sparkled off the water and the gleaming white fiberglass. Below the music that was playing were the sounds of the engine rumbling, seabirds cawing, and waves crashing against the hull. The potent smell of the ocean air almost drowned out those of beer, wood polish, and sunscreen.

For a while, all four girls had spent time in the pool with Asher—playing, laughing, swimming, and pushing him around in his inflatable car.

Later, Devon joined Tanner in the jacuzzi while Khloé, Harper, and Raini got some drinks from the wet bar and then claimed three rattan sun loungers. Keenan and Knox were now in the pool with Asher, who kicked up a fuss whenever anyone tried to get him out of the water.

The three guys were dressed in only swim shorts, so it was impossible not to objectify them for just a moment with their rock-hard abs and perfect physiques. Khloé was still a little tingly from watching Keenan emerge from the jacuzzi earlier, water pouring down his body. *No one* should be so damn enticing. It simply wasn't fair.

More annoying, he did not look like someone who was

battling the pull of an addiction. And she had to accept that he might just have been telling the truth—there was a high chance that the incubus wasn't an alcoholic.

She was hyperconscious that if she didn't make him cave and just have *one drink*, he'd be feeding from her very freaking soon. Her demon wasn't so uncomfortable with the idea. Surprise, fucking surprise.

Sitting on the lounger, she decided she'd wait for the sun to dry her off before she applied more sunscreen. It was hot as holy hell. It wasn't so hot that she wanted to retreat into the sun-shaded salon just off the main deck, though . . . despite that the sofas looked seriously comfy. Maybe later.

Raini took a sip from her glass and then placed it on the small table. "God, the air's so hot it's almost uncomfortable to breathe it in."

"Reminds me of when I went to Dubai," said Khloé. "It's a total bummer that I was banned from ever returning. It's not like I *meant* to set that building on fire."

"But you did break into one of their bank vaults," Raini reminded her.

"Yeah, but they don't know that." Khloé paused as the faint smell of meat grilling teased her nostrils. "Is it just me, or do you guys smell food cooking?"

"The crew will be prepping us dinner," said Harper. "Not sure whether we're eating in the dining salon or on the upper deck's sun terrace—you'll have to ask Knox."

Raini peered out into the distance. "Are there sharks in these waters?"

"I don't care as long as there aren't dolphins," said Harper, trying to brush away the wet hair clinging to her neck.

Raini's mouth curved. "Not all dolphins are shape-shifting demons."

"No, but they *are* twisted enough to mutilate their young, so don't be fooled by their apparent charm."

A breeze fluttered over Khloé's skin, bringing with it a featherlight spray of cool ocean water and making the loose strands of hair flutter around her face. She tucked them behind her ears and lifted her face to the sun, enjoying its warmth, hoping said warmth would chase away the strange chill that had invaded her bones last night and didn't seem to be going anywhere. Her chest *still* hurt from her encounter with Enoch, and that "drained" feeling hadn't gone anywhere. But that was off-topic and not something she cared to discuss.

"Seriously, I absolutely adore this yacht," said Khloé. "I'd totally live on it if I could."

"Me too," said Raini. "I wouldn't have thought it was possible for a yacht to have a homey feel, but it does."

Her skin reasonably dry, Khloé pulled the sunscreen from her beach bag. She squirted some lotion onto her hand and then smoothed it over her arms. Her skin prickled—not just from the heat of the sun, but from the weight of Keenan's gaze. Yeah, she knew he was watching her. She didn't look his way, though.

She'd deliberately annoyed him throughout their ride on the jet—snapping pictures of him with her cell phone, accidentally-on-purpose spilling her pink gin all over his designer tee, and purposely singing the wrong lyrics to his favorite songs. She didn't know why the latter bugged him so much, but whatever worked.

Only it hadn't worked.

He'd snarled. Growled. Cursed. He'd even tried snatching her phone. But he hadn't reached for the bottle. Or flask.

She'd pointedly ignored him since arriving on the yacht, acting as if he wasn't there, which always seemed to irritate him just as much as when she poked at him. She'd also noticed that he hadn't drunk anything but soda so far.

I think we need to step up our game with Don Juan, she told Harper.

The sphinx's eyes flicked to the pool and then cut to Khloé. "Oh, I forgot to ask how your date went."

Khloé slipped her hand beneath her bikini strap to smear sunscreen on her collarbone and shoulder. "A lady never tells."

"But you're no lady, so spill."

"You did wear your little black dress, right?" asked Raini. "There's a reason I call it your lucky dress."

Khloé nodded. "I wore it, and it did indeed bring me luck."

"I'm kind of bummed the guy didn't ask *me* out. He's hot." Raini pushed her sunglasses further up the bridge of her nose. "But he obviously goes for the small and insane type."

Khloé frowned. "I'm not *that* small."

"But you are insane."

"I find it freeing."

Harper snickered. "I can totally believe that."

After she was done applying sunscreen to her legs, Khloé looked at Raini. "Could you do my back again?"

"I'll do it."

She stiffened, because those words hadn't come from Raini. They'd come from the person behind her. *Keenan.*

He was in *hell*. Being around Khloé while having no right to touch her was hard enough. But seeing droplets of water trickle down her delectable body—droplets he wanted to lap up with his tongue—and watching her smear lotion over her skin . . . *fuck.* There was only so much a man could take.

His cock, so full and heavy it ached, was harder than a steel fucking spike. There was no easing it. Not when her wet bikini clung to her body, accentuating her delicate curves and giving him glimpses of what he couldn't have. He wanted to peel it from her, wanted to touch and taste and maybe even bite.

Still, Keenan might have been able to keep his distance if he hadn't heard she'd gone on a fucking date. Black jealousy rode him hard, taunting the possessive streak that was like a live wire around Khloé Wallis.

His demon was furious. As far as it was concerned, she was theirs; no other male had the right to touch her. It wanted to hunt down the fucker who'd taken her on a date and deliver a warning that he'd never forget. It wanted to make her understand and admit who she belonged to.

Something primitive in Keenan urged him to put his hands on her and *mark* her in some sense with his touch—something she might not see but would feel. And so he found himself standing behind her sun lounger, offering to smooth sunscreen onto her back.

She glanced at him over her shoulder but didn't reply.

He flicked up a taunting brow and waited, knowing she'd respond to the silent dare.

Her eyes narrowed. "All right." Scooting forward on the lounger, she handed him the bottle. "Just don't get it in my hair."

She turned back to Harper, as if whatever he did next would be inconsequential. Yeah? He wasn't buying it.

Keenan straddled the lounger, bracketing her body with his thighs. He kept just enough distance between their bodies that it wouldn't be awkward for him to properly apply the sunscreen.

The moment his lotion-covered hands landed on her shoulders, electricity surged through him, as if he'd plugged himself into a socket. He heard her sharp intake of breath and inwardly smiled. This would be no easier for her than it would be for him.

While she carried on an inane conversation with the others, Keenan glided his hands over her, kneading and shaping. There was nothing sensual about it. It would look almost clinical to anyone who watched. But he kept his touch firm and sure; he let her *feel* the possessive edge to it.

She didn't call him on it. Nor did she react when he dipped his fingers under the bikini strings or when he very lightly danced his fingertips over the sides of her breasts—as if she was determined to make him believe that she was barely aware of him. Bull*shit*.

He slid his mind against hers. *Just under three days left to go before our wager is over. Feeling nervous yet?*

Why would I feel nervous? she asked.

Stifling a smile, he set her sunscreen on the table and stood. *In under seventy-two hours, I'll be tasting you. Don't worry, you'll like it.*

Don't count on it. And just bear in mind that losers go to hell, you know. Oh no, wait, that's liars.

"No!" shouted Asher, glowering at his father in the pool.

"You can't stay in here all day," Knox calmly told him, heading toward the ladder.

"Can," insisted Asher.

"Can't."

"Can."

"No. You. Can't. Now let's get out of the—"

Flames burst to life around Asher, who then disappeared from his father's arms and reappeared on Khloé's sun lounger. He pouted at her. "Daddy's mean, Koey."

She picked him up and cuddled him close. "Aw, dude, your daddy just wants to put more sunscreen on you so that your skin doesn't burn."

But his little pout didn't go away.

Harper sighed and pulled out a bottle of kid's sunscreen. "Come on, little man, let's put some of this on you."

"Koey do it," he said, leaning into the female imp.

"Sure thing." Khloé took the bottle and started applying the lotion. "You hungry yet?"

He shook his little head.

"Thirsty?"

He shook his head again.

Harper leaned forward. "I think you're tired. Want a nap?"

"No," he said, but a yawn almost cracked his jaw.

Harper held her arms. "Come on, come lie here with me."

"*No nap.*"

Khloé tapped his nose. "How about you just lie here with me then and we'll cuddle?"

"'Kay," he easily agreed and then curled up beside her. Knox adjusted the position of the sun parasol so that it placed Asher in the shade.

Harper huffed at Khloé. "Why does he listen to you more than he does me?"

"Because I'm awesome and you're not," said Khloé.

Harper snorted. "If by awesome you mean 'mentally deranged,' yeah, you are. So I find it highly concerning that you have some kind of influence over my son."

"Wow, that sounds like a 'you' problem." Khloé slipped on her sunglasses. "Now, if you don't mind, I have some sunbathing to do while I snuggle my dude."

"Actually, I *do* mind—"

"Again, sounds like a 'you' problem. Good luck with that." Khloé lay back on the lounger with a contented sigh.

Harper let out an exasperated sound. "You know what, sometimes I think the ancient incantors were onto something when they said that all imps should be strangled at birth."

"And yet another 'you' problem."

Harper shot to her feet. "I need another drink."

CHAPTER SIX

Sitting on the sofa with one leg crossed over the other, twirling her ankle madly, Khloé flicked a look at the living room clock on the mantelpiece. 1:03am.

Two minutes. She had two minutes until Keenan arrived.

She'd spent the entire weekend driving him insane in every possible way. Which had been absolutely delightful, and she would sincerely treasure the memories. But no matter what she did or how pissed he got, the bastard stuck to soda and coffee. He'd looked so close to cracking when she casually talked of her brand-new vibrator and its various speeds and settings, but he'd managed to hold out. Awkward asshole.

After he'd given her and Raini a ride home from the airport earlier, he'd telepathically told Khloé to expect him at exactly 1:05am. She hadn't responded with anything other than a nonchalant shrug, but she was feeling far from blasé about this.

She'd tried distracting herself for hours—unpacking her suitcase, tackling her laundry, cleaning a kitchen that did not need cleaning. But her thoughts kept circling back to the none too small matter that, hey, Keenan would be here soon.

Shit, how had she gotten herself into this situation?

The same way she always got herself into sticky situations—she'd jumped without thinking. Which was usually fun. But now . . . huh, so *this* was what regret felt like. She happened to agree with her father—it carried the metaphorical stench of weakness.

She shook off the pointless emotion. It wouldn't *really* be so bad to have an incubus feed from her, would it? Such a thing was allegedly very enjoyable, and Khloé *liked* to enjoy herself. Ergo, she could freaking relax.

Well, she'd find that a lot easier if the incubus in question wasn't Keenan—a guy she'd wanted for years; a guy she couldn't help but measure others against; a guy who didn't want her as much as she did him or he'd have made it clear by now.

The knock on the front door made Khloé jump.

It's not a big deal, she told herself. The whole thing would take, what, three minutes? Maybe even less. Then he'd be gone, and she'd be floating on a post-orgasm cloud. That wouldn't be a bad way to end her weekend . . . or to start a new week, as it were, considering it was technically Monday morning.

Standing, she smoothed out the wrinkles in her sundress and padded into the hallway on bare feet. Taking in a deep breath, she pulled open the front door. And there he stood, tall and still. His hooded blue eyes locked on hers, full of so much heat and promise that her poor hormones went into a frenzy. And, of course, her body lit up like a Christmas tree.

Khloé stepped back, allowing him to enter. He prowled inside, exuding so much self-assurance and intense sexual energy she was surprised she didn't feel dizzy with it.

When she closed the door, he turned to face her. His eyes dropped to the pulse that was beating far too fast in her neck.

That blue gaze then snapped back to hers and drifted over her face, searching.

He took a step toward her, closing the space between them. "I won't force you, Khloé. If you want to back out, say so now."

And she knew there'd be no recriminations from him; that he'd accept her "no" and never mention it ever again. Strangely, that was what encouraged her to lift her chin a notch and say, "I don't break my word." It was quite possibly her only redeeming quality.

The air chilled as his demon surfaced, making his eyes bleed to black. "Then we will take what you owe us," it said in its usual emotionless tone.

She licked her lips. "Bring it."

Its eyes glimmered with what could have been amusement, and then it subsided. Towering over her, Keenan breezed his finger along her jawline. "You sure?"

"Just get it over with. The movie I want to watch starts soon—I ain't missing it." But he just kept on staring, and her hormones just kept on having a nervous breakdown.

Sexual tension pulsed between them like a heartbeat, and an agonizing suspense filled the air. She licked her lips. "Keenan—" Her heart thudded as a spicy, mouthwatering, aphrodisiac scent assaulted her senses. *Here we go.*

Like last time, the air turned humid and warm and stifling. Her lips parted as an unbearable heat whipped through her body so fast that she almost swayed. And then she was at the mercy of the carnal hunger that rocked her entire being.

She staggered backwards until she met the wall. Her nerve-endings turned hypersensitive. Her nipples peaked and throbbed. Her breasts swelled and ached. Her clit pulsed and tingled.

She couldn't help but moan. Her pussy . . . It was like there was a pressure inside her. Not filling her, *stretching* her open, making her keenly conscious of just how empty she was. Her inner walls spasmed, desperate to grip *something*, but there was nothing there.

A warm hand collared her throat, and Keenan's energy—so dark, so sensual—poured into her, filling her from head to toe. She slapped her palms on the wall behind her, scratching it a little with her nails.

An image flashed in her mind of him on his knees in front of her, his face in her pussy, her dress bunched around her waist. And she knew he'd planted the image there.

His mouth hovered over hers as he breathed in each moan and breath she released. But it was the sexual energy emanating from her that he was drinking in. The whole time, his eyes didn't release hers. Not even for a second. There was so much raw hunger there it made her shiver.

Phantom sensations swept over her—fingers pinching her nipples, hands cupping her breasts, a tongue lashing her clit, teeth biting her inner thigh. She groaned and whimpered and arched into him. She also cursed him through gritted teeth, because he didn't deliver any of those phantom touches to her pussy. A pussy that kept on aching and spasming.

God, she was so wet. And so damn close to coming. But he was controlling her orgasm, wasn't he? She wouldn't be able to come until he *let* her.

Bastard.

Another image flashed in her mind. An image of him fucking her right there against the wall, his teeth in her neck, his fingers digging into the thighs she'd wrapped around him.

"Ready to come?" he asked against her mouth, his lips brushing hers.

"Yes." A thick shaft plunged inside her. It wasn't real, she knew that, but it felt so fucking good. And it hit her sweet spot just right as it drove into her hard and fast and—

Then she was coming.

She sucked in a breath as pure pleasure ripped through her body, fragmenting her, devastating her, tearing a scream out of her throat.

Feeling sapped of strength, she could only sag against the wall, her chest burning with every ragged breath. She blinked at Keenan. "Well, that was—"

He slammed his mouth on hers. Hot and demanding, it ate at her own—licking, tasting, nipping. Sparks flared. Chemicals raced. Skilled hands slid over her, clutching and shaping. And she knew things were about to spiral out of control.

Keenan kissed her hard and deep, unable to get enough. Every flick of her tongue dragged him deeper under her spell. His thoughts scattered. His body tightened. His blood thickened. His heart pounded like a drum.

He hadn't thought his dick could get any harder. He'd been wrong. He was full and heavy to the point of pain.

Watching her come, tasting the sweet and delectable energy she gave off, all but shredded the leash he held over himself. But he'd known it would, hadn't he? He'd come here hoping she'd make his control slip—he could admit that to himself now.

He needed to feel her skin against his. Needed to taste and mark. Needed to answer the oppressive, relentless hunger before he went insane with it.

It was always going to happen. The carnal, primitive need that taunted them both . . . you couldn't just ignore something like that. You had no choice but to explore it; no choice but to let it play out if you ever wanted to be free of it.

Khloé gasped as she suddenly found her front pinned to the wall. Keenan pressed himself so tightly to her back that his weight held her in place. His hands were now wrapped around her wrists, keeping her own hands high above her head. Still, she struggled—which did nothing other than make the thick shaft in his jeans jerk against her back.

"Shh," he soothed, his warm breath tickling her neck. The little hairs on her nape rose, and a slight shiver made its way down her spine.

Frowning, she glanced at him over her shoulder. "Did you just shush me?" Like she was five?

"As I see it, you have two choices," he said, transferring both her wrists to one hand. "Choice number one: I walk out that door right now, and we both hope that this thing between us fades on its own at some point." He slid his free hand down her arm, along her side, and then cupped her hip. "Choice number two: I fuck you. Hard. Deep. I give us what we both need, and maybe then we can get some fucking peace. You choose."

Utterly blindsided by his words, Khloé could only stare at him. Jesus, he was serious. It wasn't exactly flattering to hear that he wanted to fuck her so he could have "some peace." Essentially, he hoped to rid his system of the attraction they'd been wrestling with for years. But, really, she could see some appeal in that. It certainly was not fun to crave someone you couldn't have. It would be nice if those cravings went away.

Plus, a night of mind-blowing sex would certainly be welcome—she would bet that Keenan could quite easily deliver that. And it would be a damn nice memory to savor. Her demon was all for it.

Still, she found herself hesitating. It was highly possible that he'd later condemn himself for sleeping with his Prime's cousin. Hell, he might even treat Khloé to one of those "it was a mistake" talks. Then she'd have to pop his head like an oversized zit.

He caught her earlobe with his teeth and softly suckled on it.

"Well, what will it be? Hmm?"

She licked her lips. "Not sure it's a good idea, Don Juan. You'll regret it afterward." She almost flinched as sharp teeth grazed her neck hard enough to sting.

"The only thing I'll regret is not doing this sooner. Spent too long jacking off to the thought of having you. I want the real thing. You going to give it to me? You going to let me fuck you hard and raw?"

Well, she was a big fan of hard and raw, so it was certainly tempting. Her body was *totally* up for it. She'd wondered more than once whether or not he'd be able to fit the full length of his dick inside her. She wanted to find out. Wanted to know if sex between them was as good as their chemistry hinted at.

He nipped her jaw. "Tell me you don't want to know how it feels to have me inside you," he said with a soft growl she felt in her core. "You can't, can you?"

No, she damn well couldn't. And she knew she'd never find herself in this situation again. If she sent him away, he'd never make another move. Then she'd always wonder just how good it could have been.

"If you're absolutely sure—and I mean *sure*—you won't regret this tomorrow, I'll go for option two."

Satisfaction flooded Keenan's veins, ramping up the need already pounding through him. "Oh, I'm sure."

His demon settled, certain that she wasn't going anywhere. It wanted him to take her there and then, but Keenan didn't want to rush this. He'd waited too long for it. He wanted to make this so good for her that she'd never forget it. Never forget *him*.

"I've wanted to fuck you since the second I met you. Did you know that?"

Her breath hitched. "I do now."

He traced the shell of her ear with the tip of his tongue.

"Shall I tell you what I'm going to do to you? I'm going to fuck you with my fingers until you come. Then I'm going to lick your pussy clean—oh yeah, I can smell how wet you are. And then I'm going to give us both what we've wanted for far too fucking long."

Sliding his hand from her hip to her stomach, Keenan kept her hips flush with his as he pulled back an inch or so. "First, I need to make one thing clear, Khloé." He snaked his hand under her dress and dipped it just enough into her panties for him to circle her clit with his finger. His cock jerked at her soft moan. "And it needs to be very, very clear."

"What?" she rasped, straining against his hold to arch into his touch.

He thrust his hand all the way into her panties and cupped her pussy. "This is mine tonight. *You* are mine tonight." If he could only have her for a single night, he'd at least fucking own her the entire time. Own her with his fingers, his tongue, his dick. "We clear?"

Khloé swallowed. Why that low-pitched, commanding tone tightened her nipples and made her lower stomach clench, she had no clue. "Uh-huh."

Humming in approval, he slipped his finger between her slick folds. "That's my girl. Now feel what I do to you."

Closing her eyes, she bit her lip as his skilled fingers began to drive her out of her mind. They went to work on her slit, stroking and teasing. They taunted her clit, flicking and pinching. And just when she thought she couldn't take anymore, they thrust into her pussy.

He groaned. "Fuck, you're tight."

Oh God, and now he was pumping those fingers hard into her pussy. She rocked into his hand over and over, grinding against the heel of his palm. Finally, she imploded with a loud cry, her knees buckling, feeling his dick throb against her back.

"Dreamed of doing that." Withdrawing his hand from her panties, he spun her to face him and took her mouth again. The kiss was hot and savage, all tongue and teeth.

She sensed then that there'd be no gentle, easy seduction. No soft words or coaxing. He meant to *take* what he wanted. Well, that was fine with her. Being ravished was always fun.

Not all that good at waiting for what she wanted, Khloé tugged at his fly. A hot, hungry growl poured down her throat and lifted the hairs on her arms. His cock sprang out and, just, *wow*. It was hot and hard and so damn *big*.

Should she touch it? Should she lick it? Should she feed it a peanut?

There was a lot of yanking and pulling as they shed each other's clothes. Naked, she trailed her hands down his chest, almost shivering at the delicious feel of all that sleek skin and pure male muscle. She gripped his shaft hard, liking the feel of it throbbing—

She blinked as she suddenly found herself sprawled on the floor with Keenan kneeling between her thighs. Hmm, this seemed promising.

Curling his powerful body over hers, he planted a hand either side of her head and then began to lick, kiss, and scrape his teeth over her neck. She bucked her hips, trying to grind her clit against his cock, but he edged out of reach. *Ugh*.

Khloé inhaled sharply as he sucked one nipple into his mouth, his hand plumping her breast. He licked and suckled—sometimes slow and soft, sometimes hard and rough. She shuddered when he moved on to her neglected breast, teasing and tasting and touching. Every time he sucked or bit her nipple, she somehow felt it in her pussy.

Arching into him, she gripped his hair. But the strands slipped through her fingers as he slid down her body. Then his mouth was on her. Oh, Jesus. That fabulous tongue licked and swirled and plunged, making her shake and writhe and moan.

She could feel another orgasm creeping up on her. Could feel the tension building and building, winding her so damn tight. And then she shattered, crying out as her body arched and shook.

Collapsing against the floor, she opened her eyes. Kneeling between her thighs once more, he snatched a condom out of his jeans' pocket and swiftly donned it. His shimmering blue gaze snapped to hers, glittering with so much heat and . . . something close to menace. Oh yeah, he was hanging by the thinnest of threads.

Keenan grabbed her legs, yanked her closer, and then roughly pushed her spread thighs up towards her chest. Usually, he had no problem keeping a woman dangling on the edge of an orgasm for hours. Desire never rode him hard. Desperation never seized him. Anticipation never filled him so fully that he couldn't hold back any longer.

Now, nothing mattered but burying himself inside Khloé. She gasped when he fed her the broad head of his cock. His shaft throbbed with the overwhelming urge to jackhammer into her over and over. Some-fucking-how, he resisted. She was so small and slight, and he worried he'd hurt her.

"Look at me," he ground out. He wanted to stare into her eyes, wanted to be sure she wasn't in any pain. He also wanted to see them glaze over with pleasure as he fucked her.

Grasping onto what little control he had, Keenan sank inside her slow and smooth. *Fuck*, he'd never been inside a pussy so goddamn tight. If she wasn't so slick, he'd struggle to enter her.

When he finally bottomed out, she let out a long, shaky breath and double-blinked. Pain pinched her brow, and she squirmed slightly.

"Shh, you're okay, I got you." He stroked her inner thighs, humming. "You took all of me like a good girl. I knew you would."

"Jesus, you're deep. My womb is like, '*What the fuck is in me?*'"

A laugh would have bubbled out of him if he wasn't grinding his teeth against the urge to pound into her. He slowly pulled back, leaving only the head of his dick inside her, and then he slammed home with such force she bucked beneath him. He did it again and again, ignoring his demon's demand for him to pick up his pace.

"Harder," she rasped. "I won't break."

"Don't want to hurt you."

"You won't." She licked her lips. "Besides, I like a little pain."

He closed his eyes, pausing mid-thrust. "Fuck, Khloé, you can't say shit like that." Not when he was precariously balancing on the knife-edge of what self-discipline he had left—and there wasn't much.

He'd never in his life felt like this. Desperate. Frantic. Shaken by the sheer intensity of the need flaring through him.

"*Harder,*" she repeated. "If it hurts, if I can't take it, I'll let you know. Come on, you know you want to."

He sank fully into her again, and her pussy rippled. "Jesus, Khloé, how can you be so tight?"

"I'm a virgin."

He blinked. "What?"

"Kidding. Sorry, there's been other guys before you." Her smile was all mischief. "And that just makes you want to fuck me so hard I'll never forget the feel of you, doesn't it?"

Yeah, it damn well did. *Tricky little witch.* He pulled back again. "You sure that's what you want?"

"Do I look unsure?" she snapped.

"No, baby, you look hungry for more of my dick." And so he gave it to her. His control a distant memory, he fucked her brutally at a merciless pace. Honest to God, it was like there was a fever in his blood.

Drowning in the hot, silken feel of her, he kept on driving hard and fast. He *couldn't* ease up. Couldn't slow down. He could only pound deep into her pussy over and over, driven by a need so basic and vicious he was helpless against it.

He wanted her to feel branded. Possessed. Owned. Greedy for more. He wanted no other man to ever again be good enough for her. Which made him a dick, but there it was.

Sexual energy swirled around her, sweet and spicy and mouth-watering. He breathed it in, let it fill his lungs. Fuck, the taste of her . . . no other beat it.

Still thrusting fast and deep, he grabbed her hand and splayed it over her stomach. "Can you feel me? Can you feel how deep I am?"

"Yes," she hissed. "God, don't stop, I'm gonna come."

She wasn't the only one. He felt the telling tingle at the base of his spine, knew he wouldn't last much longer. How could he? Those throaty fucking moans were killing him, and the inferno-hot grasp of her pussy was so gorgeously tight it was also pure torture.

He draped himself over her and gave her his weight. "I want to feel your pussy clamp down on my cock. I want to shoot my come so deep inside you, you'll swear you can taste it."

She clung to his back, pricking him with her nails. "Fuck, fuck, fuck, fuck, *fuck*."

He slipped his hand between their bodies and parted her slick folds. "Come." He brutally rammed into her, hitting her clit with his dick again and again.

Her body shook, her head fell back, and her mouth opened in a silent scream. Keenan spat a curse as her hot, snug pussy contracted around him. His thrusts turned rough and erratic as he jackhammered into her over and over. Then he drove his swelling cock balls-deep inside her and exploded so intensely he could swear he saw stars.

Feeling as pliant as melted wax, Khloé let her arms flop to her sides. Yowza. Just yowza.

They lay there for a few minutes, shaking with aftershocks and striving to catch their breath. Finally, he pulled out of her and rolled onto his back—she felt his reluctance to move, and it made her demon smug.

"Fuck, I didn't mean to be that rough. Did I hurt you?"

Khloé looked at him, knowing she wore a lazy, sated expression. "I look in pain to you?"

He didn't respond to the rhetorical question. He merely stood upright and held out his hand. She took it, allowing him to pull her to her feet. Her body ached in some very interesting places, but she liked it.

His gaze raked over her, but there was no heat this time. His expression was carefully blank. She could almost see him pulling in, pulling *away*, making sure she understood it was just sex and that he'd meant it when he said there'd be no repeat.

Khloé almost rolled her eyes. Guys were always so sure that women would get "attached." It was kind of narcissistic, really.

She hadn't once doubted that he meant what he'd said. Nor had she read anything into what just happened. But the sudden remoteness in his manner chilled her all the same. Her demon glared at him, itching to do something that would snap him out of it.

"Bathroom?" he asked.

"The downstairs one is to the left of the kitchen." Watching his naked ass stride into the bathroom, she almost hummed. Well, it was a very nice image. One she wouldn't see again. But that was okay. Really. Truly.

She reached for her clothes. By the time he reappeared from

the bathroom, having disposed of the condom, she'd slipped her dress and panties back on.

He pulled on his own clothes without a word and then turned to her, clenching his fists . . . as if not trusting that he wouldn't make a grab for her. His expression might be blank, but it was clear to her that he didn't want to leave—his reluctance was right there in his body language. That made her feel a little better, but her demon was still in a funk.

Seconds ticked by, and then he cleared his throat. "Lock up after me." He left without a second glance. How nice.

*

Every house she passed looked the same. Plain and sterile with a white, rusty car in the driveway and a small, neglected lawn. No matter how far or how fast Khloé walked along the footpath, she couldn't seem to get closer to the house on the end of the street. It always remained out of reach, just like the woman who resided in it.

Khloé dipped her hand in her pocket to feel for the house key. It wasn't there. She'd just have to ring the doorbell. Sometimes Penelope answered, sometimes she didn't. It depended how much Bourbon she'd—

A graying, smirking, suited-up guy appeared a few feet in front of Khloé. She stopped walking. Enoch. Not good. "Jolene is looking for you."

"Yes, I know." He glanced around. "Such a dull, inane dream for someone so full of life and energy."

"And just what the fuck do you want?"

He laughed, delighted. "And there's that typical Wallis attitude. But then, all imps are full of snark and sass, aren't they?"

Well, yeah.

"Your grandmother should have known better than to cross me."

Khloé rolled her eyes. Like that made him special. Her family members crossed people all the time.

"She'll pay for that. But not by my hand. You know, losing a person you love is an agony like no other. It steals your breath, pounds your soul, drags you down so low you can't see a way back up. Your grandmother's going to feel that same pain when I kill you. I would have killed her daughter to repay her for killing mine. But it's partly your fault that Molly is in that grave, so I'll destroy you instead. Then I'll have you kill Jolene." His eyes hardened, but his smirk widened. "Come, walk with me."

Her brows drew together as the air around her thickened until it felt like there was a weight on her shoulders. A weight that seemed to be pushing her deeper and deeper into . . . something. Her surroundings blurred, and the colors mashed together like a pastel painting. Only he remained clear.

He held out his hand. "Come. I can help you reach your mother's house. That is where you're heading, isn't it? We'll go there together. Maybe we'll even find her inside. Maybe she'll even be sober. Wouldn't that be nice?"

Khloé pressed a hand to her chest. The thick air she'd inhaled was like a pressure inside her ribcage. A pressure that was building and building, inflating her lungs like they were balloons.

"Come," he ordered, flexing the hand he held out. Impatience shimmered in his gaze. "Don't resist. Just obey. Just—"

Khloé's eyes flipped open—it was a move that almost hurt, since her eyelids felt so damn heavy. The darkness of her bedroom greeted her. Maybe it was a noise, she wasn't sure, but something had wrenched her out of a deep, fucked-up sleep.

Tensing, she reached out with her psychic senses. Her pulse skittered when she found two other minds. Demonic minds. Both felt *wrong* somehow.

She kicked off the bedcovers and, silent as always, snapped out her wings. She flapped them hard once, making her body zoom upwards. She plastered her palms and the soles of her feet to the ceiling and hung there like a spider—an ability that awesomely freaked out Ciaran; she'd pounced on him from above plenty of times over the years when they were kids. And adults, if she was honest.

Khloé had expected the intruders to stealthily make their way through her house. They didn't. Floorboards creaked, furniture was jostled, and doors were shoved open. And then two people barged into her room, their movements awkward and clunky.

Her nose wrinkled, and she almost gagged. They smelled of dirt and rot and . . . death. As she took in their weathered clothing and decaying bodies, she was sure as shit that they were already dead.

Well, fuckadoodledo.

The stout one grunted. The teenage corpse gargled a weird sound. Not that they were communicating—no independent thoughts drifted through their brains. They were both fully controlled by their puppet master.

In any other circumstance, Khloé would have plunged her mind into that of her enemy and taken the wheel. She could control most minds with minimal effort, but she couldn't control the dead. Only a demon with the power of necrokinesis could do that.

She could take on two reanimated corpses—they'd be unable to use whatever demonic abilities they'd possessed when alive. But Enoch might be able to attack her with some of his abilities just by looking at her through the eyes of his puppets. That wasn't good.

The dead teen suddenly jerked back, his back bowing. Then his body snapped straight, and a long breath rattled out of him. "I know you're in here, Khloé," he said, his voice rough and garbled. "You can't hide for long."

True. But she'd never intended to hide, only to observe; to study her enemy.

She dropped onto the back of the teen. Her weight was enough to send him to his knees, no doubt due to how rickety his bones were. Wicked fast, she lifted her hand and sent a powerful wave of electric fire soaring at the stout corpse. Flickering and crackling, the flames whipped him so hard he crashed into the wall.

She slapped her hands on the teen's head and emitted yet more electric fire; it buzzed and sparked beneath her palms. She might not be able to take control of his mind, but she could sure as shit fry it so that the corpse was useless to its master.

A hard, white-hot impact slammed into the back of her shoulder, barely missing her wings and knocking the breath from her lungs. *Hellfire orb.*

Gritting her teeth against the agony of her skin blistering and burning, she stood and whipped around. The stout corpse was still convulsing as shockwaves of electric fire moved through it, but her power clearly hadn't hurt Enoch, because he was still able to attack her via the corpse.

Just then, another ball of hellfire appeared in its hand. It appeared too late, though, because she'd conjured an orb of her own. She tossed it at the corpse's face, blinding it, cutting off Enoch's ability to see and hurt her. Seconds later, it slumped, and she knew the necromancing piece of shit had withdrawn from its mind.

Her shoulders dropped as she looked from one corpse to the other. Neither was a pretty sight—the teen's mush-for-brains was trickling out of his ears, mouth, and nose; the face of the other guy was blistering, charring, and peeling away, courtesy of the hellfire.

Speaking of blistering skin . . .

She peeked at the injury on the back of her shoulder. It was ugly and raw, but it wasn't very deep. Thankfully, she was a fast healer, so it should be gone within the hour.

She psychically reached out to touch Ciaran's mind. *Bro, I got a problem here—meet me in my bedroom.*

A male mind slid against hers. *Are you going to ask me for a condom again?*

She snickered. *No. I'm going to ask you to help me get rid of a couple of corpses.*

It took mere seconds for her brother to appear. After hearing her story and losing his ever-loving mind, he teleported Jolene and two of her sentinels, Orrin and Mitch, to the house. While her grandmother and the sentinels examined the bodies, Khloé told them what happened.

"You should have called for help sooner," clipped Ciaran, standing in the doorway of her bedroom, his jaw clenched, his arms folded across his chest.

Khloé blinked. "Why?"

He gritted his teeth. "Because you were up against a Lazarus demon and two corpses, why else?"

"I've been up against worse." It was the truth. "Besides, I figured I could take them. He was able to attack me with hellfire orbs through them, but he didn't toss any of those black, smoky orbs."

"There'll be limits as to what he can do through his puppets," Jolene told her.

"I don't recognize either of the bodies; they definitely weren't from our lair," said Orrin.

Jolene cursed. "So Enoch's now targeting the cemeteries of other lairs."

"He might be hoping the disappearances of the bodies will be reported and that you'll then somehow be held responsible for it all," Mitch suggested.

"Possibly." Jolene planted her hands on her hips. "I'm going to kill the bastard when I find him. And I *will* find him."

"Did you manage to locate David Shore?" asked Khloé.

"Yes. He lives in Nebraska, but he's on a business trip at the moment. We'll have to wait a few days before we can pay him a visit."

Orrin looked at Khloé. "Enoch likes to finish the jobs he started—it's a matter of pride for him. He'll be both embarrassed and furious that you thwarted him. He's not going to let it slide, and I doubt it'll be long before he strikes again. We had members of the Force watching your house, but they were distracted when two cars collided further up the street. They ran over to assist."

"Enoch probably staged it," said Jolene.

"It seems likely." Rubbing her aching head, Khloé asked, "Hey, Grams, do you know if Enoch can dream-walk? I think he visited me in my dream, because it seems an awfully big coincidence that I *just* dreamed of him telling me that he'll not only kill me but use *my corpse* to hurt *you* all in the name of revenge . . . then something woke me up, and I realized that I wasn't alone in the house."

"It sounds as if he can indeed dream-walk, but I can't say for sure," replied Jolene.

Well, that wasn't good. "Can he hurt me through my dreams?"

"No. But he may be able to alter your dreams or drag you into a deeper sleep."

Khloé felt her brows draw together as she remembered how the air in the dream had thickened and weighed her down. "I think he tried to do that tonight."

"He most likely hoped to lure you into such a deep sleep that his puppets wouldn't wake you."

"Well, it didn't work."

"Probably because you're resistant to most forms of mental manipulation. But he can hurt you in other ways, so be prepared for him. Have you told Teague what's been going on?"

"Not yet. I was going to wait until he returned from his trip."

"I'd call him and fill him in, if I were you. There's a chance he could find out through the demonic grapevine, and then he'd be upset that you kept it from him. Plus, he has a right to know. And you'd want him to contact you if the situation was reversed."

True, true. "Fine. I'll call him tomorrow."

Ciaran planted his feet. "I'll move in here for a while and stay in one of your spare bedrooms so I can teleport you out of here if anything happens."

Oh *the hell* no. She loved her brother, she truly did, but he was a nightmare for her to live with. Mostly because he ate like a horse, never tidied up after himself, "borrowed" her stuff, and thought he could tell her what to do.

"You can teleport *to* me in the blink of an eye—that means you don't *need* to stay here," Khloé pointed out.

"That would be true if I could trust that you'll call me for help straight away, but I can't," said Ciaran. "You'd rather take him on alone than pull me into a dangerous situation."

"Yeah, well, you pull the same shit with me."

"Which is why both of you are going to promise me here and now that you will telepathically call out for help if Enoch attacks," said Jolene. "Consider it an order."

Ciaran let out a sigh. "I promise."

Khloé hesitated, twisting her mouth.

Jolene took a step toward her, her expression grave. "Enoch wouldn't just kill you, Khloé. He made it very clear that he means to reanimate your corpse and send you after someone you love. Do you really want that?"

Khloé exhaled heavily. No, she didn't. "I promise I'll send out a telepathic call for help if Enoch makes another move."

"Good. Now let's get you cleaned up."

CHAPTER SEVEN

Just as the studio's lunch break began, a hand thumped on Khloé's desk. Looking up from the appointment book, she found Harper standing there, her expression tight.

The sphinx folded her arms. "Do you know how frustrating it is that passive-aggressiveness goes right over your head?"

Khloé blinked. "Huh?"

"I've been glaring at you for *hours*, and you haven't once commented on it."

"Oh."

Devon sighed. "Just ask her what's wrong, Khloé."

Putting down her pen, Khloé asked, "What's wrong?"

"You didn't call me last night after Enoch sent dead people to your house—*that's* what's wrong," said Harper.

"You're still stewing over that? I thought we dealt with this earlier." Really, there hadn't seemed a need to disturb all her girls with news of something they could do nothing about. "It's not like you found out *days* later. Jolene called you this morning and brought you up to speed. Raini didn't find out about it until this morning either, since it took a few hours for the news to fully circulate through the lair."

Khloé was guessing that Harper had shared it with her mate and sentinels, because Keenan earlier telepathically ranted at Khloé for not telling him herself. She'd snickered and then slammed a mental door on him. The guy would never learn.

"That's not the point," said Harper. "What happened was some major shit. I should have heard it from you immediately after it happened, *not* hours later from Grams."

"She hadn't given me permission to mention it to anyone outside the lair."

"But I'm your cousin! Your *favorite* cousin."

"You don't tell me everything that goes on in your lair."

Harper spluttered. "Yeah, well . . ."

"Stop being a whiny bitch."

"Hey!"

"Raini and Devon got over me not calling them last night."

"No, they didn't, which is why they've been scowling at you all morning."

Khloé felt her nose wrinkle. "They have? Really?"

"*Oh my God.*"

Shrugging one shoulder, Khloé turned to head to the break room. "Well, if you guys are so pissed, you probably won't want to hear what happened between me and Keenan before Enoch came."

Just like that, she was surrounded by all three women, causing her to halt.

"You let him feed from you?" asked Devon, her green eyes twinkling. "Was it good? It was good, wasn't it?"

"I expected him to drop the whole thing now that he'd made his point that he wasn't an alcoholic," said Raini. "He's just always been so determined to keep his hands off you. Then again, I don't suppose he needed to touch you to make you come."

"He *did* make you come, right?" asked Harper. "He didn't leave you hanging to be a prick or anything?"

"Oh, he made me come," replied Khloé. "Four times, in fact."

Devon's mouth dropped open. "Four times? You let him feed from you four— Oh my god, you slept with him, didn't you?"

"On my hallway floor."

Raini puffed out a breath. "Wow. Then what happened?"

"Then he left."

"He left?" echoed Harper, her brows lowering. "Like . . . just got dressed and walked out?"

"Pretty much," replied Khloé. "A few words were exchanged here and there. I wasn't offended or anything. He made it clear beforehand that it'd only be a one-time thing."

Harper studied her face. "And you're good with that? Because you look and sound good with it, but this is *Keenan* we're talking about. You like him a lot."

"I do," Khloé admitted. "But neither him nor I do relationships, as you well know."

"What if he wants a repeat of last night?"

"He won't get one." Khloé wasn't going to risk that he could slip through her defenses and wangle his way under her skin. He wouldn't *purposely* do it, but he had the potential to because, as Harper had pointed out, Khloé liked him a lot. Which was rather unfortunate. "Well, are we eating lunch or what? I'm starving." She shrugged past them and headed to the break room.

"Oh no, you can't just close a door on a conversation like that," protested Devon, trailing after her. "You haven't told us what it's like to be fed on by an incubus yet! Enquiring minds want to know."

Khloé crossed her eyes. No beings were more curious than hellcats.

In between bites of lunch, she told them a little more about what happened the previous night and answered each of Devon's nosy-ass questions. Once their break was over, Khloé returned to her desk and spent yet more hours talking with clients, booking appointments, and supplying the girls with coffee when need be.

It wasn't easy to power through it all when her muscles ached, her body felt weak, and the strange chill *still* hadn't left her bones. All she wanted was to go home and crash.

Ten minutes before the studio was due to close, while she was busy tidying her desk, Knox swanned in with Asher balanced on his hip. Levi followed them inside . . . as did Keenan.

They all nodded at Tanner, who sat on the sofa, waiting for Devon. Keenan's hooded, watchful eyes fixed on Khloé, focusing on her so intently her nerves went a little haywire.

Pinpricks of awareness swept over her skin, and memories of last night crawled all over her. Memories of his mouth crushing hers, of his fingers thrusting inside her, of his hands gripping her thighs tight to hold her still for his possession. Oh, and he *had* taken complete possession of her.

Being the sole focus of all that raw sexuality had been super-hot. And, damn, he'd been good with those hands. His tongue was equally skilled. And he certainly knew how to use that weapon of mass destruction in his jeans.

Seeing the hard set of his jaw and the flinty look in his eyes, she knew he was still pissed that she hadn't informed him of last night's incident. Ha, what fun. She could see that he was gasping to give her one of his "you need to be more careful and should have called me" lectures. But he'd never do it while outsiders were around, and there was currently one client still left in the studio.

"The auditions for pornos are outside and on your far right," she said.

He ground his teeth so hard it was audible. "You do know you're insane, right?"

"Insane people don't know they're insane."

Flames swallowed the pen in her hand, making it disappear. More flames burst out of Asher's palm, and then he was holding her pen.

Unable to stifle a smile, Khloé headed to her baby cousin. "Give it back, mister. That's not yours."

He offered her the pen, his eyes smiling.

"Good boy," said Khloé, taking it back. He reached for her, flexing his little fists, so she took him into her arms. "You're ridiculously adorable, you know."

Harper put her hands on her hips. "How come he so easily obeys you?"

"He knows he can't handle this much crazy yet."

Levi snickered. "Can't argue with that."

Asher pointed to the vending machine. "Candy."

"You want candy? I can make that happen." Khloé crossed to the machine and bumped the side of it with her fist. Instantly, it whirred to life and dropped a Hershey's bar.

"I do it," said Asher. He smacked the machine with his little hand, frowning when nothing happened. He huffed. "Gossake!"

Knowing it was his way of saying, "For God's sake," she had to laugh. Noticing that Harper didn't find it so amusing, Khloé said, "At least he's not spouting swear words." Yet.

Flames engulfed a bag of chips inside the machine, and then that same bag of chips appeared in a burst of fire . . . right in Asher's open hand. His face lit up, and he let out one of his infectious giggles. "Mama, look!"

"I see, I see." Smiling, Harper took him from Khloé and

nuzzled his neck. "Want to sit on the big chair again while you eat your ill-gotten goods? You guys wouldn't *believe* how many times a day he uses his gifts to steal shit from people. It makes Grams so proud," Harper added, rolling her eyes.

"He might be a sphinx like his mom," began Raini, "but he's an imp in his soul."

Khloé nodded. "And don't we all just think that's fabulous?" she said, completely serious. Everyone stared at her. Frowning, she lifted her shoulders. "What?"

*

"Thank you, Meg," Knox said to the Hispanic she-demon as she cleared the dining room table, piling dishes and silverware onto a tray.

Meg inclined her head with a fond smile and then left the room. She'd worked at Knox's estate for years and did everything from housekeeping to watching over Asher.

Full to his stomach, Keenan leaned back in his chair. He was always guaranteed a gourmet meal if he ate at Knox and Harper's home. Meg was a damn good cook.

With its spacious rooms, high ceilings, chandeliers, and bulletproof blue-tinted windows, the modern piece of architecture was the height of luxury. It wasn't showy or pretentious, though. It had both charm and warmth. Still, it wasn't until Harper came along and added personal touches to the place that it truly felt like a home.

She was currently upstairs with Asher, intending to give him a bath before putting him to bed. The toy car he'd left on the table had disappeared in a burst of flames a few moments ago, so he'd obviously called for it. The kid was a hoot.

Eying Keenan, Knox picked up his half-empty glass. "So . . . you slept with Khloé."

Keenan didn't let his expression change. "Did I?"

"It was obvious to me just by the way you were looking at her earlier, but that's only because I know you so well." Knox sipped his wine. "Was it merely a one-night stand?"

Keenan cast a quick look at the closed dining room door. He was a private person and didn't like airing his personal business.

"Meg can't hear us from here," said Knox. "She'll be busy in the kitchen for a while."

Yeah, Keenan could hear dishware clattering and water running from a faucet. "Khloé and I agreed it would be a one-time thing."

"For a person who's finally had the very thing they've wanted for years, you don't seem happy about it. Is your demon pushing you for a repeat? You usually only wear that 'don't speak to me' expression when your demon's riding you about something. You said it liked her just fine. Was that an understatement?"

It was more than a damn understatement. The demon wanted a lot more than just a repeat. It had been in a foul mood ever since Keenan left Khloé's home in the early hours of this morning, and it had gotten progressively worse throughout the day. The entity wanted to be at her side—she amused and entertained it, giving it a break from the relentless boredom that plagued all demons.

When Keenan had heard that Enoch had struck again, a fury like he'd never felt had torn through his system, just as it had coursed through his demon. They both wanted to track down the son of a bitch and kill him with their bare hands. They also wanted to yell at Khloé for not calling out to them for aid.

Yes, Keenan understood why she hadn't. He wouldn't have expected her to call out to Larkin or Levi, so it wasn't fair of Keenan to expect her to contact *him*. Nonetheless, he was pissed. And that same illogical anger hummed through his demon.

He'd purposely stayed away from her until later on, not trusting that he wouldn't chew a metaphorical chunk out of her ass—that wouldn't get him anywhere with Khloé. It wouldn't make her talk to him, and it certainly wouldn't help him convince her to contact him directly in the future if Enoch made another move.

By the time he'd seen her at the studio's closing time, he'd calmed down enough that he could talk without grinding his teeth. His demon? Not so much. So Keenan had held back on talking with her, giving his demon's foul mood the time to ease.

Considering what happened between them in the early hours of that morning, Keenan had expected her to act a little differently around him. Not awkward—that wasn't in her nature—but different . . . if for no other reason than he'd seen her naked. Plus, in his experience, a lot of women felt unnecessary shame after a one-night stand.

But Khloé had been her normal self, as if nothing had happened between them, as if it wasn't a blip on her radar. Maybe he should have been relieved that there was no weirdness, but he wasn't. Because it fucking rankled that she could just push what had happened to the back of her mind when he wasn't able to do it.

He'd fed himself a bunch of bullshit when he'd pinned her against her hallway wall—he'd lied to himself that the draw he felt toward her would disappear the moment she was no longer forbidden fruit; that taking her just once would be enough to burn out what was between them. He'd known, *known*, that all he'd want afterward was more. But he'd reached for what he craved anyway.

Could he have stopped himself? Yes. Probably. Maybe.

In any case, he hadn't wanted to stop. And now, well, he was fucked. He couldn't stop thinking about how beautiful she'd looked beneath him, accepting the hard fucking he gave her.

Usually, no matter how good the sex had been, he always felt a niggle of dissatisfaction after a one-night stand. Part of him felt . . . empty. He couldn't quite explain it.

There had been no such feeling of emptiness when he'd collapsed over Khloé, panting and shaking with aftershocks. He'd felt truly and utterly sated. In truth, sex had never been that good for him before.

But then, he wasn't exactly emotionally detached from Khloé, was he? Which was why it had been dangerous to succumb to what he wanted, but he'd done it anyway. He couldn't get the taste or feel of her out of his mind.

Realizing that Knox was waiting for an answer, Keenan sighed and said, "My demon's giving me trouble, but it's nothing I can't handle." The entity snorted, the little shit.

"Are you sure? Because if it wanted Khloé anywhere near as badly as you did, it won't so easily back down and give her up. Our demons can be quite obsessive. If it decides to fight you, you'll be in for a rough time."

"It's fought me on things before. It always subsided eventually."

Knox hummed and then set down his glass. "Would you care to tell me why you haven't touched a drop of alcohol for over a week?"

"No."

The Prime's mouth twitched. "Thought not. But it doesn't take a genius to work out that it had something to do with Khloé. You were proving to her that you aren't an alcoholic. She wanted proof of that before she allowed you in her bed?"

Sighing again, Keenan drummed his fingertips on the smooth table. "No. I proposed a wager." He relayed all the details, adding, "Naturally, I won."

"Naturally. Which, of course, you knew would happen. And

I'll bet you also knew that you'd find it next to impossible to stop at feeding from her. You were tempting fate."

"Maybe."

"I'm not judging you for any of this, Keenan. The only person who saw harm in you making a move on Khloé was you. If you don't want anything more with her, it'd be wise to keep it at a one-night stand, though, given that your demon is at risk of becoming attached to her."

Keenan felt his brow crease. "It's highly possessive of her. Wants to collect her. But it hasn't developed an attachment to her, and I can't envision it ever doing so. It doesn't form connections easily. My demon's got bigger trust issues than I have. The only people it truly trusts are you, Harper, and the other sentinels."

"Well, at least it's learned to trust." Knox's brows inched up. "It never had such faith in Thea?"

"No." And it had urged Keenan not to trust her either, but he hadn't listened.

"While we're on the subject of Thea, I called her and set up a meeting for tomorrow. I've made it clear that I'll give her one chance to be straight with me. If she was another breed of demon, I'd delve into her mind and dig out the truth for myself. But the only thing a person finds when invading a nightmare's mind is their own personal nightmare. As such, I'd like you to be at the meeting. You know her better than I do. You'll have a better shot at sensing if she's lying."

"I wouldn't be too sure of that—I bought her bullshit too many times."

"Because you *wanted* her to be telling the truth. Not because she'd fooled you."

"Maybe. Maybe not. In any case, if you need me to be at the meeting, I'll be there." But he wasn't looking forward to it.

Keenan rubbed at his forehead. "I don't suppose you've had any luck locating Enoch?"

"None whatsoever. You're still angry that Khloé didn't inform you of Enoch's attack herself?"

"Yes. I know it's irrational, but I'm still pissed. From what I heard, she didn't call out to *anyone*—not even someone from her own lair—until the threat had passed."

Knox's brow creased. "I don't think Khloé is quite as vulnerable to attack as you seem to think. If she was, Jolene would have her *very* closely guarded at all times. Harper isn't pushing for that to happen, so I can only assume that Khloé can defend herself quite well. She survived the attack, didn't she?"

"That doesn't mean she wouldn't benefit from some added protection."

"I realize that, although you're unlikely to admit it aloud, Khloé matters to you. I realize that you want to play some part in protecting her. But you've made the choice not to be in her life, Keenan. You can't have it both ways.

"Of course, you can speak to Jolene about it. She may allow you to play bodyguard for Khloé for a while. If so, Larkin can temporarily take over guarding Asher. But it's highly unlikely that Jolene will agree. In her situation, I wouldn't bring in an outsider to protect someone within my lair. I'd consider it my responsibility to keep them safe, and I wouldn't appreciate the insinuation that I wasn't able to do so."

"I'm not saying Jolene can't protect Khloé—"

"Then leave it be."

"And if it was Harper? Would you just leave it be?"

"Harper's my mate and my anchor, Keenan. To you, Khloé's quite simply the relative and employee of one of your Primes. You won't let her be anything else."

*

Settled on her sofa with a tub of ice-cream, Khloé dialed Teague's number. Jolene was right; she couldn't let him find out about Enoch's bullshit from someone else.

Her anchor answered after only a few rings. "Well, if it isn't my favorite girl in the world."

She snickered. "You're so full of it, Sullivan." Smiling, her demon rolled its eyes. It adored the hellhorse on a purely platonic level. "That's a whole lot of noise in the background." It was a wonder she could hear him. "Where are you?"

"A horse racing stadium. It's nothing like hellhorse racing, but it's still fun to watch. To what do I owe the pleasure of your call?"

She twisted her mouth. "Well . . ."

"Khloé, what is it?"

She scratched the back of her head. "I just wanted to tell you that, um . . . deadpeoplebrokeintomyhomelastnight."

"Dead people *what*?"

She quickly brought him up to speed on everything.

"Motherfucking fucker," he spat. "Tell me Jolene at least has a clue where this Enoch bastard is hiding."

"She's working on finding out."

He bit out another curse. "You shouldn't have kept this from me, Khloé. Yeah, I get *why* you did it, but I still don't like it. And I absolutely *loathe* that I've been having a blast, completely oblivious to the fact that you're dealing with this bullshit. You wouldn't like it either if it was the other way around."

No, she wouldn't, so she didn't try defending herself.

He took a long breath. "I'll be back in Vegas as soon as I can."

"You don't need to end your trip early—"

"You think I'll stay here while you have a threat hanging over you? Not happening, gorgeous. I'll be back tomorrow."

"But—"

"Don't 'but' me, Khloé. I'm pissed enough as it is. You will not talk me out of heading home early, so give it up. I'll see you some time tomorrow. In the meantime, be careful."

She sighed, knowing better than to argue with the stubborn bastard. Plus, she'd be glad to see him. "Will do. Have a safe trip."

He mumbled something and then rang off.

Snorting, Khloé tossed her phone on the coffee table. She sank further into the sofa, chose a movie on the streaming service she'd subscribed to, and pressed the "play" button on her remote. She'd watched no more than ten minutes of the movie when there was a knock at her front door.

Frowning, she stabbed her spoon into the ice-cream, put the tub on the table, and then headed to the hallway. She peered through the peephole of the front door, and her stomach took a nosedive. *Keenan.*

Her demon slinked to the surface, curious as to why he'd come. It wasn't necessarily pleased to see him, though; he'd delivered a kick to its ego when he walked out on them early this morning.

Khloé suspected he was there to piss and moan that she hadn't told him about Enoch's second attack personally. Ugh, she did not need this right now. She was tired and wanted a little "me" time.

"I know you're there," he said.

She silently cursed. It was tempting to ignore him, but that stank of cowardice. Khloé was no coward.

Blanking her expression, she pulled open the door. The sheer, sexual impact of him struck her hard, just as it always did. His eyes snared hers, bold and unflinching. He made her think of a predator refusing to lose sight of his prey.

She truly didn't have a sliver of a clue why she found it such a turn-on to have him look her so dead in the eye. But there was something inexplicably heady about being the focal point of such intense attention. Her demon melted every time.

Khlóe didn't avert her gaze. Didn't stiffen. Didn't fidget. She just stared right back at him. A familiar, irrepressible chemistry sparked to life, flickering in the air between them.

His eyes drifted over her, taking in her pigtails, printed tee, yoga pants, and bare feet—eye-fucking her as blatantly as he always did. Her nipples tightened, the traitors. What was wrong with her? She should have felt uncomfortable. Maybe even violated.

"What are you doing here?" Proud that her voice came out strong and steady, she gave herself a mental pat on the back.

"I came to see you." Like a tank, he forged his way inside and kicked the door closed behind him. The hardwood floor creaked beneath his feet as he strolled past her.

Following him into the living room, she folded her arms as he nosed around, taking in the sight of the ice-cream tub with a flick of his brow. "Why are you here?" she asked.

He turned to face her. "We need to talk." There was no note of demand in his tone, and he wasn't wearing his "you're going to give me what I want whether you like it or not" expression. He looked cool, casual, unchallenging. She didn't trust it.

"If you've come here to whine that I didn't tell you about Enoch's latest act of fuckery, you might as well just leave," she said, calm but firm. "I'm not going to apologize for it. I'm not going to say that I'll contact you if it happens again. Even if I wanted your help with Enoch, the decision would *still* be down to Jolene."

She fought not to tense as he fluidly stalked towards her, making her pulse skitter. His gaze dropped to her mouth, and it took everything she had not to lick her lips—especially when he towered over her, all sex and smolder. Having him this close was not good for her composure. Not good *at all.*

He loosely curled his fingers around one of her pigtails and then let it slide through his fist. "I haven't come here to yell at you. The fact is, whether I like it or not, I'm not a person you'll ever look to in a crisis. But I wish you would." The note of sad resignation in his tone stabbed her in the chest.

"Be fair, Keenan, I'm not a person you'd ever contact while in a tricky situation."

He gave a slow nod. "You're right. And it isn't fair of me to expect something of you that I wouldn't myself do if our positions were reversed. But I worry about you. You don't take as good a care of yourself as you do those you love. You're not treating this as seriously as you need to."

"I'm not?"

"No. Last night, you didn't call out to anyone for help. Those people who broke into your home were dead, yes, but that's what made them the perfect soldiers—they didn't feel pain, fear, or hesitation. They just did what their master forced them to do. And he'll send more your way—we both know that. I'd like you to promise me that you'll call *someone.* Jolene, your brother, Harper, I don't care who. I just don't want you facing Enoch's puppets alone." He tugged lightly on one pigtail. "Promise me."

She snorted. "I'm not promising you shit." Maybe she should have been touched by his concern, but it rankled that he'd come here acting as if he cared. "You told me, in so many words, that all you wanted from me was a one-time thing. That's fine. But you don't get to then demand promises from me—it doesn't work that way, Keenan. And I can't imagine why you'd possibly be so worried when all I am to you is the cousin of your Prime, nothing more."

Keenan's mouth snapped shut, as if he was biting back words.

But then he clipped, "You're more. That's the fucking problem."

"Excuse me?"

"You don't think you're important to me, I know that, but you are. I can't just ignore that there's a threat hanging over your head. I can't. That's not who I am."

She snorted. "If I was really that important to you, you'd have wanted more than one night. But you don't. You just wanted 'some peace.' Well, you got it."

His eyes like burning coals, he ate up the space between them in two strides. "Do I look like a man who's at fucking peace to you? You can't know how little sleep I've had since Enoch first hurt you. Knowing there's a danger to you . . . it's all I can think about. That's when I'm not thinking about how much I want to be inside you again. Every goddamn train of thought in my head somehow circles back to you, no matter what. So when I say you're important to me, it's exactly what I mean."

Keenan took a breath, inwardly cursing. He'd told himself that he'd remain calm, that he wouldn't lose his temper—he always said too much when he did that. He always blurted out things that he'd prefer to hold inside him.

It wasn't easy to keep said temper in check when his demon's agitation fueled his. And it didn't help that his body was in chaos—his blood was hot, his skin felt too tight, his dick was rock hard. A ferocious hunger bit and clawed at him, tempting him to steal another taste of her.

She was mere inches away from him. It would be so easy to tag her by her nape, yank her to him, and claim that mouth he'd had far too many fantasies about. So easy to strip them both naked and wrap her pigtails around his fists as he fucked her from behind.

He wasn't so much angry that she hadn't called out to him for help. He was angry that she wouldn't *want* to—that he wasn't someone she'd care to turn to. But that was on him, wasn't it? Which was why he was mostly angry at himself. If he didn't deliberately hold back from her, he might have been a person she instinctively called out to.

Knowing the little imp didn't respond well to pressure, Keenan had resisted the urge to push her. He'd moved slow, easy, and tried coaxing her to give him what he wanted.

It hadn't worked, which he should have anticipated. She was more stubborn than most people he knew.

"But you're not going to act on just how 'important' I am to you, are you?" she asked, taking a step back, retreating.

His demon *lunged* for her with such strength that it caught Keenan off-guard and managed to force its way to the surface. "You should stop doing that," it told her.

Her brow pinched. "What?"

"Keeping your distance from us; resisting what you want. He is doing the same to you, but he will lose the fight. And so, my little imp, will you."

Keenan wrenched back the control, forcing his demon to subside. It didn't fight him, satisfied that it had delivered its message. He silently spat a curse at the entity. It only shrugged, unbothered.

He couldn't even deny his demon's claim. Keenan fought the entity's desire to own her, fought his own need to indulge in at least one more taste of her, but he knew he wouldn't be able to hold out much longer.

Khloé eyed him warily. "Did it just use the word 'my'?"

He shrugged. "You already knew it was possessive of you."

"No, I knew *you* felt a little possessive. I didn't think your demon was in sync with you on that."

"Now you do." Flexing his fingers, he backed up a step. "I'll get going." Because he could see that she meant to question him on whether the entity had spoken the truth, and Keenan didn't want to answer.

Even as his demon lashed out at him for it, Keenan spun on his heel and walked into the hallway. He'd just pulled open the front door when she spoke from behind him.

"Is it right?" she asked. "Will you lose the fight?"

Shit. He glanced at her over his shoulder. And he found that he couldn't lie to her. "Sometimes I think I already have." Then he walked out.

CHAPTER EIGHT

Khloé had just placed the studio's phone in its receiver when the front door opened, letting in a stream of outdoor noise. She brightened when she spotted the familiar, too-hot-for-his-own-good figure who breezed inside. "Teague!" she exclaimed with a little squeal.

He grinned. "Hey, gorgeous." He crossed to the desk just as she rounded it and then he pulled her into a tight hug. "I leave for a few weeks, and everything goes to shit."

Khloé looked up at him. "Not everything. I won fifty dollars on a scratchcard yesterday."

"A scratchcard you bought or stole?"

"I don't see how that's relevant."

He snickered. "Your lunch hour starts in ten minutes, right?"

"Yep."

"Good, I'm taking you to lunch. You only gave me the bare bones of what's been happening with Enoch. I'm pretty sure there's a lot you haven't told me."

"Are we all invited?" asked Devon.

"No," he replied.

Raini sighed. "You don't think it's childish that you don't like to share her attention?"

"Can't say I give a shit either way," he said.

Devon snorted. "To be honest, Adam's the same," she said, referring to her own anchor.

"Yeah," began Harper, "so is Knox. I guess it's a guy thing."

"No, it's an alpha male thing," stated Raini. "They're all awkward motherfuckers a lot of the time."

Devon gave a slow nod. "That can't be denied."

Once her lunch break started, Khloé and Teague headed to the English-themed pub that wasn't far from the Xpress bar. They'd been there together many times before. It was louder than usual due to the group of sports fanatics that were shouting at the TV as if the football players could actually hear them.

Patrons could either settle at the long wooden bar, one of the sturdy tables, or at one of the booths. Waitresses walked around taking orders, cleaning tables, or serving drinks and food. The smells of yeasty beer, grilled meat, and onions made Khloé's stomach rumble.

She and Teague settled in a booth and each ordered a drink plus a burger with fries. Only when the waitress walked off, leaving them alone, did Khloé relay all the finer details of the Enoch situation to Teague—pausing only when someone brought over their drinks.

Done, she leaned back in the cushioned booth and picked up her soda. "And that's it."

Opposite her, Teague shook his head. "Damn, gorgeous, you really are a magnet for trouble."

"I knew I'd somehow get the blame for this shit," she mumbled into her glass before taking a long swig of her drink.

"What can I do to help find Enoch?"

"Unless you secretly have the gift to psychically locate someone, nothing," she replied. "We used to have someone with that ability in our lair, but they were lured to another."

"People with rare gifts usually are lured to larger more powerful lairs," he pointed out. "Raini has a rare one, doesn't she?" It was a stab in the dark.

"Does she?" Khloé asked airily.

"I believe so, yeah." He drank some beer from his pint glass. "I can sense she's powerful, but she keeps a low-profile and never lets off steam in the combat circle. Like she's hiding what she can do."

"Or she's a pacifist," Khloé suggested.

"Or she doesn't want to draw attention to herself." He lifted a hand. "Don't worry, I'm not expecting you to tell me anything. I know you'd never betray her trust—she's important to you."

Pausing, he took another swig of beer and then leaned back. "Enoch won't be easy to locate. I'll talk to Jolene and ask her if she has any leads. She won't tell me to butt out; not when it's you." He drummed his fingers on the scarred table. "Want me to stay with you at your house until all this has blown over?"

"I'll be fine on my own." She set her glass on the coaster that displayed the pub's logo. "Ciaran can be by my side at the drop of a hat."

"It would still be good if you had someone close to you. I'm surprised Keenan's not insisting on playing bodyguard, claiming you need his backup—he usually shoves his way into your business. Of course, he's more interested in getting you on your back. Preferably on a bed, but I doubt he'd be too fussy on the 'where' so long as he got what he wanted. And you know what would happen afterward? Nothing. He'd carry on as if it never happened."

Her chest tightened, because that was *exactly* how it had all gone down.

His departing comment from last night after she'd asked if he'd lose "the fight" drifted through her mind . . .

"Sometimes I think I already have."

She still wasn't sure how she felt about that. A part of her wanted him to lose it because, hello, he knew his way around a woman's body for sure—no one had *ever* fucked her like that before or made her come so hard so many times. But the sensible part of her—which rarely spoke up—knew that no good could come of it and thought it was best to go cold turkey.

"I don't have anything against him as a person," Teague went on. "But he's a guy who goes through women like they're a dying breed and watches you with too much territorialism. I don't want you getting hurt. He *would* hurt you. Then I'd have to kill him."

"I've got bigger things to worry about than whether some guy wants to get in my panties. Anyway, Mr. Hit-and-Run, you're not much different from him."

"What does that mean?"

"It means you spread yourself around and leave broken hearts wherever you go, which is why I forbade you from making moves on my friends."

"Do they all know you made me take a blood oath that I wouldn't try to date any of them without first asking you?"

"Yes."

He drained his glass. "You know, for the record, I think making me take a blood oath was a little dramatic."

Khloé shrugged. "Aunt Mildred told me it was best to insist on one if I expected someone to keep their word."

His brows dipped. "You have an Aunt Mildred?"

"I can't *believe* no one remembers her."

*

Leaning against the wall, Keenan watched as Thea gingerly took a seat opposite his Primes. With a stilted smile, she crossed one leg over the other and tucked her hands under her thighs—probably to stop herself from fidgeting. She looked as nervous as a knocked-up teenager.

She glanced at Keenan, as if seeking reassurance. That was something he couldn't give her. How this meeting went would depend solely on her willingness to be truthful.

Her gaze slid back to his Primes, who sat behind Knox's desk. "Thank you for agreeing to see me." She peered over her shoulder at the closed office door, a worried look on her face.

"Your son will be fine with Larkin," Harper assured her. "Now, why don't you tell us what happened with your ex-mate?"

Turning back to face the Primes, she looked the sphinx dead in the eye. "I didn't kill him."

"He cheated on you," said Harper.

"Yes, he did," confirmed Thea, her expression hard. "Which was why, when he came to collect his stuff, he found that I'd shredded his clothes and wrecked his other belongings. I wouldn't have killed him for cheating. I *didn't*. Gavril did."

"Why?" asked Knox, drumming his fingers on his desk.

"Lee-Roy . . . opposed him," Thea replied vaguely. "Gavril doesn't like anyone opposing him. And he wants me out of the picture."

"Explain," said Knox.

Instead, she closed her eyes.

Swift impatience flickered across Knox's face. "You don't have to tell us your secrets, Thea. Keep them if you wish. But then you'll have to seek sanctuary from another lair. We won't provide protection for someone who isn't being honest with us."

Thea's eyes met his. "It's just hard to trust others with this. If I make a mistake, if I take a chance on the wrong person, I could lose my son." Her gaze slid to Harper. "You're a mother. If you needed to keep a secret for your child's sake, you would, wouldn't you?"

Harper nodded. "I would."

Hell, she *was* keeping secrets to protect Asher. Keenan was one of the very few people who knew of those secrets.

"But that doesn't erase the issue—we can't offer you protection unless we're fully aware of the situation," added Harper.

Thea leaned forward slightly. "Will you promise me that, no matter what I tell you, you won't take Lane from me?"

Knox twisted his mouth. "I can promise you that, yes . . . *providing* he isn't in any danger from you."

"He's not."

"Then tell us your story. Or leave—one or the other."

Thea shifted in her seat and squared her shoulders. "Lane has a rare and substantial gift. One that Gavril wants to exploit. He called for a meeting with me and Lee-Roy after we first separated. Gavril convinced him that it would be a good idea to 'rent' Lane to demons who'll pay enough money to utilize his gift in some way; he promised to give us a percentage of whatever money Lane earned."

Keenan exchanged a look with Levi, who was lounging on the sofa, looking deceptively relaxed. It wasn't uncommon for Primes to rent out their demons, but that only happened with adults, and those adults had to consent to such a thing.

"I went *ballistic*," Thea continued. "I made it abundantly clear that I would *never* allow anyone to use my son. Jesus, he's *four*." She raked a hand through her hair.

"What happened next?" prodded Harper.

"I stormed out of the meeting. Lee-Roy turned up at my home

that night. He tried to convince me to change my mind. We had a huge row. I reminded him that it was his job to *protect* our son, not to allow someone to exploit him. He marched out, furious that I wouldn't 'see reason.'"

Well then, wasn't he a miserable piece of shit.

"Gavril called me the next morning," Thea went on. "He asked how Lane was doing; said it must be so hard for me to be a single parent; said he could see how stressed I was, and that maybe I'd find it easier if Lane went to live with Lee-Roy. It was a threat, plain and simple—if I didn't come around to his way of thinking, he'd take Lane from me."

Thea looked at Keenan. "That was when I first tried contacting you. I knew that, because of your past and how protective you are of children, you'd see a *boy* when you looked at Lane, not a thing to be used. I knew you wouldn't ignore that he needed help. But you wouldn't return my calls."

"I won't be made to feel guilty for that," Keenan told her. "You could have explained to Knox why you wanted to speak with me; you could have at least mentioned that you wanted help for your son. You didn't."

"Because I didn't feel I could trust anyone but you with the information. Now I have no choice but to take a chance."

"What happened next?" asked Harper.

Thea turned back to the Primes. "Lee-Roy came to me the night he was killed. He said that I was right; that he was a bastard for even thinking of trying to profit from our son's gift. Said he intended to tell Gavril that he'd have to wait until Lane was eighteen. I was *so* relieved.

"He called Gavril and invited him to my house. Gavril fumed at Lee-Roy for 'switching sides' and threatened to take Lane from us if we didn't cooperate. I don't know which of them attacked first, but the living room turned into a battleground. Lee-Roy screamed at me to get out of there.

"I teleported upstairs, grabbed my getaway bag, headed to Lane's room, and then teleported us both as far away from the house as I could—which, sad to say, wasn't much further than a few blocks. My teleportation gift isn't very strong, and it weakens me fast. I stole a car and drove us out of the neighborhood before Gavril could send his goons after us. We've been dodging them ever since, but I don't know how much longer we can manage it."

Unless she left the country, Gavril would probably find her soon enough. She could use glamor to disguise her appearance, but it was a lot harder to disguise a person's scent. That meant hellhounds would have a good chance of tracking her.

"He's telling people I killed Lee-Roy so that no one will harbor me, and so that he has an excuse to kill me . . . at which point Lane will be left without parents to protect him, and Gavril can do whatever he wants with him."

Knox tilted his head. "What is it that Lane can do?"

Thea hesitated. "It's nothing *bad*. It's just . . . substantial."

"What can he do?" Knox persisted.

She licked her lips. "He . . . he can steal people's abilities. But only temporarily," she hurried to add. "It only lasts a few hours, and it knocks him unconscious every time—he's too young to control any of the abilities he absorbs."

Shock struck Keenan hard. It was an *extremely* rare gift, and people tended to be wary of those who possessed it. They also tended to exploit them in much the same way that Gavril wished to exploit Lane. After all, people would indeed pay a chunk of money to have someone weaken their enemies for them—even if the effect only lasted a short time.

"Can he pass the gifts on to others?" Harper asked.

"No," replied Thea. "He just touches someone, pulls in their ability, and then collapses."

Knox pursed his lips. "Does he have adequate control of the gift?"

"No. But he doesn't go around doing it all the time—it's very hard for him to do it; he has to *really* concentrate. If he's weak, tired, or in some way distracted, he can't do it." Thea clasped her hands. "Please help my son. *Please*. I can't protect him by myself. I'm literally begging for your help."

Knox exchanged a brief look with his mate and then cut his gaze back to Thea. "I'd like you to wait outside my office with Lane and Larkin. I'll call you back in after I've spoken with Harper."

Thea blinked. "O-okay." She awkwardly rose from her seat and, offering Keenan a weak, trembly smile, crossed to the door.

Once she'd left the room, Levi asked, "Well, do we believe her?"

"I think she's telling the truth," said Harper. "Her fear is certainly very real."

Knox nodded. "You know her better than any of us, Keenan. What are your thoughts?"

"In my opinion, she's not lying," Keenan replied. "But that's not to say that there isn't something she's not telling us. I'm not saying she *is* hiding something; just that she could be."

Harper scratched her cheek. "This makes me a bitch, I know, but I'm not so comfortable with having a kid around us who could just waltz over and steal our abilities. At the same time, I can't bring myself to turn them away."

Knox stared ahead, deep in thought. "Call Ella, Levi," he said, referring to the reaper's friend who was also an incantor. "Ask if she'd be able to bind a child's power with her magick."

Levi's brows lifted. "Sure." He headed to the corner of the room to make the call.

Knox looked at his mate. "If Thea will agree to have Lane's

ability bound for as long as he's with us, I'll be willing to agree to give them sanctuary. You?"

"I can live with that," replied Harper. "It'll be better for the kid anyway, considering he collapses after using the ability, so Thea should be up for it. I wouldn't like to see Asher out cold."

After ending his call, Levi sidled up to the office desk. "Ella said it's doable, but that the magick could be undone—there's no way to permanently bind a power with magick."

"That's fine. I don't wish to permanently bind it. Call Thea back inside."

The reaper inclined his head and did as ordered.

Rubbing at her thighs, Thea shuffled back into the room and retook her seat.

Knox braced his arms on the desk. "If you'll agree for an incantor to bind Lane's gift temporarily, we'll agree to give you sanctuary."

Her mouth bobbed open and closed. "Bind it?"

"Yes. He'll be unable to use it until the magick has been unraveled. That's our deal. Take it or leave it."

"I'll take it. I'll do anything that will help him." A faint, wobbly smile curved Thea's mouth. "Thank you. Thank you so much."

Her mind slid against Keenan's. *And thank you, too. I know you must have put in a good word for me.*

I didn't, Keenan replied, just as annoyed as his demon that she'd touch his mind. It wasn't an intimacy, no, but demons weren't casual about touch—psychic or physical.

Her brow furrowed, but she didn't glance his way.

Keenan looked at his Primes. "There are some things I need to see to. Call if you need me."

*

Frowning, Khloé picked up her mojito from the table. "It's not 'nice' that he wants to protect me from Enoch, it's annoying."

"He said you mean something to him," Raini reminded her.

"And it may in fact be true, but I don't believe he's all that happy about it." Khloé sipped her drink, relishing the burst of sweetness on her tongue. "If he could make whatever he feels for me vanish, he totally would." Which didn't hurt. Nope. Not even a little.

"I'd like to disagree with that, but I can't." Raini dipped her hand into the complimentary bowl of nuts that she'd swiped from the long bar. "I've always gotten the feeling that he doesn't want to care for you. I don't think he wants to care for *anyone*. He never seems to keep a woman around long enough for him to develop any feelings for her."

"Yeah, I've noticed." It made Khloé wonder why exactly that was, but she'd never ask him such a personal question. Unlike him, she didn't pry. Most of the time.

She let her gaze sweep their surroundings. The Xpress bar was as busy as always. She and Raini had headed there straight after work a couple of hours ago. They didn't intend to get drunk. They just wanted to wind down and get a little buzz going. Harper and Devon would have come if they hadn't already had plans.

After Khloé and Raini had settled at a VIP table and ordered some drinks, Khloé had finally told her all about her conversation with Keenan the evening before.

"I figured the pushy incubus would try involving himself in all this," said Raini.

"If he could kill Enoch, I'd be *all* for it—I want the motherfucker dead. But Keenan doesn't have the power to end him. He can't help our lair better than anyone else can."

"What we need is that blade he mentioned. Do you know if Larkin has had any luck finding one on the black market?"

"She told Grams that she found one, but that it's up for auction. A seven-day-long auction. Larkin said not to worry, though, she'd make sure we were the highest bidder."

"Well, that's good news, at least." Raini drank some of her cosmo. "Although I like that Keenan's worried for you and wants you protected, it's unfair of him to try involving himself in your problems. He can't pick and choose how he's there for you. He's either a part of your life or he's not."

Khloé nodded. "I made a similar point to him. He dances around the edge of my life, but he's not *part* of it. He's never crossed that line."

"Other than when he slept with you."

"That was just sex. He fucks women all the time without stepping a foot into their lives."

"True. Why are you only telling me this now? Why didn't you mention any of this in front of Harper and Devon?"

"Because they'll most likely tell me I should accept whatever help and protection I can get. *You* know what it's like to have someone messing in your life, trying to have the best of both worlds." Maddox wouldn't leave Raini alone but nor would he claim her as his anchor.

The succubus sighed again. "Yes, I do."

"Devon had a similar struggle with Tanner before they got together when he was intent on helping track whoever put the bounty on her head, but he was clear to her that he'd give her a relationship if he could. He wasn't just being a meddler. Keenan would never offer me anything. Like you said, he can't pick and choose how he's there for me."

"He clearly thinks he can, though. God, male demons can be *so* annoying. Especially ones in positions of power, like Primes and sentinels. They tend to forget that their authority only extends so far."

They both looked up as two cute male demons approached their table.

"Ladies," greeted the taller of the two. "We were hoping we might be able to join you."

"Sure," Raini replied, gesturing at the empty seats.

Khloé wasn't really in the mood, but as they began to talk, she quickly discovered that they were . . . nice. Funny. Confident of their own allure, but not cocky or sleazy.

The one on her left, Deke, was quite the charmer, and he turned those charms on her. Her prickly demon wasn't interested in being wooed, so it aimed a sullen glare his way. But he managed to wrench a few smiles out of Khloé as he talked.

He teased her, didn't take himself too seriously, made her laugh. He was also flirty without touching her, which she liked. Far too many male demons tried shoving their way into a woman's personal space.

But, truly, he wasn't the guy she wished was flirting with her. Wasn't the guy she wished was wanting her as much as she did him. There was nothing she could do about that, though. And there was no sense in pushing another man away because of it.

Listening intently to his story of how he tied his drunken brother-in-law to a tree the night before the guy's mating celebration, she felt herself begin to relax. Making it better, Raini was having fun with Deke's friend Court.

Having finished his tale, Deke shrugged. "He swears he'll get me back for that, and I can't say I'd blame him for it."

"Yeah, it would be fair to say you have it coming," agreed Khloé.

He brushed his hand over her hair, his smile a little on the impish side. "Love how thick and sleek your hair is." He shifted his body ever so slightly, and she knew he intended to lean in and kiss her.

She was distantly aware of Raini laughing at something Court said. That laugh abruptly cut off, and she muttered, "Oh, shit."

Khloé looked at her. "What?"

Just then, a tall shadow fell over them.

Khloé looked up and felt her stomach drop. What the fuck was *he* doing here? Her demon's sullen mood vanished in an instant.

Staring at her, his face cold, his eyes blazing, Keenan held out his hand. "Come."

Oh, he had some balls. Like *mega* balls.

A hush fell over the table. Khloé felt Deke stiffen beside her. She also noticed his friend sit up a little straighter.

"Khloé," drawled Keenan.

"You don't have to go anywhere," Deke said to her. To his credit, he didn't flinch at the dark look Keenan shot him. But if she didn't do something to defuse the situation before Deke tried being a hero, the guy would get his ass kicked for sure. He wouldn't stand a *chance* against Keenan. And she'd really rather that they didn't all get kicked out of the bar.

She was more worried by the fact that her demon was intent on going with the sentinel. Khloé didn't trust that the entity wouldn't surface, take over, and do something stupid like kiss him right there—it was certainly considering it, since its ego was no longer smarting after he'd admitted she was "important" to him.

With an inward sigh, Khloé slowly pushed out of her chair. "Five minutes," she said to the incubus. Her demon practically clapped its hands in glee. Ugh.

"Khloé," said Raini.

"I'll be fine," Khloé told her, although her friend didn't look so worried. In fact, there was a devilish glint in her eyes. Knowing Raini, she found the whole thing swoon-worthy.

His jaw hard, Keenan snatched Khloé's hand and started dragging her away.

She dug in her heels. "Now wait a—"

"Don't fight me. Not right now." He hauled her across the room and through a door marked "Private." It was a break room, she quickly realized.

A stout male stood at the kitchenette, washing a cup. He glowered, protesting, "Hey, you can't come . . ." He trailed off, his eyes flickering, as Keenan just glared at him. The guy sighed. "Yeah, okay." He trudged out of the room, leaving her alone with the sentinel, who shut the door and flicked the lock.

Keenan backed her into the wall, his eyes gleaming with something dark and dangerous that perversely made her body roar to life. "You let him touch you," he ground out. "You let him touch you *right in fucking front of me.*"

Khloé swallowed at the lethal whisper. His fury was so hot it was almost palpable. A fury he had no right to feel. She felt anger flicker to life in the pit of her belly. But that didn't stop the good ole sexual tension from flaring up and charging the atmosphere. Her demon basked in it, finding the blatant danger emanating from him a total aphrodisiac.

There had to be something wrong with Khloé—the display of jealousy made her blood heat even as it annoyed her. He'd just spent so long masking his emotions around her that there was something heady about the sight of his control fraying.

Maybe another person would have urged him to calm down, placated him, tried to pet the anger out of him—something. Instead, Khloé arched a taunting brow. "You got a good reason why I *shouldn't* have let him touch me?"

He let out a sexy little snarl that made her nipples pebble. "Oh, I've got lots of them."

"Dazzle me."

Slamming a hand either side of her head, he put his mouth to her ear. "One, you don't want him. You *want* to want him, but you don't. Two, you can do better than a weak asshole who tries to pick you up in a bar—notice he didn't follow you into this room to make sure you're okay. Three, your demon loathed his touch." Keenan met her eyes. "I'm having the same goddamn issue with my demon; it doesn't want anyone but you. And neither do I."

Okay, *that* took her off-guard—it also made her stomach flutter and her demon purr. But Khloé noticed he hadn't said that he intended to act on it.

He smoothed his hand over her hair, as if wiping away Deke's touch. "He touches you again, I'll break his fucking hand."

Khloé shook her head. "I don't know where you get off on thinking you have the right to pull this shit, but you don't. At all. We fucked. That's it. And then you couldn't get out of there fast enough. Yes, you were underlining that it meant nothing—I get that. It's not as if you weren't clear beforehand that it would just be sex. But you don't get to then demand that I keep away from other guys."

His eyes flared. "And how would you have felt if you'd glanced over to see me sitting there with some female lounging all over me?"

Like someone had stabbed a blade through her chest. Her demon probably would have lost its shit.

"I spent years craving you; wanting you just about every way I could get you," he said. "Having you just once was supposed to help. It didn't. It only made things worse; only made me need you more."

Every word dripped with hunger and stroked her skin like the sweetest caress. She couldn't deny that they also wriggled their way through her defenses.

His gaze lowered to her mouth and blazed so hot her breath hitched. "Sometimes, I could swear I can taste you." He smoothed his hand up her thigh and tugged her dress around her waist.

"Wh-what are you doing?"

He pressed his body flush to hers and planted his forearms flat on the wall, settling his cock against her clit. Fuck, he was hard. And he'd no doubt feel her taut nipples stabbing his chest. Awesome.

She gasped as he ground his hips against hers. Trying to ignore the carnal hunger trickling through her like warm syrup, Khloé said, "Now hold on a second." Her demon frowned at her—it didn't want him to stop.

"I might have lasted another day or so before giving in. Maybe even a week, I don't know. But I would have ended up at your door at some point." Squeezing her ass, he rocked his hips, eliciting another soft gasp from her. "Want you more than I've ever wanted any damn thing in my life. And I'm fucking done fighting it." He tore off her panties and slammed his mouth on hers.

CHAPTER NINE

Keenan greedily feasted on her, drowning in her delectable taste. There was no forgetting it—he'd tried that. He'd failed. Being away from her had only made him crave it more. Crave *her* more.

Egged on by his demon, he kissed her harder, possessing her mouth until she melted against him. A growl rumbled in his chest and poured down her throat. She shivered a little, digging her fingers harder into his arms.

He was still furious that she'd allowed the other male to touch her; that she'd wanted it; that she'd even been able to tolerate another man's touch. Hell, his demon wouldn't even tolerate another woman's flirtations—it had snarled at the blonde who'd kept strolling past Keenan's table, flashing him sultry smiles.

He'd kept his distance from Khloé at first, not wanting her to realize he was watching over her. But the moment he'd sensed that the asshole at her side meant to kiss her, he'd shot out of his seat. There was no way Keenan could have watched that. No way he wouldn't have sucker-punched the other male for tasting her.

Keenan had not only lost the fight to stay away from her, he'd willfully lost it. He just hadn't realized it until right at that very moment when someone else moved to kiss her.

He hadn't been able to stop himself from intervening. Hadn't been able to resist getting her alone so he could take her again and make it clear to his little imp that her body was off-limits to every male but him.

Now, within the confines of his jeans, his cock throbbed at the scorching heat of her pussy pressed against him. "Need to be in you." Wicked fast, he snapped open his fly, freed his dick, slipped on a condom, and lifted her. The moment she wrapped her legs around his waist, he lined up the broad head to the slick entrance of her pussy. "This is going to be fast and rough, baby."

"Don't call me that."

"Why? That's what you are. My baby." He yanked her down hard, slamming her onto his dick, forcing her to take every inch. She sucked in a breath, digging her nails into his back through his tee.

He groaned as her inferno hot pussy tightened and rippled around him. "So fucking good. Have you missed my cock?"

"It's your only redeeming quality," she all but snarled. His demon chuckled.

"That's probably true." Gripping her ass tight, Keenan hammered into her. Brutal. Savage. Merciless. Loving the prick of her nails, her husky little moans, and the erotic sound of flesh slapping flesh.

She was small, but she took all of him, demanding *more, harder, faster*. He gave her what she asked for, needing it just as much as she did.

He hated that there was a condom between them. He wanted to feel her, skin to skin; wanted to pump every ounce of his come inside her. One day, he thought. He'd take her without a condom one day.

Out of control, he relentless powered into her. The spicy, delectable taste of the sexual energy spilling from her spurred him on. He breathed it in, absorbed it into his system, took her inside him. Nothing tasted better than her. Nothing.

He wanted her to walk out of the break room with her lips swollen from his kisses, smelling of him and sex. He wanted people to understand that she was now officially off-limits.

He couldn't yet do as his demon demanded and claim her as his mate—it was too soon for that. Neither she nor Keenan were ready for it. But they were now in a relationship whether she liked it or not, and he wouldn't be sharing her with others. He delivered that message with every hard, territorial thrust.

Khloé dug her heels into his lower back, moaning at the feel of his dick furiously ramming into her over and over, winding her tight as a damn drum. He rutted on her—there was no other word for it. He kept his face buried in the crook of her neck, grunting and growling like a wild animal. All that raw sexual aggression only made her hotter.

Her demon relished it, wanting more. Only more. It was greedy for whatever he would give.

His hands clutched her ass tight, digging his fingers so hard into her flesh that she knew he'd leave bruises. She didn't care. Didn't care that he was leaving suckling little bites of ownership on her neck. She only cared about the orgasm that was so close.

Every cell in her body seemed coiled tight with a tension that just kept on building and building. She was going to come so damn hard . . . if only he'd let her.

She licked her lips. "Keenan." What she'd intended to be a demand came out sounding more like a plea for mercy.

His teeth nipped her neck. "I know what you want." He

shifted his angle so that he was hitting her sweet spot with every hard, perfect thrust. "Come for me."

She imploded as a shockingly powerful orgasm smashed into her system. Her eyes went blind. Her back arched like a bow. A scream tore out of her throat, but Keenan swallowed it as he closed his mouth over hers. He thrust harder, faster, rougher.

With a guttural growl, he yanked her down one last time just as he jammed his cock impossibly deep inside her. Then he exploded.

Breathing hard, she collapsed against him, resting her head on his shoulder. Little aftershocks rocked her sated body, and she couldn't help but let out a contented hum.

Just as satisfied, her demon stretched. It was smug that it had gotten what it wanted; smug that he'd done as his own entity predicted and "lost the fight."

Not entirely sure what exactly that meant for her, Khloé lifted her head. "I'm not asking for any promises from you, but I need you to know I'm not interested in being a girl whose door you go knocking on whenever you feel like a quickie." She had nothing against fuck-buddy arrangements, but they weren't a good idea if you cared for the buddy.

He danced his fingertips down the side of her face. "I don't want something casual from you. I want more than that."

Everything in her stilled, including her demon. "More?"

A hint of amusement entered his eyes. "Yes, the dreaded 'more.'"

"Neither of us do relationships, remember. You avoid commitment, and my maternal line is—"

"Cursed, yeah, I heard you mention it to someone once. I'll take my chances." He rested his forehead against hers. "We'd both be lying if we said we're now out of each other's system and can easily go our separate ways. That's far from the truth. We'd end up back in bed together at some point. And that would happen again. And again. And again. So why don't we act like fucking adults and just admit that to keep on fighting this would be stupid and pointless?"

Khloé closed her eyes. She wanted to reach for what he was offering, but what did she know about relationships? Nothing. She'd never tried "more" before, and it hadn't ever panned out well for either of her parents, until recently when Richie mated.

She was much like her father—a pain in the padded ass who pushed people's buttons on a regular basis. Which she took pride in, to be honest. Keenan knew that about her and seemed to want her in spite of it, sure, but . . . well . . . ugh, she didn't know what to do.

"You said you don't want promises from me," Keenan went on. "That's good, because I can't make you any. My past attempts at relationships didn't work so well. But that doesn't mean this is doomed to end. I'm not asking you to move in with me or make an irrevocable commitment. I'm asking you to agree to take this slow and see what happens."

He talked as if they were already together and she just needed to acknowledge it. "And if it takes us nowhere?"

"At least we'll know."

She bit her lip. "What about your demon? Is it onboard with this?"

"Oh yeah, it's onboard. And it's pretty sure yours is, too. Is that true?"

"Yes. I don't get why, but my demon weirdly likes you."

His lips twitched. "Then be done hesitating."

Sighing, she scratched at her head. "Okay, we can try this more-thing and see what happens, whatever that even entails. But I can't guarantee I'll be any good at it—I've never done it before."

A smile tugged at one corner of his mouth. "That's all right. I can be patient."

She snorted. "Patient. Right."

He cupped her chin. "You know that this is exclusive, right? There'll be no other men for you, and there'll be no other women for me."

She nodded. "I can agree to that."

A knock sounded at the door. "Khloé, you okay in there?" Raini called out.

"I'm fine, I just need two minutes!" Khloé replied. She puffed out a breath. "I guess we better get out there," she told him.

When he set her down on her feet, she straightened her dress and cast a forlorn look at her torn panties. "You didn't need to ruin them."

Closing his fly, he shrugged. "They were in my way." He scooped them up off the floor and stuffed them in the back pocket of his jeans. Once he'd disposed of the condom, he took her hand, led her to the door, and then pulled it open.

Raini took one look at them and grinned. "Did you guys have an allergic reaction to something? Your lips are *awfully* swollen."

"Fuck off," muttered Khloé.

The succubus just laughed.

*

Having wrapped the soft towel around her, Khloé did a long stretch, feeling deliciously sore. Keenan had followed her home from the Xpress bar yesterday evening and tumbled her into bed. They'd spent the night talking, laughing, teasing, and fucking.

He'd left an hour ago, since—as Asher's bodyguard—he needed to join Harper, Knox, and Asher on their trip to an amusement park. He'd made it clear that he planned to return to her afterward.

Raini must have excitedly spilled the beans to Harper and

Devon, because the two she-demons had called Khloé to ask if she and Keenan were truly a thing now. Harper was *beyond* thrilled. Devon was just as happy, but she was also worried what it would do to Khloé if things went south.

Khloé wasn't afraid to take the risk that she might get hurt, because just maybe the outcome of that risk would be something good. What *did* weigh on her was the knowledge that if the relationship came to an end, she wouldn't be able to cut him out of her everyday life.

He was a staple in her cousin's life—not only as Harper's sentinel, but as Asher's bodyguard. For that reason alone, Khloé came into contact with the incubus at least twice a week. He also attended most of her lair's celebratory events, since Harper and Asher were usually in attendance. And he was of course present at each of Harper's events.

If the relationship came to a screeching halt, there would really be no way for him and Khloé to avoid each other. They couldn't truly go their separate ways—their lives were too interlinked. Seeing him so regularly would be hard enough. But it would also mean she'd always hear about whatever women came after her. And if he found himself serious about someone again, Khloé wouldn't be able to enjoy the bliss of ignorance.

It would hurt. Badly. And if she desperately needed to get away or put some space between them, she'd have to give up her job and maybe even move out of Vegas.

So, yeah, she was taking a big risk here. But she'd tried ignoring what she felt for him, and it hadn't worked. Besides, she'd gotten the distinct impression that if she'd said no, Keenan wouldn't have let it alone. Like her, he seemed tired of wrestling with what he wanted. All they could do was take a gamble and hope it paid off.

In her bedroom, she dressed and dried her hair. Humming to

herself, she headed downstairs and went to the kitchen. Khloé frowned at the male who was sitting at her breakfast bar, munching on cereal. "What are you doing?"

Ciaran spared her a brief glance. "Eating while I waited for you to get your boney ass downstairs."

"My ass is not boney." She crossed to one of the cupboards and pulled out a Danish pasty. "Why are you here?"

"Orrin managed to locate David Shore. Grams wants to pay him a visit in an hour. You interested in coming?"

Khloé's demon perked up. "Oh, yeah, definitely."

"Figured as much." He spooned more cereal. "So . . . want to tell me why Keenan's jacket is hanging on your coat rack?"

She tensed. "No, not really."

Ciaran smirked. "Oh, so it's like that, huh? Thought so. I would have assumed you guys are just bed-buddies, but he wouldn't have deliberately left his jacket here to mark his territory if it wasn't more serious than that."

She frowned. "He's not marking his territory. He just forgot to take it with him."

Sighing, Ciaran leaned forward. "Khlo, commitment-phobic demons like Keenan are extremely careful not to leave their shit at a woman's house—they don't want to lead her on or have to go back. I'm telling you, he left that jacket as a message to any guy who comes here."

Khloé made an exasperated sound. "Male demons are so weird."

Once she'd eaten breakfast, Ciaran teleported her to their grandmother's house. Khloé's brows lifted when she saw that her father was waiting with Jolene and Orrin. He'd seemingly convinced his mother to allow him to come along. Well, it wasn't like he wouldn't be useful—Richie was very good at interrogations.

It turned out that David Shore lived at an apartment

complex in Michigan. The building was pretty decent and had good security. No security was good enough to keep out imps, though—especially one who could teleport. So, it wasn't long before Khloé and her lair members were standing outside David's apartment.

Taking the lead, Jolene knocked on his front door. When there was no answer, she knocked again. Still nothing. She pressed her ear to the door. "I can't hear any activity going on inside."

"Maybe he's not home," said Ciaran.

"Maybe," Jolene allowed. Still, she knocked again.

"Want me to teleport inside and see if the place is empty?" Ciaran asked.

Just then, the elevator behind them *pinged*. They turned just as a thin figure stepped out of the elevator with a grocery bag tucked under his arm, his eyes fixed on the screen of the cell phone in his hand.

He certainly matched the description of the guy they were looking for, so it was no surprise that he walked toward David's apartment. He froze when he finally spotted the demons gathered there.

Jolene gave him a pleasant smile. "David Shore?"

He threw the bag and ran through the door that led to the stairwell.

They all dashed after him, their feet thundering down the stairs, throwing hellfire orbs and yelling for him to stop. One orb hit his hand, causing him to drop his cell phone. He hissed in pain but kept on running.

Reaching the first level, he rocketed toward the exit. Ciaran appeared in front of it, causing David to skid to a halt. He turned to run, but the other imps surrounded him.

His chest heaving, David spun in a circle, searching for a

weakness in their defenses, finding none. The burned flesh on his hand hissed and blistered as the hellfire ate at it. The orb sure got him good.

Planting his feet, Ciaran glanced at Khloé. "Now, sis, why would he run from us?"

"Good question," she said. "The move screamed 'guilty conscience' to me."

Her chin up, Jolene took a step toward the familiar. "You know who I am. Yes?"

Cradling his burned hand, David gave a short nod, eying her warily. "Jolene Wallis."

Her smile was all politeness. "Very good. As you may already have guessed, these people you see here are members of my lair. We're not here to hurt you, David. We hope to speak to a friend of yours. I think you know who I mean."

He averted his gaze for the briefest moment. "I-I don't."

"Really?"

"Really."

Khloé tilted her head. "Why do you think he's lying, Grams?"

Jolene pursed her lips. "I'm not yet sure. But we'll find out."

His eyes wide, he shook his head. "I'm not lying, I swear."

Jolene flicked her hand. A blast of hot air swept him up and mercilessly flung him at the wall so hard that the plaster cracked. He dropped to the ground like a rock, groaning.

Ouch.

"Maybe you should rethink your answer, Mr. Shore," suggested Orrin.

Richie nodded. "Yeah, I think that would be for the best."

Coughing, David pushed to his feet. "I can't tell you what I don't know."

A nauseating crack split the air. David cried out as his now-broken leg crumpled beneath him. He stared open-mouthed at the bone protruding out of his calf. "*Fuck.*"

Khloé winced at the sight, though she had to admit she envied her father's ability to break bones with his mind. She could cause *so* much shit with a gift like that. Which was why it was no doubt for the best that she didn't have it.

Jolene brushed an imaginary piece of lint from her blouse. "Let's not play games, David. They bore me. Where's Enoch?"

Panting, David licked his lips. "He left my lair a long time ago." He coughed again. "We haven't been in contact since then."

Khloé twisted her mouth. "Yeah, I'm still not believing him. Pops, break his femur this time—I've heard that hurts like a bitch."

"No!" shouted David. "No, no, don't!"

"Then answer Jolene's question truthfully," said Richie. "Tell us where we'll find Enoch."

David weakly shook his head. "I'd tell you if I could, but I honestly don't know." The sound of his femur bone breaking echoed throughout the stairwell. He cried out again, his fingers retracting like claws. "*Fuck, fuck, fuck, fuck, fuck.*"

His face contorting with anger and pain, he slung a ball of hellfire at Jolene. She popped up her shield, which absorbed the orb, and then gave him a bored look.

"Bad move," said Orrin.

David's head whipped to the side, and blood spurted out of his mouth. Khloé knew the sentinel had dealt him a telepathic punch.

Jolene sighed. "I really am tired of your pointless denials, David. Each time you lie to us, we're going to hurt you. There are lots of ways we can do that. Weird and wonderful and *delightfully* agonizing ways. Must we really demonstrate? Or shall we skip straight to the part where you tell me what I want to know?"

David spat a blob on the floor. Among the saliva and blood were two teeth. Ew.

He stared up at the Prime, lines of pain carved into his pale face. "You'll kill me even if I do."

"Nonsense," said Jolene. "I'll only kill you if you continue to refuse to cooperate."

"If I were you, I wouldn't worry too much about dying," Khloé told him. "Enoch will no doubt resurrect you. You'll probably be his favorite toy."

David blanched as his expression morphed into one of pure horror. Yeah, she wouldn't like the thought of her dead body being used as a puppet either.

Jolene folded her arms. "No more lies. When did you last see him?"

David closed his eyes, his shoulders sagging. "A week ago," he admitted, his voice like gravel. "He said he needed some money and a place to lay low for a while. I gave him what money I had on me. Fifty or sixty dollars—something like that."

"And just where is he laying low?" Jolene persisted.

"My uncle's hunting cabin. It's not far from here." He rattled off the address.

Jolene smiled. "Thank you, David, you've been most helpful." She turned to her lair members. "Shall we go?"

Ciaran pushed open the exit door, and they all began to file outside.

Khloé looked at David, who seemed shocked that they were actually allowing him to live. "Just in case you get any mad ideas to borrow a cell phone and call Enoch to warn him that we're coming . . ." She raised her hand and zapped him with a high charge of electric fire. It coursed through his body, making him shake and convulse. Then he sagged, out cold.

Turning back to the exit, she shrugged at Ciaran, who was still holding the door open. "He'll wake up in a few hours," she said.

"He'll also have one fuck of a headache to go with those broken bones."

"You gotta love electric fire."

CHAPTER TEN

"Seems like no one's home," said Orrin, sweeping the open-plan log cabin with his gaze.

Khloé reached out with her mind, searching for others. The only ones she found were those of her lair members. "He was here very recently." There was evidence of his presence all around them—the dirty skillet on the cooking stove, the remnants of recently burned wood in the stone fireplace, the pile of unlaundered clothes on the floor, the unwashed dishware that had been plonked in the sink.

She felt her nose wrinkle. "Not the tidiest guy in the world, is he?" She could *never* live like this. The sight of the mess actually made her shudder.

The cabin was pretty basic. In terms of furniture, there was a couch, small dining table, two wooden chairs, a bed, a nightstand, and a few outdated appliances in the kitchenette. It might have been cozy if it was in better shape.

A fine layer of dust coated most surfaces. Streaks of grime

stained the windows. Flakes of mud and fragments of dead grass littered the floor and were wedged between the wooden planks. It surprised her that there were no patches of rot or evidence of leaks.

"Maybe he went for a walk," suggested Ciaran, studying the empty gun rack near the front door. "What else is there for him to do around here? It's not like he'd have to worry about being spotted by people who'd then report his whereabouts. This place is out in the middle of nowhere."

Very true. Khloé peered out of a grimy window. There didn't seem to be anything out there other than trees, thickets, and long grass.

"Can we be sure the cabin's current guest is Enoch?" asked Richie. "David could have lied about his whereabouts."

"It's Enoch." Kneeling near the nightstand, Orrin held out a framed picture. "Found this in the drawer."

Jolene took the picture, and her face softened. "Molly. She was such a sweet kid." The Prime tapped her nail on the silver frame. "I can't envision him leaving this photo behind, so I don't think he up and left. He's around here somewhere, and he'll be back sooner or later."

"I say we lie in wait; surprise him," proposed Ciaran.

"Maybe he never left," mused Orrin, flexing his foot on a particularly creaky floorboard. He kicked aside the rug that covered it, revealing a cellar door.

Khloé exchanged a look with Ciaran.

Orrin dropped to his knees and put an ear to the hatch. "There's movement coming from down there. I can hear scuffling sounds."

"I doubt it's Enoch," said Jolene. "He'd do his best to stay still so that we wouldn't hear him. Plus, he'd have had a hell of a time placing the rug over the hatch after closing it."

"Not if he's telekinetic," Orrin pointed out, lifting his head to meet her gaze. "He isn't known to have that ability, but we demons like to keep our secrets, don't we?"

True enough. "I can't feel any other minds here," said Khloé. "Not even that of an animal, so it can't be some form of wildlife scurrying around down there."

"*Something's* moving," he said. "And my gut's screaming at me to find out what it is."

"Then do it, though I'm not sure what you expect to find." Jolene cut her gaze to Richie, who stood near the front window. "Watch out for any signs of Enoch."

Orrin unfastened the rusty bolt and then hauled open the heavy wooden door, making the hinges creak. Khloé peered down into the dark cellar. Dust motes danced in the shaft of sunlight that streamed through the open hatch and shined over a rickety ladder, a bare lightbulb, and the stack of boxes near the base of the steps. But it was what she could *smell* that snatched her attention.

Khloé backed away fast and put the back of her hand against her nose. "Something's dead down there." There was *no* mistaking the scents of death and decay.

Jolene's mouth twisted in distaste. "It can't be one of his puppets. We'd have felt their mind."

"I'm guessing he killed and stashed someone down there," said Orrin. "Only one way to find out." He began a slow, careful walk down the creaky cellar steps.

Khloé looked at her father. "Any sign of Enoch, Pops?"

"None," Richie replied without turning his gaze from the window.

Orrin paused halfway down the steps and tugged on the pull string near the bulb. The light didn't flicker on. "Great. Anyone got a—"

A pale hand snapped out of the darkness and cuffed his ankle. It yanked hard, dragging him down the stairs. Orrin hit the floor hard and crashed into the boxes. Three rotting corpses stumbled out of the shadows and descended on him. His hoarse cries mingled with their grunts.

"Fuck." Ciaran raised his hand and let out a telekinetic blast that swept the corpses off their feet and sent them sailing away from Orrin. He then teleported to the sentinel, grabbed his arm, and teleported him to Jolene's side.

"Mother*fuckers*," Orrin spat, covered in scratches, bites, and streaks of dirt.

Her heart thudding, Khloé quickly closed the cellar door and bolted it shut. "How the fuck didn't we feel their minds? I can feel them *now*." She could also hear them moving around, so Enoch clearly hadn't withdrawn from their minds yet. "Shit, I say we get out of here right—"

The window near the kitchenette smashed as a black, smoky orb zoomed into the cabin and smacked Ciaran's head. Khloé's heart leaped into her throat as her brother fell to his knees, coughing and gagging. *Fuck, no.* Her demon hissed in pure fury.

In an instant, Jolene popped up her shield while Khloé and the others ducked and took cover. More black orbs were pitched through the air. They crashed into walls or furniture, rotting whatever they touched. Some hit Jolene's shield but did no damage.

"Get behind me!" Jolene yelled.

Richie and Orrin followed the order but, seeing that Ciaran was struggling to fight off the strange gas, Khloé crawled to her brother.

"I'll help," she told him. "Combining our power did the trick last time."

Sucking in air like a drowning man, Ciaran shook his head.

It'll wipe us out. You can't afford to be weak right now.

Neither can you. Khloé clasped his hand and shoved some of her power inside him. His own rose to meet hers, and they melded into a powerful force that leapt on the gas, aiming to chase it from Ciaran's lungs.

Even as Jolene, Orrin, and Richie launched balls of hellfire in the same direction that the black orbs were coming from, the imps all moved to stand in front of Khloé and Ciaran so that the shield would protect them too.

"Can you guys see him?" Khloé asked them.

"Yes," replied Richie. "The fucker has a forcefield surrounding him. I can't work out whether he's trying to lure us outside or pin us in place."

Or maybe he was keeping them distracted, she mused. But why?

Finally, Ciaran inhaled a long breath. "I'm good now," he croaked, releasing her hand. He coughed and cleared his throat. "But I can't teleport us out of here yet. Not strong enough."

"There's five of us against one of him," Richie reminded him. "We've got this."

The front door burst open. Corpses shuffled inside, slow and clunky with disturbingly vacant eyes. The ones in front were humans. Behind them on the porch were animals—a bear, a cougar, and several wolves.

Khloé felt her mouth drop open, and her equally shocked demon could only stare. *Shit.* None looked like fresh kills. They'd been dead a few days. And she strongly suspected they'd all died at Enoch's hands.

"I can't move my shield to block them or Enoch's orbs will hit us," said Jolene.

"You keep him occupied," Orrin told her. "The rest of us will deal with his puppets."

And then the cabin became a battlefield. Khloé set her sights on the bear, blasting it with a current of electric fire. Richie took on the humans, snapping their bones like twigs. Orrin concentrated on the wolves, hitting them with telepathic punches that knocked them off their feet. Ciaran fought off the cougar with telekinesis and hellfire, keeping it at a distance.

It would be fair to say that chaos reigned. Hellfire orbs sizzled. Electric fire crackled. Bones snapped in half. Bodies slumped to the floor. Voices cursed or cried out. Corpses grunted or growled.

Neither she nor Ciaran were at their strongest, due to having combined their powers only minutes earlier, but they kept up the pressure. Still, it helped that the corpses couldn't move quickly, or they'd have pounced on the imps in a flash. That didn't make the puppets much easier to fight, though. They were, as Keenan had once commented, the perfect soldiers.

You could knock them to the ground with pure power, but they'd get back up without a wince. You could shoot them with bullets of electric fire, but they'd do no more than flinch with the impact. You could break their necks or limbs, but they'd keep on coming—even if they had to slink like a worm along the floor.

And the human corpses could throw balls of hellfire. Two of which hit Khloé—one on her shoulder, one on her leg. Both hurt like holy hell, and the smell of her burning, blistering flesh was just as nauseating as that of the corpses that *just kept on coming.*

"Try to blind them," Khloé advised. "If Enoch can't see through their eyes, he can't attack us."

The imps smacked the faces of the corpses with hellfire, aiming for their eyes. Some dropped like stones, blinded and useless. Others kept coming, having dodged the orbs in time.

The corpses in front of them weren't the only threat.

Enoch continued to sling black orbs through the broken window, uncaring that they couldn't penetrate Jolene's shield. Moreover, the corpses in the cellar had managed to punch enough holes through the hatch that one of them would no doubt crawl out of it any moment now.

"*Motherfucking motherfucker*," cursed Ciaran, his voice thick with pain.

Khloé looked to see that the cougar had knocked her brother onto his back, its rear claws digging into his stomach, its teeth snapping at his face. Only the arm he'd placed against its throat kept it from biting down.

He wasn't using his telekinesis to buck it off, which meant his reserves had to be super low. Her own were sadly no better. She flicked her hand, sending out a wave of electric fire that was strong enough to lash the wild cat like a whip and cause it to topple over.

She screamed through gritted teeth as hot pain knifed through her leg. Powerful jaws had clamped around it like a fucking bear trap. Khloé glared down at the dead wolf, knowing Enoch was looking back at her through the one eye that hadn't yet been blinded. Well, she could fix that. She zapped its good eye with electric fire just as there was a loud crack. His broken jaws went slack.

She gave her father a grateful nod and pulled free of the wolf. Only then did she realize that all the puppets lay blind and still at their feet. The one that had half-crawled out of the hatch had taken a hellfire orb to the face, and its limp body blocked the other corpses from being able to exit the cellar.

"You're all looking a little worse for wear," said a voice that grated on her nerves and made her demon snarl.

Khloé snapped her gaze to the doorway. Enoch stood there, surrounded by his forcefield. Jolene had moved to block him with her shield, which was probably the only reason he hadn't started hurling more of his weird black orbs at them.

"Khloé," said Jolene.

Enoch laughed. "She's too weak to destroy my forcefield at the moment. So, it would seem we're at an impasse. I can't penetrate your shield, and you can't damage mine. I suppose we'll have to continue this another day."

"You think Molly would be proud if she could see you now?" asked Jolene.

His face hardened. "Don't you speak of her."

"We cared for her too, you know. We all mourned her. Her death was a tragedy—"

"Death is not the end. My power proves that. She could have lived, but you just *had* to interfere, and now I've lost her forever. I warned Khloé in her dream that I'd get my revenge on you both. It may not have worked today, but there's always next time."

"Molly was already lost to you, and you know it. Reanimating her body was selfish on your part. You treated her body like it was a doll, and you did it rather than deal with your own grief. If your mate had been alive, she'd have hated you for it. Just as your siblings hate you for resurrecting your parents and others they cared for."

"Not all see the beauty in what I do. But I think you'll be surprised to find out just how many people do." A sly smile curved his mouth. "Bet you didn't know some of the demons in your precious lair sought—and paid well for—my services when they lost their loved ones. It's been happening under your nose for years."

Khloé tensed. He could *not* be serious.

She almost jumped when Ciaran's fingers linked with hers. The spurt of power that shot into her body wasn't very potent, but it quickly blended with hers, strengthening her. *We'll probably pass out after this, you know that, right?* she asked him. Melding their powers twice in a day never failed to leave them unconscious.

I know, he replied, *but it has to be done.*

He wasn't wrong.

"I'm sure we'll all see each other again soon," said Enoch, giving them a little wave.

Adrenaline spiked through her. That rat bastard was going nowhere. She lifted her hand and let out a wave of electric fire that rippled through the air. It surrounded Enoch's forcefield in a flash of speed, crackling and hissing.

His eyes widened, and his face fell. "No!"

Her demon smirked. "Oh, fucking yes," hissed Khloé. She snapped her fist closed, cutting through the forcefield.

Jolene, Orrin, and Richie attacked as one, hitting the bastard with hellfire, telekinetic punches, and a snap of power that broke his neck. Enoch burst into a cloud of ashes that swiftly flew away. The corpses that were struggling to get out of the cellar instantly collapsed due to the breaking of the psi-connection. And Khloé, well, the world viciously spun around her.

Her vision blurred. A feeling of weightlessness filled her. Nausea roiled her stomach. The voices around her faded as the world just kept on spinning and spinning and spinning.

And then it went black.

*

"Drink it, Khloé, it'll help you heal faster," said Jolene, sitting beside her on the sofa.

Feeling her nose wrinkle, Khloé looked down into the mug, watching her tepid herbal tea whirl ever so slowly. She'd tried sipping at it, but her stomach felt jittery. Plus . . . "It tastes like swamp water."

"Drink it in one gulp and get it over with," advised Raini.

Khloé set the cup on a square coaster on the mahogany table. "I'd just vomit it back up again."

She'd woken a few minutes ago, but Ciaran was still out cold upstairs in the spare bedroom. Jolene's living area was packed with people. All were deep in conversation about Enoch, debating on what the lair's next step should be.

The Prime was rarely alone. People waltzed in and out of Jolene's house all the time, particularly kids looking for juice boxes, cookies, or other snacks. It wasn't just that their lair members liked to be near the Prime. There was just such a welcoming feel to Jolene's house. Who wouldn't feel relaxed surrounded by the scents of baked cookies, lavender, and fresh coffee?

The earthy colors made the house feel even homier, as did the keepsakes, photos, and knickknacks. Jolene liked to be surrounded by the many memories she cherished.

Khloé let out a long breath. All she wanted to do was go home, shower the battle away, and just relax for a while. Her demon needed the downtime, too. But her parents seemed determined to keep her in their sight until her wounds healed a little more. To be fair, the burns were still ugly and raw.

A fist pounded on the front door. Khloé's head snapped up.

"That's probably Harper and whoever's come along with her," said Raini, who then walked out into the hallway.

The succubus had called the sphinx about what happened while Khloé was still in dreamland—something Khloé only knew of because Keenan had telepathically ranted at her *the very second* that she woke up for not calling him . . . hence why she'd slammed a mental door on him again. She didn't need someone's angry voice reverberating around her aching head.

Keenan stalked into the room, his face darkening as he caught sight of Khloé's injuries. "The fuck? You said you were fine."

"I am," said Khloé.

His eyes blazed. "You're covered in blisters, bruises, and puncture wounds! And you smell like death!"

Affronted, her demon gave him a haughty sniff. "Careful or all these compliments will go right to my head," said Khloé, deadpan.

"Don't downplay this. Why the fuck didn't you call me and tell me you were attacked? I had to hear it from Harper, who heard it from Raini."

"I was out cold until a few minutes ago. And before you rant at me for not giving you a telepathic holler for help, note that you wouldn't have done it if the situation was reversed. Now I have a bitch of a headache, courtesy of expending a truck load of psi-energy earlier, so I'd appreciate it if you quit yelling."

Keenan stared at her, his chest heaving. Then he leaned down, fisted the front of her tee, and slammed his mouth on hers. He kissed her hard, and she tasted his panic and relief. "I officially fucking loathe Enoch. Never met him, but I loathe him." *Don't ever scare me like that again,* he telepathically added.

He perched himself on the arm of the sofa, paying no attention to the imps who stared at them in open-mouthed fascination. Yeah, word hadn't yet gotten around her lair that she and him had a thing going on.

Her mother looked pleased. Her father? Not so much. But then, he never liked *any* male sniffing around his daughters.

Knox frowned as his gaze swept the room. "Why do several of you look as though you went a few rounds with a tiger?"

"We can thank Enoch's puppets for that," griped Khloé. Her own claw marks and bites still stung like a bitch. She was supremely thankful that demons healed fast.

Harper folded her arms. "Can someone please walk me through what happened?"

"It was a trap," said Jolene, a cup of coffee in hand. "Enoch knew we'd question the people he might seek help from. He knew David wouldn't hold out against us. And he knew we'd come, expecting to find him all alone and an easy target. So he built himself a small army and waited. He planned to murder us all there and then."

Orrin nodded. "He'd killed and stashed people in the cellar. They looked like dead hikers to me, but I can't be sure. We couldn't feel their minds at first, so my guess is that he kept them inside a forcefield until he was ready to pounce. Khloé managed to bolt the hatch shut before they could get out. That was when Enoch struck."

"He targeted Ciaran immediately so that he couldn't teleport us all away," Jolene added. "I put up my shield to protect us while we struck back at him, but nothing hit him—he'd surrounded himself with a repellant forcefield. I realized too late that it was only a diversion."

"Diversion?" echoed Devon.

"Yes," replied Jolene. "He didn't want us to see that he'd sent a small army of corpses to the cabin—some human, some animal. While I was fighting Enoch, the others dealt with his puppets, but it wasn't easy. Eventually, only Enoch was left standing. We killed him, but not for good. He'll be back."

Keenan's brow knitted. "How did you get him to drop his shield so you could kill him?"

Khloé lifted her hand. "With this." She let flickers of electric fire play across the surface of her palm.

His brows shot up, and he looked sincerely impressed. "You can conjure electric fire? I've heard of the ability, but I don't think I've ever before met anyone who possessed it."

"It's an uncommon gift," commented Knox. He looked at Jolene, his lips curving. "It must aggravate you deeply that she hasn't joined your ranks."

Jolene's mouth tightened. "Oh, it's aggravating all right. She'd be a tremendous addition to my Force. Loyal. Organized. Meticulous."

"But I think we can all agree that the people under my command would eventually unite to kill me," said Khloé. She'd drive them insane. Often. Totally on purpose.

Harper tilted her head. "I think Devon once made a similar point."

The hellcat nodded. "I did."

"What's the latest word on this blade that's up for auction?" Jolene asked Knox. "I know there's only two days left before the auction closes, but would the seller be open to canceling it and settling on a price?"

"I already tried that avenue; it got me nowhere," said Knox. "He's intent on going through with the auction. Be sure that I won't allow anyone to outbid us. You'll soon have the blade in your possession."

Harper's shoulders lost some of their stiffness. "Which means it's only a matter of time before you have what you need to defeat Enoch. Good. Because he needs to die in a *major* freaking way."

"Agreed. But we can't kill him with the blade until he surfaces again," Richie pointed out. "It'll be a few days before his body has regenerated; he may attack immediately; he may wait." A frown marred his brow. "He said that people from our lair paid him to resurrect their dead. Could he have been telling the truth?"

"I'd like to think not," said Jolene. "But people can do irrational things when deep in grief."

Tanner nodded. "It might be worth looking into."

Jolene pushed to her feet and crossed to the fireplace, a restless edge to her movements. "He's been part of our lair for over a decade now. We need to check how many of our demons have died within that period and have someone take a look at their graves."

"Me and Mitch will do it," said Orrin. "If we can't positively say any of the graves haven't been disturbed, we'll pay a visit to their relatives—if there are dead bodies somewhere in their house, I doubt we'll have a problem sniffing them out."

Khloé sighed. "I need to go home and take a shower."

"You need to heal a little more first," Penelope insisted. "The hot water will hurt your burns."

"But I *reek*." Khloé looked up on hearing sounds coming from upstairs. "Ciaran must be awake."

Relief fluttered across her mother's face. "Thank God. I'm proud of him for joining your ranks, Jolene, but I still worry for him." Penelope looked at Khloé. "Since you're *not* a member of her ranks, is there any way you can spare me the worry I went through today and just leave this stuff to the people whose job it is to protect our lair?"

"None of them can destroy Enoch's forcefields, so, no."

Penelope's shoulders slumped. Honestly, Khloé was surprised the woman wasn't slurring. It was clear she'd been drinking a lot today—probably to calm her nerves, since one of her worst fears was that she'd lose another of her children.

Just then, Ciaran padded into the living room, his face soft and flushed with sleep. He frowned at Khloé. "You woke before me?"

"Blame Keenan," she said. "He telepathically yelled at me, and I'm pretty sure it's what yanked me out of sleep."

The incubus curved a hand around her nape. "I needed to hear your voice and know you were okay. Slamming a mental door on me was mean."

"Yet fun."

"Will you always find joy in pissing me off?"

"It's looking likely."

He sighed. "I feel so cared for."

"Do you? How strange."

He just shook his head.

A little while later, imps began to trickle out of the house. Richie had to usher Penelope out, though, as she wouldn't stop faffing over Ciaran and Khloé.

"We should all probably head out, too," Harper told her lair members.

"I'll be staying with Khloé," Keenan stated.

"I figured as much," said the sphinx.

"I'm glad you two finally got your acts together," Jolene said, her eyes dancing from Khloé to Keenan. "You've been circling each other for far too long."

"My thoughts exactly," said Ciaran. Groaning, he leaned back in his chair. "God, I feel awful. My throat is raw, and my chest hurts."

"I feel your pain. Literally." Khloé grimaced. "It's been two weeks since I inhaled whatever gas Enoch produces, and I still feel like a bag of shit."

Keenan frowned. "Why didn't you say something sooner?"

She shrugged. "I didn't see any reason to. My body had to tussle hard to fight the gas, so I'm not surprised I'm feeling the after effects of that."

"What sort of after effects?" asked Raini.

"Nothing major," said Khloé. "Sore throat. Achy chest. Tiredness. The occasional headache. I have a weird chill in my bones that I can't explain, too."

"Describe the gas for me," said Knox. "Was it transparent? Did it have a scent? Was it like a hazy breeze?"

"No, none of that," said Khloé. "It was a black, smoky sphere. He threw it at me. It tasted like rot and decay, and it burned like a bitch." Her stomach sank when Levi swore and exchanged a grim look with his Prime. She looked from one male to the other and asked, "What? What's wrong?"

"Yes, what *is* wrong?" demanded Keenan, his muscles suddenly rigid.

"That wasn't a gas," said Knox. "Not even close."

Ciaran leaned forward in his seat. "Then what was it?"

Knox stroked his mate's back, who'd turned to him, the image of anxiety. "The essence of death," he said softly.

A boom of silence hit the room.

"No. *No.*" Jolene shook her head. "Nobody has the ability to conjure that. The ability doesn't truly exist. It's a myth."

"No, it's not," said Levi. "It's just so exceedingly rare that most believe it isn't real."

Knox nodded. "I had a childhood friend who could conjure it. I saw him throw an orb just like that at a cat. The animal died within minutes."

"But I didn't," Khloé pointed out. "I fought it off. So did Ciaran." By combining their powers, but that was something she'd keep to herself.

"You're alive, but it's possible that the orb did some damage to you," said Knox.

Keenan cursed a blue streak, still stiff as a board. "What kind of damage are we talking about?"

"I don't believe I've met anyone who survived such an attack, so I can't say for sure," said Knox. "There's no way of knowing."

"Maybe there is." Jolene grabbed her cell phone from the table. "I'm going to call Vivian and have her take a look at you both."

Keenan took Khloé's hand. "Who's Vivian?"

"An incantor within our lair who works as a nurse in a local hospital," replied Khloé. "What makes her an excellent nurse is that she can see *inside* a person's body." So perhaps she could give them the answers they sought.

Khloé looked at her brother, who was staring into space. Raini was talking to him, but he didn't appear to be listening.

It didn't take long for Vivian to arrive. Jolene invited her to settle in the armchair and then told her about the whole death essence extravaganza.

Vivian studied Khloé closely. "Your cheeks are a little flushed. Do you feel hot, even with the chill in your bones?"

"Sometimes," replied Khloé.

"Let's take a closer look at you. After that, I'll examine Ciaran." Vivian knelt in front of her and weaved a pattern in the air with her hands. A light breeze built around them, and then Vivian stared hard at Khloé's body.

A tense hush fell around the room as everyone watched and waited.

Vivian's brow creased, and she jerked back a little. "What *is* that?"

Khloé tensed, her gut rolling. "What's what?" But the incantor didn't answer. "Tell me what you see."

"Just a minute, honey," said Vivian, her eyes roaming over every inch of Khloé.

A horrible tension built inside Khloé, and her inner demon went on high alert.

Tapping her foot, Jolene glared at the incantor. "*Vivian*, what do you see?"

Finally, the nurse sat back on her heels, her face a mask of concern. "I hate to say this, Khloé, but . . . it looks as if you didn't drive all of the death essence out of your system, because tiny particles of it are floating around your bloodstream."

Gasps and curses filled the room.

Khloé felt herself pale. "You're sure?"

Vivian nodded, clearly distressed. "I can't honestly say what the particles are doing to you, only that it isn't good. I suppose it's much like an infection. Or a virus. You're feeling the symptoms of it. And given that you've been infected with death itself . . ."

Bile burned the back of Keenan's throat, and he pressed his lips tight together. He heard what the nurse didn't say. *Khloé will probably die if she doesn't get help.*

His nostrils flared. This could not be fucking happening. It couldn't.

For all his power, he could do *nothing* to protect the person who mattered most to him. He couldn't kill Enoch permanently, and he couldn't destroy the infection that would no doubt soon ravage her body if they didn't find a way to stop it. Which they *would*. Keenan wouldn't accept anything less.

"How quickly will the infection progress?" Keenan asked Vivian, who was now examining Ciaran.

"I don't know," she replied, her gaze on the male imp. "I've never come across a case like this before." Once she'd finished her examination, Vivian swallowed. "You have a small dose of it in you, Ciaran, just as your sister does."

Ciaran cursed. "This is just fucking *great*."

"Shit, fuck, shit," Harper hissed. "Is there anything you can do for them, Vivian?"

The nurse lifted her shoulders. "I could form protective shields around their vital organs, but that's pretty much it. And those shields won't last more than a month—the particles will eventually rot them."

"The only thing that will combat death essence is pure life," Knox added.

"Meaning only an angel can heal them," Devon guessed.

Hope spiked through Keenan. "There are angels who'll heal for a fee."

"True, so the twins' situation isn't hopeless," said Tanner. "But angels are always on the move, so they can be hard to find and pin down. Also, they won't always intervene—sometimes they claim a person's death is 'meant to be.'"

Her eyes glittering, Jolene pulled in a breath through her nose. "Well, neither Khloé nor Ciaran are 'meant' to die yet—it's nowhere near close to their time."

Too right it isn't, thought Khloé. "Where do we look for an angel? They spend most of their time at hospitals, clinics, and homeless shelters, right?"

"Places like that, yes," said Vivian. "One visits my hospital twice a month, posing as a doctor so he can help heal some of the human patients. I've never met any others."

Jolene's eyes sharpened. "When did the angel last visit your hospital?"

"A week ago. If he sticks to his usual pattern, he'll be back in seven days."

"With any luck, we'll have found another angel before then," said Jolene. "If we don't, we'll speak with him. We *will* get you healed," she told Khloé and Ciaran.

"I know you will." Khloé had every faith in her grandmother.

"I'll do what I can to locate one," said Knox.

Nobody argued it was lair business. Not when two lives were on the line.

Jolene's gaze slid back to Vivian. "Get building those shields around their vital organs—that's step one to fighting this thing."

The incantor knelt in front of Khloé again and bit her lip. "The sensation isn't going to be pleasant."

Khloé sighed. "I had a feeling you'd say that."

Vivian hadn't been kidding. The magick crackled through Khloé's body like mini jolts of electricity. She flinched a few times but was mostly able to hold still.

Done, the incantor tilted her head. "How do you feel?"

"Edgy and jittery."

"It'll pass soon, once the magick fully settles into your cells."

"Good." Khloé looked at her grandmother. "My mom can't find out what's happening, Grams. She's *terrified* of losing another one of her kids. It keeps her a prisoner in her own mind. Don't put her through the worry and panic that this would cause her. She's been through enough."

Jolene sighed. "I know, but—"

"Khloé's right," said Ciaran. "Our mom doesn't *need* to know. We'll find an angel soon and then all will be fine."

"It will," agreed Keenan. "Because there's no way either you or Khloé are dying. No fucking way."

CHAPTER ELEVEN

As she stood under the hot spray of her shower, an exceedingly rare thought crossed Khloé's mind. *I should have listened to my mother.* The feel of the water pattering on her wounds was bad enough. But the heat of said water made her burns and blisters sting like a bitch.

Keenan's hands were gentle and almost . . . reverent as they soaped her down, careful not to touch any of her injuries. He seemed much calmer, but she could feel his anger—it was almost like a hum in her bones. That anger wasn't directed at her. It was directed at the bastard he held responsible for her wounds and the infection that had taken hold of her body.

Her demon was just as infuriated, especially since Khloé wasn't the only one infected. Khloé still couldn't quite believe that Enoch had also poisoned her brother. Her other half. The person she was closest to in the world. She wanted to kill that cock-smoking, monkey-loving, necrokinetic motherfucker for that alone.

She was pissed with herself, too. Maybe if she'd mentioned her "after effects" to someone sooner, she'd have realized that they weren't normal. Everyone would have been aware of Enoch's nifty ability, and they would have been ready for it. And then maybe her brother wouldn't be infected.

"You and Ciaran are both going to be fine," said Keenan, no doubt sensing her tension. "All we have to do is find an angel—it's not like they're rare."

She had the feeling he was reassuring himself of that just as much as he was her. "I know. And I know we'll both be fine." She *had* to believe that. "It's just . . ."

"You're mad at yourself for not speaking up about the after effects before now."

"Good guess."

"You had no way of knowing that Enoch had infected you with something. None of us knew for sure until Vivian confirmed it. I highly doubt Ciaran or anyone else blames you."

"They'd have been better prepared to deal with Enoch if I'd said—"

"No, they wouldn't have. Not unless the people you mentioned it to were Knox or Levi, because no one else knew what those black orbs really were. Even if they *had* known, your lair still would have gone after Enoch." He pressed a kiss to her forehead. "I could happily spend the rest of my days torturing that fucker."

"We all could."

"I wish you'd called out to me earlier. I know why you didn't, but I wish you had."

"It's not like you could have teleported to my side or anything," she pointed out.

"A member of my Force is a teleporter. He could have taken me to you."

And then he'd have been smack-bam in the middle of a battle during which he could have been badly hurt—that wasn't an appealing thought. "Ever think that your sudden appearance would have been a distraction we didn't need?" she asked as they rinsed off the soap.

He tilted his head, his eyes sharpening. "You didn't want to drag me into a dangerous situation, did you?"

Busted. "Why does that make you smile?"

He brushed his mouth over hers. "Because it's nice to know you care."

"Hmm, well, let me just remind you that I didn't call on *anyone.* I didn't need to. I already had several powerful demons with me."

"*Today* you did." He turned off the shower and stepped out of the stall. "But Enoch could try to get you alone next time, and it worries the shit out of me that you'd face him and his armies alone before you'd risk the safety of people you care for. It has my gut all tied up in knots."

"God, you worry like an old woman. I already promised Jolene that I'd call for help if anything happens. I won't break it."

He held open a towel in invitation, so she exited the stall and let him wrap it around her. "I'd like you to adjust the conditions of that promise."

"Adjust the conditions?"

"Yes. I'd like you to call out to *me* if something happens. It would be a lot easier if I could shadow you at all times, but you'll never go for that."

"I don't need a bodyguard. An attractive male to perform household chores while naked? Now *that* I need. Interested?"

He framed her face with his hands. "Give me this, Khloé."

She frowned as she sensed something. "It hurts you that I don't rely on you."

"Yeah. It's a kick to my pride too—I won't lie about that. I might not have a gift that can wipe Enoch off the face of the Earth, but I make pretty powerful back up. I have gifts that you don't know of."

Her demon hummed, intrigued. "Really? Do tell."

"I'd rather show you."

"But you're not going to unless we're fighting side by side, right?"

"If that'll help persuade you to call on me, yes." He sobered. "You know Enoch wouldn't simply kill you."

"He'd resurrect me and use me as one of his minions, I know."

"*And* sic you on someone you care for. All of that plays on my mind far too fucking much."

Her demon sniffed, confident that it didn't need such over-protection, but it was prepared to make the concession. As he'd pointed out, he'd be powerful backup—that was never a bad thing. Khloé exhaled heavily. "If you'll cease with the moaning, I'll agree to call out to *you* if I need help."

Relief blew through Keenan. He rested his forehead on hers. "Thank you." He wouldn't have functioned well without knowing she'd call on him. The only person he truly trusted to protect and defend her was him. "Will your grandmother give you any shit over it?"

"Now that we're together, no."

"Good." He pressed a kiss to her temple.

"And *you'll* call out to me if danger comes knocking on *your* door, right?"

He hesitated. That hadn't been part of his plan at all. "Well—"

"Right?" she repeated, her tone empty of negotiation.

Shit. His demon was fine with the idea, since it considered the imp to be its equal and liked that she'd want to fight at its side. Keenan . . . no, he wasn't so at ease with the idea of placing her in danger. But he'd be a damn hypocrite if he tried using that excuse. He'd also be a piece of shit to not make the same concession she had.

He sighed, conceding, "Right." But he didn't like it.

She gave him a pointed look. "Don't think I won't hold you to that."

"I'd expect nothing less."

"Now can we move on from the subject of Enoch, please? I've had enough of him for one day."

Yeah, so had he. "I'm all for that." But it wouldn't be so easy to put it out of his mind. Not when his insides were all knotted up. And not when he worried that she'd suddenly declare, feeling rightfully vengeful, that she wanted to go hunting for Enoch. If the bastard hit her with another orb, he might just kill her on the spot, given she was already infected. The thought was enough to steal the breath from his lungs.

"We should have a lazy day tomorrow," he said.

"A lazy day?"

"It's Sunday tomorrow, so you won't be working. We should just hang out here—eat, binge watch TV, fuck, eat some more, maybe shower, then fuck again." Which would keep her indoors, where she'd be safer. "After all the shit that's gone on lately, you could use a day to wind down."

She narrowed her eyes, and he wondered if she sensed he had an ulterior motive. But then she shrugged. "I can go with that."

"Good." Watching a droplet of water trickle over her collarbone and settle on the swell of her breast, he felt his gut clench. Keenan scooped up the droplet with his tongue, and a flush swept up her neck and face. His demon wanted him to lick a few other choice places.

Keenan put his mouth to her ear and nipped the lobe. "Go into the bedroom, drop the towel on the floor, lay on the bed, and spread your legs for me. Wide. I want to eat your pussy before I fuck you."

Her eyes lit up. "Hmm, I approve of this plan."

*

The female attendant pulled a pair of bowling shoes out of a cubby and placed them on the counter. "Here you go," she said to Harper, who smiled and thanked her.

Slipping on her own pair of rental shoes, Devon spoke to Khloé. "I can't believe you bought your own bowling shoes."

"You think I'm going to wear sweaty rental shoes that are no doubt hosts to all kinds of bacteria and fungi?" Khloé snorted. "No thanks, I'll pass."

Behind her, Keenan slid his arms around her waist. "Now that you've put it like that, I'm not so sure I like wearing rental shoes either."

Tired, Khloé leaned into him. In truth, she wasn't in the mood to go bowling or anything else. She'd been looking forward to the original plan for her and Keenan to spend their Sunday afternoon together alone, but the girls had turned up with their mates and Levi and had proposed a group outing.

She knew why, of course. They not only wanted to take her mind off what was going on, they wanted to keep a close watch on her and figured this was a covert way to do it. Like she wouldn't know what they were up to.

She hadn't called them on it, though. Purely because Keenan was ten times more wound up than she was, and he hadn't been able to relax. He'd tried, but it wasn't working. She supposed it raked at his insides that he couldn't do anything to heal her.

As a sentinel, he no doubt wasn't used to feeling powerless, and the emotional state seemed to be tormenting him somehow . . . as if it was bringing back painful memories, maybe? She didn't know and didn't want to ask. If there was anything to tell, he'd confide in her when he was ready.

Khloé had asked Ciaran to come with them, but her brother was spending time with his girlfriend, who Khloé happened to like. He generally had bad taste in women. Or maybe, like Khloé, he had so many issues with relationships that he was reluctant to get involved with anyone he thought he might fall for.

When demons fell, they fell hard.

Waiting for the others to slip on their rental shoes, she glanced around the Underground's bowling alley. There were several lanes, all of which included cushioned benches, a plastic table, and a ball-return machine. Electronic score boards hung from the ceiling, occasionally showing animated action replays of the players' throws.

The sounds of balls rolling, pins clattering, and people cheering echoed through the large space. Music videos played on the widescreen, wall-mounted TVs. There was also a lot of dinging, bleeping, chiming, and gunshot sounds coming from the arcade area.

"Just so you all know, I'm hitting the arcade before we leave," said Khloé.

"That machine over in the corner near the ATM is my favorite," said Raini. "I always get a prize, every time."

Levi frowned at the blonde. "That's a vending machine."

"I know," said Raini.

"How many pins are in the lanes?" asked Tanner, leaning against the counter. "Fourteen? Sixteen?"

Devon gave him a patronizing smile. "Sweetie, there's actually a reason they call it *ten* pin bowling."

Khloé looked at the hellhound. "Wait, you've never bowled before?"

Tanner just shook his head.

"Want some pointers?" asked Devon.

Tanner snorted. "You just throw a ball at the pins to make them fall down—how hard can it be?"

Khloé exchanged a smile with Devon. The hellhound was *so* going down.

"I had to book two lanes because there are eight of us," said Knox. Well-groomed and smartly dressed, he should have looked out of place. Somehow, though, he always seemed to "fit" into his surroundings. Probably because he was always at total ease with himself. "We'll need to split into two groups."

"Ooh, the girls vs. the boys," suggested Raini.

"But that won't be fair to you girls," said Levi.

Raini's spine snapped straight. "Why? Because an all-male team would win for sure?"

Levi spluttered. "No, because . . . Tanner, you explain."

The hellhound scowled. "Don't expect *me* to dig your way out of your hole."

Khloé rolled her eyes. "Let's just head to our lanes."

Once they'd entered their names into the scoreboards, they grabbed drinks from the concession area and chose which balls to put in the ball-return machine.

Up first, Khloé lifted one of the smooth balls. The weight was just right. The soles of her shoes squeaked against the floor as she crossed to the glossy bowling lane, careful not to step over the red line. She planted her feet wide, held the ball tight between her hands, bent over and—

"Wait, you do the granny roll?" asked Keenan, who stood at the mouth of the neighboring lane. "Seriously?"

Straightening, Khloé frowned at him. "Think of how many people have stuck their fingers into the ball. I highly doubt the workers clean them after every game—hell, I'll be surprised if they clean them more than once a year. Ergo, I am *not* sticking my fingers into those germ-infested holes." Just the thought made her shudder.

"And she says she's not OCD," muttered Harper from the bench.

"You can't bowl like that," insisted Keenan. "You'll hurt your back."

"More importantly, you'll lose," said Levi.

Keenan scowled at him. "*That's* more important?"

Khloé shook her head in a "whatever" gesture and turned back to the pins. "I won't lose." She had the granny roll down to a *science*.

She assumed her prior position and rolled the ball *hard*. It rushed down the lane fast and crashed into the white pins, knocking all ten of them to the floor. Smug, Khloé strolled back to the bench. "Now, that's how I roll. Pun intended."

Having also scored a strike, Keenan grinned at his little imp. "I'd high-five you, but something tells me you're not going to touch my hands until I've washed them."

"Washed them *and* used antibacterial gel. I have some in my purse."

"Of course you do." Keenan took a seat. "You're up, Tanner." And he did not see this going well for his friend, but he said nothing.

The hellhound mimicked Devon as she slipped her thumb and two of her fingers into the holes of a ball and carefully lifted it. Both she and Tanner then headed to the start of their respective lanes. The couple counted to three and then released their balls. Devon's zipped along the lane and whacked the pins hard, sending all but one crashing to the floor. Tanner's ball rolled sideways and found its home in the gutter.

Devon gave her mate a look of mock sympathy. "Bad luck, Pooch."

Tanner threw her a glare and returned to the bench.

"You sure you don't want any pointers, Tanner?" asked Keenan.

"Fuck off," muttered the hellhound.

Keenan just laughed.

Both teams threw themselves into the game. A lot of trash talk went on, mostly between Keenan and his teammates. Tanner, who was gracefully losing, repeatedly reminded everyone it was just a game. Until it started to look as though he had a shot at overtaking others—then he began to take the game *uber* seriously. He even tried mimicking Khloé's granny rolls to see if it brought him any luck. It didn't—she just made it look easy.

After scoring yet another strike, Keenan crossed to Khloé, who was standing near the table between the benches, drinking her soda. "I see you're winning."

"Of course I'm winning," she said. "I was taught by the best."

"Who?"

"My Aunt Mildred."

Devon threw back her head. "*Oh my god.*"

Khloé's brow creased. "You really don't remember her? She had a scar on her lip. A really deep dimple in her chin. Wore cloying rose perfume all the time. And she had a strawberry birthmark on her neck that was shaped a little like the UK."

Devon burst out, "*You do not have an Aunt Mildred.* Keenan, there's a high chance I'll grab her by the throat if you don't move her right now."

"Can't let you do that, Devon," he said. "No one touches my girl."

The hellcat just about melted. "Awwwwwww."

Having taken her turn, Harper crossed to them. "I broke another nail."

"You also have a little mascara goop in the corner of your eye," Raini told her.

Harper went to wipe it with her finger, but Khloé grabbed her hand and said, "Don't."

The sphinx frowned. "What?"

"Touch your eye without washing your germ-covered hands first."

Harper's eyes twinkled. "So . . . I really shouldn't lick my fingers either?"

"What? No, of course not. Wait, no. No, no, no, don't do it. Don't—*oh my god, you're such a freak!*"

Keenan almost laughed, but his good humor fled him when a sobering sight caught his attention. Gavril was standing near the entrance of the bowling alley with two of his sentinels, and the Prime's eyes were fixed on Keenan. *Son of a bitch.*

His inner demon slinked to the surface, wanting the other male *far* away from Khloé; detesting that he'd impinged on Keenan's time with her.

Telepathically reaching out to Knox, Keenan said, *Gavril's here.*

The Prime sidled up to him. *I know. He just telepathed me. He'd like five minutes of your time. You're free to turn down his request.*

I'd rather see what he wants. Maybe the asshole would then run along and disappear from Khloé's general vicinity.

"What's wrong?" she asked, leaning into him, clearly sensing his change of mood.

Looking down at her, Keenan cupped her nape and brushed it with his thumb. "Nothing. I just need to speak with someone. I'll be five minutes. Take my turn for me." He gave Harper a look that said, "Don't let her out of your sight."

With that, he and Knox headed to the bowling alley's entrance. Knox must have telepathically ordered the other sentinels to remain with the women, because they didn't try to follow—not even Levi, who liked to guard the male Prime at all times.

As Keenan and Knox halted a few feet away from Gavril, Keenan's inner demon curled its upper lip. All it had ever sensed when it looked at the harbinger was weakness.

Gavril straightened his shoulders. "Knox."

"Gavril," was all Knox said in return before exchanging nods with the other Prime's sentinels.

Gavril briefly inclined his head at Keenan and then slid his gaze back to Knox. "I wouldn't have thought a bowling alley was your scene."

"I was about to say the same to you," said Knox.

"I confess, I only came because I heard you and your sentinels were here," said Gavril. His eyes danced from Knox to Keenan. "I was hoping to speak to you both in person."

"Then speak," said Knox.

Gavril pursed his lips. "Has Thea been in contact with either of you?"

"No."

Gavril's jaw tightened. "I have it on good authority that a female and young boy recently joined your lair." He looked at Keenan, daring him to deny it.

Keenan shrugged. "I wouldn't term it 'good' authority, since it's untrue." They were giving Thea and Lane sanctuary—that was different from offering them a place in their lair. Which was the only reason Keenan's demon wasn't sulking about it.

"Not according to my sources," said Gavril. "Your new members' descriptions don't match those of Thea and Lane, but she'll of course be using glamor."

"You should consider finding new sources," Knox advised.

Gavril's nostrils flared. "I don't know what lies she has told you. But know that Thea is dangerous and unstable. She killed her ex-mate, the father of her son. I cannot—will not—allow that to go unpunished, so do not think you can hide her from me. It is in your best interests to hand her over."

Knox took a slow step toward him. "If I didn't know any better, I'd think that was a threat. That can't possibly be true, though, can it? Because you wouldn't be stupid enough to believe you would get away with threatening me."

"It was not a threat," Gavril assured him. "When I say it is in your best interests, I mean that she is not a person who can be trusted. She would betray you as easily as she betrayed her ex-mate."

"Then it is a good thing I haven't welcomed her into my lair, isn't it?"

Gavril's gaze snapped back to Keenan. "She will come to you eventually. She will tell you lies; will claim that she is oh so innocent and desperately needs a white knight. She may even profess an undying love for you. Do not fall for her act."

Keenan's demon puffed up, affronted that the other male would believe it could be so easily deceived. "Thanks for the advice," he said, his voice dry.

Gavril's mouth tightened, but he and his sentinels then left without another word.

Keenan stared after them. He didn't speak until they were a safe distance away. "He was convincing enough to have me wondering if there's some truth to what he's saying. But Thea was pretty convincing, too."

Knox nodded. "It's possible that both are lying; that each are mixing enough truth with fiction to make their sides of the story believable. It's a shame I can't read her mind."

"Did Ella manage to successfully bind Lane's power?"

"Yes. She also agreed to check on him weekly to be sure that no one has undone her magick."

Keenan felt his brow pinch. "You don't trust that Thea wouldn't hire someone to unbind his gift?"

"I simply don't trust *her*, so I intend to keep a close eye on the situation. If she is lying, we'll find out soon enough. I just hope it won't be in a way that leaves us dealing with a lot of blowback."

CHAPTER TWELVE

Sitting on the chair in the studio's break room, Khloé watched Teague pace up and down, a mass of restless energy. She'd called him yesterday when she'd returned from the bowling alley and asked him to meet her at her house today after work. She had a few things to share with him, and she didn't want to tell him about her damn infection over the phone.

Khloé planned to keep it from as many people as possible for two reasons. One, it was never good for demons to know you were weak. Two, the news would then be less likely to reach her mother. But Teague's loyalty was primarily to Khloé; he'd never divulge anything that she told him in private.

He'd agreed to meet with her at her house. But, having heard from someone that she and Keenan had been all handsy with each other at the bowling alley yesterday, he'd stormed to the studio. He'd been furious at the idea that she was letting Keenan "use" her, but he'd settled a little on hearing that she and the incubus weren't simply sleeping together.

She'd also explained that she had bigger worries than if the relationship would crash and burn. To say that Teague hadn't taken the news of her infection well was something of an understatement.

"Enoch's got a lot to fucking answer for." Clenching his fists, he shot Khloé a look full of censure. "I'm not happy that you didn't mention this until now."

"I only learned about it recently," she reminded him. "I didn't tell you immediately because it wasn't something I wanted to share over the phone."

"You could have told me sooner."

"Keenan and the girls pretty much commandeered my entire day yesterday, wanting to keep my mind occupied on other things. I wanted you and I to be alone when we had this conversation." Because Teague was a private person; he didn't like sharing his emotions with outsiders—it made him feel vulnerable—and she knew he'd need the opportunity to vent a little. He'd done plenty of that in the last ten minutes.

He stopped pacing and shoved a hand through his hair. "What's the plan for how to handle this?"

"In short, we need the help of an angel." She crossed one leg over the other. "Jolene and Knox are trying to locate one."

"I don't personally know any, but I'll ask around." Teague flopped onto the chair beside hers. "I hate that there's nothing else I can do."

"You and me both."

"Does no one have any idea where Enoch could be?"

"Not right now, no. He'll lay very, very low while his body regenerates. The auction I told you about finishes today. With any luck, the blade will be ours. Then we can kill him for real." Her demon relished the idea.

"Would his death somehow rid you and Ciaran of the infection?"

She felt her nose wrinkle. "I doubt it. I think our best bet is to find an angel."

Teague rubbed his nape. "How is Ciaran?"

"Physically, he's still groggy and showing signs of the infection. Emotionally, he's pissed as all hell and is more worried about me than he is about himself. But that goes both ways."

"You can't die, Khlo," said Teague, his voice rough.

"I'm not going to. Do you really think my grandmother would let that happen?"

"There are some things you can't control."

She tucked her hands between her crossed thighs. "Yeah, I know. But I have to believe that this will all work out, Teague. I have to."

He slid an arm around her and pulled her close. She leaned into him, accepting comfort and giving it. Her demon burrowed into him too, not liking that he was hurting.

The door to the break room slowly swung open, and none other than Keenan breezed inside.

*

Keenan held himself very still as Khloé sat up with a smile. There was no guilt on her face at having been caught hugging another man, and there shouldn't be—she'd done nothing wrong. Teague was her anchor; there was nothing sexual between them. Still, jealously and possessiveness churned in Keenan's stomach, and his demon all but roared.

His muscles ached with the effort to stay still. He wanted to stalk over to Khloé and yank her away from Teague. Wanted to take her mouth right there and make it clear that she was his.

His demon snorted at the sour look the hellhorse tossed him. The entity saw him as no threat. But it still hated the sight of Teague's arm draped over her shoulders.

Seeing the lines of concern etched into Teague's face, Keenan figured she'd told him about the traces of death essence coursing through her system. Keenan wasn't going to lie, it bothered him that she'd confided in another man. Yeah, Teague was her anchor and had no mate, so his loyalty was primarily to Khloé—there was every reason for her to confide in him. But the possessive heart of Keenan *hated* it.

"I came to see if you were ready to leave," Keenan said to her, his voice deceptively calm. He wasn't going to be an ass toward her and, in doing so, punish her for his pointless jealousy.

Her brow furrowed. "Is it closing time already?"

"Almost," he replied.

"Well, we're talking, as you can see," clipped Teague.

Keenan didn't even look at him. "You need more time, baby?" he asked her. Yeah, he'd used the endearment on purpose, hoping to prick at the hellhorse's temper. Immature, yes, but Keenan had never liked him.

"Baby?" echoed Teague. He snickered. "Oh yeah, I heard that you two are dating," he said, going for nonchalant, as if not wanting Keenan to know just how much it got to him.

"You heard right."

"It's . . . nice that she'll have you around to protect her if need be." Yeah? Teague didn't *sound* like he thought it was nice.

"But there's no need for you to be around her so much anymore," the hellhorse went on. "I'm here now."

"That doesn't fill me with confidence. You don't exactly have a good track record of keeping her safe."

Teague rumbled a growl and stood. "You son of a bitch."

Keenan shrugged. "It's only the truth. She's a magnet for trouble. And if she's not attracting it, she's causing it—most of the time, she does it on purpose. I've pulled her out of far more scrapes than you have."

Khloé rolled her eyes. "Ugh, can you two not engage in one of your dick-measuring contests again? I mean, I know hell-horses are naturally *extremely* well endowed, but Keenan has one monster—"

"Stop," both he and Teague said.

She just shrugged.

Keenan cut his gaze back to Teague. "I get that you don't want me in her life—you made that clear a long time ago. But I'm not going anywhere. You can support her in this, or you can just stay out of it and give me and Khloé a chance to make this work. But what you won't do is give her grief over this. She's got enough to deal with. She doesn't need any more shit being thrown at her, especially not from her anchor."

Teague watched him closely, seeming . . . impressed. "I never intended to give Khloé grief. But you? Yeah, I'll give it to you when I'm in the mood."

"Knock yourself out." Because Keenan couldn't care less.

Teague's phone buzzed. He pulled it out of his pocket and looked at the screen. Cursing, he turned to Khloé. "There's something I need to take care of. If you need me for anything, call me and I'll come straight to you. Okay?"

"Okay," she replied, pushing to her feet.

Teague pulled her into a tight hug. Keenan's chest burned and ached like a bitch. He couldn't even say the hellhorse was doing it to get a rise out of him. No, it was a genuine display of affection. Teague might be an ass, but he cared for her.

Pain spiked along Keenan's jaw from how hard he was clench-ing his teeth. Seeing another man's hands on her was hard enough. But seeing her looking so relaxed in said man's arms, her affection for him clear on her face, made it hurt for Keenan to breathe . . . as if his ribcage was too tight.

Fairly vibrating with the same black jealousy, his inner demon seethed. It had never despised anyone as much as it did Teague in that moment.

The only reason the entity hadn't surfaced to attack the other male was that, as Khloé's anchor, Teague's death would cause her actual physical pain—a pain that could even become chronic. The demon would never do anything that would bring her harm.

Pulling back, Teague stroked her hair away from her face. "You take care of yourself."

She saluted him. "Will do."

Snorting, he let her go. Only then did Keenan's demon stop pacing. Teague shot him a narrow-eyed look as he passed. Like Keenan could give a fuck.

Khloé sighed. "I want a donut."

Keenan blinked. She could be so random, but he found he liked that. He held out his hand. "Then let's go get you a donut. After that, we'll have dinner."

"Where?" she asked, taking his hand.

"Wherever you want to go."

*

Meandering around Keenan's living room later on, Khloé said, "I just knew your place would be swanky." It was all style and luxury with the elegant décor, the quality furnishings, the ridiculously wide TV, and the high windows that provided a truly great view. The layout seemed very similar to Tanner's apartment. Oh, how the other half lived.

Standing near the doorway, Keenan frowned. "Swanky? Is that a compliment, or a criticism?"

"Neither. Simply an observation. I like it." It wasn't the stylishness that gave it her tick of approval, though, it was the cleanliness. That ticked Khloé's acceptability box.

"Then why are you making that face?"

"I'm just surprised that you don't have any antiques. I mean, you've been on this earth a long time. I figured you'd have kept *some* pieces of furniture."

"I never developed an attachment to any of it."

She got the sense that Keenan rarely developed attachments to anything or anyone. Knox owned quite a few antiques which, according to Harper, he'd collected over the centuries. But the male Prime was a demon who liked to own and possess things.

"How many rooms do you have?" she asked.

Stalking toward her, Keenan replied, "Aside from this one, there's the kitchen/dining area, the master bedroom, the office, the workout room, and the spare bedroom." He tilted his head. "Want a drink?"

A little bloated from the ethnic meal they'd just eaten at the Underground, she said, "Nah, I'm good."

He curled his arms around her and drew her close, his steel-blue gaze snaring her. "I've wanted to get you alone all day. Wanted to bring you here so I could fuck you in my bed."

She'd never known anyone who made such bold, direct eye-contact. Keenan didn't just look *at* you, he stared right into your eyes with a laser-focus that made you feel the center of his world.

She would have thought that being the focal point of such intense attention would make her uncomfortable. But to have someone look at you as if, in that moment, they found you the only person worth their notice . . . it was a heady thing. "Is that so?"

"Yes, it is so. I've lay in my bed many times, jacking off to the thought of you."

"Now I feel bad."

"Why?"

"Because you only had your hand to make you come. When

I got myself off thinking of you, I had my vibrator."

Keenan froze as all kinds of explicit images exploded through his brain and made his cock throb. He felt her wicked smile in his balls. The little minx knew *exactly* what she was doing to him.

"It's not nice to tease me that way." He scraped his teeth over her lower lip, liking her little gasp. "You'll have to introduce me to your vibrator. We can have some fun with it."

"Not sure if—"

The intercom beeped, and he inwardly sighed. If that was one of the sentinels needing his help with something, he was going to be pissed.

Keenan dabbed a kiss on one corner of her mouth. "Just give me a sec." He crossed to the small screen near his front door that showed who was on the doorstep of the building. An unfamiliar female stood there, looking edgy as hell. Curiosity alone made him push the "speak" button and ask, "Yes?"

"It's me. Thea," she added, lowering her voice. "Can I come in?"

Anger spiked through Keenan, and his demon spat a curse. If he was looking at someone on a photograph or video feed, he couldn't see through their glamor. It hadn't occurred to him that it could be her; that she would actually come to his building again.

She had some fucking front to turn up here and expect him to welcome her inside. Those days were long gone. "No," he said. "You need to leave."

Her face fell. "Please? I just want to talk. I won't stay long."

"No. Leave." He turned away from the screen and headed back to Khloé. The intercom beeped again, but he ignored it. He rested a possessive hand on her hip, not liking the blank look on her face. "Sorry about that," he said.

"Want to tell me who Thea is?"

No, he really didn't. "It's complicated."

Khloé's scalp prickled. If he'd said something like, "Just some woman who wants to get in my pants," Khloé would have been pissed, but she wouldn't have demanded more info. He was an incubus; he'd *always* have women wanting to get in his pants, which meant Khloé would be delivering bitch slaps for years to come. But hearing the words "it's complicated" made unease churn in her belly.

She stepped back. "If a guy came knocking at my door, asking to come inside, you'd—"

"Beat the shit out of him so he didn't repeat that mistake."

She rolled her eyes. "You'd want to know who he was, so don't be a hypocrite and blow me off. Look, it's not that I expect you to answer to me. You're a grown man. You don't have to tell me your every secret. But if there's a woman sniffing around you and the situation is 'complicated,' I'm going to want to know about it. So give me *something*." Or she'd walk. She would. She needed to be able to trust that he'd be upfront when it counted.

Sighing, he crossed to the sofa and sank onto it. "All right." He patted his thighs. "Come sit here and I'll tell you about her."

Khloé frowned. He looked so tired all of a sudden, and she sensed that this conversation might take a lot out of him. She considered letting him off the hook and saying it didn't matter, but it *did* matter. Her demon, *pissed* that another woman would come here, wasn't going to let it go. So Khloé did as he asked and settled her hands on his chest.

He cupped her hips and pulled her closer. "That's better." He slid his hands up her back. "You know that me, Knox, and the sentinels spent most of our childhood at an orphanage for demonic children, right?"

She nodded. "Yes." She'd heard enough about the place to

know it had been a hellhole, and she admired them all for surviving it.

"Thea was there, too. I cared about her, and she claimed to care for me. But she refused to come with us when we left—she wanted to go her own way; didn't want to belong to a lair again. She didn't have great experiences with those. Plus, having spent so long under the control of militant staff, she needed to feel free. Needed to make her own decisions and not answer to anyone, which I can understand. She asked me to go with her, but I wouldn't. I needed to feel grounded just as much as she needed to feel unbound."

Getting it, Khloé nodded again and moved her hands to his shoulders.

"She'd turn up now and then," Keenan went on. "Every few years or so. She'd always give me the same spiel—she was ready to settle down now, to put down some roots, to try 'lair-life,' as she called it. But a few weeks would go by, and then she'd be gone again. She never said goodbye, never even left a note. She'd just disappear."

Khloé's lips parted. "That's fucking cowardly, not to mention a *total* bitch-move."

"I'd call her on it the next time she showed up, and she'd always say the same thing—she found goodbyes too hard. She'd also always claim it wouldn't happen again; that she was back for good this time. I bought it, because I wanted to. I don't like to give up on people, and I hated that she seemed to have given up on herself, so I gave her more chances than I should have."

"What made you stop giving her chances?"

He slipped his hands under Khloé's tee and splayed them on her back. "When she turned up at my doorstep nine years ago, I'd already decided I was done—I'd accepted that she wasn't going to change. I was also involved with someone at the time.

It was just a fling, nothing serious. But it was exclusive.

"Thea cried. Claimed to love me. Claimed she really meant to stay with me. She made me all kinds of promises, and she may have even meant them for a short time. Or maybe she just didn't like that I was involved with another woman and wanted to be sure I ended it." He sighed. "I should have known better than to buy her bullshit."

"She disappeared again?"

"Yes. And then I was officially done. My demon had already given up on her long before that, so it was pleased that she'd be out of the picture from then on." He trailed his fingers down Khloé's back, tracing the bumps of her spine. "She turned up again six years ago. She came out with the same spiel, but her words meant nothing to me. I wasn't even tempted to buy her promises. I told her I was done, and I wasn't nice about it. She could see that I meant it, and she left in tears. I wasn't moved by them. The sad thing for her is that . . . her promises might not have been empty that time."

"Why do you say that?"

"A few weeks later, she joined another lair. Soon after that, she took a mate, and she eventually had a child with him."

Ah. Khloé fingered the small, bumpy logo on his tee. "Do you regret not giving her one last chance?"

"No. I was glad she was done with the stray lifestyle—it's fucking dangerous. But little by little over the years, she'd killed everything I felt for her. I'd never have been able to trust a word she said. Trust is important to me."

Khloé had sensed that much for herself. "Why did she come to your building just now?"

He pinned her gaze with his. "If I answer that question, you'd need to keep the story to yourself. Only a select number of people in my lair know about this. If you don't feel comfortable keeping secrets from your Prime or your girls, you need to let this go."

"I would never betray a person's confidence. Whatever you tell me stays between us."

Keenan figured that, given how jaded and cynical he was, he should have experienced a moment of doubt. But he found that he trusted Khloé to keep his secrets, and so did his demon.

Nodding, he started doodling circles on her lower back. "Thea came to our lair recently, seeking sanctuary." He told her everything—about the death of Thea's mate, about Gavril's accusation, about Thea's claim that her Prime was telling lies and simply wanted to get his hands on her son. "It makes me a bastard, I know, but I probably would have turned her away if it hadn't been for her kid. You see, I know what it's like to be that kid."

Khloé smoothed her hands over his shoulders. "What do you mean?"

He hated revisiting his past. Hated it. But he worried that Khloé would think he hadn't objected to Thea's request for sanctuary because he still cared for her. He needed his little imp to understand why he'd felt unable to turn his back on the boy.

"My mother got pregnant to a mated demon in her lair," he said. "The son of the Prime. He'd seduced her with his gifts, putting her into a suggestible state—incubi can do that. My mother was a chameleon. She could change her appearance, become *anyone*. And he lied and said that she had posed as his mate. Said mate believed him and insisted on her being tossed out of the lair."

"Fucking assholes."

Keenan couldn't agree more. "We mostly lived on the streets. She sought help and protection from many people, especially if we encountered trouble with other demons, but they always turned her—us—away. Being a stray demon is shit, Khloé. There are so many dangers out there, and you have no protection at all. If my mother had been given help, maybe she wouldn't have been assaulted and killed by a group of twisted male demons."

Khloé gasped, her face a mask of compassion. "And you feel that turning away Thea and Lane would make you as bad as the people who turned their backs on you and your mother."

"Yeah," he replied, relieved that she got it.

"I think you're right; I think Thea was counting on that. Manipulative bitch."

"She isn't a bad person, Khloé, she just—"

"Oh, I disagree. I'm sorry if she had a bad childhood. I can't even imagine how hard life at Ramsbrook must have been for you guys. Every one of you is strong for surviving it. But having issues doesn't give a person the right to trample over others. She knew *you* had issues too, and she didn't let that stop her from playing you again and again.

"Maybe she *wanted* to mean the spiel she fed you, but she didn't mean it. And she shouldn't have made promises to you if she couldn't be sure she'd keep them. Hell, she didn't even have the decency to tell you when she was leaving—she'd just up and go. If she was really a good person, she'd have had more respect for you than to do that shit over and over. God, I feel like slapping her."

Keenan felt his mouth twitch, touched by her vigorous defense of him. "It's not a thing anymore, Khloé. I'm over it."

"Yeah? Well maybe she's not so sure you're over *her*, because why else would she turn up at your apartment, expecting entry?"

He frowned. "I've given her no reason to think I'm not done with her."

"*Except* not object to her seeking sanctuary from your lair. She might be thinking it means you still care for her."

"I only care if *you* think that, because it couldn't be further from the truth. I was looking out for the boy, not her. You believe that, right? You understand?"

"Hearing about your childhood, yes, I understand. And if you say she's not who you want, I believe you."

Keenan hummed. "Good." He dragged his fingertips down the sides of her breasts and bit her lower lip. "Because the only woman I want is sitting right here, exactly where she's supposed to be. So, can we move on from this topic or do you have more questions?"

"No more questions. I appreciate you telling me all that. Trusting me with it. I won't repeat a word of it. Not to anyone."

He pressed a kiss to her mouth. "I know you won't." His imp was reckless, impulsive, and crazy at times, but she was also loyal to the bone, and her word was gold. "Now that we've got all that out of the way, are you ready to get to the good stuff?"

"The good stuff?"

"Yes. All this talking is interfering with my plans."

"Hmm, what plans?"

He nuzzled her neck. "Plans that involve you naked and coming hard for me."

Khloé almost shivered. Damn if her hormones didn't do a mighty cheer. It was a little surprising her libido woke up, given they'd just been discussing some heavy stuff. But then, she had no actual defenses against the epitome of seduction, did she? That was what he was.

He was also hurting—she could see it clear as day. Talking about all that crap had taken its toll on him. She wanted to make him forget it, wanted to help him shake it all off.

Leaning into him, she said, "I'm totally game, just in case there was any doubt."

"There was no doubt."

"Cocky bastard."

His mouth, so hot and hungry, took hers. It was like every cell in her body ignited. Need—so hot and raw and primal—fired through her. She kissed him back, just as greedy. The growl that rattled his chest vibrated with power and a dark dominance.

The kiss went on and on and on, turning her brain into pudding. Gripping her jaw to hold her still, he slanted his head and sank his tongue deeper into her mouth. He kissed her hard, stealing her breath. The feel of his blunt nails scraping her scalp made her groan. She liked the little sting.

She tore her lips from his, gasping for breath. With a snarl, he grabbed her nape and took her mouth back; fucked it with his tongue until she was a pile of melted goo.

Needing more of him, she snaked her hands under his tee and smoothed them up his chest, exploring all that hard, male muscle; feeling the power that purred beneath his skin and seemed to reach for her.

He yanked off his tee and then pulled the tie out of her hair, letting her hair tumble down her back in sleek waves. "I want to feel your lips wrapped around my dick. Want to watch it disappear into your mouth again and again." He scraped his teeth over her neck, scoring the skin. "You going to give me that?"

"Keenan, I'm not fucking magic. There's no way I'll be able to deepthroat that monster."

He felt his lips twitch. "Not asking you to deepthroat me. Just want to feel your mouth on my cock." He unbuttoned her fly. "Stand up and take your jeans and panties off. Good, now the rest. I want you naked." Once she'd stripped and kicked her clothes aside, he lowered his zipper, let his dick spring free, and then spread his thighs. "Come here, baby. I want you on your knees in front of me."

She did as he asked and, no shyness, curled her fingers around his dick. The breath slammed out of his lungs as she squeezed him. "Yeah, like that," he said. She fisted him tight as she pumped, her tongue flicking out to touch her lower lip. His gut clenched. "Suck."

She circled the broad tip of his dick with her thumb, smearing the drop of pre-come there. "Patience." Her hot tongue licked his shaft from base to tip—it was like a lash of fire.

He gripped her nape and gave it a cautioning squeeze. She rolled her eyes at the silent warning, but then she closed her mouth over the head of his cock and sucked, bathing him in liquid heat. "Yeah, baby, that's what I need."

She sucked hard, hollowing her cheeks, gliding her tongue along the underside of his shaft. He was captivated by the sight of him disappearing into her mouth, over and over. Pure masculine possession lived and breathed inside him—a raw, relentless force that yanked every thought from his brain bar one: *Mine.*

He'd never felt so possessive of anyone or anything. He hadn't thought he had such a deep territorial streak in him. Maybe he hadn't until Khloé came along. Maybe she sparked it to life.

He groaned as he hit the back of her throat. She kept bopping her head up and down, keeping the suction perfectly tight. Right then, she was intoxicating his senses with her delectable taste, her sexy little moans, and the sight of her perfect mouth sucking him. It took everything he had not punch up his hips and fuck that mouth he'd fantasized about for years.

A crushing, incessant urge to take her pounded through him so hard it was dizzying. *Not yet.* He wanted to blow his load down her throat first. He needed it. His demon needed it. "That's it, suck me hard."

Without pausing, Khloé flicked her eyes to his, needing to see his expression. Sheer unadulterated pleasure was stamped into every line of his face. She gasped as a phantom finger fluttered over her slick folds.

"I'm going to play with your pussy while you suck me off," he said.

Oh, Jesus. A phantom finger alternated between circling and flicking her clit, stoking the fire inside her. She kept sucking and licking, her lips stretched tight around him. Every time she moaned or whimpered, the long shaft jerked or throbbed.

He sent telepathic whispers into her mind. Told her how much he loved her mouth, how much she pleased him, how badly he wanted to pour his come down her throat. He carved his fingers through her hair and fisted it. His hold was gentle yet screamed ownership.

She moaned as a phantom finger slid through her folds and then dipped inside her. At the same time, his cock swelled, becoming impossibly thicker.

"Swallow all of it, Khloé," he growled. "Drink my come." His hand tightened in her hair as he punched up his hips and exploded, his shaft pulsing with each blast of come. She swallowed it all and then sat back on her heels.

His face was all languid and lazy, and his eyes gleamed with satisfaction. "Damn, you're good with that mouth."

"Right back at you."

"Up here, baby. Straddle me again."

CHAPTER THIRTEEN

In something of a sensual daze thanks to those phantom fingers, Khloé stood. "You're still hard," she noted as she straddled him. Yip-fucking-pee.

He roughly squeezed her breast, his hold undeniably possessive. "I'm an incubus, baby. I can stay hard for as long as I want to." He swooped down and latched onto her nipple, suckling *hard*.

Khloé gripped his head. She really did love that mouth of his. "Keenan—" She gasped as two blunt fingers thrust inside her.

"Slick already." He withdrew his fingers and held them up to her face, all shiny and wet. "See?" He licked both fingers. "Hmm." His steel-blue eyes glittered with so much heat and possession that it took her breath away. "I want you even wetter."

That oh-so-familiar aphrodisiac scent laced the air, turning it thick and sultry. She dug her fingertips into his upper arms, holding on for dear life as heat swept through her like a tidal wave—making her hard nipples throb, her aching breasts swell, and her pulsing clit scream to be touched.

He splayed his hand over her throat, and his dark energy flooded her in an instant. He kept his mouth flush to hers, drawing every breath she released into his lungs, feeding on her own sexual energy.

Meanwhile, his damn pheromones played havoc with her mind and body. Her composure flitted away, along with every sane thought in her brain. Right then, there was no thinking, only feeling.

"I want you to ride me right here." He lowered her, lining the head of his dick to the entrance of her pussy.

Close to trembling with the electric anticipation that taunted her body, she reminded him, "Condom."

"Want to come inside you, baby. You on the pill?"

She licked her lips. "Yes."

"Never went ungloved before. I always wore a condom."

"So why switch it up now?"

"The others weren't mine. You are." He draped his arms over the back of the sofa. "Lower yourself on my cock. *Slowly*."

Khloé almost shivered. The note of pure, masculine demand played across her nerve-endings and made her lower stomach clench. She bore down, gasping as the broad head inched inside her, stretching her until it burned.

"That's it. Want you to feel every inch of me."

Every thick, long inch, she thought. Her inner muscles stretched and fluttered, showing a little resistance, but she kept on lowering herself, determined to have him buried deep inside her. The bite of pain and the immense pressure of his size filling her only made it better.

Once she was finally fully impaled on him, she let out a shaky breath. She felt every vein. Every ridge. Every throb. Every fast beat of his heart.

Keeping her pace slow, she impaled herself on him over and over, flooded by feel-good chemicals and a desperate, unrelenting need for *more*. She tried to move faster, needing—

He gave her ass a sharp slap, and her pussy clamped down on him. "No. Not ready for you to fuck me hard yet." He lazily slid her up his cock. "Keep it slow. You'll be rewarded," he added, his eyes smoldering with such carnal promise, her pussy quaked.

"You're an asshole," she croaked.

He draped his arms over the back of the sofa again. "I know."

Well, then, good. Digging her fingertips into the smooth flesh of his wide shoulders, she went back to impaling herself slowly. He didn't release her gaze for even a moment, as if he didn't want to miss even a flicker of emotion that glimmered there.

When she gave him a lazy, spiral, downward thrust, Keenan grunted and fisted his hands. He itched to touch her, palm her gorgeous breasts, tangle his fingers in all that glorious hair. But he kept his hands where they were, not wanting it to end.

The roasting hot clasp of her inner muscles was almost excruciatingly tight. He loved that he was taking her skin to skin, feeling *everything*. Loved the way she stared right at him, her eyes glazed, her lips parted. The desperation flickering in those smoky eyes twisted his gut and tightened his balls.

Everything about her drove him and his demon wild—they were hooked on her, pure and simple. The entity pushed him to take over; to fuck her with hard, territorial thrusts that would drive home who she belonged to.

Most of all, it wanted Keenan to officially claim her. Keenan wanted it just as much, but he sensed she still wasn't ready for that yet. He didn't want to do anything to scare her off or make her retreat.

"You've been a very good girl, haven't you?" Keenan grabbed a fistful of her hair and snatched her head to the side. He put his mouth to her ear. "Ready to fuck me harder now?" He punched his hips upwards, giving her a rough, shallow thrust.

"You know I am."

"Then do it."

Thank fucking God. Khloé didn't hesitate. She rode him hard, feeling close to drunk on the sexual endorphins pumping through her.

So many sensations assailed her as his phantom hands drove her insane—they plumped her breasts, pinched her nipples, squeezed her throat, toyed with her clit.

Shaking with the avalanche of sensation he was subjecting her to, she kept riding him hard. She desperately wanted to come but couldn't. Not until he let her. It was like having an elastic band wrapped around all the tension inside her, keeping it trapped. She couldn't take much more.

"Keenan," she rasped, her mouth dry. "I need—"

"Look at you . . . eyes all sex-drunk. Lips swollen. Nipples hard. Tits swaying." He teasingly skimmed his fingers over the swells of her breasts; the calloused pads of his fingers felt like flickers of fire to her super-sensitized nerve-endings. "Don't know what's hotter. Watching you ride me, or watching you suck me off."

"Make me come." Her voice cracked.

"Not yet."

She hissed. "You're a fucking prick, Keenan!" She paused with only the head of his cock inside her. "I'm not moving until you promise you'll make me come."

A chill brushed over her skin as his eyes bled to black. The demon stared at her, not looking all too happy with her. Its large hands snapped tight around her, spanning her narrow waist.

It mercilessly yanked her down, impaling her on its dick, stuffing her full. "Now I take you." It pumped its hips, drilling into her, slamming deep. And, oh God, that felt so good.

Her own demon liked how rough and demanding it was. Liked that it so boldly took what it wanted. The entity found it a total turn-on.

Wound so tight she was close to sobbing, she held on tight, enjoying the ride . . . right up until the flesh beneath its hands started to prickle and burn. Realization hit her like a slap. She widened her eyes. "No—"

"Fucking yes," it growled, ruthlessly slamming her down on its cock while still thrusting its hips upwards. It took her mouth, rough and savage. The demon was beyond brutal. It demanded everything from her. The skin beneath its hands kept on burning yet, somehow, it felt unbelievably good—there was no way to explain it.

Black eyes once more became blue as the demon subsided. Keenan's hands gripped her ass as he impaled her on him again and again, rough and frantic, punching up his hips each time. She wanted him this way; liked it. Liked seeing the cool, controlled surface he presented to the world completely obliterate.

Her breath caught as his dick began to swell. The tension inside her built once more, and anticipation buzzed through her as she felt the elastic band around all that tension loosen.

"Come for me," he ordered. And then the elastic band snapped.

Her release thundered through her in violent waves, bowing her back and trapping a scream in her throat. Her pussy squeezed and quaked around him, milking him.

Keenan grunted. "*Fuck*, yeah." He forcefully slammed her onto his cock one last time and detonated. Jet after jet of hot come burst out of him.

Limp and sated, Khloé leaned into him, her chest burning for air. Yow-damn-za. She'd never had an orgasm that intense before in her life; hadn't even known it was possible.

He palmed her nape and dropped a kiss on her hair. "You good?"

"Just riding my buzz." She kept her eyes closed, enjoying the way he dragged the pads of his fingers over whatever part of her body he could reach, as if he was tracing and mapping her.

When those fingers lightly danced over the suddenly sensitive skin on her waist, Khloé sat up. "Your demon branded me," she remembered. She glanced down, examining the tattoo-like brand. It was . . . well, it was pretty. And bold as hell.

His finger traced the thin, intricate pattern that spanned her stomach from hip to hip like a belt. The occasional "K" was woven inside the pattern. "I like it," he said.

She met his gaze, searching for any signs that he was unhappy with his demon's decision to mark her. When their entities were possessive of someone, they sometimes branded their skin. Those brands would fade once the entities lost interest. "You do?"

"Yes. My demon has good taste."

"You're not at all mad?"

He frowned. "Why would I be?"

"Some people don't like it when their demons mark others."

"If it had branded anyone other than you, I would have been pissed. How does your demon feel about it?"

"It generally balks at possessiveness, but it's rather pleased."

"Good, then all is fine." He swatted her ass. "Shower."

She blinked at the abrupt change of subject. Apparently, he truly wasn't bothered by the brand.

Keeping hold of her, he stood and carried her through the apartment, giving her glimpses of the other rooms. Her brows lifted when they entered the master bedroom. It was as spacious as every other room in the apartment, and she particularly liked the French doors and small terrace.

The off-white shade of paint on the walls made her think of clotted cream, and it matched the color of the lush bedding. It also went nicely with the smooth pine flooring and the built-in pine wardrobe. The rest of the furniture was just as sleek and modern.

He pressed a button on the hi-tech sensor on the wall near an abstract painting, and the ceiling spotlights instantly dimmed.

He padded into the attached private bathroom, which was just as stylish and contemporary. She liked the white/gold color scheme and the luxury walk-in shower.

Pausing, he lowered her to the floor. It was only when she looked up that she saw his gaze had turned inward—a classic sign that he was talking to someone telepathically. Finally, he blinked, and his eyes cleared.

"Everything okay?" she asked.

"That was Knox. He outbid everyone on the auction. The blade now belongs to Jolene."

Satisfaction flared inside her. Khloé smirked. "And it'll soon be buried in Enoch's precious little black heart." She could. Not. *Wait.*

"That's the plan. I think we need to celebrate."

"Oh yeah?"

"Yeah. After our shower, I'm going to lay you on my bed and make you come again and again, until you can't take anymore."

"I'm up for that."

*

A few days later, Raini rested her coffee takeout cup in the front passenger seat's cupholder. "I get that people will do irrational things when deep in grief. But keeping a resurrected dead relative in your basement or outhouse goes *beyond* irrational."

Khloé nodded, switching gears. "I was really hoping Enoch was lying when he said that members of our lair hired him to reanimate their deceased loved ones. According to Grams, they hadn't known their relative would be nothing but a walking corpse. Enoch allegedly made it sound like it was another state of life."

"But they had to have realized that was untrue when the spiritual echoes faded from their relative's body."

"They did, but Enoch refused to undo what he'd done, and they were too scared to ask Jolene for help in case she went psycho on their asses."

The corpses had since been destroyed and reburied, just as the others had.

"Promise me that if anyone tries to have my dead body reanimated, you'll step in and put a stop to that shit," said Raini.

Khloé coughed around a dry throat. Her mouth felt all tacky and dry. "I promise. But I want the same promise right back."

"I solemnly swear I won't allow it." Raini grimaced. "Ugh, this song is the height of annoying." She turned off the radio. "You know, you don't look so good."

Khloé didn't *feel* so good. As if the cough and dry chest weren't annoying enough, fatigue badgered her every minute of the day. Her eyes felt dry and itchy, and it took everything she had not to rub them. The headaches came and went, and they always made her want to curl up in a ball and drown out the rest of the world.

In truth, she was getting worse every day. And no matter how much she strived to hide it from those around her, they didn't buy her attempts to play it down. In fact, it only made them pissed at her, so she'd stopped trying to kid them.

"I feel like crap, but I'll be fine," she told Raini. "We just need to get some angelic assistance."

"Has Vivian seen anything of the angel who frequents the hospital where she works?"

"Not yet, but she said she was expecting him in a week's time. It's only been four days since then. To be honest, I thought we'd have managed to locate another angel by now, but finding one is proving to be a lot harder than I'd anticipated."

"I honestly thought Knox would have located one. I mean, the guy has contacts everywhere."

"Yeah, but he's a seriously powerful demon, Raini. Not the sort of person who'd attract angelic attention. They'll naturally prefer to avoid him. Enoch, the bastard, is making it just as difficult for us all to find him. It's driving my grandmother insane. She called each of the guy's siblings, but they all claimed they'd still heard nothing from Enoch. Ciaran's been helping the sentinels try to track the fucker, but there's been no sign of him."

"I saw Ciaran yesterday," said Raini. "He didn't look anywhere near as bad as you do, which is probably because you were infected much earlier than he was, but he looked drained . . . like someone had sucked all the energy from him."

Khloé swallowed. "I know." She felt her hands flex on the steering wheel. "I hate that I can't do anything to help him."

"He said the same thing to me about you. He's super worried about losing you. Keenan seems just as worried. Knowing how incredibly impatient he is, I'm guessing he's seriously wound up that the angel hunt isn't getting us anywhere."

"'Wound up' would be an understatement. I keep trying to distract him with sex, but it only works for a little while."

Raini snorted. "He's no doubt very aware you're trying to distract him. I'll bet the only reason he hasn't called you on it is that he's enjoying reaping the benefits."

"Probably."

"Things seem to be going good between you two."

Hearing the questioning note in the succubus' tone, Khloé said, "They are. He doesn't seem to get as annoyed with me these days. Which I'll admit is disappointing."

Raini snickered. "I don't think you ever truly annoyed him. I think he just didn't do so well with battling all his sexual frustration. Will you be seeing him tonight?"

"After he's back from accompanying Knox, Harper, and Asher on a mini outing, yes. He should only be a few hours at most." Khloé cast the rearview mirror a swift glance. "You may have noticed that two members of his Force now follow me everywhere. It doesn't matter to him that Jolene already has people tailing me—Keenan's determined to put his own people on me."

"Well, of course he is. He needs to feel that he's actually doing *something* to protect you. That's only natural for someone like Keenan."

Which was one of the reasons why Khloé didn't give him shit over it. The other reason was that she didn't want him distracted worrying about her all the time. A lot of risk and danger came with being a sentinel—she wanted his mind on the game.

Raini fiddled with the sleeve of her top. "I actually think that—" She cut off so abruptly that Khloé frowned.

Stealing a quick glance at the succubus, Khloé noticed her eyes seemed unfocused and her jaw had tightened. "Is Maddox telepathing you again?"

Raini sighed, her shoulders slumping. "Yes. He's been doing it a lot more since all the trouble started with Enoch."

"He's worried you'll get caught in the crossfire?"

"Maybe, I don't know." Raini gave her head a quick shake. "But we're not going to talk about that or him. We're going to go to your place, have some margaritas, and watch a feel-good movie. Like *I Spit on Your Grave*."

Khloé brightened. "Ooh, I like how you think."

They went ahead with Raini's plan with only a minor modification—they also ordered a Thai takeout to spice things up. By the end of the fun evening, they had a real good buzz going on, and Khloé's stomach hurt from laughing so much.

Feeling all warm and tingly, she escorted Raini to the door and said her goodbyes. Walking pretty well for a tipsy girl, the succubus sang as she made her way home. Khloé remained on her doorstep until Raini was no longer in sight.

Returning inside, Khloé headed to the living area. She needed to clean up the mess. Humming to herself, she righted the cushions on the sofa, switched off the TV, put the glasses and cutlery into the dishwasher, and dumped takeout containers and other rubbish into the trash. There were a few other things to do but, desperate to pee, she dashed to the small downstairs bathroom.

She'd no sooner sat on the toilet when a male mind touched hers. *Hey baby, I'm on my way to your place now,* said Keenan.

Her demon stirred, pleased that he'd contacted them. *'Kay,* Khloé replied. It was a telepathic slur.

A chuckle echoed through her mind. *I take it you and Raini had a few drinks. Drunk sex with you should be an adventure.*

She was about to ask how the hell he knew Raini had been here, but then she remembered he'd assigned two demons to watch over her. *We only had one or two drinks.* Ha, such a lie.

You sound out of it. You sure you're awake?

Yup. But she was sure she could quite easily fall asleep right there. It wasn't like she hadn't done it before.

Good. What you up to right now?

Peeing.

A vibe of pure male amusement touched her mind, but the vibe quickly faded. *You're not serious, are you?*

Yup.

He broke the connection so fast, she snickered.

Having done her business, Khloé washed her hands and stumbled out of the bathroom and into the hallway. Coffee. She should drink coffee and sober—

A door burst open and slammed into a wall.

Khloé sharply turned. The bottom fell out of her stomach as partly decomposed corpses began to slowly and unsteadily file through the back door and into her kitchen, their eyes wide and vacant, their skin pale and dirty.

CHAPTER FOURTEEN

For a mere moment, her thoughts blanked as her fuzzy mind struggled to process what she was seeing. Her demon stared, equally stunned. Then reality slapped them both hard, sobering Khloé in an instant. Panic quickly kicked in, and with it came a shot of pure adrenaline.

She planted her feet as power hummed in her belly, eager to be released. She gladly gave it what it wanted. The flickering blue/amber electric flames crackled and hissed as they sliced through the air and lashed the intruders like whips.

Three corpses collapsed, their bodies jerking as shockwaves coursed through them. Even so, Enoch was able to make them conjure hellfire orbs and throw them Khloé's way. *Bastard.*

Wicked fast, she slammed the orbs with a wave of electric fire that sent them crashing into the wall hard enough to make the plaster crack. A picture frame crashed to the floor, and glass shattered.

Keenan! she telepathically yelled, remembering her promise.

I could use a little help here, she told him, slinging balls of hellfire at the intruders, aiming to blind them so she could cut off Enoch's ability to use them. More of his puppets stumbled past the fallen and began to shuffle out of the kitchen, their steps slow and awkward.

Keenan's mind brushed hers, vibrating with urgency. *What's happening?*

Short version: dead people broke into the house through the back door. I took out a few of them, but there's at least half a dozen still here.

Keenan swore. *I'll have someone teleport me to you; sit tight.*

Oh, there'd be no sitting. She needed to deal with these fuckers. Her demon was furious that its enemy had not only penetrated its home and launched an attack, but that said enemy wasn't physically within reach.

Khloé ducked as a series of hellfire orbs came flying at her at an incredible speed. The first two missed. The third grazed her temple; it was like the slice of a hot blade. The fourth orb rammed into her thigh and, *fuck*, the searing hot pain almost sent her to her knees.

The hellfire ate the denim of her jeans and scorched the skin beneath, making it sizzle and blister and burn like a motherfucker. Her demon's fury hit a *whole* new level.

She could smell her flesh burning, but that horrid scent was *nothing* compared to the nauseating smell of dead flesh burning. It was like someone was roasting rotten meat. Her stomach rolled, and she would have gagged if she wasn't so busy fending off Enoch's puppets.

She swiftly sidestepped another orb, gritting her teeth as the move aggravated her thigh wound. Seething as much as her demon, she tossed a succession of hellfire balls at the heads of the corpses, aiming for their eyes, blinding some but only wounding others.

Fuck, I can't get inside your house, growled Keenan.

She tensed. *What?*

There's a translucent shield surrounding it—my teleporter can't bypass it.

Shit, shit, shit.

Collapse the shield, he added.

I can't unless I can see it. Right now, I need to knock down the people coming at me. She sent out a wave of electric fire strong enough to knock all the corpses down like bowling pins. Those she'd blinded stayed down, but the others awkwardly struggled to stand.

We'll keep trying to get inside.

Okay. But she had absolutely no confidence that they'd manage to penetrate it.

Khloé fired a series of electric-fire "bullets" out of her hand. Skulls burst and brain matter splattered on the floor as corpses toppled to the ground. But others only jerked as the bullets sank harmlessly into non-vital body parts.

As she'd already learned, it wasn't so simple to incapacitate people who were already dead. Especially since, even while they were jerking with electric shockwaves or suffering from horrific burns, Enoch—completely unaffected by their injuries—could still use them to attack her.

Khloé inhaled sharply as a hellfire orb smacked into her chest, almost winding her. She hissed through her teeth at the blazing pain. "Fuck this shit."

Shelving the pain as best she could, she kept on fighting. Enoch upped the ante, using his puppets to throw balls of hellfire and even a few psychic slaps that stung like a bitch. But it wasn't much longer before all the corpses were flat on the ground, to her demon's utter satisfaction.

Walking toward the only body that was still moving, Khloé said, "And then there was one."

Enoch glared at her through his puppet's eyes. He couldn't attack her again, since the corpse's arms had all but disintegrated, courtesy of the amount of hellfire it had been hit with. "It is only a matter of time before you are dead," he said, the words weak and garbled.

Her demon hissed, but Khloé gave him an "oh you're so cute" smile and said, "Sweetie, you don't get to be so cocky when you're too chicken shit to come out and face me yourself. Hiding behind corpses? I guess I should feel flattered that you fear me."

His upper lip curled. "I fear no one."

"Yeah? Prove it. Come face me." With that, she sank a bullet of electric fire into the corpse's head.

Sighing, Khloé glanced around. What a fucking mess. Her hallway floor was littered with pieces of skull and brain, and blistered, battered bodies—many of which were leaking slushy brain matter out of their noses, mouths, and ears.

The front door flew open, and Keenan rushed inside with several others hot on his heels. He went to grab Khloé, but one look at her injuries made him halt. "Jesus, *fuck*," he bit out.

Khloé peered down at the ugly wounds. "I've had worse. The hellfire isn't eating at my skin anymore." The pain was still unreal, though. "If Enoch popped his shield up around my house, he couldn't have been far away."

"Which is why I have several members of my Force searching the area," said Jolene, her eyes scanning the space. Power rippled through the air. The windows rattled. The walls shook. Vibrations hummed through the ground.

"Grams, please don't huff and puff and blow my house down," said Khloé.

Her grandmother turned to her and exhaled heavily; the disturbance slowly eased off. She strode toward Khloé, her face creased in concern. "Are you all right, sweetheart?"

"No, she's fucking not," Keenan snapped. His gaze, so cold and hard, swept over the remains of the corpses. "It's a good thing you're so damn powerful, because the bastard sent a small goddamn army. Were the corpses already here when I first telepathed you?" His unnaturally calm voice was coated in so much ice she was surprised the air didn't fog.

What, he thought she'd tried battling them herself for a short while? "No. They burst through the door after I finished in the bathroom. I telepathed you mere moments later. But thanks for assuming I broke my promise."

He closed his eyes and let out a long breath. "I didn't assume that, I just—"

"Forget it, it's not important right now. Grams, I don't recognize any of these people. Do you?"

"No, none." Jolene licked her lower lip. "You know, I'm glad Enoch's not easy to kill. Because it will be glorious to hurt him badly over and over and over . . . and not have to worry that he'll die too soon. Don't you agree?"

Khloé pursed her lips. "Actually, I kind of do."

Since no one could stand the putrid stench a moment longer, they all got the hell out of there and walked to Jolene's house. They gathered around the Prime's kitchen island as she barked orders down the phone to her sentinels. Ciaran, Beck, and a few others soon arrived.

Khloé almost fell off her stool when Harper, Knox, and Levi showed up. Apparently, Keenan had telepathically filled them in on what had happened—something he hadn't cared to share with the rest of the class. She shot him a glare, but he only stared at her, his jaw clenched so tightly shut she figured he had to be in pain.

He was being uncharacteristically quiet, which was a tell-tale sign that his black temper was riding him hard. He never trusted himself to speak when he was so exponentially pissed.

Knox and Levi kept flicking him looks, as if waiting for him to blow, while Harper launched into an "Enoch needs to die" tirade. The whole time, the sphinx patted Khloé's back gently . . . like she was traumatized or something.

Khloé batted her hand away. "I'm fine."

Harper glowered at her. "I'll be the judge of that."

"Why?"

"Because."

Khloé rolled her eyes. "All my injuries are healing, so stop stressing."

"Did anyone think to try stabbing Enoch's shield with the blade?" Knox asked no one in particular.

Having ended her call, Jolene said, "I tried. It didn't work. Are you sure it will permanently kill him?"

"Absolutely positive," replied Knox.

"But it's useless to us if he won't surface," Ciaran pointed out.

Beck began handing out steaming mugs of coffee. "He's going to keep coming after you, Khloé. And he'll probably send even *more* corpses next time."

"Maybe," she said, cradling a hot cup with both hands. "I challenged him to come at me directly."

"He won't do that," said Beck. "Using corpses is a low-risk method of attack for him—he'll keep on doing it until you're dead."

"You shouldn't be alone at your house anymore, Khloé," said Ciaran. "He's attacked you there *twice* now. Either I move in with you, or you move in with me."

Not going to happen. "We'd kill each other within forty-eight hours. You know that. And I'm not staying with anyone else either. I can think of something better."

Harper folded her arms across her chest. "Such as?"

"Staying in one of the Underground hotels." Khloé sipped at her coffee. "Enoch doesn't seem willing to come after me in person. If he sends corpses to the Underground, they'll be destroyed by the doormen. He could pay someone to teleport them down there, yes, but they'd be seen and obliterated by any demons who came across them. Enoch will have to then come for me himself. So not only will staying in an Underground hotel help keep me safe, it'll help bring him out into the open."

Levi blinked. "That is a good plan. And it might just work. If nothing else, you'll be safe from his zombie friends there."

"Knox and I have a penthouse suite in the hotel across the road from Urban Ink," said Harper, her arms slipping to her sides. "You could stay there until all this blows over."

"Works for me." Khloé had been to the penthouse several times. She and the girls mostly went there just to change from work clothes into dresses-worthy-of-a-bar-crawl before having a girls' night out.

"I'll be staying there with you," Keenan told her, his voice still glacier cold.

Yeah, she'd figured he'd say that. She'd have demanded the same if their situations were reversed. "Fine," said Khloé. Sex on tap sounded good to her.

"I like the idea of you staying in the penthouse," said Jolene. "Even if Enoch manages to slip past the doormen guarding the entrance of the Underground, he'll have a hell of a time bypassing the hotel's security and gaining access to the penthouse. Even I had trouble breaking into it."

Harper glared at Jolene. "You broke into my penthouse?"

Jolene gave an unapologetic shrug. "I was merely testing the security measures."

Harper opened her mouth wide, looking like she might verbally lay into the woman, but then she shook her head and turned back to Khloé. "Knox and I will get you settled there before we head home. I won't be able to relax until I know you're safe."

"I'll teleport you back to your house so you can pack some stuff." Ciaran stood. "Are members of the Force still there cleaning up the mess, Grams?"

Jolene nodded. "It will no doubt take them a while." Her face softened as her gaze slid to Khloé. "We won't let this—Enoch—taint your home, sweetheart. He doesn't get to have that power. Before you go anywhere, you need to call both your parents and tell them what happened tonight."

Fuck, those conversations wouldn't go well. "I'll do it when I'm packing my stuff."

Of course, both her parents lost their mind on hearing that Enoch had struck again. They both also tried convincing her to stay with them for a while, but they eventually conceded that staying in the Underground would be a better option.

Keenan came with her to her house while she packed, but he didn't say a word. Nor did he speak when, as promised, Harper helped her get settled into the penthouse. It really was gorgeous with the shiny marble flooring, the stylish custom furnishings, the unique artwork, and the floor-to-ceiling windows. It was also as freakishly clean as Khloé's home, so that was enough to make it feel homey for her.

Khloé doubted she'd make use of the gym during her stay—she was far too lazy for that. But she'd be happy to try out the sauna at some point.

As the couple were leaving, Knox said, "If you need anything, if there's a problem of any kind, press this." He gestured at a button on the keypad attached to the entryway wall. "It will alert the hotel staff. You probably won't need to, of course, given that you'll have Keenan with you." He looked at the sentinel, who was staring out of the window overlooking the Underground.

"Sleep well," said Harper, giving Khloé a quick hug. "See you tomorrow, Keenan."

The couple then stepped into the elevator, which soon began to descend.

Khloé turned and walked into the living area, her feet dragging. God, she was dog tired. Which was unsurprising, given that she'd expended a whole lot of psychic energy tonight. "I need to go shower and clean my wounds—I'm sure you've noticed I absolutely reek," she said to Keenan's back.

He slowly turned to face her, and his eyes swept over her injuries again. He crossed to her, tension in every line of his body. A sense of helplessness poured off him, making her chest ache.

He skimmed his hand up her arm. "I hate seeing you wounded," he said, his voice thick with suppressed anger. "It makes me want to kill."

"Yeah, me too."

He rested his forehead on hers and closed his eyes. "I couldn't get to you." He almost choked on the words. "You kept your promise, you called out to me. But I couldn't do my part and get to you." Guilt dripped from his voice.

She loosely fisted his shirt with one hand while combing her fingers through his hair. "That wasn't your fault."

Shame snaking through his system, Keenan opened his eyes. "You could be dead now. Worse, you could be one of Enoch's fucking puppets." Just the thought of her shuffling toward him, her eyes empty, her face pale and slack, made his stomach lurch.

There would have been only one thing that Keenan could have done for her—destroy her, just as she'd destroyed those other corpses tonight. But it would have killed something inside him to do it. Something that never would have healed.

Khloé was laughter and mischief and *life*. Enoch was intending on snuffing that out. The worst of it was . . . Enoch could do it without ever again touching her, because she was already ill, and it was getting worse.

Every moment of every day, it played on his mind that she was riddled with a fucking infection—one he had no way of fighting. Not without divine help. Literally. And so far, he'd had no luck getting it for her.

He felt like he was letting her down. Felt like the biggest fucking failure. What good was all his power and training if he couldn't protect the person who mattered most to him?

His demon didn't do "guilt," so it felt none of the shame that assailed Keenan. But the entity was all eaten up by the powerlessness that taunted them both. It had no intention of losing Khloé but, like Keenan, it could almost feel her slipping away.

Earlier, he'd paced outside her house with the others who'd gathered there on noticing the shield. He'd struck it with power over and over, but the shield hadn't once faltered. Not even when he, Jolene, and the sentinels worked together to try taking it down. They'd needed Khloé for that—the person *inside* it.

"You have no reason to feel guilty, Keenan. Nothing that happened tonight was on you. What went down was bad, I know, but you're missing the positives. His plan was an epic failure. He didn't manage to trap me. He didn't manage to kill me via his puppets or even severely wound me. I saw how much that infuriated him when I spoke to him—the defeat was hard for him to take.

"We have a better chance of making him surface again now. If he comes at me directly, we'll *all* be waiting for him. And, more importantly, I'll have the blade with me—Grams even gave me a knife sheath to strap on my thigh so that I can carry the blade at all times, but I prefer tucking it inside my boot. He doesn't know about the knife yet, which gives us an advantage."

Keenan curved his hand around the side of her neck. "It should make me feel better, but it doesn't. You're forgetting one very important thing. If he manages to rip that blade from your hand and stab you with it, there'll be no healing your wound. The steel is fatal to *all* demons—that's the only reason it can kill him."

A line creased her brow, and he could see she hadn't thought of that. "But I'm more at risk from dying at his hand if I don't get rid of him fast," she said. "There's only so many times he and I can do the same dance before he gets lucky and manages to kill me."

"I know. That's exactly why, from now on, I'll be shadowing you whenever you go somewhere. No, don't argue. I know you're powerful, and I know it'll be hard for him to get to you here. But I won't be able to function if I don't at least escort you from place to place. I don't trust anyone else to protect you as vigorously as I will." He stroked his thumb down the column of her throat. "Give me that peace of mind. I need it."

She would have fought him on it, but she could see that he really *did* need it. And since it wasn't as big of a deal to her as it was to him, she sighed and said, "I don't think it's necessary, but fine. You want to follow me around, knock yourself out. But don't whine when you get bored."

"You're many things, Khloé, but you're never boring."

"Why, thank you."

He took her hand. "Come on, let's get you cleaned up."

*

Khloé ambled along the footpath, passing house after house after house. All looked the same, just like every car and driveway and lawn looked the same.

It was the house at the end of the street she needed to reach, but it seemed so far away. She sped up, eager to get there. But the street seemed to stretch and elongate, keeping the house away from her. She walked faster and faster but couldn't seem to get any closer to it.

She began to jog and slipped her hand into her pocket. No key. She'd lost it. Which meant she'd only get inside if Penelope let her in.

Khloé slowed as she noticed a man lounging on the roof of a car up ahead. Realizing it was Enoch, she hissed.

He turned his head and pinned her with his gaze, smiling. "I'll bet you're pleased with yourself, aren't you, Miss Wallis?"

"Pleased?"

"Well, you killed all those people I sent your way."

"They weren't exactly people." But he was not getting that. "I made their state of death more final, though, yeah. And I think they would have thanked me for it. But since I destroyed the corpses of people who'd never done a damn thing to me, no, I'm not pleased." She planted her feet. "I'd much rather fight you. But you're hardly ever around."

"I was at every attack."

"Not always bodily."

Humor lit his eyes. "And you think that means I fear you."

"No. I think you want to draw this all out as long as you can; make us suffer as you feel that you're suffering."

He gave a slow clap and sat up. "Clever girl."

"But you're still a chicken shit."

He stiffened but didn't drop his smile. "Really?"

"Well, it's not like I can actually kill you for good. You could fight me in person and survive it just fine. Instead, you use puppets."

"It hurts to die, and then I'm weak for days until my body regrows—not something I enjoy. Why not get my revenge from the comfort of a chair?"

She tilted her head. "You really think Molly would want you to do this? To turn on your lair? To try to kill the sister of one of her best friends? To live as a stray and always looking over your shoulder?"

Fury flashed across his face. "I think she'd rather be alive. But *your grandmother killed her. Jolene will die soon, too. And she'll die at your decomposing hands, but not before she's felt the pain of your passing. We'll see just how easy it is for her to accept someone she loves is dead; we'll see if she can bring herself to destroy her resurrected granddaughter.*

"Jolene didn't kill your little girl. Molly was already gone."

"No, she was gone *after you sliced through the shield that protected her, leaving her vulnerable. I couldn't keep my psychic grip on her after that. I lost her. And it is something that both you and your grandmother will pay for.*"

He conjured a black orb and tossed it at Khloé so fast she couldn't dodge it. It crashed into her head and—

Khloé's eyes snapped open, and she clenched the coverlet hard as her surroundings sank in. There was no pain, no Enoch, no street, no black orb. Instead, she was lying on the luxurious bed in the penthouse's guest bedroom.

Beside her, Keenan curled an arm around her waist and drew her close. "You all right?" he asked, his voice thick with sleep.

"Yes. It was just a shitty dream." And yet *not* entirely a dream. Enoch had invaded her sleep *again*. Was it another distraction so that he could send in his puppets?

She reached out with her mind and scanned the penthouse. Aside from Keenan's, there were no other minds present, demonic or otherwise.

Keenan slid a hand up her back. "What was the dream about?"

She hesitated, not wanting to worry him.

"Khloé."

She sighed. "I think Enoch went for a stroll through my dreams again." She relayed what happened. "He's obviously pissed and needed to vent a little."

"It's more than that. He doesn't want you to feel safe. He wants to make you feel that he can get to you anywhere, any-place—even in your dreams."

"Huh. Never thought of it like that." Khloé blew out a breath and rubbed a hand down her face. "I'm not going to be able to get back to sleep." In all honestly, she was reluctant to drift off in case he went strolling into her dream again. Plus, her demon was too restless to settle any time soon, and its edginess would keep her awake.

Keenan tossed back the covers. "Then let's go make some coffee. I'll ask Levi to contact his incantor friend, Ella, and see if there's a way to block Enoch from entering your dreams."

Khloé lifted her brows. "Do you think it could be done?"

"There's only one way to find out."

CHAPTER FIFTEEN

It turned out that it *could* be done, so Levi brought Ella to the penthouse an hour later. Khloé's inner demon stirred, sensing the female was powerful. Khloé had met the slim, leggy redhead once or twice before. There was something very striking about her. It wasn't just her rich ruby red hair or her piercing inky blue eyes. She carried herself with a confidence that said she could take out anyone without breaking a sweat—Khloé liked that.

"Levi told me someone keeps going for a stroll in your dreams," said Ella, settling on the sofa beside her. "I can use magick to help. Normally, it would be pain free. But Levi said that someone built protective shields around your vital organs. I'll first have to unravel the one around your brain and then rebuild it afterward—both processes will hurt."

Yeah, Khloé remembered the pain from when Vivian first constructed the psychic shield. Going through it again would be worth it if it meant keeping Enoch out of her dreams. Her demon was still in a tizzy about it.

Jolene had been just as furious to hear that he'd pulled that shit yet again. In fact, so was Teague—Khloé had called him shortly after last night's attack, not wanting him to find out about it from anyone else, but she'd called him again after the dream incident. He went freaking *nuclear*.

"That's why I have a tub of ice-cream on my lap," Khloé told her. "I'm hoping that eating it will distract me."

"One can but hope," said Ella, twisting in her seat to face her.

Khloé did the same and spooned some ice-cream. "Ready when you are."

Keenan loomed over them, seeming almost manic with restlessness. "How does this work?" he asked Ella. "You plant a psychic wall in her mind to keep him out?"

"If I did that, she wouldn't be able to telepath anyone," said Ella. "What I'm going to do is embed a sort of 'tripwire' in her mind that will become active when she sleeps. If anyone tries to invade her dream, it will flick the tripwire, which will snap her awake." She smiled at Khloé. "Let's get started."

Ella's fingertips danced in the air, and she chanted under her breath. Her magick punched its way into Khloé and crackled through her body, just as Vivian's power had. Her demon stiffened, disliking the sensation, but it didn't fight back; it simply watched the incantor closely as she worked.

The entire time, Keenan sat behind Khloé with his arms curled around her waist, keeping her and her demon anchored. Eating the ice-cream didn't distract her much, but she hadn't really expected it to.

"Done. Now I'm going to plant the psychic tripwire," said Ella.

Khloé grimaced. "Is it going to hurt?"

"No. You might feel a strange sensation in your head, like a butterfly is trapped in one place just beneath your scalp, but it will pass."

'Strange sensations' she could cope with just fine. While Ella did her thing, Khloé said, "It'll infuriate Enoch that he can't reach me, which will further bait him into coming at me."

Keenan rumbled a low growl against her neck. "Don't remind me. I want him out in the open. But I don't want him near you."

"I know, but—" Khloé blinked. "Wow, that really does feel like a butterfly's trapped up here, flapping its wings." She pressed down on the spot. "I can't feel it with my fingers when I touch my scalp, though. Oh, wait, it stopped."

"Because the tripwire is now in place," said Ella. "Now I just need to rebuild the shield around your brain."

Again, magick jolted through Khloé's head and unsettled her demon, but the entity again put up no resistance. Khloé leaned back against Keenan and ate her ice-cream, not really tasting it. Finally, the crackling sensations faded.

Ella smiled and said, "All done. If anyone tries slipping into your dream, you'll wake immediately."

Feeling fidgety and jumpy, Khloé let out a long breath. "Thank you, Ella. I know it's a long shot, but is there anything you can do to fight the infection?"

"I already asked her during our drive here; it can't be done," said Levi, his tone heavy with regret.

"Only pure life can destroy that sort of darkness," said Ella.

Khloé sighed, not particularly surprised by the answer. "I don't suppose you know any angels, do you?"

The incantor shook her head. "No, sorry. I've never come across one. They provide their services to many preternatural creatures—for a price, of course—but they're less likely to work with demons. Hey, Lucifer was once an angel. Maybe he could help."

"He gradually lost his power to heal after eons of living in hell," Khloé told her. "He's been whining about it ever since, according to my grandmother."

"He probably wouldn't have helped you anyway," said Keenan, resting his chin on her shoulder. "He doesn't involve himself in Earth matters—they apparently bore him."

"I think most things bore him, with the exception of Asher," said Khloé. The Devil seemed to have a genuine fondness for her little cousin. But then, Asher could win anyone over. His dimply smiles could melt even the hardest heart.

"Lou's currently trying to convince Harper and Knox to allow him to 'mentor' Asher," groused Levi. "Lou feels that, as the boy's honorary uncle, he'd be the best choice."

Khloé shook her head, and her demon rolled its eyes. "Unreal."

"A whole lot of power lives in that child—I sensed it when I first saw him—so it's unsurprising that the Devil would want to be around him," said Ella. "Lucifer would no doubt try to use him for his own purposes."

"Neither Knox nor Harper would allow that to happen," Levi stated.

Damn right they wouldn't. Lou was darkly powerful, yes, but he wasn't the most powerful entity in existence or even the cruelest. There were far worse things in hell than Lucifer— he'd just made a home for himself there and brought some order to it.

Just then, Keenan's phone began to chime. He dug it out of his pocket and stood. "I'll be right back." He headed to the kitchen to take the call.

Looking at Levi, Ella tilted her head. "On another note, how's the kid you asked me to spell?"

"Fine, from what we've seen," replied the sentinel. "He and his mother are being watched at all times."

Khloé pursed her lips, wondering if they were referring to

Thea and Lane. She didn't ask, unsure if Keenan would have to deal with some blowback for telling her lair business.

A tickle built in the back of her throat. She coughed and sat up straighter, patting her chest hard.

Ella shot her a look full of regret. "I'm sorry that there's nothing I can do about the infection."

So did Khloé. Like yesterday, she felt tired and drained. Her throat was still dry and sore, and her chest still ached like a mother.

"I hate that I can't help in some way," added Ella.

"Thankfully, we won't need your help," said Keenan, crossing to the sofa. He looked down at Khloé, his eyes gleaming. "We have ourselves an angel."

*

Anticipation riding every muscle in his body, Keenan strode inside Knox's office with Khloé just a step behind him. He inclined his head at Larkin, who was lounging on the sofa, but most of Keenan's attention was on the tall, ethereal male in the center of the room who was glaring at the Prime.

Keenan's entity watched the angel very closely, like a predator focused on potential prey—it would pounce for sure if the angel refused to help them, but Keenan didn't believe it would come to that. The angel would bluster and frown at the prospect of working with demons, but he'd be attracted by the promise of payment—mostly because having money allowed them to give more help and support to charities. Although they were stationed on Earth, they could earn a permanent place up above if they did enough good deeds, but that could take eons.

Personally, Keenan doubted that they *always* donated their wages and lived a total frugal lifestyle. Angels were no more perfect than anyone else.

"I don't appreciate being kept somewhere against my will," said the angel, his body rigid.

Knox shrugged. "You're free to walk out at any time."

"I did," the male bit out. He pointed at Larkin. "*She* keeps bringing me back."

"Because it's necessary that we speak with you," said Keenan, planting his feet.

The angel spun and gave him a quick head-to-toe inspection. He sniffed, all ego and superiority. "And just who are you?"

Well, wasn't he an arrogant fucker. Keenan didn't give a shit—the guy could be as much of an asshole as he wanted so long as he healed Khloé. That was all Keenan and his demon cared about. "I'm the person who had you brought here."

The moment Keenan's source contacted him with the angel's details and location, Keenan had sent a teleporting member of his Force to pick up the angel and bring him to Knox's Underground office. "It's Eric, right?"

The angel lifted his chin. "What do you want?"

"You can heal illnesses."

"Of course," said Eric, arrogance dripping from his tone. "It's a standard ability for my kind."

"I need you to heal two people. You'll be paid for your services."

Eric flicked a dismissive hand. "I don't work for or with demons."

"You do now," said Keenan, his tone non-negotiable.

Eric narrowed his eyes. "You think I'm afraid of you?"

Keenan stalked toward him. "No. I think you're kicking up a fuss because you think it's the best way to make us offer you more money to do our bidding."

"We don't have time to sit down and go back and forth while we settle on a price with you," said Khloé, speaking for the first time. "Two people have been hit with death essence, and they need your aid."

"Impossible," scoffed Eric. "If they'd been hit by death essence, they'd be dead."

"Obviously that's not *always* the case or I wouldn't be standing here right now," she said. "Both my brother and I were able to drive the death essence from our bodies, but small particles of it remained, and those particles are slowly killing us. See for yourself."

Eric lifted his hand and waved it, shining a beam of light at Khloé. Keenan frowned. It was no different than someone aiming a torch at her, but that divine light must have enabled the angel to see something he didn't, because Eric's face paled. "How is it that your organs haven't failed?"

"They're currently protected by magick, but those protections won't last forever. My brother and I need your help, and we need it *now*. So let's stop pussyfooting around—name your price so that I can contact my Prime and we can all move forward with the situation."

"If Knox Thorne is not your Prime, who is?"

"Jolene Wallis."

His upper lip curled. "I've heard of her."

Khloé's lips twitch. "I take it you don't like imps much."

"The last time I refused to assist an imp, they emptied my bank accounts, stole the contents from my home-safe, took out bank loans in my name, and posted my address on a BDSM online forum declaring I was having a party and that all were invited. I lost my teaching job after that fiasco."

Keenan's demon chuckled, despite its dark mood.

Khloé shrugged. "Sounds pretty tame to me. My grandmother will go to *any* measure to ensure that my brother and I are healed—I'm not saying she'll physically harm you, but she has ways of making your life an endless cycle of hell."

Larkin crossed one leg over the other and said, "The big G can't help you—he and Lucifer made an agreement not to personally interfere in fights between angels and demons, since past attempts almost resulted in the two deities going to war. Neither likes war, and the Earth would never survive such a battle intact. In other words, you can't rely on divine help. Be smart, cooperate, and name your price."

Eric tightened his mouth, staring at Khloé hard. Finally, he jutted out his chin and said, "Twenty thousand dollars *each*. And before you tell me that's extortionate, remember that you can't put a true price on life."

Thinking he was something of a greedy fucker but relieved that he'd agreed to help, Khloé telepathically reached out to Jolene. *Grams, we got an angel here. He says he'll heal Ciaran and me, but he wants to charge you twenty grand per person.*

Jolene's mind practically leapt at hers. *An angel? Where?*

Knox's office. Will you agree to his price?

Of course, her grandmother replied without hesitation. *I would have expected him to demand more.*

I think he's too afraid of you and imps in general to test our patience.

So he should be. I'll contact Ciaran and be with you shortly.

Khloé switched her focus back to Eric. "Jolene has agreed to your price."

Eric nodded. "When will she get here?"

"Soon."

It couldn't have been more than a minute later that Ciaran, Jolene, Orrin, and Vivian abruptly appeared in the middle of the office. Khloé frowned. Why had she brought along Vivian?

Ciaran sidled up to Khloé and gave her a nod, fairly vibrating with optimism. "You okay?"

"Hopefully both of us will be in, say, five minutes' time," she replied.

As regal as ever, Jolene fixed her attention on the angel. "I am Jolene Wallis. And you are?"

He licked his lips. "Eric Carlton."

"Eric Carlton," she echoed, flashing him a courteous smile. "I will agree to your price, Eric. But only if my grandchildren are *fully* healed. A member of my lair here can see illness in a person. She will tell me if you failed."

Ah, that explained Vivian's presence.

Eric gave Jolene a look that was all haughty. "I am an angel; we do not fail when it comes to healing." His eyes turned wary. "How do I know you'll stick to your end of the bargain and actually pay me?"

"My word would mean nothing as a Prime if I went back on it whenever I pleased. It is a weakness that can lead to people losing their position. I would much prefer to keep mine. Let us get this done, shall we?"

Ciaran nudged Khloé. "You first, sis."

Khloé frowned at him. "I was going to say the same to you."

"You're sicker than I am," he pointed out.

"He's right, Khloé," said Jolene. "You should go first."

"Fine." Khloé rolled back her shoulders and crossed to Eric. Keenan stood behind her like a sentry, so damn tense that his muscles probably hurt. And she knew he'd pounce on the angel in a flash if the guy made a wrong move. Eric saw that easily enough, because he cast Keenan a nervous glance.

"What do I need to do?" she asked the angel.

Eric held up his hand. "Just place your palm flat against mine."

Wary of feeling a perfect stranger's power course through her, she hesitated. But this had to be done, didn't it? Khloé followed his directive and waited. Her breath caught when his entire palm glowed. A gentle wind drifted through her, warm and comforting. She felt flares of heat here and there, felt—

Her body pitched forward as the wind disappeared in a rush, as if sucked out of her by a hoover or something. The only reason she didn't fall was that Keenan caught her by her waist. Her demon rushed close to the surface, bracing itself to attack.

"What the fuck just happened?" the incubus demanded, a growl rumbling in his chest.

Eric looked at his palm, his lips parted. "I-I don't know. My power . . . it was as if your system regurgitated it," he told Khloé.

Jolene stepped toward him. "Try again." It was an order.

The angel obeyed, and the same damn thing happened.

Stiff, Jolene turned to the incantor. "Vivian, check her."

Vivian weaved a pattern in the air with her hands, staring at Khloé's body. She bit her lip. "She's still infected, Jolene. It doesn't look as if his power did anything to help her."

Khloé felt the blood leave her face, along with every ounce of hope that had sat in her belly.

Keenan spat a vicious curse. "Why isn't it working?"

Eric lifted his shoulders. "I have no idea. Perhaps the infection has had too much time to set into her cells—do not forget, it is the essence of death; it will not react like a normal virus of any sort."

"Try to heal Ciaran," Khloé told him, her chest tight. "He hasn't had the infection long."

"If it didn't work for you, it's not going to work for me," said Ciaran.

"It might." Jolene motioned him toward the angel. "Let Eric try."

Ciaran's lips thinned. "But—"

"I understand that you'll feel guilty if he's able to heal you when he wasn't able to heal Khloé," began Jolene, "but that's not a reason to refuse help. Plus, we *have* to know if this infection can in fact be beaten. If he's able to heal you, we know Khloé has a chance; that we just need to find someone strong enough to help her."

Ciaran exhaled heavily. "All right. But the same thing's going to happen to me that just happened to her."

It didn't happen, though. Eric's power effortlessly flowed through Ciaran. When both males lowered their arms, Jolene quickly asked, "How do you feel?"

Ciaran's brow knitted. "The fatigue and discomfort have gone."

"Vivian, tell me what you see," Jolene told her, waving her toward him.

The incantor checked him, and her face relaxed. "He's fully healed."

Relief surged through Khloé so fast, she was surprised her knees didn't buckle.

Ciaran's eyes fell shut. But he didn't look relieved. He looked pained. "So, what, we need a more powerful angel to heal Khloé?"

"An archangel could heal her, of course," said Eric. "But they do not come to Earth. They never leave heaven. *Ever.* Not for anything."

"Well, that needs to change," Keenan clipped, his heart pounding. He paced up and down like a caged animal. He couldn't keep still; couldn't find any calm, no matter how deep he dug for it. "Contact one."

"I'm unable to," Eric told him. "They serve heaven; they do not concern themselves with angel business or anything that happens outside of their realm. Even if I *could* contact one, no amount of money or threats of violence would persuade one to come here. To put it simply, they wouldn't care, just as you probably wouldn't care to save the life of a carpet mite. The creatures down here mean nothing to them."

Keenan's demon snarled, wanting to punch and smash and destroy. He grabbed Khloé's hand and raised it. "Try again, Eric."

The angel shook his head. "But I—"

"Just *try*," insisted Keenan and his demon, battling for control of their vocal cords, making the words come out loud, deep, and mechanical.

Swallowing hard, his eyes wide with fear, Eric did as he was ordered. But, again, his attempt to heal her didn't work.

Anger whipped through Keenan like a bolt of red-hot lightning. He swiped the office desk, sending everything on the surface crashing to the floor. No one moved, no one tried to calm or placate him. They waited, trusting him to get ahold of his temper.

His breaths coming hard and fast, he glared up at the ceiling. He'd come here expecting to have Khloé healed; to be able to take her back to the penthouse, healthy and free of what Enoch left inside her. Instead . . . *Fuck.*

A familiar female mind softly stroked his own. A touch that was meant to comfort and calm him. He swallowed around the lump in his throat. He loved that she'd try to soothe him, but he hated that she felt the need to do it. She shouldn't *have* to worry about him—*she* was the one who was riddled with an infection. He wouldn't be a selfish bastard and make this all about him.

Forcing himself to think past the rage clawing at his insides and the hardness that had settled in his gut, he said, "There *has* to be other preternatural creatures that can help her. Some shifters can heal. Even some vampires have the power to do it."

"But none of them produce pure life like an angel," Eric pointed out. "They wouldn't be able to combat death essence."

Keenan raised a brow at him. "Can you say that for certain?"

Eric faltered. "Well, no—"

"Then we don't give up." Keenan turned to Knox. "You once

met with vampires. Can you talk to them and find out if they have one who could heal Khloé?"

Knox gave a slow nod. "I can ask them."

"I'm in contact with some practitioners," said Vivian. "I could see if any of them could be of any aid to Khloé."

"Do it," Keenan told her. "I have a contact who's a lone bear shifter. I'll speak with him and see if he knows a shifter who's also a powerful healer." He looked down at his imp. "The situation isn't hopeless, Khloé. There are millions of preternatural creatures on this Earth. At least *one* of them has to be able to help you. We just have to find out who they are and then get their ass here."

CHAPTER SIXTEEN

Khloé picked up the remote and switched off the TV. She hadn't been able to follow the movie because her mind was elsewhere. It just kept replaying those earlier moments when Eric's attempts to heal her had failed. She hadn't expected that. She'd taken it for granted that all she needed to do was find an angel. Any ole angel.

She'd been wrong.

The only saving grace was that her brother was no longer infected. Not that Ciaran seemed so happy about it. She'd almost slapped him across the head for stupidly feeling guilty.

Khloé hadn't given up hope that there was a way of ridding her of the infection. Nope, not at all. She didn't admit defeat so easily. Keenan was right—the law of probability said that at least *one* of the preternatural creatures out there had a gift that could help her. Khloé trusted that her loved ones would do everything in their power to find such a person, just as she would have done for them.

With both her lair and Keenan's working together on this, it would surely only be a matter of time before she found herself standing in front of someone who could heal her. In fact, that could even happen, shortly. Keenan was currently meeting with the bear shifter he'd mentioned; he might return with positive news.

In-keeping with her plan to stay in the Underground out of Enoch's reach, she'd remained at the penthouse. And now, bored out of her mind, she wished the time would tick faster so she could head to work and do *something*.

Having heard from Knox that Eric's attempt to heal Khloé came to nothing, Harper had immediately called her, offering for Khloé to take the day off. Raini and Devon—who'd also called her—thought she should stay at the penthouse and rest. Khloé didn't think "rest" would really help much. The infection didn't work as viral infections did. Plus, she needed to distract herself from all the bullshit, so she fully intended to go to work.

Hearing the intercom system beep, Khloé headed to the entryway and pressed the audio button. "Hello?"

"Good morning, Miss Wallis," said the hotel's receptionist. "You have a visitor."

"A visitor?" echoed Khloé.

"Well, technically two. A woman wishes to speak with you. She introduced herself as Raini. She has a young boy with her."

Khloé straightened. A boy? Raini could have brought Asher along, but surely not without an escort. "They have no one else with them?"

"No."

"How old is the kid?"

"About four or five."

Suspiciousness pricked at her. Keenan said that Thea could use glamor. Could she be posing as Raini, hoping that Khloé would allow her inside? Possibly. It wouldn't take much digging to learn details about Khloé such as who her friends were and where she worked.

Not prepared to take any chances, Khloé said, "I'll be right down." If it was Raini, she'd invite her up. If it was Thea, well, Khloé would tell her to fuck right off. It might even be fun. If nothing else, it would be a nice distraction.

She slipped on her shoes and took the elevator down to the first floor. Raini was waiting there, her hand clenched tightly around the strap of her purse. Only it wasn't Raini. Because Raini didn't slouch, wear conservative clothing, or own that boring jacket.

Did Thea really think Khloé so easily fooled? It would seem so. How silly. Khloé's inner demon sniffed in affront.

Raini's mimic forced a smile. "Hey, girl. Can I come up?"

Hey, girl? Ugh. Stepping out of the elevator, Khloé scanned the large reception area and spotted a boy sitting on one of the sofas playing on his tablet. Keeping her voice low, she said, "I'm guessing that's your kiddo over there, and I'm guessing you're Thea."

Surprise flickered across the female's face.

"I know all about you. And no, we can't go somewhere and talk in private, if that's what you're hoping. I don't know what you want, but I'd rather you got this over with fast." Her inner demon pushed close to the surface, intent on watching the other woman very carefully. It didn't like her. Didn't like that she'd hurt Keenan.

Thea forced a smile and said, "Girl, have you been drinking? Who is this 'Thea' person?"

Lord deliver me. "Look, I ain't gonna lie, I see the appeal in playing head games with people. It's the best time-passer ever. I'd normally play along with it just to see how far you'd take the act, but I'm not in the mood right now. So we'll have to content ourselves with you getting down to the nitty fucking gritty and telling me why you're polluting my air."

Thea drew in a breath, dropped the vapid smile, and inclined her head. "Very well. I heard that you and Keenan are allegedly a . . . couple now."

She'd said "couple' like it was a dirty word. "You went through the trouble of finding me just to tell me that?"

"Someone mentioned they thought you were staying here and I, well, I need to ask you something. And I need the truth. *Are* you and Keenan really a couple? Or is he secretly pretending to be in a relationship so that no one will guess I'm around?"

"It wouldn't be a secret if I denied or confirmed it, would it?" And it was more fun to keep the woman in the dark.

Thea briefly closed her eyes. "Please just tell me."

"Why?"

"Because I planned to try to fix things with him, but I never go after men who are spoken for. If he has moved on, I'll back off."

Khloé's demon hissed. The bitch wanted him back, huh? Well, too fucking bad. "In your shoes, I'd quite simply just back off anyway, since he wants nothing to do with you."

"He's just mad at me. And rightly so." Thea curled her hair behind her ear. "Keenan doesn't forgive easily. I knew it would take time to win back his trust and earn a place in his life. But he's worth the wait and effort, so I would have been as patient as he needed me to be. If he's with someone else and he's happy, though, I'll step aside. So, please just answer my question. Are you and him together?"

Khloé eyed her closely, seeing right through all the bullshit. "You wouldn't truly step aside. You're here to size up who you see as a possible opponent." Khloé took a step toward her. "You

think I can't sense that? You think I don't know how hard it is
for you to keep up this noble act when what you really want to
do is warn me away from Keenan?"

"I don't—"

"Come on, be a big girl and say whatever you *really* want to
say. I'll even pretend to care, if you like."

The softness left Thea's expression. "Keenan and I had something special. I messed up, and I hurt him so bad he's never
recovered from it enough to try a relationship. I'm not saying
I think he pines for me. I'm saying he's holding onto that pain
and using it as a shield to keep others away. Because he knows,
deep down, he's never going to find anything that special with
someone else. It only comes around once in a lifetime."

A flare of jealousy fired through Khloé. It shouldn't have hurt
that he'd had "special" with another woman, but it did. Just as
it hurt that this bitch could well be right—a subconscious part
of him could be clinging to what he'd lost, desperate to have it
back. Khloé sure hoped that wasn't the case, because she'd hate
to have to mangle him.

"He and I can start over," Thea went on. "I'm here, I'll fix what
I broke, and I'll make him so happy he'll never regret taking a
second chance on me. So if you are with Keenan, if you care
about him at all, you'll walk away and let him have that something special again."

"That's a real pretty way of putting '*stay away from Keenan, he's
mine, mine, mine.*' That *is* what you mean to say, isn't it?"

Thea's mouth tightened. She gave a tight shrug. "I suppose
you could sum it up that way."

"And if I tell you to go squat and piss up a tree, what will you
do? I truly am interested to know."

"I'll fight for him, if I have to."

Khloé perked up. "Fight for him as in, like, challenge me to a duel?" Her demon stretched inside her, more than happy to take this bitch on.

"No. I just mean that I'd put in the effort to prove *myself* to him."

How boring. "You don't think it would be a waste of time, considering he's indicated that he doesn't want you back in his life?"

"He doesn't want to risk that I'll hurt him again—that's different from him not wanting me around. You can't understand unless you've ever loved someone so deeply that they almost feel part of you. He loved me that way once. You can't just shake off something like that, no matter how much you might wish you could. It stays with . . ." She trailed off as her eyes darted to something behind Khloé.

Her brows knitting together, Khloé glanced over her shoulder. Her stomach flipped at the sight of Keenan fluidly stalking through the reception area, anger in every step . . . like a pissed-off leopard intent on punishing whoever had intruded on his territory. The danger emanating from him right then almost made her demon purr.

Thea backed up a few steps as he advanced on her, his eyes cold and flinty. She raised her hand, as if it would protect her. "Keenan—"

"Don't know why the fuck you're here, but you need to get out of my sight," he clipped, his nostrils flaring. His hold on his temper was clearly wafer-thin.

"But I just—"

"*Don't*," he bit out. "I'm not interested in anything you have to say. I thought I made that clear."

"I'm not trying to upset you, I swear. I just wanted to talk to Khloé, I wanted to—" Thea cut off as he put his face close to hers, a snarl tugging at his features.

"You stay away from Khloé," he ordered in a menacing whisper. "You hear me? You don't approach her. You don't talk to her. You don't even *look* at her. She's no one to you."

Pain flickered in Thea's eyes. "But she's someone to you? Is that what you're saying?"

"That's exactly what I'm saying. So do the smart thing and stay the fuck away from her. You know me. You know how far I'll go to protect what's mine." He took Khloé's arm and ushered her toward the private elevator. "Go," he told Thea. "There's nothing for you here. I'm not interested in you or anything you have to say."

Khloé raised her finger and said, "I did try to tell you that, *Raini*." She gave a dramatic wink. "It was *lovely* chatting with you."

After he'd swiped his keycard and punched in the code, the metal doors slid open. He shepherded Khloé into the elevator and jabbed the up button. Thea hadn't moved. She was staring at him, her eyes wet and hurt. Security guards surrounded her just as the shiny doors closed.

Keenan spun Khloé to face him, his eyes hard and dark with anger. "Why the fuck would you give her the time of day?"

"She came here posing as Raini."

"You obviously suspected it wasn't Raini, because you didn't let her up to the penthouse. You had to at least also suspect it was Thea, given that she had a kid with her. But even if you *didn't* think it was her, you shouldn't have gone down to *see a total stranger*."

Her brow furrowed. "Don't you growl at me."

"I'm serious, Khloé. Enoch is going to try all sorts of ways to get to you. He might even hire an assassin to do the job for him. So if a stranger comes calling, you tell the receptionist to send. Them. Away. You hear me?"

"Look, I get that your emotions are still all over the place after what happened earlier—"

"Tell me you'll do that, Khloé," he said, ignoring her words. "Tell me you'll send any strangers away."

"Or what, Don Juan?"

He towered over her, all sex and fury, and curved a hand tight around her nape. "Or I'll fuck the answer I want right out of you." He took her mouth with a territorial snarl, sweeping away any other objection she might have made. The kiss was hard and wet and hungry, and it woke her body in an instant.

Need—so raw and terrible—roared through her. Her blood heated. Her nerve-endings tingled. Her hormones went haywire.

Keenan kissed her hard and deep, so greedy for her he almost shook with it. A powerful, primitive need crawled through him, thick and hot. He wanted to fuck her. Possess her. Pleasure her. *Claim* her.

His fear of losing her to the fucking infection sat like a lump of lead in the pit of his stomach, driving him to officially make her his. He couldn't imagine not having her in his life. Her smile, her laugh, her way of making him feel alive—even when she was poking at his patience—warmed his soul. Just *looking* at her each morning set him up for the day.

He got why committing to a mating would be scary for her, but he wasn't going to give her up. Not to her fears. Not to the infection. Not to *anything*.

He was done holding back on claiming her. He couldn't do it any longer. He needed her in a way he'd never needed another person. Needed her to belong solely to him, because he sure as fuck belonged solely to her—all the way from cell to bone.

Struggling to breathe, Khloe tore her mouth free. "Wait."

"No." He bit down on the crook of her neck. "You're mine, and I'm going to claim what's mine."

Khloe's heart thudded. Claim? A contradictory mixture of panic and joy spiked through her.

Realizing they'd arrived at the penthouse, she backed out of the elevator. "You don't really want this. You're not thinking straight because you're mad and—"

"Mad?" He prowled toward her, his face cold, his eyes alive with something that made her stomach twist. "I'm mad about a lot of things. I'm mad that my ex came here. I'm mad that you've got an infection ravaging your system. I'm mad that Enoch's sending dead fucking bodies after you. I don't do well with feeling helpless, Khloé. But I'm helpless to protect you, and I absolutely fucking hate it."

She kept on backing away, but he just kept on stalking her. She licked her lips. "I'm doing what I can to stay safe—"

"Doesn't matter. It wouldn't matter if you were surrounded by armed fucking guards every single minute of the damn day. I'd still worry."

"Then I'd say it's a control issue for you. You don't like that you can't take charge of this situation," she accused, expecting him to go on the defensive.

"You're right, I don't. Control is important to me for a number of reasons. But you've been shooting mine to shit since day one."

The surprise of that made her halt. She frowned. "How? By poking at you?"

And then he was eating up her personal space. "No. By making me hard as a fucking rock against my own damn will. Yeah, that's right, I can't control my body around you. I never have been able to."

Pure shock hit her first. But it quickly gave way to sheer incredulity when she realized . . . "Oh my God, you're mad at me for this," she said, backpedaling again. "How is it *my* fault?"

"It's not. But I wish it was, because then I could be pissed at you. And maybe if I was pissed at you, I wouldn't want you so damn much I can barely fucking think straight. It's like you're imprinted in my system. I can't get you out, and I don't even want to." His anger melted away, replaced by a firm resolve that made her scalp prickle. "Come here."

Her pulse jumped. "Why?"

"So I can claim what belongs to me. I know why that scares you. You hear the word 'mate', and you don't think 'safe.' Why would you? I don't know your family well, but it's no secret that your mother's relationships have been nothing short of dysfunctional—all violence and verbal abuse and binge drinking. It's also no secret that your father wasn't faithful to his past partners and that he struggled to settle down. Although he's now mated, you're probably not confident that it'll last."

Khloé opened her mouth to argue . . . but she couldn't. He was right. He was right about all of it.

He closed the space between them in one slow step. "People have been walking in and out of your life since you were a kid. Some were good, some weren't. It probably became a reflex for you not to form attachments to anyone new, because taking a chance on them sticking around usually never worked out. And that's mostly why you fear taking me as your mate—you don't have any faith that I won't leave you at some point."

She swallowed hard and closed her eyes for a moment. She hated that he'd seen right through her. It made her feel too exposed.

"It's no easier for me to take this risk, Khloé. I know what it's like to get used to having people around, to learn to trust them, only to have them shit on that trust. I can't promise you that our mating will be all flowers and rainbows. I can only assure you that I'll give this all I have; that I'd never give up on us."

He swept his thumb over her jaw. "We could play it safe and

just go on as we are, sure. But neither of us would happily waltz through life with no regrets that we didn't take a shot at mating. You know that." He framed her face with his hands. "What scares you most? That there'll be no going back—and there won't be, Khloé; neither me nor my demon would ever let you go—or that you love me?"

She jerked back, but he didn't release her face. "Love you?" she echoed. "You think I love you?"

"Don't you?"

She spluttered. "Well, I . . . it's . . . I don't . . . Why are you . . ." She closed her eyes. "Fuck."

"You love me," he said softly. "And I get why you'd find that scary. I love you more than I've ever loved anyone or anything, and it fucking terrifies me."

Her eyes popped open. "You . . . you love me?"

He let out a soft chuckle. "Yeah. How could I not?"

"Easily. I'm the ultimate pain in the ass. Proudly. I put a whole lot of effort into it, as it happens."

"Hmm, yes, you do. But you're my pain in the ass." He took her mouth, sweeping his tongue inside to flick her own, feasting and consuming and dominating.

Khloé broke the kiss as a spicy, aphrodisiac scent laced the air and seemed to curl around her. The room instantly felt too warm and humid. Heat flashed through her system, making her breasts ache, her nipples harden, her clit pulse, and her core spasm. "Wait. We're not done talking."

"Sure we are," he said easily, sliding his fingers into her hair. "What is there to talk about?"

A phantom finger slid through her folds and then circled her clit. She sucked in a breath and moaned. "Not fair."

His brows lifted. "Did you think I'd play fair when it comes to something this important to me? If I thought you didn't want the same things I do, I'd back off. Maybe. But you do want this, Khloé."

Fuck if she could deny that. "What about your demon? It might be possessive of me, but I highly doubt it's interested in claiming me." She gasped as phantom fingers pinched her nipples, making her pulse clench and ache.

"My demon wants to straight-up own you. Wants to brand you both inside and out. As far as its concerned, it has waited long enough for both you and me to get with the program. It doesn't want to wait any longer, and neither do I." He put his mouth to her ear and bit the lobe. "More importantly, neither do you."

An image flashed in her mind of her tied spread-eagle to a bed while Keenan hammered into her, his skin glimmering with a fine sheen of sweat.

"Do you want me inside you, Khloé?" he asked, his voice low and velvety; it feathered over her tingling skin, teasing every nerve-ending. "Do you want to feel my cock filling you? Stretching you? Shooting my come in you?"

Phantom lips suckled on her clit, making her stumble backwards and collide with the side of the sofa. "Oh, Jesus." Each wet tug on her clit made her pussy spasm and ache. "You need to stop." But he didn't. Those lips suckled a little faster.

She reached behind her to rest her hands on the arm of the sofa. "You're such a prick," she hissed. "You can't seduce me into accepting your claim."

Keenan combed his fingers through her hair. "You already have accepted it, baby. You just haven't said it out loud yet. Do it, Khloé. Say it. Say you'll take this gamble on me, on *us*."

She drew in a shaky breath, trembling with the unadulterated need rocketing through her bloodstream. "I can't think when my body's screaming for you like this."

"What's there to think about? You want this. I want this. So, let's stop dicking around and do what every other couple does—take a chance."

She squeezed her eyes shut. She could admit, if only to herself, that he was right—she didn't need to "think." She knew what she wanted; she was just hesitant to reach for it.

That made her want to slap herself, because she'd once resolved that she'd be nothing like her parents, who allowed their issues and fears to rule them when it came to relationships. Yet, here she was, doing that very thing.

He'd been right about something else, too. She loved the annoying bastard. She'd loved him for longer than she cared to admit. She'd denied it to herself for years because it had made it easier to deal with the idea that she'd never have him. But now she did have him, and now those feelings she'd tried to bury swamped her entire system.

Her demon had no fears about taking this chance with Keenan. It considered him a worthy mate for Khloé; believed he would protect and care for her. It wanted Khloé to do as he'd suggested and stop dancing around the decision.

She opened her eyes. "This could blow up in our faces," she whispered.

"Or it could be the best fucking thing we ever did." He cupped her jaw. "Take this gamble with me, Khloé."

She swallowed hard. "Fine. But if my family curse interferes at some point and you find yourself alone and miserable, don't whine to me about it."

Masculine satisfaction glimmered in those blue eyes. "Noted." He closed his mouth over hers and sank his tongue inside to lick her own. He plundered and devastated her mouth. Bit and licked and feasted.

She tasted relief, triumph, and smugness. Tasted a primal

possession that she knew was riding him hard. She sure hoped he'd ride *her* hard.

He slowly lowered the zipper of her jeans. "I can smell how wet you are."

Explicit image after explicit image shot to the forefront of her mind while he quickly stripped her of her clothes. At the same time, a phantom tongue licked at her nipples.

She inhaled a shaky breath. "*Keenan.*"

"Ah, there's my pussy." He drove his finger inside, groaning when she tightened around them. "Missed this."

"Seriously, Keenan, you need to do something. You put the ache there, now deal with it." That sounded petulant even to her.

His free hand closed over her aching breast and squeezed just right. The finger inside her swirled. "Tell me what you want, Khloé."

"*You know.*"

"I know you want to come. But how shall I make you come? With my abilities? With my fingers? With my mouth? With my cock? Tell me what you want."

She hissed out a breath. "I don't care, just make me come."

He pushed her thighs further apart, dropped to his knees, and clamped his mouth around her pussy.

Oh, God, yes. She gripped his hair for dear life as he ate her out, using that talented tongue to push her closer and closer to coming. But she didn't come. Couldn't. Not until he let her.

Wound so tight it was almost painful, Khloé tugged on his hair in demand, shamelessly pulling his face closer. He plunged his tongue so deep her head fell back. "Now, now, now." And then the orgasm crashed into her like a freight train, yanking her under, making her shake and cry out.

Once she'd finally pulled herself together, she opened her eyes just in time to see him stand and whip off his T-shirt. She swallowed at the sight of all that hard, male muscle. It was *criminal* that he looked that good. Criminal. But as that scorching hot body now belonged only to her, she was fine with it.

He swiped his tongue over his lower lip. "Nothing tastes better than you," he said, his voice thick and deep with a raw hunger that mirrored her own. "Turn around and bend over."

Just the phrase she wanted to hear. Khloé did as he asked, gripping the arm of the sofa. She heard a zipper lower. Felt his cock slap her ass as it sprang out of his jeans.

Her heart pounded. Her breaths started coming faster. Her body went tight as a bow with anticipation.

Her skin felt too hot, too sensitive. He'd made her come, yes, but the orgasm hadn't completely sated her—he hadn't let it, wanting her to need more.

Khloé gasped as the thick tip of his cock inched into her pussy. Her inner muscles gave a little resistance, but he relentlessly pushed his way inside, mercilessly stretching her.

Keenan slowly pulled back until only the broad head was inside her. "You feel so fucking good." He smoothly drove deep, groaning through gritted teeth at the feel of all that tight, wet heat sheathing him. It was like being squeezed by a slick, blazing hot fist. His demon loved it. Loved that she'd accepted their claim on her.

The sexual energy pouring off her filled him. Invigorated him. Rushed straight to his dick.

In the grip of a carnal desire that inflamed him both inside and out, he gave her another achingly slow thrust, wanting her to really *feel* every inch of him. Wanting her to feel branded to the bone.

"I'm not looking for soft and slow, Don Juan," she snarked. "*Harder.*"

He raised his brow. "Now that's not my name, is it?"

"Suits you, though."

Feeling his mouth twitch, he gave her another lazy thrust.

She hissed at him over her shoulder. "I said, *harder*."

"Say my name, and I'll give you what you want."

"Oh my God, just fuck me!"

He leaned over and licked the back of her shoulder. "You're not going to have the control when we're in bed, baby. It won't happen. You already know that. Now . . ." He fisted her hair and yanked her head back. "Say my fucking name."

"Keenan," she ground out.

Releasing her hair, he splayed one hand on her back and gripped her hip with the other. "Good girl. Now you get what you want." Keeping her pinned in place, he rode her hard, evoking every response that her body had to give.

There was nothing gentle about the way he took her. He didn't *feel* gentle. He felt frantic, feverish, possessive.

"Feel me, Khloé. Feel my cock slamming into you. Owning you." He savagely took her, relishing the feel of her tight muscles sucking at his shaft, as if to hold him inside. "Love how greedy your pussy is for me."

Her inner muscles rippled, and hot liquid drenched him. *Fuck.*

A slave to the primal drive to jackhammer into her, Keenan slammed hard and deep again and again, losing himself in her. With each breath he took, he filled his lungs with the cock-hardening scent of her need; he drank in the succulent, spicy taste of the sexual energy spilling from her. It made his demon close to drunk.

"You love getting fucked by my cock, don't you?"

"Yes," rasped Khloé, holding tight to the arm of the sofa as he ruthlessly powered into her. The feel of his fat dick slicing through her super-sensitized inner muscles was sheer heaven.

She tried throwing her hips back to meet each thrust, but he held her still, forcing her to take only what he gave her—something that *totally* flipped her demon's switch. All Khloé could do was moan and whimper as he possessed and used and claimed her body like he had every right. It was exactly what she'd granted him.

A cool draft hit her back, and then his thrusts changed; they became rougher, aggressive, almost feral. And she knew she was getting fucked by his demon. It told her she was theirs, made for them, and that they'd never let her go.

Over and over Keenan and the entity switched, taking turns fucking her body. No, *claiming* it. She'd be sore tomorrow for sure, because the demon was pitiless in its intent to make her feel utterly branded.

Feeling her orgasm creep up on her, she dug her fingertips into the sofa's arm. "I'm gonna come."

Phantom sensations suddenly swamped her—tongues lashing her nipples, teeth biting her breasts, a thumb pressing down on her clit, a wet finger probing the bud of her ass. The assault to her body was too much; the pleasure was too all-consuming.

"Come," Keenan ordered.

Violent wave after violent wave of sheer bliss washed over and through her, making her body shatter into a million pieces. Her eyes went blind. Her head shot up as she screamed.

Behind her, Keenan went wild, hammering into her so hard it jolted the sofa. His cock swelled impossibly as he jammed it *so fucking deep* and exploded with a growl of her name.

*

Sprawled flat on her stomach on the bed, Khloé opened her eyes to peek at Keenan. He was lying on his side, mapping her back with the pads of his fingers, looking more peaceful than she'd ever seen him. Which made her imp nature shake its hands in gleeful anticipation of just how entertaining it would be to poke at him. But Khloé shoved it aside. Later. She'd torment him later.

They'd gravitated from the living room to the shower, where he'd fucked her against the tiled wall. Then they'd tumbled into bed, where he'd taken her yet again. The guy was insatiable, and that was not something she saw any need to complain about.

"You're quiet," she said.

His eyes briefly slid to hers. "I'm busy."

"Doing what?"

"Indulging myself." He traced the bumps of her spine. "I like touching you. Spent a long time fighting the need to do it. Now that I don't have to anymore, I'm never going to."

Well, that was fine with her. "All right."

"How do you get your skin this soft?"

"Soaking in the blood of virgins."

His mouth twitched. "I can see how that would work."

"I highly recommend trying it. Though results may vary."

He gently tugged the tie out of her hair, letting the thick strands flow over her back. He bunched his hand in it, looking as intrigued as a cat with a ball of yarn. "Love your hair."

"Why, thank you. I grow it myself." She let her eyes fall shut as he massaged her head with just the right amount of pressure. The feel of his fingertips digging, kneading, and gliding along her scalp felt heavenly. She could easily drift off to sleep like this, but she had an important question to ask first.

She met his gaze. "Now that you're a lot calmer, are you going to tell me what the bear shifter said?"

He sighed. "He says that no shifter healer will be able to help you. They can heal wounds, but not sicknesses. But that doesn't mean we need to give up, Khloé. Just because shifters can't help doesn't mean other preternatural breeds can't."

Although disappointment flooded her, she said, "I know that, and I have no intention of admitting defeat."

He dropped a kiss on her hair. "Good."

Hearing her phone beep, she grabbed it from the nightstand and read the text. A smile tugged at her mouth.

"Who is it?" asked Keenan.

"God, you're nosy. It's Teague. He's checking to see how I'm doing, and he's invited me to the racetrack on Saturday to watch his demon compete." She *loved* the tracks.

"He won't like that I've claimed you."

No, he wouldn't . . . which reminded her that she'd need to tell him herself so that he didn't find out from others. "Neither will Thea."

"The difference is, I couldn't give a fuck what she thinks about anything. Teague matters to you."

Khloé bit her lip. "Are you sure she doesn't mean anything to you anymore? She talked as if you guys were fated. Kept saying you'd had 'something special.' She's convinced you can get it back."

"I cared about her at one time, but those feelings just . . . died. She killed them. I look at her, and I feel nothing. My demon has no time or patience for her. The fucked-up thing about me is that I can shut people out so easily if they betray or hurt me. It's like a switch gets flipped, and it numbs whatever I'm feeling."

It sounded like a self-protective measure to her. The thought that he'd subconsciously developed one just about broke her heart. Wanting to lighten the mood, she asked, "I didn't flip that switch even once, despite my best efforts to rile you?"

The corner of his mouth hitched up. "You push plenty of my buttons, but never that one. You managed to work your way under my skin—it didn't matter how hard I fought it; you made a place for yourself there without even trying. I was determined to find a way under yours."

"You found it," she admitted in a whisper.

His eyes flared, and then he smiled. "I know. It's a good thing, because it makes us even." He smoothed his hand down her belly, over her navel, and cupped her pussy. "All mine." He thrust a finger inside her and groaned. "I can feel my come in you."

She licked her lips as he began to fuck her with his finger. "You're gonna get me all hot and bothered if you keep that up."

"Good. I want you again."

"I've got to get ready for work."

"I won't let you be late." Nipping and kissing her neck, he kept on pumping his finger inside her, building the tension, dragging her into a realm of pure sensation where she lost all sense of time and—

Her phone rang, snapping her out of the moment. It had slipped out of her hand and was resting on the covers.

Stilling his talented finger, Keenan picked up the cell and said, "It's Teague; you should answer it. He'll be worried if you don't." He swiped his thumb across the screen and then handed her the phone.

She took it and said—well, croaked, "Hello?"

"Why didn't you text me back?" Teague demanded.

"I wasn't ignoring you; I just needed a minute."

"You took more than a minute. I panicked, thinking something might have happened to you."

"I'm sorry, I didn't mean to worry you. I'm just kind of in the middle of something." She widened her eyes at Keenan when he began pumping his finger inside her again. *Stop*, she mouthed, but he didn't.

"What are you doing that's more important than replying to your anchor's message?" sniped Teague.

"Um . . . you don't really want to know." She glared at Keenan and mouthed, *Seriously, stop.*

Keenan withdrew his finger ever so slowly, but then he rolled her onto her back and slid down her body. Oh, fuck.

"Why wouldn't I want to know?" asked Teague.

She almost gasped as Keenan's swiped his tongue through her folds. She gripped his hair and tugged, but he didn't move away. He lavished attention on her clit and folds with that blessed tongue.

"Khloé, answer me," said Teague. "What's going on?"

Keenan looked at her, his eyes twinkling. "Don't forget to share our news with him, baby." Then he went back to toying with her clit.

"Did I just hear the incubus?" asked Teague—as a hellbeast, his hearing was very acute. "What does he mean by 'news'? What news, Khloé?"

Her hips bucked when Keenan suckled on her clit. Her eyes almost rolled back into her head. "Um, well . . . can we talk about this later?"

"No, I want to know now. What. News?"

A phantom tongue stabbed inside her. She gasped, arching, and the phone fell out of her hand.

CHAPTER SEVENTEEN

Feeling thoroughly claimed from the inside out, Khloé walked into Urban Ink. She was never late for work, so it was no surprise that the girls sent her a few raised brows. No clients had arrived yet, thankfully.

Before she could say anything, Keenan spun her to face him and took her mouth. His lips moved soft and slow against hers. The kiss was deep and languid and lazy, and it just about melted her.

Pliant against him, she fisted the sides of his tee as she kissed him back. Her inner demon practically purred, arching into the proprietary way he touched her. He swept one hand down her back to settle on the curve of her spine just above her butt—an unmistakable display of pure masculine possession.

Pulling back, he caught her face in his hands and just looked at her for a few moments, his eyes all soft and warm. His crooked smile hit her right in her core. "Call out to me if you need to leave here for any reason—even if it's only for five minutes," he said.

She licked her lips, a little dazed by his kiss. "Will do."

"Good." He nodded at the girls, gave her one last kiss, and then breezed out of the studio. And, yep, she watched his ass the entire time. Well, it was one very fine ass. He hadn't been impressed when she'd scrawled her name on it with a sharpie, but she couldn't say her apology had been whatsoever heartfelt.

Turning to face the others, Khloé saw that they were all gaping. She frowned. "What?"

"He looks . . . happy," said Harper. "And I mean *really* happy. Keenan can often be in a good mood, but he's never actually happy. Considering there's all kinds of shit going on around you right now, I expected him to be in the foulest mood ever. What gives?"

Khloé tapped her fingertips on her thighs. "Well . . . he decided to claim me earlier, and I accepted his claim."

Raini sighed. "*Khloé.*"

Surprised, she widened her eyes. "What? Why is this bad?"

"It's not. But I now owe Devon thirty dollars."

Smug, the hellcat folded her arms. "I bet Raini that you and Keenan would claim each other before all this Enoch business was over—as far as I was concerned, it was a done deal. But Raini thought it would take longer for you guys to get past all your issues."

"*I* didn't participate in the bet because I thought it was juvenile," said Harper, all haughty.

Devon snorted. "You didn't participate in the bet because you had no clue what would happen, and you didn't want to be wrong."

Harper waved that away and slid her gaze back to Khloé. "So, you're happy?"

Khloé inhaled deeply. "Yes, I am. The claiming feels a little surreal, though. I never thought it would happen. Ever. Like

Raini once said, Keenan seemed so set on keeping me at a distance."

"And he failed in an epic way," said Devon. "I always knew he would."

Khloé frowned. "No, you didn't."

"I *so* did."

Slipping off her jacket, Khloé rolled her eyes. "Whatever."

"How are you feeling today?" asked Raini.

"No different than I felt yesterday," replied Khloé as she hung her jacket on the coat rack. "Which is both good and bad."

Harper put a hand to her forehead. "I'm still so shocked that the angel couldn't help you."

"Keenan spoke with a shifter who made it clear that his kind wouldn't be able to heal me. That didn't go down well with Grams." Khloé had telepathically passed on the news to Jolene earlier.

"We *will* find someone who can, Khloé," Harper told her, her expression hard and determined.

"I know. I'm not admitting defeat." And neither was her demon.

The sphinx nodded, satisfied. "Good. Have you been keeping Teague updated on everything?"

"Yes. I spoke to him on the phone this morning, in fact." She almost blushed as she remembered what else happened during that conversation.

"I'll bet he wasn't too pleased to hear that Keenan claimed you," hedged Raini.

Khloé rubbed her nape. "Actually, he took the news pretty well."

Raini blinked. "What did he say?"

"Something along the lines of '*I will slit his fucking throat if he hurts you in any way, shape, or form.*'"

Raini put a hand to her chest. "Oh, that's a relief. I expected Teague to try to kill him for claiming you."

"I don't think he dislikes Keenan. I think he disliked the idea of Keenan using me. Now that he knows that's not the case, he'll deal, but he'll also take time to warm up to the mating—in Teague's mind, no one will ever be good enough for his anchor. On another note, Teague invited us to the racetrack on Saturday. You guys up for it?"

All three women brightened and immediately accepted the invitation.

"Watching hellhorses race is always entertaining," said Devon. "Mostly because they're psychotic."

Khloé felt her brow furrow. "They're not psychotic. Just wild."

"*And* crazy," added Devon. "*And* vicious. *And* cannibalistic."

"You're so judgy."

Devon scrunched up her face. "Is that even a word?"

"Yes. My Aunt Mildred used to say it all the time and— *Hey, sheathe those claws, feline.*" Khloé backed up a step and wagged her finger. "Don't think I won't dig out the water spray bottle."

"*Don't even try it.*"

"Stop hissing, it's rude."

"And antagonizing others isn't rude?"

Khloé pursed her lips. "I don't know. Never really thought about it."

"Harper, get her away from me before I strangle her."

"Damn, you're moody today, Dev," said Khloé. "You surfing the crimson wave, sweetie? I have spare tampons if you need them."

Devon looked ready to pounce on her, but then the studio door swung open.

Harper quickly slid between the two females and planted a hand on both their chests. "Oh look, our first client has arrived," she said far too brightly. "Devon, head to your station. Khloé, please go greet Macie."

"No problem." Khloé crossed to the reception desk and smiled at the she-demon standing there. She was a regular client who had dozens upon dozens of super cool tattoos. "Morning, Macie."

"Morning," the woman greeted. Her smile faltered as her gaze landed on something behind Khloé. "Is Devon okay?"

"Oh, yeah," Khloé assured her with a flick of her hand. "The poor thing's just having her monthly code red situation, that's all—you know how it is."

Devon made an exasperated sound. "That's it, Harper, I'm killing her, I am."

Hearing footsteps stomping toward her, Khloé turned just as Raini and Harper restrained the hellcat and dragged her away. "Such a drama kitten," said Khloé, shaking her head. "God, there's no need to be so embarrassed about it, Devon. It's natural. We all have to check into the Red Roof Inn sometimes, it's—*Stop with the hissing, you freak!*"

*

The door of the hotel's boardroom opened just as Keenan made his way toward it. Several Primes filed out with their sentinels, until only Knox and Levi remained inside.

Entering the large room, Keenan asked, "Does Harper know she just missed a Prime-meeting?"

Switching off the media screen, Knox looked up. "She knows. Those demons simply had a business proposal to put to me—she had no interest in hearing it."

Levi eyed Keenan closely. "You look . . . different. Settled. It's hard to explain."

He *felt* settled, deep inside. Felt centered. All would be perfect in Keenan's world if only his mate was well.

"You found someone who can heal Khloé?" asked Knox.

Keenan felt his jaw tighten. "Not yet, no. The bear made it clear that shifters won't be of any help. Have you talked to the vampires?"

"I've reached out to them, but they haven't yet responded," replied Knox, closing his laptop.

"I tried to find someone who might know how to contact an archangel, but there literally doesn't seem to be anyone on Earth who can," said Levi, dropping into one of the chairs. "They all said exactly what Eric said; that archangels aren't concerned with angels or what goes on down here. I'll keep asking around, though."

Gathering the papers together that were fanned out around the teleconferencing phone, Knox briefly glanced at Keenan. "Want to explain why you're not in a black mood anymore?"

Planting his feet, Keenan lifted his chin a notch. "I claimed Khloé."

"It's about fucking time," said Levi. "I mean, congrats."

Knox's mouth curved. "Yes, congrats. It's nice to have some good news for a change."

Keenan lifted the pitcher of ice water from the center of the long table and poured himself a glass. "I need you to have a talk with Thea." Just hearing her name made his demon flex its fists.

Knox's brow pinched. "Thea? Why?"

"She turned up at the hotel to see Khloé, posing as Raini in the hope that Khloé would be fooled and let her up to the penthouse."

Levi straightened in his seat. "What the fuck is she playing at?"

"Khloé gave me a recap of the conversation. In sum, Thea was warning her away from me. It seems she has some ridiculous idea that she and I can make another go of things." Keenan sipped at his water. "It was bad enough that she turned up at my apartment and put me in the position of having to tell Khloé everything or risk losing her." Thankfully, the Prime hadn't been pissed at Keenan for telling an outsider.

Knox sighed, settling in his chair at the head of the table. "Thea's supposed to be keeping a low profile."

"Well, she's not. I won't have her bugging Khloé. I told Thea to stay away from her, but I'm not so sure she'll listen to me."

"She'll think that, with the history between you, there's no way you'd arrange for her to be punished for anything," said Levi.

Keenan nodded and took the seat opposite the reaper. "I need you to talk with her, Knox, and reiterate that she's to keep her distance from my mate. Khloé's got enough going on right now. She doesn't need any added stressors on top of all that. And I don't want my past tainting my present or my future."

"It's done." Knox scratched his chin. "I think you, Levi, and the other sentinels should all be present for the conversation. In such situations, we usually hold meetings together to show a united front. I want Thea to grasp that although she comes from Ramsbrook like us, we won't show leniency toward her; she will still answer to us the same as others would. Find her and bring her here, Levi. Keenan, you get hold of Larkin and Tanner. We might as well hold the meeting here."

"What about Harper?" asked Keenan. "I know she doesn't always attend disciplinary meetings, but Khloé's her cousin."

"Which is why I would rather my mate wasn't here. She's all knotted up with fear for Khloé right now; she wouldn't stay calm while in the same room as someone who wishes to cause Khloé distress."

"Fair enough." Keenan telepathically called both Larkin and Tanner while Levi left to find Thea.

Larkin arrived at the boardroom first, and Tanner appeared mere minutes later. Keenan quickly relayed the issue once they had settled at the long table.

Larkin sighed. "Thea is her own worst enemy at times."

Keenan would have to agree with her on that. "You should also know I've claimed Khloé," he added, pride in every syllable.

A smile split Larkin's face. "Really? That's amazing news. Not wholly unexpected, of course—I figured it'd happen sooner or later. Congratulations, Keenan. I'm super pleased for you both."

"Same here. I was tired of watching the two of you dance around each other," said Tanner. "On a more somber note, how *is* Khloé?"

Keenan's stomach twisted. "No better, no worse."

"Levi's just telepathed me," Knox cut in. "He and Thea are almost here. She's brought Lane with her, so one of our Force will stand with him outside the room."

They all fell silent as they waited. When knuckles rapped on the door, Knox bid them to enter. Levi returned to his seat, but Thea hovered near the closed door, biting her lip. Tense and agitated, Keenan's inner demon licked its front teeth.

She swept her gaze over each person there, no doubt noting their blank expressions. No one spoke or greeted her in any way. The only sounds were the whirring of the ceiling fan and the drone of the air-conditioning unit.

"Hello," she finally said.

"Sit," Knox invited.

Thea reluctantly walked to the table and gingerly sat on the chair beside Larkin. "Levi said you wanted to speak with me."

"Yes," said Knox. "Why do you think I've called you here?"

"I'm assuming that Gavril's been in touch with you again or something." Her face fell. "You're not going to withdraw your protection from me and Lane, are you?"

"It's not my intention. But my protection will mean nothing if you persist on being careless."

"Careless?"

"The plan was for you to keep a low profile, yes?"

She gave a slow nod. "Yes."

"Going to one of my Underground hotels and asking to speak with one of my guests isn't lying low, is it?"

Color flooded her cheeks. "I wore glamor."

"You posed as Khloé Wallis's friend. Why is that?"

Thea slid Keenan a quick look and tucked her hair behind her ear. "I just wanted to talk to her."

Knox's brow hiked up. "And you didn't think she'd guess that she wasn't speaking with one of her closest friends?"

Thea gave a weak shrug. "Most people don't."

"Did you even consider what *could* have happened? It's no secret that she currently has somebody trying to kill her. If she hadn't already known about you from Keenan, she could have thought you were sent by the person who wants her dead; she could have killed you, leaving Lane without a mother."

She blanched. "I would have teleported me and Lane to safety *immediately* if she tried to attack. Look, I'm sorry for seeking her out. I just wanted to speak with her. I didn't upset her or anything. Did I, Keenan?"

Keenan said nothing, making it clear that he wasn't there to vouch for her.

Knox cocked his head. "You think he'll defend you. This confuses me."

Yeah, it confused Keenan and his demon just the same.

Thea licked her lips. "I don't blame Khloé for reporting what I did—"

"Khloé didn't report your behavior. Keenan did."

Her gaze flared and shot to Keenan. "She insisted on *you* telling tales *for* her?"

"Khloé didn't ask me to tell anyone anything," said Keenan. "I reported you to Knox because one, it's my job to report such things, and two, I won't allow *anyone* to fuck with my mate."

Thea's mouth fell open. "Your mate?" She shook her head, skepticism written all over her face. "No. You'd never take a mate. Not ever. I've known you practically all my life. Your commitment issues run too deep for you to ever give all of yourself to a relationship."

Keenan shrugged, not caring what she thought. "Believe what you want; just stay away from Khloé."

Thea's eyes narrowed, and she studied him carefully. "Oh, I get it. You're pretending to be her mate hoping it will scare away the person who's after her. Admirable, I guess."

"Make no mistake about it—Khloé is my mate."

"I don't believe you."

"I don't care. Just do as I say and keep your distance from her."

She gripped the edge of the table. "Are you saying all this to hurt me because I mated with someone else? You are, aren't you? Damn it, Keenan, that's unfair. I would have taken you as my mate in a heartbeat if things had been different."

"I'm not even going to ask what that means." It might have mattered to him once, but not now.

"I came back to you time and time again, but *nothing* ever changed. You'd ask me to stay, but I could see I wouldn't have been your priority. Your position as sentinel came first. Hell, Knox and the other sentinels came before I did."

"Oh my god, are you for real?" Larkin cut in, glaring at her. "You spent years trying to lead him around by his dick. You'd turn up, jump in his bed, say all the right things, give him hope, but then you'd flounce off again without a goodbye. And you really think he should have offered to take you as his *mate*? You think that he should have made you his priority when he clearly wasn't yours?"

Thea's face hardened. "That's not how it was. I love him. I've always loved him. But I know too well that sentinels never put their mates first—I've seen firsthand what that does to a woman. Being second best wrecked my mother." She looked at Keenan. "You knew I wouldn't repeat her mistakes. You knew I wouldn't commit to a sentinel, but you never once offered to give up that position."

"You never asked me to," he pointed out.

"I shouldn't have had to. You knew what held me back."

Maybe he had, deep down. And maybe he'd ignored it because it suited him; because choosing between her and his position would have been too hard. If so, yeah, that probably made him a selfish asshole. But she'd never been willing to give a relationship with a sentinel a chance, had she? She'd wanted things her way or no way at all. Wasn't that just as selfish?

You should want someone for who they were, not for who you wished them to be. Thea had only wanted him on *her* terms, and she would have molded him into someone else. She'd never understood and accepted him as he was. Which should have hurt, but . . . "None of this even matters now."

"It matters to me," she clipped, her eyes wet. "*You* matter to me. Why couldn't you just love me, Keenan? You cared for me; I know that. But you didn't love me."

No, he hadn't, he realized. "You never gave me a chance to see if I could have."

"I knew I loved you even as a child."

"Not all of us find it so easy to bond with people. In any case, all this is moot. Even if I wasn't with Khloé, I wouldn't want you. I don't say that to hurt you, I say it because it's true and because I need you to get it. I need it to sink into your brain so that you don't make the mistake of bothering her again—you wouldn't like the consequences."

Thea snickered. "Why? What will she do to me?"

"She won't need to do anything, Thea," said Knox, his voice soft but grave and menacing. "I gave you sanctuary, and that means you answer to *me* just as my lair members do. If you step out of line, you'll be punished." He leaned forward, pinning her gaze with his. "You are to stay away from Khloé Wallis. You're not to make contact with her in any way. If you do, you'll have me to deal with. And trust me, Thea, you won't enjoy what happens next. Nobody ever does."

Thea swallowed hard, her eyes flickering. "She's not part of your lair."

"Doesn't matter," said Knox. "Khloé's under my protection. Not only as Keenan's mate, but as the cousin of *my* mate and son. To me, she's family. And nobody fucks with my family. Nobody."

Hurt flashed across Thea's face. "After our shared experiences, you don't think of me as family?"

"No. You could have been one of us, but you chose to go your own way. You built your own family, and if you want to keep that family safe—namely, Lane—you need to buck the fuck up and stop doing things that put him at risk. In other words, you need to keep a low profile *as you were instructed to do*. You should be putting your son's safety before your apparent need to meddle in Keenan's affairs."

Thea's hand balled up into a fist, but she took in a breath and blanked her expression. "You're right," she said with forced calm. "I was being selfish. It won't happen again."

"And you understand exactly what will happen if you do?"

"I understand."

"Good. You're dismissed."

Thea pushed out of her chair and looked at Keenan. "Do you love her?"

Keenan felt his brow crease. Tired, he sighed. "You really want to know the answer to that question?"

"I wouldn't have asked it if I didn't. Do you?" she pushed.

Well, he wasn't going to lie to spare her feelings. "Yeah, I love her."

Thea flinched. "She makes you happy?"

"Yes."

She swallowed hard. "Then I hope things work out for the two of you."

"They will." Keenan would do everything in his power to ensure that they did.

Keeping her chin up, Thea walked out of the boardroom and closed the door behind her. Glad she was gone, his inner demon rolled back its shoulders.

Tanner looked at Keenan. "It's a good thing we had that talk with her, because my gut says she had plans to come between you and Khloé in whatever ways she could. She'll back off now that she knows she has nothing to gain from it."

"I don't know about that." Larkin braced her elbow on the table and rested her chin on her hand. "I mean, she had nothing to gain from fucking up the fling he was having all those years ago, but she did it anyway."

Levi nodded. "Jealousy can make a person do the weirdest shit. But she's more likely to bide her time and lure us into thinking she's letting it go."

"Either way, she won't get near Khloé again," said Keenan. "I won't allow it."

"None of us will allow it—she's your mate; that means something to us." Knox tilted his head. "How hard do you think it will be to convince Khloé to join our lair?"

Keenan grimaced. "I don't know. She'd have Harper and Devon here, but she's very close to Ciaran and Jolene; she wouldn't easily agree to leave them."

"I really don't think Khloé would ask you to move to her

lair—she knows you; knows how close you are to each of us and that it would take something out of you to give up your position here," said Larkin. "But she'll find it hard to leave her lair. Maybe you could come up with some kind of compromise."

"Compromise?" echoed Keenan.

The harpy rolled her eyes. "You don't have to say it with dread. Yes, a *compromise*. Maybe you could agree to move into her house so that she's still close to her family. Then she won't feel as though she's truly *leaving* them if she switches to our lair. It'll just be more like she's answering to a different Prime."

"It's a good idea," said Tanner. "You could tighten the security around her house, Keenan. A few of our lair members live in and around that neighborhood, so you wouldn't feel all alone out there."

"But I would be surrounded by imps," said Keenan.

"The good thing about imps, though, is that they only cause trouble for outsiders," Tanner pointed out. "If they consider you one of theirs, they'll protect and defend you. Being Khloé's mate, they'll consider you one of them even though you answer to Knox."

"That's true," conceded Keenan. If it was the only way to get her to agree to move to his lair, he'd do it. "I'll talk with her about it later. Right now, my main worry is the infection that's slowly killing her."

Larkin leaned forward. "You're not going to lose her, Keenan."

"I know I'm not." But he was living minute to minute in fear that he would.

CHAPTER EIGHTEEN

Now that the studio was ready to be closed, Khloé began gathering her things together. She'd no sooner slipped on her jacket than Keenan stalked inside, oozing as much sex and smolder and sin as always. Her demon instantly perked up and, of course, her hormones let out dreamy sighs.

He exchanged greetings with everyone as he made a beeline for her. Pulling her into his arms, he pressed a soft kiss to her mouth. "How was your day?"

Khloé splayed her hands on his hard chest. "I almost drove Devon to tears, so very good—she's a tough nut to crack, in an emotional sense." She tilted her head. "What about you?"

"Other than for one particular event, it was an okay day," he replied vaguely.

"Expand on 'particular event.'"

"I'll tell you all about it when we get to the penthouse."

Satisfied that he didn't intend to blow her off, Khloé nodded. "All right." Having said her goodbyes to everyone, she allowed him to shepherd her out of the studio.

Radiating protectiveness, he practically glued himself to her side as they strolled down the strip, passing an endless number of pedestrians. Many businesses were now closing and pulling down aluminum roller shutters. Others were only just opening, and "Closed" signs were being flipped around.

"Do you miss guarding Asher?" she asked as they walked into the hotel.

Keenan gave her a sideways glance. "I miss seeing him every day—I got used to it. But there's no way I'd protect him properly when I'm so worried about you. I'd be distracted, so I'd be no good to him. Plus, I just need to be near you right now. I won't function well if I'm not."

Warmth bloomed in her stomach. The dude said the best stuff sometimes. Her demon might have melted if its emotional repertoire wasn't so stunted.

Once inside the elevator that would take them up the penthouse, Khloé said, "Although I don't think it's strictly necessary for you to always be local in the event that I'll need you, I do appreciate that you'd put some of your responsibilities temporarily aside for me—I know that can't be easy for you. You take your position very seriously." She respected and admired his dedication and drive.

He gave her an odd look that was close to hopeful, and his face softened. "I do."

Reaching the top floor, she stepped out of the elevator and made her way to the fancy kitchen with Keenan hot on her heels. He leaned against the counter, watching as she prepped the coffee machine and then switched it on . . . as if every little move she made fascinated him.

She grabbed two mugs out of the cupboard. "So, tell me what happened that tainted your otherwise okay day."

He straightened, sighing. "Knox called Thea in for a disciplinary meeting. I asked him to speak with her and make it clear that she was not to bother you again. I wasn't so confident that she'd heed my warnings."

Khloé would have liked to have been there, but she understood why she hadn't been invited—lair business was lair business. And, yeah, she'd have probably stirred shit up. "I'm guessing she wasn't too pleased about the whole thing." Which made Khloé feel all warm and fuzzy inside.

"No, she wasn't," he confirmed.

"Did she make excuses about why she approached me?"

"She just said she wanted to talk to you." He gently tugged out the tie binding her hair and watched as it tumbled down her back like a black river. His gaze followed the movement of his hand as he smoothed it over the dark strands. "She didn't seem to see any wrong in that, though she did say she could understand why her behavior would be reported."

"Which she no doubt said in the hope that it would placate Knox."

"Probably." Coffees in hand, they settled on the stools at the kitchen island, angling their bodies to face each other. "She found it hard to believe that I'd truly taken you as my mate," Keenan added.

Her demon huffed. "Found it hard to believe or simply didn't *want* to believe it?" asked Khloé.

"Probably a little of both, considering she claimed that she wouldn't have kept walking out of my life if only I'd chosen her over my position of sentinel."

Khloé jerked back. "Say what?"

"She felt that she wouldn't have been my priority."

"Because you have a demanding job? That's bullshit. It's more likely that she felt threatened by how close you are to Knox and the other sentinels. She wanted to weaken the bonds between you and them."

Keenan pursed his lips, considering that. "Possibly." Honestly, he couldn't give a shit either way anymore. "But she wouldn't be the first person to find being mated to a sentinel very difficult," he said, knots in his stomach. It was a probing comment, and she clearly sensed it.

His little imp sipped at her coffee. "If you're asking, in a round-about way, whether it will be a problem for *me*, the answer is no."

With hope budding inside him, he waited for her to elaborate, but she didn't. "Just no?" he asked.

"Just no."

He inwardly sighed. That was the thing about imps—you'd only get the right answer if you asked the right question. "Any particular reason why my position won't be a problem for you?"

"For one thing, I like that you have your own life and a sense of purpose—not everybody does, and it can make them feel lost."

"Like your mother," he mused.

"Like my mother. And Lucian, for that matter."

Keenan gave a slow nod, in total agreement that Harper's father—the ultimate nomad—was in fact lost. His demon didn't have even an inkling of respect for the other male.

"Also," Khloé went on, "the hours you work aren't going to bother me because I'm not a person who needs company twenty-four/seven. And if I *do* want company or I get bored, I have an endless number of family members who will keep me occupied."

"In ways that are legal and moral?"

"I'm not comfortable answering that question. Back to your original one . . . I know how important your position is to you; I know you wouldn't feel whole or happy without it. If something's important to you, it's important to me."

Hearing the ring of sincerity in her tone, Keenan swallowed, and the knots in his stomach unraveled. He splayed a possessive hand on her thigh and gave it a little squeeze. "Thank you for understanding."

If she'd asked him to choose between her and his position, he would have chosen her—he didn't want to live a life that didn't have her in it. He'd tried that, and it hadn't worked. But it would have destroyed something inside him to have walked away from his lair, Knox, and the other sentinels.

"Does that mean you won't ask me to join your lair?" he asked.

"Yes, that's what it means."

"You'll join mine?"

She set her mug down, a pained look briefly shaping her face. "I'll have to, I know that. But I won't lie, it's going to be super hard."

His chest squeezed. He hated the thought of her hurting, especially when she was being so fucking understanding and supportive of him. He could do no less for her.

Keenan picked up her hand and stroked her palm with his thumb. "What if we live at your place instead of mine? Would that make moving lairs less difficult for you?"

Straightening, she studied his face carefully. "You'd really do that? You'd really leave your swanky apartment and live among imps?"

"I want you to be happy, just as you want me to be happy. If being close to your family is important to you, then it's important to me," he said, paraphrasing something she'd said. Her face brightened, and everything inside him settled in an instant.

"Really?"

"Really."

"You're sure?"

"I'm sure."

Surprised she hadn't choked on the knot of emotion clogging her throat—God, he was turning her into such a girl—Khloé bit her lip. "Thank you." She would never have expected him to make such a concession. Even her demon was touched.

He rubbed her thigh and looked as though he was about to speak again, but then his eyes clouded, and that *Keenan's not home right now* expression took over his face.

She waited for him to finish his telepathic conversation, praying that he was receiving some good news. But when his eyes cleared and his face darkened, her stomach sank. "Something wrong?"

Grinding his teeth, he set down his mug. "That was Knox. He spoke with the vampires."

"They can't help," she guessed. *Fuck.*

"They have a vampire in the ranks of their army who can heal, but she does it by taking a wound and transferring it to another person. You have no wound. Even if you did, she'd be unable to help you. Apparently, she's come up against death essence before, and she couldn't combat it."

Any other time, Khloé might have commented on what a pretty cool gift that was. But right then, her devastation was too great. Especially since . . . "I spoke to Grams half an hour ago—something I meant to tell you once our conversation was over. Vivian consulted the practitioners she knows. Their response, well, it's not good news."

"Tell me."

"They claim that it's possible that blood magick would help me, but that someone would have to die in order for me to live. And, considering we'd be fighting pure death, we'd need pure innocence to truly have a chance against it. In other words, we'd have to sacrifice a newborn baby—they're the only beings that are without sin. I wouldn't even consider that shit."

He closed his eyes and cursed. "It makes me an evil bastard that my mind didn't immediately recoil at that idea. I just—"

"You don't want me to die, I know. There's a lot of things I'd be willing to try in the hope of combating the death essence, but never the sacrifice of a newborn baby. You'd never be able to go through with it either."

He bit out another curse. "Blood magick can often backfire anyway."

Very true. "Vivian also managed to speak with the angel who frequents the hospital where she works. He claimed that only an archangel could heal me. Grams is having no luck getting in touch with one."

"Levi's had no success with that either." Keenan squeezed her hand. "There are other preternatural creatures out there with various gifts—dragons, elementals, fey. The list goes on and on. I'm not buying that the only being in existence that can fight death essence is an archangel."

"Same here." She twisted her mouth. "Do you think it's possible that Enoch could somehow undo what he did to me? That he could call the death essence out of my system or something?"

Keenan's brow hiked up slightly. He hadn't considered that. "Maybe. We'll ask him that very question when we get ahold of him. It won't be long until we do."

"So I shouldn't kill him with the blade if I come across him?"

"If it seems like you have no choice but to kill him to survive a confrontation with him, then don't hesitate. There will be another way to save you. We just have to find it."

"And we will."

Keenan curved his hand around the side of her neck. She was fucking amazing. Other people might have wallowed, given up hope of being healed, and drowned in self-pity. Not Khloé. She remained sturdy and strong, refusing to give in to whatever worries she might have. His demon loved that spine of steel she had.

Needing to be closer to her, Keenan gripped her by the waist, lifted her, and then sat her on his lap so that she straddled him. "That's better." Locking his arms tight around her, he took her mouth, needing and relishing the taste of her, loving how she melted into him.

When he finally pulled back, he rested his forehead against hers. "Missed you today."

"Missed you right back. Which kind of annoyed me. It was very distracting."

"I know what you mean. But you've been distracting me for years, so I'm used to it."

She toyed with the collar of his tee. "Devon said I wear your scent now."

A smile quirked his mouth. "Tanner said I wear yours." If two demons were intimate on more than one level, their skin often became embedded with each other's scent. "Does it bother you?"

"No. You?"

"Not at all. I like it." He took her mouth again, feasting and consuming her. Hunger crawled through him, thick and hot and carnal. He embraced it, desperate to forget for just a short time that she was getting closer to death every single day; desperate to drown out the clawing fear that rode him day and night.

He snaked his hand beneath her tank top and slid it up her back, wanting—no, *needing*—the skin-to-skin contact. More, he needed to be inside her; needed to lose himself in her; needed the glorious oblivion that only Khloé had ever been able to give him.

She tore her mouth free and raked her fingers through his hair. "I'm curious. Do you have anything against the idea of

bending me over the kitchen island while you shove your delightfully large schlong in me?"

He felt one side of his mouth tip up. "My what?"

*

As a deep male voice made an announcement over the racing
stadium's intercom, Khloé smiled. "Teague's horse is up next,"
she said without turning away from the wall of glass that overlooked the dirt track.

Beams of bright light slashed through the air and illumi-
nated both the track and artificial grass, courtesy of the rows of
high-powered floodlights. Spectators were everywhere—the tiered
grandstand, the indoor cafeteria, the outdoor picnic area, and
some even stood near the white fence that bordered the track.

Khloé took another bite of her hotdog, despite the fact that
her stomach kept doing annoying little flips. She loved watching Teague's stallion race. It was, without a doubt, the fastest of
its kind, which was why it was a favorite among the gambling
addicts. She wasn't really nervous on its behalf—she never
doubted that it would win—but her stomach still often went all
jittery with anticipation.

Hellhorse racing was bloody, gory, and intense as hell. Which
was why she and her demon loved to observe it.

Normal horses might be prey animals, but hellhorses sure
weren't. There was nothing placid or timid about them. They
were ferocious, aggressive, mercurial creatures with notoriously
bad tempers.

Keenan curled his arms around Khloé from behind and
locked her to him. "I'll admit, this VIP box is way cooler than
the one at the hellhound stadium," he said.

Khloé smiled. "Ain't it, though?"

Like the VIP boxes at the hellhound racing stadiums, it had

chic leather seating, multiple TVs, and a personal waiter who would enter whenever summoned. But it had a few extra luxuries, such as the cool mini bar, complimentary champagne, the small buffet of finger-foods, and the sliding glass door that led to a private balcony.

Sidling up to them, Devon tipped back her champagne flute and sipped at her drink. "As much as I love watching hellhorses race, I'll never quite understand why they put themselves through this. I mean, some of those obstacles are *horrendous*."

The hellcat wasn't wrong. It wasn't so much the eight-foot tall hedges and stone walls—it was the ditches that were placed to either side of them. Said ditches contained some horrible shit—simmering lava, short flaming wooden spears, clumps of hyped-up poisonous snakes, and red-hot iron spikes to name but a few.

"The person who comes up with ideas for the hurdles has to be a sadist," said Harper, comfortably perched on a leather seat with Asher on her lap. "You'd better hope said sadist doesn't turn his attention to hellhound racing, Tanner. You guys already have it hard with the hot oily pits and bubbling puddles of boiling water."

Seated opposite the sphinx with Larkin beside him, Tanner said, "Those puddles burn like a son of a . . ." He trailed off as his eyes flicked to Asher, who was playing with his fake cell phone. "Gun," he finished lamely.

Keenan nuzzled Khloé's neck. "You going to give me a bite of that hotdog?"

Her nose wrinkled. "Nah."

"But I'm hungry. And I shared my chips with you."

"I don't see your point. Hey!" she whined when he leaned over and bit a chunk out of the hotdog.

He quickly chewed it and said, "I'll make it up to you later."

Devon gently nudged her. "Is Ciaran not coming?"

Khloé sighed. "I don't think so. I invited him, but . . . he's been avoiding me."

"It's guilt, sweetie," said Raini, leaning against the window. "He hates that he's healed and you're not. Also, he seems to be throwing all his energy and time into finding someone who can heal you."

Khloé was well aware of that, and she couldn't say she'd have acted any different in his position, but . . . "It would have been good for him to take a break and just chill for half an hour."

Devon touched the glass. "Ooh, we have movement down there."

Khloé watched as, sure-footed and impressively built, twenty hellhorses padded onto the oval track, their heads high and proud. Spectators cheered and whistled.

The steeds lined up, side by side, near the start line. Some looked hyper and edgy, swishing their tails and trotting on the spot. Others were calm and still, like they were about to go for a leisurely walk through the woods or something. They had no jockeys, so there were no reins or saddles.

"Horsies!" shouted Asher, leaning forward to get a better look at them.

"Sort of," said Harper. "They're hellhorses."

The kid pointed at his chest. "For me."

"No, little man, they're not for you." Harper rolled her eyes. "I'm thankful he can't pyroport very far right now, or he'd probably plop himself on top of one of the hellhorses."

"That would be a bad idea, dude," Devon told him. "No one rides a hellhorse unless they're crazy."

Khloé frowned. "I've ridden Teague's steed a few times."

"I rest my case," said the hellcat.

Snorting, Khloé turned back to the view of the track.

"Hellhorses might be insane, but there's no denying that they're beautiful," said Larkin.

Beautiful was an understatement, in Khloé's opinion. They were regal and elegant with their arched neck, long legs, inward-turned ear tips, and their long, high-carried tail. Their metallic coat and lush mane were as dark as their all-black, wide-set eyes. In a word, they were breathtaking.

Teague's stallion was easily identifiable due to the large scar that slashed across its neck, but Khloé would have recognized it anyway. It had a little extra, indefinable *something* that made it so much more magnificent and majestic than the others. It was also packed with more muscle and had an intimidatingly confident air.

It was favorite to win, like always. Every person in the VIP box—other than Asher, of course—had placed a bet on it.

Raini grinned. "I love how Teague's hellhorse just stands there very still while the others try to irritate it by snapping their teeth or puffing smoke out of their nostrils. It doesn't even look their way, as if it believes it's above all that."

"I honestly don't know why anyone would even bother to race against it," said Devon. "That stallion never loses."

"That's exactly *why* people want to race against it," said Keenan. "They know that if they *do* miraculously win, they'll make an instant name for themselves."

The hellcat lifted her brows. "Never thought of it like that."

"See the female hellhorse on the far right?" asked Khloé. "She's the smallest of all the competitors."

"I see her," said Keenan. "I've seen her race before. She's fast, especially for her size."

"She is," Khloé confirmed. "She's been hounding Teague to father her child, ignoring his refusals. I know that hellbeasts often choose fathers for their kids who are fit and strong and powerful. But of all the reasons to ask someone to father your child, she actually asked Teague so that their offspring might be a hellhorse racing champion."

"Sounds like she's hoping to achieve something through her child that she can't achieve herself," said Larkin. "Some parents are like that. Ooh, looks like the race is about to start."

Done with her hotdog, Khloé placed her napkin in the trash and then opened the sliding glass door. As she stepped out onto the private balcony, the scents of dirt, horses, and concession food drifted to her. Keenan and the others joined her on the balcony, their gazes locked on the hellhorses.

A hush had fallen upon the stadium, and the steeds had all stilled. The air was taut with intensity, excitement, and anticipation. It was enough to make Khloé's stomach flutter again.

A horn beeped, signaling the start of the race. The hellhorses burst into action and flew across the track. Their hooves thundered along the ground, kicking up so much dirt that dust clouded the air.

Teague's stallion kept its pace steady but swift as it fell into something like, what, seventh place? It was hard to tell straight off. There were so many competitors. The hellhorses didn't stay in their own lanes. They ran as a tight herd, biting and body-slamming each other as they strived to reach first place.

Voices gave a fast commentary over the loudspeaker, but Khloé wasn't really listening. She was focused on the track, calling out Teague's name and cheering on his demon.

"I like the way Teague's hellhorse hangs back a little, like it knows it's a given that it'll win," said Devon.

"The race is still hard to watch," began Harper, "because you know there's no way that they'll walk off that track without *some* injuries. Shit, they're coming to the first hurdle."

Khloé held her breath as Teague's stallion jumped high,

clearing the wall and ditches. A couple of the others weren't so lucky—one scraped its belly on the pieces of broken glass that studded the top of the stone wall. Another landed awkwardly, and one foreleg crumpled beneath it. In both cases, the steeds tumbled into the ditch of spears.

Raini flinched. "It's painful to watch."

Khloé nodded. "That had to hurt like a *mother*." Her demon loved the mercilessness of it all, the freak.

She bit her lip as the rest of the hellhorses rocketed across the track, their legs a blur. They galloped through pools of flaming water, leapt over hedges that blazed with hellfire, and cleared walls that were embedded with thorns and spikes—always striving to avoid the ditches. Some succeeded, but not all.

"There's fourteen steeds left," said Keenan. "Thirteen," he corrected when a hellhorse tumbled into a lava ditch. Its squeals of agony made her chest hurt.

The other steeds paid it no attention, needing to focus. They bolted, their hooves thudding so hard on the ground she would bet the spectators near the fence could feel the vibrations.

Her heart sank when she glimpsed the next hurdle. It wasn't simply a high wall. Short swords stabbed out of its sides and surface every few seconds. Swords which could easily slice the knees, legs, or stomach of the hellhorses.

As the steeds approached the hurdle, the one beside Teague's swung its head, neck extended, and bit Teague's shoulder hard enough to make it nicker and shake its head.

"That mothertrucker," Khloé hissed, remembering not to swear in front of Asher. She suspected that said mothertrucker had hoped to distract Teague's steed from adequately prepping itself to jump. She mentally crossed her fingers and toes, hoping the dirty trick wouldn't work.

Time seemed to slow for her as she watched her anchor push

off its hindlegs and leap into the air. Khloé squeezed Keenan's hand, fighting the temptation to close her eyes. The hellhorse soared, all grace and power . . . and it cleared the hurdle.

She practically sagged. "Thank freaking God."

A few of the other steeds didn't manage to clear the wall, and the swords sliced through their stomachs. Wincing, she flinched as—to make their pain even worse—they fell into a ditch of boiling water. One of them was the mothertrucker who'd bitten Teague's steed. Well hello, karma.

"They're dropping like flies," said Keenan. "There's only ten left."

All ten rocketed along the track. Some were tiring and falling behind while others, including her anchor, purposely surged forward. They tackled more hurdles, and most cleared them. Two found themselves in ditches, leaving only eight competitors.

As they neared another hurdle, one steed breathed fire onto the rear legs of the one in front of it. The surprise and pain must have been enough to put the hellhorse off its game, because it lost its momentum and didn't quite make the next jump. Worse, it fell onto a bed of red-hot iron spikes.

The fucking firestarter targeted Teague's steed next, blowing flames at his hindlegs and tail. *Shit, no.*

Her anchor let out a throaty whine, and its pace faltered slightly, making her stomach drop. But then it put on a burst of speed, even as its tail blazed with hellfire.

Devon bounced lightly on her toes. "That's it, run, you psycho, run!"

Khloé joined her hands together and put them against her mouth. "Come on, faster. *You got this.*"

It picked up speed again and leaped over the next hurdle . . . neatly skating right into third place.

Keenan rested a hand on her shoulder. "It's third, baby."

"I know." Khloé fanned her face. "Okay, they're almost at the final part of the track." The hurdles there were the worst, and some were close together.

The remaining competitors galloped along the track, their coats gleaming with a fine sheen of sweat. They also attacked each other—biting, body-slamming, breathing fire, and puffing out smoke in an effort to fog the others' vision. The pain and distractions sometimes worked, causing some to fall or trip up. The rest forged onward.

The voices coming from the tiered stands became louder, and the commentator's voice became thick with urgency.

Khloé's heart jumped as Teague's hellhorse slid into second place. "That's it, that's it, keep going."

The small female hellhorse was hot on its heels. It moved closer, and closer, and closer.

"Okay, they're coming up to the last hurdle," said Harper, bouncing from foot to foot.

And it was a bitch of a hurdle, too. The flaming hedge was wrapped in thick, thorny vines that snapped out like small whips.

"Go, go, go!" yelled Raini.

Just as the remaining steeds neared the hurdle, the female hellhorse slammed its body so hard into Teague's stallion that the male almost crashed into the fence that bordered the track. Worse, the move put the steed at an angle that made it awkward for it to clear the hurdle.

"What a devious little bitch," spat Khloé, forgetting she wasn't supposed to swear.

She almost covered her face with her hands as the stallion and the female leapt into the air. Teague's steed successfully jumped the hurdle, to her utter relief. The female, however, wasn't so successful—its leg buckled as it landed, and it went down hard, tripping up another competitor and taking them both out of the race.

Khloé grabbed Keenan's arm as her anchor hurtled into first place. The people around her yelled encouragements at the steed, but she held her breath. Finally, it ran over the finish line.

She beamed. "It won!"

An applause broke out, and the spectators went wild. Some people in the neighboring box began swearing and kicking up a fuss. Apparently, they'd bet on the wrong hellhorse.

Cocky and proud, it slowed to a trot and tossed its head, flicking its luxurious mane.

"I *totally* knew it would win," said Devon.

Khloé winced at its injuries. "It's hurt, though." It had cleared the hurdles, but it had come away with burns, puncture wounds, and ugly cuts.

"They're all wounded," Harper pointed out.

Keenan turned his little imp to face him and tucked a stray strand of hair behind her ear. "Feel better now that it's over?" he asked.

"Yes, I do." She blew out a breath. "I gotta pee, though. The intensity is always too much for my bladder."

Harper chuckled. "I'll come with you. I'm potty training Asher, so I take him to the toilet every now and then to keep on top of it."

Keenan nodded, taking his mate's hand in his. "Larkin and I will escort you."

Larkin put down her soda and crossed to them. "Ready when you guys are."

He stayed in the front while Larkin took up the rear as all five of them exited the VIP box. They headed down the empty hall-way toward the restrooms. Hinges creaked as a door up ahead of them opened, and a small child stepped out.

Unbelievably fast, Lane raised his hand and sent out a stream of magnetic energy. A stream that careened toward Asher.

Everyone acted at once. Larkin pushed Harper and Asher to the floor and snapped out her wings to help shield them. Keenan tackled Khloé to the floor and covered her with his body.

But the blue steam soared toward Asher, as if it was destined to hit whatever it was aimed at. Asher didn't pop up his protective shield. Something black and oily seemed to splutter out of the little boy's hand, and that "something" crashed into the stream and seemed to . . . *consume* it, turning it just as black, and rushed toward Lane. It poured into his eyes, nose, and mouth, making his head jerk back. Thea's son then promptly blacked out and hit the floor.

Before anyone could react, Thea appeared in front of Lane, gripped his arm, and teleported him away.

Everyone jumped to their feet, looking from Asher to the spot where Lane and Thea had just been.

"What in the everloving fuck just happened?" demanded Khloé.

"I don't know," said Harper, examining Asher closely.

"Is he okay?" asked Keenan. The kid was pouting but otherwise looked fine.

"Not sure," replied Harper. "I don't understand what—" She cut off, her eyes widening. "Khloé, behind you!"

Keenan spun just as Thea looped her arm around Khloé's neck and teleported away.

CHAPTER NINETEEN

Shock numbed Keenan for all of three seconds, blanking his thoughts. Then reality hit him like a blow to the jaw. His demon roared, and his mind *lunged* for hers. *Khloé?*

Oh, I'm gonna murder the shit out of this bitch. Khloé hissed in pain, and a weak vibe of dizziness touched his mind. *Mother—* Her voice cut off with a crackle, as if their mental frequency had been jammed somehow.

His heart slammed against his ribcage. *Khloé? Khloé?*

Nothing but white noise.

He spat a curse. "Something's blocking my telepathic connection to Khloé—all I can hear is a faint crackling."

Rubbing Asher's back, a pale Harper said, "I can't reach her either. It's like there's psychic interference of some kind."

Keenan glanced around him, as if there would be a clue as to what was happening or where his mate might be. He dragged his hands through his hair. "I have to go fi—"

Fire roared to life beside Harper, hot and bright. The flames died away, revealing Knox and Levi. Keenan could only assume that Harper had called out to her mate.

Radiating fury, Knox took Asher into his arms and held him close as he looked him over. "What exactly just happened?"

Keenan gave him a quick recap and then scrubbed a hand down his face. "I can't reach Khloé telepathically—something's blocking the connection. But Thea can't teleport far. I might be able to find them."

"I can see that you're eager to go out searching for Khloé, but that's not the best move," Knox told him.

Keenan bristled. He felt his face go tight and wouldn't be surprised if his skin looked like it had been stretched tight around his skull. "Knox—"

"Just hear me out. Thea may not be able to go far in one teleport, but she can 'hop' from place to place with that ability. There's no saying where they are. Your best bet is to contact Khloé."

"I told you, *I've tried*. So has Harper. It didn't work."

"Yes, but there's someone who probably *will* be able to reach her, because they're so interlinked with each other that no number of psychic blocks could keep their minds from connecting."

Keenan frowned. "Teague?"

"No. Ciaran. Twins often have their own frequency, and it's often far too strong to jam."

Harper's brows lifted. "You're right. Let me call out to Grams and Ciaran."

"Tell them to meet us at our home," Knox said to her. "Asher will be safer there."

Before Keenan could object, flames sprung to life around them all and licked at his skin. When the flames died down, they were all stood in the living room of the mansion.

Keenan felt his nostrils flare. "I need to look for Khloé."

"I get why you're raring to leave," said Knox. "But it makes more sense for you to be here in case Ciaran can reach her. The moment I have her location, I can pyroport you to her. If you're out searching, I'll have to go without you."

"You could pick me up along the way—"

"Which would take mere seconds, yes, but anything could happen to Khloé in those precious seconds. Do you really want them to be wasted?"

Keenan ground his teeth, hating that the Prime made sense. He wanted to move, act, search, kill. A chilling, incapacitating fear had tightened every muscle in his body and wound itself around every bone. But he couldn't, *wouldn't*, let it rule him.

"All right," he said to his Prime, his voice strained.

Knox nodded, satisfied. "I'll telepath Tanner and ask him to take Devon and Raini home before he joins us. They'll have to—"

Just then, Jolene, Ciaran, Beck, and Khloé's aunt Martina appeared in the center of the room. All looked as grim and infuriated as Keenan felt.

While Harper brought them up to speed, Keenan paced up and down the room, clenching his fists so tight his knuckles turned white. He couldn't stand still. He felt too edgy, twitchy, and restless.

His demon was no calmer. Not much rattled the entity, but it was absolutely freaking the fuck out. Because this was Khloé—its mate, the only being whose life mattered more to it than its own.

Realizing his breaths were starting to come quick and shallow, Keenan took a long, centering breath—he couldn't afford to lose his shit. But no matter how hard he focused on breathing normally, he felt as if he couldn't get enough oxygen.

Being so helpless threw him back to another time and plucked at old memories. He shoved all that shit aside. This wasn't about him. It was about Khloé. His mate. The only woman he'd ever loved.

"You think I can reach her?" Ciaran asked Harper.

The sphinx nodded. "She's your twin. Khloé once told me that her mind used to automatically reach for yours all the time before she was old enough to control it, and vice versa. Tap into that frequency now, Ciaran. Ask her where she is so that we can go get her."

The male imp's gaze focused inward, and his eyes clouded.

Keenan went very still, watching Ciaran closely, his guts tied in knots. Seconds ticked by as the guy said nothing at all. Keenan didn't realize he was holding his breath until he felt the strain in his chest. "Can you reach her or not?"

"I can reach her," replied Ciaran without focusing his gaze on Keenan. "But there's a lot of static, like when you're trying to talk to someone on a cell phone and there's a bad connection."

"At least we know for sure that she's alive," said Jolene. "Can you tune out the static enough to understand her?"

"I won't know until she wakes," replied Ciaran. "She's unconscious right now."

Keenan bit out a harsh expletive. Panic threatened to make his thoughts go blank again. He couldn't have that. He needed to think. Needed to focus. His mate's life might very well depend on it.

Khloé, baby, wake up and answer me.

There was still nothing but white noise.

He kept on pacing. It felt like his muscles were straining against his skin, trying to force him to act on the need to do *something*. Anything. It rankled that he couldn't. His demon hated it just as much. The entity had no patience at the best of times. It wanted immediate action. Wanted to hunt and destroy the person who'd taken its mate from it.

Come on, baby, talk to me, Keenan pleaded. But there was still no response.

So much adrenaline pumped through his system, he was surprised his hands weren't shaking with it. He wanted to pound his fists into the wall. Wanted to release the terrible wrath that had coiled in his stomach and demanded a target.

His demon's rage fed his, making it hard to think. So many dark images and scenarios tore through his mind. The mental overload was too much.

Harper rubbed her arms, as if to warm them. "I don't know why Thea would have taken Khloé. I *do* know someone must have undone the spell that bound Lane's gift, because he just used it on Asher. The power he let out was magnetic. It meant to steal something from him."

Jolene's eyes narrowed. "Do you think it worked?"

"I'm not sure," replied Harper, looking at her son, who was idly fiddling with his father's collar. "He doesn't seem to have decreased in power."

Knox nodded. "I agree. And his demon isn't worried."

"But *something* zoomed out of Asher and into Lane," Larkin pointed out. "Could it have been one of his smaller gifts?"

"I truly don't know," replied Knox. "I've asked his demon—it's avoiding the question, which is never good."

Harper swore beneath her breath.

Beck rubbed at his brow. "Anyone have an idea of why Thea would take Khloé?"

"It could be a simple case of her wanting revenge on Keenan for claiming Khloé instead of her," suggested Levi. "Scorned she-demons can be vengeful creatures."

Martina frowned. "If it was that, wouldn't Thea have killed her already?"

"Not if she wishes to make Khloé suffer for a while first," said Levi.

Jolene sniffed. "Khloé would overpower her in an instant."

Ciaran nodded. "Then maybe she wants to sic her kid on Khloé to strip her of her gifts so that she's helpless against Thea during torture—Lane's presently unconscious, so Thea would need to keep hold of Khloé until he wakes and can use his gift on her the way he did on Asher."

Harper looked at her son again and stroked his hair. "I can't understand why she targeted him. I mean, what difference would it make to her if he's stripped of his powers for a few hours?"

Knox scraped his jaw with his hand. "Thea said that Lane couldn't temporarily transfer the gifts he stole from people onto others. What if that was untrue? What if Thea wanted to strip Asher of his powers so that she could have them for a short while?"

Harper hissed out a breath. "It's possible. Maybe even probable. But why would she want them? And why would she want them enough to risk making an enemy of us? That's plain suicidal."

Keenan flicked a look at the wall clock, wishing time would move faster; wishing his woman would wake; wishing he hadn't taken pity on Thea and Lane's situation. Maybe if he'd turned her away, she never would have taken Khloé. Given how spiteful Thea could be, he thought it likely that she'd make his mate suffer in some way if she could.

Khloé wouldn't meekly sit still while someone kept her captive. She'd do what she did best—she'd annoy the holy fuck out of her captor until she pushed them too far. That was what worried him most.

Dread sat like a heavy weight on his chest. It weighed him down until he came to a halt, feeling rooted to the spot. "I should have seen it coming. I should have known that Thea would retaliate after the things I said to her at the disciplinary meeting."

Larkin took a step toward him, but he backed away, not wanting to be touched. He felt too tense, too edgy, too close to violence.

The pounding in his ears wouldn't slow or quieten. His fists felt hot, and his jaw ached from how hard he'd been clenching it.

He fought the urge to lash out at those around him. He couldn't afford to lose control. He needed to keep his shit together. He was no fucking good to her like this.

Keenan breathed deeply through his nose and cast all worst-case scenarios out of his mind. Instead of trying to fight the cold rage, he reached for it. He pulled it around him like a cloak of icy calm, using it to numb the other emotions overpowering him. Fear and anxiety didn't have any place here.

"You're not to blame, Keenan," said Larkin. "This happened purely because Thea—for a reason we can't be sure of—stupidly decided it would be a good idea to snatch Khloé."

Levi nodded. "You didn't do anything wrong at the hearing, Keenan. You were just honest with Thea. It's not your fault that she couldn't handle that honesty."

"It doesn't necessarily follow that this is about vengeance, though," said Ciaran. "If it's true that Lane can transfer powers to others, maybe Thea took Khloé because she wants one or more of her gifts. It's well known that Khloé can control most minds—that's an ability that many people covet."

"Right now, I don't particularly care why Thea took her," said Keenan. "I care about getting her back." He touched her mind again and said, Khloé, I need you to wake up and talk to me. Come on, tell me where you are. But his words yet again went unanswered.

*

A telepathic voice hammered at Khloé's consciousness, playing into her dream and slowly pulling her out of sleep. She would have sunk her head further into the pillow, only there was no pillow. In fact, there was no bed. She was lying on a cold, hard floor that—

Memories came crashing down on her. Lane. Thea. A strange male. A sonic scream that sliced through her psyche and made her world go black.

Khloé froze but didn't open her eyes, unsure if she was being watched by the people she could hear arguing. Her demon shot to full alertness in an instant, ready to attack.

She might have sprung to her feet if her ankles weren't tied together. Moreover, her wrists were bound behind her back, which was probably why her shoulders ached something awful.

Khloé let her eyelids flutter partially open so she could examine her surroundings. The world was on a tilt and . . . oh, dear God, they'd actually locked her in a goddamn crate like an animal. The metal glimmered blue and gold here and there. Magick, she thought. Someone had woven magick into the metal. It was spelled shut.

These fuckers were *so* going to pay for this shit.

Again, a telepathic voice invaded Khloé's mind, badgering her to wake. Her heart leaped. The connection was spotty, but she recognized her brother's voice.

She reached out to him and replied, *I'm awake.* Pain lanced through her head, sharp as a scalpel. *Fuck.* Had the sonic scream done some damage to her mind? It was possible. Her sister could release sonic screams that gave people a *wicked* headache. Jolene often talked of how those screams might cause lasting damage to people if Heidi grew in power as she aged.

Careful, Khloé tried to touch Keenan's mind, but it was like there was a mental wall in place. A wall that also stopped her from reaching out to Jolene and Harper. It was as if her psyche was contained by . . . something. The crate?

Was it containing her mind as well as her body so that she couldn't call for help? If that was the case, she'd probably also be unable to use her abilities while inside the crate. Containment spells hampered the mind, body, and psyche.

Testing that theory, she tried conjuring a flicker of electric fire inside her closed fist. But the power swirling in her belly, eager for release, didn't come to her aid. *Hell.*

A vibe of relief touched her mind just as Ciaran's voice breezed inside. *Jesus, sis . . . scared . . . shit out of me. Where . . . you?*

Not sure yet, she replied, almost hissing out a breath at a second shard of pain. She *really* needed to get out of this damn cage. It was a good thing she wasn't claustrophobic.

There was another crackle in her mind just before Ciaran spoke again. *Fucking static . . . Give me a minute to . . .* She almost flinched at the sharp ringing sound that pierced her ears, but then the static eased away. *Can you hear me better?*

Her pulse jumped. *Yes, I hear you just fine.* More pain streaked through her skull. Their frequency might have improved, but using telepathy still hurt like a bitch, thanks to the goddamn containment spell. Whoever designed it should have accounted for the twin bond. She was thankful that the dumb bastard hadn't.

It would have been much easier to use her cell phone, but she'd already seen that it was resting on a nearby coffee table, and it had been smashed to shit.

Are you alone? asked Ciaran.

No, Thea's here. Ignoring the agony slicing through her head, she went on. *So is Lane and three guys I don't recognize.* She rattled off quick descriptions of the males. *Is Keenan with you?*

There was a long pause before Ciaran replied, *Yeah, he's with me. He said to tell you he'll come for you. You should know he's mere minutes from going postal. Also, he said the guys you described sound like Thea's Prime, Gavril, and two of his sentinels. No one can understand why she'd take you to Gavril, though.*

They're having some kind of standoff right now. Not wanting to draw attention to herself, Khloé remained very still as she discreetly glanced around. *I have no clue where I am, but I can tell you that it's fancy. I'm in a Victorian-style parlor.*

Can you get out of there?

Sure. Once I undo the binds and get out of the crate.

The 'crate'?

As she tackled the binds, Khloé kept her eyes on her captors, who were still arguing.

"The plan was simple, so I can't understand why you had such difficulty following it," Gavril berated Thea.

The woman looked nervous, but not cowed. "It wasn't easy to get close to Knox. People tend to keep their distance from demons with Lane's ability—you know that. Stealing the ability from Asher seemed simpler. You yourself said he probably inherited it from his father."

"Yes, *probably*," said Gavril. "But I can't be sure. You should have waited until you had an opportunity to steal it from Knox. It shouldn't have been so hard for you to integrate yourself into his life. You've known him since childhood, for shit's sake."

Thea's lips thinned. "I warned you that he was unlikely to trust me. Knox trusts very few people—I've never been one of them."

"But you were once close to one of his sentinels. All you had to do was get close to Keenan again so that you'd have access to Knox."

"I tried! Keenan always had that bitch with him!" She jabbed at finger at Khloé but didn't move her gaze from Gavril.

"Then you should have tried *harder*."

"Keenan wouldn't give me the time of day, and he went ballistic when I spoke to her. Knox warned me that I'd be punished if I went near her again. He, his mate, and their sentinels apparently consider *her* to be their family, not *me*. If she really is Keenan's mate, it will only be a matter of time before she joins his lair. If I was still around, she'd have requested that I be gone from the picture. Then I'd have lost any chance of getting the power you want. I had to act now."

"What good was *acting now* if the child doesn't even possess the power to call on the flames of hell?"

"I believe he does, and I believe that Lane can give you the power when he wakes."

"That's all well and good. But the idea was to strip Knox of his powers so that he'd be vulnerable. I planned to kill him with his own gifts. Now I can't."

"Not true," she objected. "Nothing's impervious to the flames of hell, which means you could still kill Knox with them. He just won't be helpless while you do."

Hmm, it would seem Gavril thinks that Knox can truly call on the flames of hell, and he wanted Lane to get the power for him—Thea was in on it, said Khloé, trying to ignore the pain pounding through her skull. *She believes the rumor that Asher also possesses the gift, so she had Lane try to steal it from him instead.*

Why the fuck would she help Gavril?

Don't know. Gavril has another reason for wanting Knox stripped of his powers, though. He wants Knox to be vulnerable to attack so that Gavril can kill him. He's not too happy that Thea went off script and targeted Asher.

Gavril sighed and looked at Lane, who was curled up on a chair, asleep. "How long will it be before he's conscious again?"

"Not long," said Thea. "Then you'll get what you want, and he and I will be on our way."

"Not until you've helped me deliver the imp. Then my sentinels will take you and Lane wherever you want to go."

Khloé stiffened. *Apparently, they plan to "deliver" me somewhere. What? Where?*

I don't know yet.

Thea's eyes narrowed at the Prime. "Thanks, but Lane and I can make our own way."

Gavril smiled. "You don't trust that I'll stick to my end of the deal and let you both go?"

"Of course I do. I just don't like to take chances."

Also, Thea and Gavril made a deal that he'd leave both her and Lane be if she had the kid use his gift for him this one time. In other words, she played Knox.

It was a few moments before Ciarán responded. *I just relayed all that to everyone. Believe me when I say that Thea and Gavril will pay. But we're more worried about finding you before you get "delivered." We need some clues as to where you are. What can you see? What can you hear?*

Like I said, it's just some fancy Victorian-style parlor. I feel like I've stepped back in time. I can't hear any voices coming from outside the room. Don't bother trying to track me through GPS—they trashed my cell.

Yeah, we figured that when Larkin's attempt to track you didn't work. Can you see anything out of the windows?

She lifted her head and peered out of the nearest window. *A dull sky. Clouds. Trees. That's it.*

"Ah, you're awake," said Gavril, his gaze now on Khloé. "Excellent."

Shit. Gavril's noticed I'm conscious.

Are you able to attack him?

Not until I'm out of the crate. There's a containment spell in place.

Well, shit.

She tensed as Gavril's heavy footsteps headed her way, his boots scuffing the hardwood floor. Her heart kicked into high gear, but she kept her expression blank as she awkwardly sat up and drew her knees up to her chest.

Thea trailed after him but didn't move to his side when he halted in front of the crate. She stopped a few feet behind him. Khloé's demon sent her a haughty sniff. It intended to make that bitch pay in blood. A fine plan.

Gavril stared at Khloé curiously. "You don't look afraid, which means you're thinking someone will come to help you." He sighed. "Think again. No one knows where you are, and they have no way of finding out. So, don't make a fuss or start screaming. I don't like that shit. You'll be out of here in . . ." He glanced at his watch. "Ten minutes. Sit tight until then."

Khloé narrowed her eyes. "And where exactly will I be going?"

"To a person who offered me enough money to retrieve you. Apparently, he wants to kill and then resurrect you or something."

Her demon's lips pulled back in disgust. "Enoch."

"Yes." Gavril's brows dipped. "Strange fellow. He heard that I had what you might call a terse conversation with Keenan at the bowling alley; he thought that the sentinel and I were enemies, and that I might like to partake in the downfall of Keenan's woman.

"Really, I couldn't give a rat's ass what happens to you. But no one is going to assume I've been part of this plan; they'll assume that Enoch's involved. They'll probably reason that he's working with Thea and that she used Lane to distract Keenan just so that she could take you to Enoch. That means they'll concentrate on finding *him* after you're dead—they won't think to look at me for this."

Wrong, because she'd telepathically filled Ciaran in on what was happening, but there was no need for Gavril to know that, was there?

"Are the rumors true?" he asked. "Can young Asher truly call on the flames of hell?"

"I don't know."

"He's your cousin, and you don't know?"

"Do you honestly think that Harper and Knox will divulge things about their son that could get him hurt?" Khloé shook her head. "No, they keep their secrets. That protects the rest of the family, too—we can't be tortured into sharing info we don't have."

"Does Knox have the gift?"

"I don't know."

"What breed of demon is he?"

"I don't know."

A muscle in his cheek ticked. "What *do* you know?"

Her demon, its ego balking at being huddled in a freaking crate, pushed to the surface and glared at him. "What I know . . . is that you are going to die tonight," it told him.

There was a moment of pure silence. And then he bust a gut laughing. "You think so? Sorry to burst your bubble, but that won't happen."

"You cannot keep an imp anywhere they do not want to be," the entity warned him. Then it pulled back, allowing Khloé to have control again.

"You don't have a prayer of escaping that crate," said Gavril. "Now why don't you sit nice and quiet like a good little girl? This will all be over soon." He turned, dismissing her—which chafed her pride but was a good thing, because she didn't want him to watch her closely—and headed to his sentinels.

Thea didn't follow him. She glared at Khloé, balling her hands up into fists.

Khloé leaned against the back of the crate, feigning nonchalance. "So, you made a deal with that asshole."

Thea stepped closer. "I originally wasn't going to live up to my end of the bargain, you know," she said, her voice too low for her words to carry to the others. "I never intended to sic Lane on Knox. I genuinely went to the Prime for sanctuary. I hoped to get back together with Keenan and start afresh with him."

Such pain and indignation flashed across the woman's face that Khloé tensed, expecting an attack. But the attack didn't come.

Thea flexed her fingers. "He made it clear that *you're* who he wants, though. If you really are his mate—and everyone I've spoken to seems convinced that it's true—you'll join his lair, and I'd have had a front seat to the Keenan-and-Khloé show. I can't watch that. I can't watch while he builds a life with someone else. I don't have that in me."

"Oh, I see. Well, that *totally* justifies you using your own son as a weapon."

Thea flinched. "I had no choice."

"Sure you did. And you made the wrong one. Now he's suffering for it. Look at him. He's not even conscious."

"He'll be fine."

"That's so not the point. You not only made him use his gift on someone, you made him use it on another child. Trust me, he won't forget that. He'll always carry the guilt of it." Not that Khloé was all that convinced that Lane's attempt to drain Asher of power had worked, but still. "And if you think Gavril will really stick to *his* end of the bargain and let you and Lane walk off into the sunset, you're thick as pig shit."

"He'll stick to it," Thea insisted.

"He isn't going to give up the kind of power your son has. If you have any sense, you'll grab the kid and teleport out of here while you still can."

That would not only save Lane further harm, it would mean that Thea couldn't "deliver" Khloé anywhere. Also, Khloé would then have one less foe to worry about. She could hunt Thea down at a later date. The Prime and Enoch were the main threats.

"I gave Gavril my word," said Thea.

"So? You gave your word to Keenan lots of times. You never had any trouble going back on it."

Thea winced, and an angry flush swept up her neck and face. "Bitch." She leaned forward, her eyes blazing. "I'm going to watch while this Enoch guy kills you, and I'm going to enjoy every moment of it."

"And then you'll die because you'll no longer be of use to Gavril, and your son will be taken back to your lair to be used like a tool for the rest of his days."

"*You'll* be the tool. Enoch intends to use you in all sorts of ways."

Oh, Khloé didn't doubt it. "I don't plan to stick around. Not really feeling the vibe here, you know."

"Thea," Gavril called out. "Get over here and wake the boy."

Thea threw Khloé one last glare and crossed to her Prime. "It's not so simple," she told him, looking down at her son.

"Make it simple. Slap his face or something."

"I'm not going to *slap* my child."

Gavril lifted a brow. "Surely you're not going to get all high and mighty now—you just happily used him to strip another child of his powers."

"I didn't do it 'happily.' You gave me no choice."

The Prime gave a soft snort. "Don't kid yourself, Thea. You agreed to my deal because you liked the idea of Knox being vulnerable enough that I could kill him. You want him hurt. You want him to suffer. What did he do, forbid you from joining his lair all those centuries ago?"

"No. I *chose* to be a stray."

"And Keenan chose to stay with Knox instead of leave with you. Is that what this is about? You blame Knox for the choice Keenan made, or do you simply hate the Prime because he means more to the incubus than you ever did; that Keenan's loyalty is to him instead of to you?"

Thea's face reddened. "It's neither of those things."

"I don't believe you," said Gavril.

Hell, neither did Khloé. The asshole had a good little theory going on.

"And I have to wonder if you targeted Asher because you knew it would hurt not only Knox and Keenan but Harper and the other sentinels," Gavril went on. "They don't consider you part of the family they've made—you said so yourself. So you struck at the heart of that family to punish them all, didn't you?"

Thea's eyes flickered. "You are way off base, Gavril," she firmly stated, but Khloé heard the deceptive note to her voice.

The Prime must have heard it as well, because he shook his head and smirked. "I don't think so."

"And I don't care."

Khloé reached out to Ciaran again. *Listen, there's something you should know. They're taking me to Enoch.*

A vibe of anger smacked her mind. *What?*

Apparently, he's offered to pay Gavril a lot of money to do so.

Her twin bit out a vicious curse. *Do you still have the blade?*

Yes, it's still in my boot. No one thought to check inside my boots for weapons, thankfully.

Gavril let out an exasperated breath. "If the boy isn't close to waking, we might as well take the imp to Enoch while we wait."

Thea frowned. "I'm not leaving Lane."

"He'll be fine with my men."

"I'm not leaving his side. I want to be there when he wakes."

"You mean you don't trust that I'll *return* you to his side?"

Thea lifted her chin and shrugged one shoulder. "I like to err on the side of caution."

"Then we shall all leave as one party. I want the imp off my hands so I can concentrate on what's important."

Khloé tensed. *Um . . . it appears we're leaving now.*

To go where?

I don't know, but I do know that Enoch will be there.

Fuck, fuck, fuck.

Don't worry. I've already undone the binds, so I'm not as helpless as he'll be hoping I'll be. And remember, I have the blade. Have a little faith in me, would you.

CHAPTER TWENTY

"A dull sky, clouds, and trees," echoed Keenan. "If Khloé can see those things, she's not being kept in the Underground."

The moment Ciaran had told him that he felt Khloé's mind stir, a shudder had racked Keenan. The depth of his relief almost made his knees give out. His demon, equally relieved, had rolled back its shoulders. The entity had been keeping itself occupied by plotting lots of torturous ways to make Thea suffer.

Knox twisted his mouth. "I'd say Gavril has her in one of his properties. I would imagine that he has many, but I doubt if all are Victorian-style houses, so that may narrow it down. Larkin, I need you to find out if Gavril owns any such properties. You can use the computer in my office. Be as thorough but as fast as you can—Khloé's depending on us."

"I'm on it." The harpy stalked out of the room and dashed up the stairs.

Her face hard, Harper planted her hands on her hips. "I'm infuriated with myself for letting Thea fool me."

Keenan flexed his fingers. "Same here. I should have seen that she was playing the damsel in distress card in the hope that I'd keep her close so that she'd have access to Knox."

"You couldn't really have seen that so clearly," said Ciaran.

Harper ground her teeth. "We should have at least *considered* that that might have been the case. I didn't trust her, but I also didn't think she'd use her son that way. She seemed genuinely afraid for him."

"She probably was—she has to fear that Gavril won't live up to his end of the deal," said Levi.

"Whatever the case, she dies tonight," declared Jolene. "Thea and her son both do."

"Damn fucking straight," said Keenan.

Just then, Tanner prowled inside the living room and sighed. "You have no idea how difficult it was to convince Devon and Raini to remain at my apartment and wait for an update on what was happening. Any developments since we last spoke, Knox?"

The Prime brought him up to speed, his expression hard.

Tanner muttered something under his breath. "Can't Khloé use her gifts to free herself?"

"She's in the grip of a containment spell," Keenan told him. "She can only telepathically connect with Ciaran."

Ciaran abruptly stiffened and then bit out a harsh expletive. "We have a major fucking problem," he announced to the room.

Keenan stilled. "What problem?"

Ciaran's nostrils flared. "She's being delivered to Enoch. He apparently paid Gavril to acquire her."

People spat curses, forgetting to be careful of not doing so around Asher.

Rage slammed into Keenan, making his icy calm falter for a moment. "*What?*" He listened carefully while the imp explained.

Despite that Khloé seemed confident she could escape the crate, fear still battered at his cold calm, threatened to crack it open and shatter it.

Jolene turned to Ciaran. "Do you know if she has her blade with her? The one that can kill Enoch for good?"

"She has it," the imp confirmed.

"But she can't use it until she's out of the crate," Tanner pointed out. "Enoch might not plan on releasing her from it."

Jolene sniffed, all haughty. "As if a crate could contain an imp. It's insulting that Gavril would think differently."

"If he's so sure she can't get out of it, the containment spell is probably very potent," said Tanner.

"It won't make a difference," Jolene told him. "She'll get out. We need to be there to help defend her when she does—she'll be facing Enoch, Thea, *and* Gavril."

Harper nodded. "Thea will gladly kill her if Enoch doesn't. And I think we can safely say that Gavril would have no desire to keep Khloé alive, though he might not necessarily want her dead. He'd kill her out of spite."

Tanner took Asher's hand, who gave him a dimply smile. "How are you doing, little man?"

"He's fine," said Harper. "Whatever Lane did doesn't seem to have harmed him or even stolen any of his powers." She frowned. "I don't know what leapt from him to Lane, but I'm not so sure it was an ability. And if I were Thea, I'd be nervous as hell right now."

Asher touched his mother's face. "Want Koey."

Harper kissed his palm. "Yeah, we all want Khloé, sweetheart. She'll be here soon." She looked at Tanner. "He saw her be taken, so he's a little upset and—"

A hiss escaped Ciaran through gritted teeth. "They're taking her to Enoch now."

The bottom fell out of Keenan's stomach. "*Where* exactly are they taking her?"

"She doesn't know yet," said Ciaran, his voice strained. "But she'll tell us when she gets there."

*

Khloé's stomach rolled as Thea took them on yet another short teleporting trip—the woman's gift didn't take them far, so they were having to make seconds'-long pit stops along the way to wherever Enoch waited.

Khloé braced herself for another teleport, but it didn't come. Apparently, they'd reached their destination. Still inside the crate, she found herself sitting in the middle of a dirt street. She blinked, feeling like she'd traveled back through time to the old west.

Dilapidated wooden buildings were all around her—saloons, a blacksmith, hotels, banks, and a jail and sheriff's office but to name a few. Many windows had been shattered or boarded up. Wooden planks were rotting, and metal was badly rusted. It made her itch for a tetanus shot.

Shale, pebbles, and debris littered the rocky sand. The remains of broken barrels, wagons, and crates could be seen here and there.

The place had clearly been deserted for many years. There were no people around that she could see—not even Enoch. The only sign of life was the black birds that rested on the posts and roofs, flapping their wings and cawing.

A hot breeze fluttered over her, rustling the weeds and making the sagging doors creak. It also brought with it the scents of rust and dust that laced the stale air.

She reached out to Ciaran, wincing at the shot of psychic pain. *I'm in an old western ghost town*, she told him. *If it's used as a tourist attraction, it's closed today for sure, because there's no one around.* But Enoch was probably already here.

Ciaran's mind touched hers. *There are ghost towns all over the world. Do you have any idea where you are?*

Khloé tried seeing beyond the deserted town. There was only sand, cacti, and mountains, but . . . *I think we're still in Nevada.*

Why?

Because Thea can't teleport far, and it only took her four "hops" to get here.

But we don't know for sure that the Victorian house was in Vegas. Larkin's looking into what properties Gavril owns. If we can locate it, we can look for the nearest ghost towns. Can you see anything that will help us narrow down our search? Any landmarks? Any signs?

No. It just looks like your average wild, wild west ghost town.

Up ahead, a shutter saloon door swung open, and Enoch stepped out onto the wooden deck. Adrenaline spiked through Khloé, and the entity within her bared its teeth.

Gavril pasted a polite smile on his face. "Hello again, Enoch."

"Gavril," the Lazarus demon greeted simply. His grating voice was like nails on a chalkboard.

The Prime flicked a hand in Khloé's direction. "I've brought her to you, bound and caged."

Enoch's gaze locked on her, and the hairs on Khloé's nape lifted. Choosing to no longer hide that her binds were undone, she let her arms casually hang over her raised knees.

Enoch cut his gaze back to Gavril. "*Bound* and caged?" he challenged.

His lips thinning, the Prime amended, "Caged, then."

Enoch turned back to the saloon and pushed open the shutter door. "Bring her inside."

Looking none too happy by the order, Gavril nonetheless nodded at Thea, who then teleported their small party of people into the saloon. Khloé gazed around the dusty, cobweb-filled space, taking in the bar, stools, tables, chairs, piano . . . and the two corpses flanking Enoch—their skin pale and rotting, their vacant eyes staring into space.

"Oh, God," muttered Thea, taking a step back.

Similarly, Gavril and his sentinels—one of whom was carrying Lane—recoiled as they stared in horror at the corpses.

A shudder of disgust swept through Khloé. Her fingers itched for the blade that was tucked into her boot. Both corpses were dressed in filthy, ratty clothes from the wild west era. The town must have its own cemetery—most places like this did.

Enoch stalked toward the crate and stared down at Khloé. "I had thought you'd be dead by now. The infection should have contaminated your organs."

"I'm not easy to kill," she said.

"Maybe not, but you *will* die here tonight. I warned you that I'd one day kill you; that I'd use your corpse to attack the people you love."

"You'll have to open this door to kill me," she pointed out.

He smirked. "Oh, and you think you can strike at me when I do?"

"Would you expect anything less?"

"I suppose not." He tilted his head. "You haven't tried to escape," he mused, a note of suspicion in his voice.

"Why would I, when these people here intend to take you out as soon as you've handed over the money you owe them?" asked Khloé.

Thea's eyes widened. "That's a lie!"

"Indeed," said Gavril. "Now, pay me and we will leave you and the imp in peace, Enoch. Thea and I have things to do."

"Like take Enoch out when his back is turned," said Khloé.

Gavril glowered at her. "Ignore her, Enoch. She's just trying to mess with your head—it's what imps do."

"They do, yes," agreed Enoch, his eyes narrowed in suspicion as he stared at the Prime. "But they don't wait around to be killed. They're escape artists. She undid her binds, but she hasn't tried to get out."

"She *can't* get out," clipped Gavril. "A containment spell is woven into the metal of the crate."

"The kid's waking up," declared one of Gavril's sentinels.

Thea blinked at her son and tried taking him from the sentinel, but the guy held tight. Lane's eyelids fluttered, and his little fingers flexed. Thea palmed his cheek. "Lane, honey, it's Mommy. Can you wake up for me?"

His eyes opened, and he looked up at his mother, his gaze startlingly blank.

She gently stroked his face. "Are you okay, sweetheart?" She frowned when he blinked at her but didn't reply. "Lane?"

"Let us return to the manor so we can get this done," said Gavril, his tone rife with agitation. "I want that power. I'm done waiting."

Thea rubbed her son's arm. "He'll need a few moments, Gavril. He's still disorientated."

Khloé snickered. "Oh, puh*lease.*"

Gavril glared at her. "What is that supposed to mean?"

Khloé rolled her eyes. "It's so obvious that she wants you to believe Lane's too weak to help you—in reality, she wants him to give *her* the power he stole. *Come on*, you didn't think she'd let you use her son as a pawn unless she thought she'd get something big out of it—not to mention a guarantee that you'd never come after her—did you? Your death would certainly guarantee that, wouldn't it? Not that I blame her for wanting you gone *permanently*. She has to know you'll kill her before you'll let her have Lane all to herself. Why else would your sentinel be holding him so tight?"

"Divide and conquer," said Thea. "An old and effective trick, but it won't work here."

"Prove it and have little Lane transfer Asher's ability to Gavril," Khloé dared.

The woman's face hardened. "He can't yet, he's still not fully awake."

"How convenient."

"Will you shut the fuck up!"

Khloé sighed. "Fine."

Enoch turned to Gavril. "What ability does the child have that's so important?"

The Prime's spine snapped straight. "That's not your concern."

Lane's body jerked violently, as if it had been zapped by a high voltage of electricity.

"Lane?" said Thea, her voice heavy with anxiety.

He jerked again and slapped a hand on his chest. Then he was coughing and hacking like he was trapped in a burning building.

"Gavril, something's wrong with him. What do—" Thea cut off as the coughing fit ended. She rubbed her son's arm. "That's it, honey, you're fine."

His eyes bled to black as his demon surged to the surface and glared at her.

"It's okay," she told it. "Everything is okay."

The demon gave a short shake of the head. "You threatened him," it said, its voice empty of emotion. "You scared him. You used him. All is not okay."

She swallowed. "I did what had to be done for my sake and his own."

"Not true," it argued. Then the coughing started up again. Its whole body bucked as it coughed and gagged and heaved. Then it doubled-over and retched, puking up something black and oily all over the floor at its mother's feet.

Khloé stared at the small puddle. It swirled and bubbled and steamed like a potion in a cauldron. But said movements slowly began to fade, and the puddle dried up until it was a mere black stain on the wooden floor.

Thea backed away from it. "What is that?"

"Power," said Enoch. "Extinguished power."

Thea's brows snapped together. "What do you mean, extinguished power?"

"I mean it is dead power," Enoch told her. "Something or someone made him vomit up his own personal store of power."

Gavril gaped. "That is not possible."

"I assure you, it is," said Enoch. "I haven't witnessed such a thing before, but I've heard of it. Some demons allegedly possess the defensive ability to purge others of their powers."

Gavril whirled on Thea. "What exactly happened at the stadium?"

"Lane used his gift to steal Asher's," Thea replied. "Something jumped from Asher into him. I thought it was the toddler's abilities."

Gavril flicked his hand in the air. "He is now *useless* to me. He's as good as human. Did you do this to him, Thea? Did you do this to escape the deal we made?"

Her eyes widened. "I didn't do anything! It was the Thorne kid!"

Ciaran's mind touched Khloé's. *Larkin came through for us—she found that Gavril has a Victorian house a few miles away from Harper and Knox's estate. We're going to pay a visit to the nearest ghost towns. If you're in none of them, we'll check the others.*

Relief fluttered through Khloé. *You need to look inside the saloons,* she told him.

Just then, another mind touched hers—young, powerful, familiar. Recognizing Asher's touch, she smiled to herself. How he'd managed to bypass the psychic shield keeping her from telepathing others, she had no idea. *Hey, kiddo,* she said, keeping her tone cheery. *I'll come see you soon.*

There was a small movement beside her. And then she could only gape. Asher was there. Yet he wasn't. His body was partly transparent, which meant she could very well be seeing shit. Either that or he was truly—in some sense—beside her in the crate, smiling shyly at her.

She glanced at the others to see if any could see him, but none were looking her way. They were observing Thea and Gavril, who were arguing yet again.

Turning back to Asher, Khloé flashed him a smile and reached out to her brother. *Ciaran, what's Asher doing right now?*

He was sleeping a few minutes ago when we left him at the estate with Meg, Dan, Larkin, Martina, and Beck. Why?

Because I'm looking right at him.

What?

He's partly transparent, but he's here. Sort of.

"What the fuck?" burst out Gavril.

Khloé tensed as the others crowded the crate, their mouths open wide as they stared at Asher. Only Enoch's two puppets and Lane—whose demon was still in control—remained far back.

Enoch squinted at Khloé. "You create illusions, do you?"

Gavril crouched. "This is no illusion. The boy must have the ability to astral project." His eyes narrowed, glittering with sheer cunning. "How interesting. He should not have been able to get inside that crate—no one should, whether in astral form or any other. Hello, little boy."

"Want Kooey," Asher said around the finger he'd stuffed into his mouth.

Gavril's brows raised. "Then you should stay with us. I'm sure she'd like your company."

"Kooey go home."

"I'm sorry, young one, but Khloé won't be going home."

The air chilled as Asher's eyes bled to black. The demon—so unbelievably cold and callous—curved its lips into a dimply smile that held an edge of arrogance. It opened its small hand, and a gold spark flickered to life on its palm.

Thea gasped. "What's it doing?"

The entity looked at the ceiling, and then the spark on its palm became a *stream* of gold power that punched a hole through the top of the crate and through the roof of the building, sending bits of wood flying through the air . . . and breaking the containment spell.

Khloé's heart leaped and, hearing a chorus of caws, she peered through the hole in the roof. She felt her lips part in surprise. Crows were flying and dancing there, as if drawn by the lingering energy of the power display . . . or by Asher himself, she wasn't sure.

Asher's form shimmered and then disappeared. The others spun, searching the room with their eyes. Khloé figured he'd returned his astral ass home, but then he reappeared near the bar. Or, more to the point, his demon did. And it was still wearing that arrogant smirk.

She *felt* power gather in the air as the others braced themselves to attack. Her stomach sank, her demon tensed, and a shot of pure adrenaline rushed through her. She didn't know if Asher's astral body could truly be hurt or not, but she wasn't about to risk it.

You guys need to get here fast, bro, she told her twin.

We don't know where "here" is yet, he pointed out.

Just look for the flock of crows. Wasting no time, Khloé snapped out her leg and kicked the crate door open. She thrust out her palms and called to the power humming in her belly. Whips of electric fire lashed her captors, making them cry out and fall to their knees.

She crawled out of the crate just as a golden wave of pure power swept out of Asher's demon and crashed into its foes, including the two corpses—hurling them all across the room. *Well, damn.* Her own entity was mightily impressed.

She itched to stand at astral-Asher's side, but it would serve them both better if they remained separate targets—it would divide the attention of their foes.

Lane ran out of the saloon mere seconds before crows flew through the front door. Their wings flapping like crazy, the birds descended on Enoch, Gavril, Thea, the sentinels, and the puppets before any of them even had the chance to stand upright. Voices cried out and cursed as the crows pecked with their beaks and raked with their talons.

Enoch batted them away and then surrounded himself with his forcefield. Ugh. He snarled at Khloé as he stood. "You will not survive this night."

"Worried that you'll *fail* yet again, old man?" she taunted.

Growling, he pitched several death orbs through the air. She deflected them with her own power, and they harmlessly crashed into the wall, leaving patches of rot.

The asshole threw more black, smoky orbs at her. She evaded them just as another surge of golden power swept out of Asher. It crashed into Enoch's forcefield, causing spiderweb-like cracks to form in the construction, but the bastard quickly bolstered it and repaired the damage—

She winced as a high-pitched sound built in the air, hitting a note so high it threatened to burst her eardrums and once more damage her psyche. Khloé hurled a ball of hellfire at Gavril's head, and the sound cut off.

Sensing he was the most powerful of her foes besides Enoch, Khloé plunged her mind into that of the Prime and seized control. "You will protect me and fight alongside me."

Gavril didn't hesitate to whirl on the spot and attack Enoch. He couldn't pierce the protective forcefield, but he was able to telekinetically bat away every death orb that came at her. Awesome.

Unlike Enoch, she couldn't control more than one person at a time, but Gavril proved to be very good backup. He essentially held off Enoch while Khloé blasted the others with strong currents of electric fire again and again, managing to obliterate one puppet pretty much instantly.

She inhaled sharply as one of the sentinels all but dazed her with a telepathic punch that made her stagger like a drunk. *Bastard.* Still, she fought on. At the same time, the crows kept biting and raking, and Asher kept on releasing gold waves of such crushing power it almost took her breath away.

The combined attack took the two sentinels and the second puppet out of the equation, but Thea teleported to the other side of the saloon and out of harm's way. Enraged, Khloé's demon hissed through its teeth.

Worried that the woman would teleport out of the building and escape, Khloé taunted, "Yes, that's it, flee and leave the others to fight your battle. Keenan told me what a coward you are. How many times was it that you left him without even a goodbye?" Khloé replicated Jolene's haughty sniff that could make a person feel an inch tall.

Covered in bites and scratches, Thea sneered. "Think you're better than me just because he calls you his mate?"

"No. I think I'm better than you *because* I'm better than you."

"Bitch." Her upper lip curling, Thea released a series of hellfire orbs.

Khloé ducked, dodged, and weaved, but the latter orb

connected. She jerked back at the punch of hot pain to her ear. *Fuck* it burned as the hellfire blistered and ate at her skin.

Thea laughed. "You won't be so pretty once I'm done fucking you up."

"Right now, you're no spring chicken yourself." Khloé retaliated; a flickering wave of electric fire soared toward Thea and lashed her so hard she flew backwards and crashed into the metal crate.

Even as she fell, Thea flicked her hand at Khloé. A ribbon of ice-cold energy whipped Khloé's face and sliced the skin like a blade. *Fucking ow.*

Khloé tossed several hellfire orbs at the little skank, who teleported away and took cover behind the piano. "Fuck." Another ribbon of frosty energy came flying at Khloé. She jerked back, but it slashed her chest, ripping her tee and flaying her skin.

Just then, a ripple of golden power swept up both Thea and the piano. They slammed into the wall, and Thea slumped to the floor, unmoving. Excellent.

Khloé slanted Asher a quick glance, needing to be sure he was okay, and saw that his demon was still firmly in charge. She also saw its form flicker, and she knew its power—a force that its psyche was too young to adequately wield—was beginning to burn out.

A death orb came sailing toward her. Khloé's heart jumped into her throat. She ducked, barely avoiding the orb. It was only then she realized that Gavril was dead. *Shit.*

"Oops, did I kill your puppet?" asked Enoch, smirking. "Shame the woman is dead. You could have made her your new pup—" He cut off as Khloé unleased more electric fire. It crackled and hissed as it sailed through the air and covered his forcefield.

She closed her hand, and the electric fire severed the forcefield in an instant, leaving him vulnerable. Wicked fast, she sprayed him with bullets of electric fire. But all harmlessly bounced off the forcefield he swiftly re-erected. Crap.

He chuckled. "It won't be that easy to hurt me, little imp."

He and Khloé did the same dance again and again. The fucker always popped up another forcefield in time to protect himself. Khloé hissed, and fury poured through her demon like lava.

Boards creaked as several figures staggered into the saloon, their movements awkward and clunky, their clothes in tatters, their flesh practically nonexistent—bringing with them the stomach-curdling scents of rot, dirt, and death.

They began to converge on Khloé. "Hell." Swearing beneath her breath, she let loose on them in a rage. Flames of electric fire sliced through the air and whipped the corpses, sending them tumbling to the floor.

Even as she dodged or deflected Enoch's death orbs, she peppered his puppets with bullets of electric fire, aiming for their brains and eyes. Some bullets hit their marks, but some fucking didn't.

Several of the fallen stayed down, useless to their master. Others staggered to their feet and shuffled toward her. Asher's demon kept Enoch occupied while she attacked the puppets, taking several out of the equation—some took hellfire orbs to the face; some took bullets of electric fire to the brain.

Undeterred, the other corpses staggered toward her. A few of them tripped over the fallen, but they picked themselves up and kept moving. Worse still, more and more poured into the saloon. *Fuck.*

It was like he had the entire cemetery out there, waiting their turn to take her down. There were too many of them, and she couldn't possibly hold them *all* off. So many parts of her body ached and burned, and each move she made tugged on her injuries. Her breaths were coming quick—

A sharp psychic slap shocked a gasp out of her. Her face stung so bad her eyes watered, but she shelved the pain and fought on, trying to pretend she wasn't tiring.

She heard a roar of fire outside followed by a guttural hellhound growl. Hope unfurled in her belly. Help had arrived, and that help would no doubt take down the army of puppets who were trying to get inside the saloon.

Moments later, Keenan dropped through the hole in the roof and landed a few feet away from her. Relief surged through her so fast it nearly made her dizzy. "Thank fuck you're here," she said.

His mind brushed hers, vibrating with rage. "Thank fuck you're alive."

CHAPTER TWENTY-ONE

Seeing his mate alive and well—albeit injured—made something in Keenan settle even as a need for vengeance crept through him and infiltrated every cell in his body. He wanted to haul her to him and kiss her hard, but that could wait. It would have to wait. Even his demon, who was desperate to reach and touch her, understood that.

He noticed Asher's partial form wink out just as Ciaran and Jolene teleported to Khloé's side. The female Prime instantly slammed up her shield to protect them, blocking the barrage of death orbs that came their way.

Ciaran emitted a powerful blast of telekinetic energy that flattened his targets. Only Enoch, protected by his forcefield, remained on his feet.

You keep her safe, Keenan ordered Jolene, resisting the urge to wade through the corpses and get to Khloé's side. He wanted to pile the pressure on Enoch by striking at him from another angle.

Don't worry, Jolene told him. *Enoch can't reach her.*

As a unit, they attacked the motherfucker and his puppets. Pure mayhem commenced. Balls of hellfire, death orbs, and ripples of telekinetic power zoomed around the large space. Old elixir bottles smashed or exploded. Tables and chairs broke or splintered. Patches of rot and scorch marks stained the walls and floor.

The crowd of corpses soon divided. Most headed for Khloé, Jolene, and Ciaran, but the others came at Keenan, attacking with balls of hellfire. One clipped his shoulder, burning his tee and eating at his flesh. Another hit his solar plexus so hard it was like a scorching hot fist slammed into his chest and knocked the breath from his body.

His demon roared in anger, flexing its fists. Winded and clenching his teeth against the pain of his flesh charring and peeling away, Keenan retaliated with hellfire orbs of his own—his were hotter, more lethal.

The whole time, he kept a mental eye on Khloé. She was a force to be fucking reckoned with, tossing out waves, beams, and bullets of electric fire—making both him and his demon proud as fucking hell, even as they worried for her.

Enoch repeatedly targeted her, despite the fact that she was safely behind Jolene's shield—as if he hoped that by attacking said shield hard enough, he'd eventually crack it.

The corpses' numbers dropped fast. The blinded ones slumped to the floor. But, unhampered by pain or emotion, the rest forged onward, no matter how horribly wounded they were. Keenan could almost taste the sickening scents of rot, blood, seared flesh, charred wood, and burned rancid meat.

Tossing flaming orbs at the remaining puppets, he inched closer to Enoch and exuded dark pheromones that would fuck with his system and make the bastard feel sick, disoriented, and afraid. It took a few minutes for the pheromones to truly take hold, but Keenan saw the moment when Enoch fell victim to their effects. Sweat beaded his forehead, the color drained from his face, and his hands began to shake.

His forcefield didn't falter. Yet. But it would.

Tanner's hound charged into the saloon with a throaty snarl and crashed into the crowd of corpses. A millisecond later, Harper, Knox, Levi, and the hellhound rushed through the front door, their expressions hard as stone.

Tell me the puppets outside are out of commission, Keenan said to Knox as his lair members joined the attack.

They're out, confirmed the Prime.

The air burned hot with the stream of fire that flowed from Knox's palm, lighting up corpse after corpse. Harper lifted small objects, infused them with hellfire, and hurled them at their enemies' heads while Tanner's hound ravaged them with claws and teeth. Levi joined Jolene and Ciaran in attacking with telekinesis—lifting corpses and bashing their heads on the floor or against the walls.

The air rang with the sounds of electric fire crackling, hellfire spitting, wood splintering, corpses grunting and gargling, and voices crying out in pain or anger.

Enoch's puppets stood no chance against so many foes. It was a massacre, really. Finally, all of them littered the floor, along with bits of skull, bone, and brain matter and, of course, the bodies of Thea, Gavril, and his two sentinels.

Only Enoch remained alive, still safe within his damn forcefield. A forcefield that was finally beginning to weaken. Sweat was pouring off Enoch who, his neck corded and his expression fierce, was clearly struggling to keep up the shield. But he *was* keeping it up—that was the problem. Even though he'd vomited twice and was obviously tiring, he'd held out.

Keenan reached out to his Prime again. *The bastard's stronger than I gave him credit for. Look, I know why you don't call on the flames of hell in front of outsiders, I get why you won't publicly confirm you possess that ability—hell, we're in this situation with Gavril because people worry you possess it—but we need Enoch dead.*

Don't worry, Keenan, I won't let your mate die, was Knox's only response. Translation: he'd call on the flames if it seemed to be the only way to kill Enoch, but he'd give Khloé the chance to kill the fucker with the blade first.

Keenan ground his teeth. He understood, he did, but—

His heart jumped as Thea suddenly appeared behind Khloé, much as she had earlier at the stadium. This time, though, she held a jagged piece of glass to his mate's throat. Fuck, he'd thought she was dead. His demon rumbled a growl, slinking closer to the surface.

"Oh, I really wouldn't move if I were you," Thea told her.

Everyone went still, raring to act but hesitant to risk that Thea would slice his mate's throat. And Keenan *knew* the little bitch would happily do it and then teleport away. He guessed the only reason she hadn't already done it was that she'd rather hand his mate over to Enoch—someone who'd make her suffer both in life and in death. Hell, Thea would probably teleport herself, Enoch, Khloé, and Lane—wherever the kid was hiding—out of there. *Shit.*

Khloé didn't look in the slightest bit nervous. In fact, she seemed more exasperated than anything else. "Can't you see we're busy here, Thea?"

Stay still, Keenan told his mate. *We'll make our move once she gives us an opening.*

Enoch let out a darkly satisfied chuckle. "Bring her to me," he told Thea.

Thea smiled, but then that smile faltered and she blinked hard. Her hand slowly and mechanically moved away from Khloé's throat. She'd seized Thea's mind, he realized.

His imp instantly spun and gripped her attacker by the head. Blue/amber flickers of electric fire hissed and snapped beneath the imp's palms. Thea's eyes rolled back in her head, and then she slumped to the ground, convulsing with the shockwaves of electric fire that coursed through her body. Finally, she went still. Dead.

Thank. Fuck.

While her inner demon all but laughed in delight, Khloé looked at Enoch and felt her mouth curve. "Seems like you've lost your last ally. How very sad for you."

With a growl of rage, the Lazarus demon fired more death orbs at her grandmother's shield. They seemed stronger, darker . . . as if powered by his fury. Khloé gasped when a crack formed in Jolene's shield. And another crack. And another. *Fuck.* She hadn't thought he'd ever be able to penetrate the shield. But then, Jolene's shield had never taken such a beating from him before.

Khloé pulled the blade out of her boot but didn't throw it. She had to get the timing just right. *Keenan, I need you to distract Enoch from slamming up another forcefield so I can stab him with this blade. I'll probably only get one chance.*

Make your move, and then I'll make mine, said Keenan.

Khloé lifted her trembling hand and let out a surge of electric fire that surrounded Enoch's forcefield. With a mere gesture of her hand, the construction severed, and Keenan tossed a hellfire orb at Enoch's side, making him flinch and curse. It was the distraction she needed.

Her heart hammering in her chest, she hurled the blade fast. It found its home right in his fucking eye, sinking all the way through to his brain . . . but not before he tossed another death orb at Khloé. It sailed through the air just as Jolene's shield cracked again and—*oh God*—went down. The orb smacked Khloé's face and poured up her nose and into her mouth.

Motherfucker. She fell to her knees, coughing and heaving, just as Enoch burst into a cloud of ashes. This time, the ashes didn't fly away. They floated to the floor.

Unable to catch her breath, she tried sucking in air, but it was as if her airways were blocked. Her body jerked as Ciaran slapped her back. His power rushed inside her and seemed to blow air into her lungs. The force within her reached to meld with his power, but it couldn't. It wasn't strong enough. *She* wasn't strong enough.

The death essence powered the infection in her body, and she could almost feel the protective shields around her organs begin to crumble. Panicked, her demon went absolutely fucking ballistic.

Warm hands cradled her face just as her vision swam. "Baby?" Keenan's voice was thick with fear. "Fuck, you're going to be fine. You are."

No, she wasn't. "Keenan," she rasped. The world began to spin and fade as the darkness came to swallow her. Then she passed out.

*

Sitting on a chair in his crowded bedroom, Keenan stared at the woman lying on the bed. Despair stabbed his gut and sliced through his heart, the emotion so strong and consuming it was like a living entity inside him. It threatened to drown him, to wipe away every bit of his sanity.

His elbows braced on the mattress, he held Khloé's hand between his, his thumb pressed against the pulse on her wrist. The back of his throat ached, and it hurt to swallow.

She felt cold to the touch. *Too* cold. Too still. Too . . . lifeless.

Khloé was all spirit and laughter and mischief. Now, though, she was so deathly pale he was surprised her heart still beat.

There were dark shadows under her eyes, and her lips seemed to have whitened. Worse, her pulse was so weak it was a wonder he could detect it.

Her body was shutting down. He knew it. They all knew it. And there was fuck all they could do about it. The infection had now settled into Khloé's organs and it was systematically killing her.

Tears stung the back of his eyes, clogged his throat, and tightened his chest, but the tears didn't fall. He never cried. The Ramsbrook staff had beaten that out of him.

The air in the room was thick with anguish and hopelessness, and it almost hurt to breathe it in. His bedroom was packed with people—many from Khloé's lair, many from his. Some spoke in hushed tones, some quietly wept, some paced and sniped at others.

No one tried to give him false assurances. He was glad of that. Because he was pretty sure he'd explode on anyone who tried it.

He was conscious of the time ticking away. She was weakening with every minute that passed, taking him that little bit closer to losing her. A profound loneliness hovered at the edges of his being, ready to swallow him whole. His world would be a dark, cold place without her. It wasn't a world he had any interest in living in.

A debilitating grief smothered him and made his ribs feel too tight. He'd always believed that he'd find some way to save her. He'd *had* to believe it. So he'd stayed positive and held onto hope.

That hope had vanished.

Now, he felt defeated. Drained. Flayed open right down to his soul.

His demon was still and silent, angry at the situation; angry that it was helpless to save her; angry that the universe would take her from it. It wanted to rant and rave and scorch the Earth. Maybe Levi sensed that, because he stuck close to him, a silent pillar of support.

Keenan wanted to tell him to leave. He wanted to tell them *all* to leave. He wanted to be left alone with her. The only thing stopping him from emptying the room was that he knew she wouldn't have wanted him to deprive her loved ones of these last moments with her.

Sick to his stomach, Keenan squeezed his eyes shut. To think that he'd held back from her for so long, to think he'd *wasted* all that time they could have spent together . . .

His shoulders bowed. Part of him was irrationally angry with her for leaving him, and he hated that part of himself.

Hearing the scrape of wood on wood, he opened his eyes to see that Teague had moved his chair to the other side of the bed. The hellhorse watched her, his eyes as vacant as those of Enoch's puppets. The guy looked numb—probably with shock and despair.

Strangely, Teague's presence didn't piss off Keenan or his demon. Maybe it was because they were both buried too deep in anguish to care about anything other than the woman lying so still on the bed.

Keenan pressed a kiss to her hand. She didn't stir. She hadn't responded to anyone since she'd passed out—not even telepathically.

That awful moment when she'd toppled to the saloon floor like a dead weight . . . *fuck*. He kept mentally replaying it over and over, as if his subconscious was determined to torture him with it.

"There are so many powerful demons in this room," said Teague. "Yet not one of them—hell, not even all our power put together—could heal her. How is that fucking fair?"

Keenan met the man's eyes, knowing his own gaze was flat and dead. "It isn't," he said around the thick lump clogging his throat. *None* of it was fucking fair. If anyone deserved to live a long, happy, fulfilling life, it was Khloé.

"I tried to help her." Ciaran's voice wavered, and his Adam's apple bobbed. "It usually works. Why didn't it work?" he asked no one in particular.

Jolene put a hand on his back. "Because she was weak from the infection and the battle." Her eyes grew wet. "You don't bear any blame here, Ciaran. No one in this room does."

Keenan disagreed. If Knox had just called on the flames of hell when Keenan had asked, this would not have happened. Yes, she'd still be infected, but they might have had time to find some way to heal her. Now, they'd run out of time.

"We got to her as fast as we could," Jolene added.

"But not fast enough." Harper's lips trembled, and she pressed them tight together. He'd never seen his female Prime look frail. Not until right then, as she leaned into her own mate with silent tears dripping down her ashen face. Larkin stood at her other side, rubbing the sphinx's back, her own eyes red and puffy.

Penelope blew her nose on a tissue. "I can't lose her, Richie. I can't lose another child."

His shoulders tight, Richie rested a comforting hand on her shoulder but didn't speak. His mate stood at Penelope's other side, stroking her arm, clearly sensing how close the woman was to breaking.

Penelope fisted her tissue. "There must be *someone* who can do *something*."

"If there is, we never managed to find them," Devon whispered, as if her voice lacked strength. She buried her face in Tanner's chest and wept.

"What about Vivian?" Penelope persisted. "Can't she build more protective shields around Khloé's organs?"

Wiping her wet cheeks with her fingers, Jolene shook her head. "Vivian said it's too late for that. The infection has progressed too far. Khloé won't . . ." She took in a shaky breath.

Penelope narrowed her eyes at the Prime. "You were supposed to protect her. You said you would. You *promised* me you would."

Jolene's eyes fell shut. "And I failed."

"*No,*" Martina cut in, clutching Beck as if he was the only thing keeping her on her feet. "You didn't fail, Mom. Enoch was just too powerful."

"Fucking Lazarus demons always are," Beck gritted out.

"Which is why he *never* should have been allowed to join our lair," spat Penelope. "He shouldn't have—"

"I know you're looking for someone to blame, Penelope, but that's not going to help. Nothing is going to help." Richie cleared his throat. "At this point, there's nothing we can do except be with Khloé during her final moments," he said, unshed tears in his hoarse voice.

Penelope lifted her chin. "I don't accept that. No. I *refuse* to accept it. She's going to live. She is."

Meredith touched her hair. "Penelope . . ." It was a soft entreaty.

A sob wracked Penelope. The strength seemed to leave her legs in an instant, and she dropped to the floor, wailing. Richie and Meredith crouched beside her, just as broken.

Keenan couldn't bring himself to feel for them. A strange apathy had taken him over. Maybe it had also settled into Teague, because the hellhorse paid them no attention. He was hyper-focused on Khloé, as if staring at her hard enough might just wake her.

Keenan wished that were the case. He took in a long breath,

and his chest expanded, but the tightness remained. Resting his forehead on the cool hand he still held between his own, he closed his eyes.

Conversation continued around him, but he tuned it out, concentrating on the weak, unsteady pulse that beat against his thumb. Even as it weakened, there was something comforting about it.

"Keenan?"

He tensed at the sound of Knox's voice. The Prime had moved closer to him, but Levi stood between them—a good thing, because the thought of punching Knox was far too fucking tempting.

Keenan couldn't even *look* at him as he said, "Not now." Bile burned the back of his throat. "It would be better if you left." Because the moment his mate's heart stopped beating, sheer rage would take Keenan over. He'd lash out for sure, and he'd lash out at the one person who could have prevented the second death orb from hitting her if he'd just called on the flames of hell to begin with.

Female arms surrounded Keenan from behind. *Harper.* Her shoulders were shaking with silent tears. He wondered if she too blamed her mate. Probably not. She was soft beneath the hard shell she presented to the world. She wouldn't pin the blame on anyone but Enoch.

Keenan didn't lean into her touch. He didn't want comfort. He wanted his mate to wake the fuck up and *live*. But it wasn't going to happen. Khloé was a fighter through and through, but not even she could power through this.

She was already gone, really. Her heart might beat, and her soul might even still be in there somewhere, but she wasn't going to wake up. For the first time in a while, he itched to reach for his flask, and he knew he'd do that very thing once she passed.

"Raini, what the hell?" asked Harper, straightening.

Keenan looked up and frowned. Biting her lip, Raini stood in the doorway with Maddox Quentin. Keenan and his demon both tensed. "What the fuck is this?"

"What is he doing here?" demanded Jolene.

"I went to find him," replied Raini. Keenan hadn't even realized she'd left his apartment.

Maddox looked at him. "I can help your mate."

Everything in Keenan went still. "What?"

"I can heal her," said Maddox. "Save her."

Hope and skepticism swirled inside Keenan, vying for supremacy. "How?"

Maddox shrugged. "I just can. Do you want me to do it or not?" It was clear the matter was neither here nor there to him.

"She's been hit by death orbs," Keenan told him.

"I know. Raini explained everything." Maddox glanced at Khloé's pale form. "If you want your imp to live, you need to let me act now. She won't live much longer."

"You're so sure he's not here to hurt her, Raini?" Teague asked, his eyes narrowed.

"I'm sure." The blonde sighed. "Look, we have nothing to lose by letting him try to heal Khloé. If we don't, she'll die anyway."

Fuck if she wasn't right.

"I say we let him," Penelope immediately piped up. Others agreed while some remained silent, unsure.

Sensing that all eyes were on him, Keenan nodded at Maddox. "But if you harm her, you die."

"And you die hard," Teague added.

Looking unaffected by the threat, Maddox walked to the bed and took Khloé's free hand. He didn't hold it. He held his palm flat to hers, just as Eric had done.

Keenan's demon coiled inside him, ready to pounce and attack

Maddox if he made a wrong move. Keeping her other hand tight in his, Keenan tensed as the descendant's palm began to glow with a blood-red light. That light seemed to shoot into Khloé, illuminating her veins; pumping through them like a transfusion of some kind.

Power snapped the air taut and heated the room, making his skin prickle and every hair on his body lift. Hope and skepticism still played havoc with his system, causing his stomach to cramp and his muscles to tighten.

Keenan's heart leaped as the pulse beating against his thumb steadied and strengthened. The rise and fall of her chest was no longer so gentle or subtle. A little color returned to her face, making her look haggard but not near death's door.

As the red glow spread to the veins in her face and scalp, Khloé's back bowed almost violently. Her eyes snapped open, and she took a shaky breath.

His heart thudding, Keenan sat on the edge of the bed and squeezed her hand. "Baby?"

She blinked at him. "Feel like I got hit by a freight train," she rasped.

Relief shuddered through him and made his throat thicken. Keenan lifted her and set her on his lap. Pressing his mouth to her hair, he curled his arms tight around her, holding her close as everyone crowded and fussed over her, some still crying.

Penelope tried taking her from him, but Keenan wasn't having any of it. Yeah, it made him selfish, but he could live with that.

"It's good that I came here when I did," said Maddox. "She didn't have long left."

Keenan stared at him. "How were you able to do that? To heal her? You're not an archangel."

"Far from it," Maddox easily agreed.

Sensing the male wasn't going to elaborate, Keenan said, "I owe you."

"No, you don't." Maddox's gaze cut to Raini and gleamed with possession. "But you do. Don't forget our agreement."

The succubus lifted her chin a notch. "I won't."

With that, Maddox left, his arm brushing Raini's as he passed.

Khloé frowned. "What agreement?"

Ignoring the question, Raini came closer and gently rubbed Khloé's leg. "How do you feel?"

Taking stock of herself, Khloé replied, "Like shit, but . . . alive." More alive than she'd felt in a while. She let out a shaky breath. "He really did heal me. The infection is completely gone—I can feel it." Her demon leaned into Keenan, relieved and tired.

"Well, thank the holy mother of fuck for that," clipped Ciaran, scrubbing a hand down his face.

"No, we have Maddox to thank," said Khloé. And after feeling a taste of his power, she could confirm . . . "He's far from holy."

Knox took a step toward Raini. "You said you went to find him. Why?"

"I heard from someone that a small number of archangels fell from heaven a long, long, *long* time ago," replied Raini. "I heard that they fell and copulated with demons, much like normal angels did, and that they produced children. Those children grew up among the Nephilim, but they were different; stronger; more dangerous."

Khloé felt her brow furrow. She hadn't heard of that.

Raini went on, "I thought that maybe Maddox might know someone who descended from archangels—it seemed a slight chance that they'd have the power to heal or fight the essence of death, but I figured it was worth asking."

"And it turns out that Maddox has that power," said Jolene, her eyes narrowed.

Raini swallowed. "It would seem so."

Harper sidled up to the succubus. "You know what that means, don't you?"

Raini nodded. "He just said that he could heal Khloé; he didn't explain why. But it can only mean that he's the descendant of an archangel."

"A very, very powerful one," said Levi. "Add in all the demonic blood that flows through his system, and it makes him seriously fucking dangerous."

"More dangerous than we'd previously imagined," added Tanner.

He wasn't wrong there. What had surged through Khloé was archangelic power with a dark twist. "He didn't fight the death essence with pure life. He fought it with something else. It had life—so much life—but it wasn't pure. And it was so much more potent than the death orbs that Enoch hit me with. I could *never* have expelled out of my system whatever Maddox just sent into me." Not with Ciaran's aid, not with anyone's.

Keenan looked down at her, his brow creased in concern. "But you're okay?"

"I'm fine," she assured him. "His power didn't harm me in the slightest."

Folding her arms, Devon looked at Raini. "He didn't help her out of the goodness of his heart. What did you agree to do? Tell me you're now not officially his sex slave or something."

Raini rolled her eyes. "Of course not. You come out with the weirdest stuff."

"It was a valid question," insisted Devon. "Right, Tanner?"

The hound's mouth bopped open and closed. "I wouldn't know." He let out an *oof* when Devon jabbed his ribs with her elbow.

"He's not a guy who'd want an unwilling female in his bed. He said so himself the first time I met him," said Raini.

Khloé remembered that. Looking up at Raini, she gave her a faint smile and swallowed. "Thank you for what you did. I know that going to Maddox for something couldn't have been easy for you."

"No thanks needed," said Raini. "There's nothing I wouldn't do for my girls."

Yeah, that was kind of what worried Khloé.

CHAPTER TWENTY-TWO

Sitting on the small, plastic slide, Khloé shifted slightly to get comfier and then took another swig of her pink gin. "I wonder if Little Bo Peep ever found her sheep. Or maybe she got new ones. Like for her birthday or something."

"If I lost some, I'd put 'new sheep' on my birthday gift list," said Raini, using her heel to gently rock the swing backward and forward. "And a sheepdog because, you know, it would just make things a whole lot easier."

On the other swing, Devon pointed a finger at the succubus. "Bo Peep should've thought of that. She was *such* a disappointment, as shepherdesses go." The hellcat flicked her hair over her shoulder. "I'd have been so much better at that job. I should totally try it."

Sitting cross-legged on the lawn, Harper frowned. "But we need you to pierce people and help with tattoos."

Devon sighed, disappointed. "Life always gets in the way." She sipped from her red plastic cup. "We might need to head back inside soon; I'm almost out of gin."

They'd come out to Jolene's backyard to get a little fresh air. The air inside was hot and stuffy, since the living room, dining room, kitchen, hallway, and backyard were packed with people who'd come to celebrate Martina's birthday.

Music blasted out of the open window, along with the sounds of people laughing, singing, and yelling to be heard. The birthday girl was currently in the dining room, *killing* Gloria Gaynor's "I Will Survive" on the karaoke. The imps on the outdoor deck were doing the Conga dance while singing along. Another was using the green hose as a microphone while dramatically mouthing the lyrics.

Khloé figured it was a good thing that the neighbors were lair members or Jolene would be getting a high number of complaints about the noise. Especially since their family parties could go on all night and might even bleed into the late morning hours.

A breeze brushed over her skin and ruffled the grass and leaves. Khloé lifted her plastic cup to her mouth and took another sip of her pink gin. The sweet taste exploded on her tongue.

Raini leaned the side of her face against one swing chain. "You know, it kind of amazes me that Keenan left your side, Khlo. He's been your shadow for weeks now."

He had indeed. And he hadn't once snapped at her mother for turning up at the house on a daily basis just to faff around Khloé. She suspected that was partly because he was glad Penelope had tossed out her useless boyfriend and was back on the sobriety wagon. Hopefully she didn't fall off it again.

Keenan often watched Khloé like a hawk, as if searching for signs that the infection might have returned. It hadn't. Maddox had definitely either neutralized or overpowered it, because even Vivian had confirmed that there wasn't so much as a dot of death essence in Khloé's system.

"He seems to have calmed a little since he slid this on my finger," said Khloé, smiling down at the black diamond ring, just as she did many times a day. Such jewelry was a symbol of the ultimate commitment, so demons only ever exchanged them with partners they were utterly certain of.

Keenan had given Khloé hers the day after Maddox had healed her, saying that watching her almost die had made him realize that he never wanted to be without her. Since she felt the same, she'd asked him to wear the masculine matching ring. It had settled something in him.

"I wouldn't say he's calmed," objected Devon. "Every time he has to leave you at the studio, he looks like he might spontaneously combust."

"She almost died; the guy got a scare," said Harper.

"We *all* got a scare." Devon squinted at Khloé. "Don't ever almost-die again."

"Why, did you cry?" asked Khloé.

The hellcat sniffed. "No."

"You lie, Pinocchio."

"God, that puppet was *such* a whiner," said Devon. "'*Poor me, poor me, I'm made of wood.*' A lot of women would be happy with a guy whose nose grew like that. We'd always know when he was lying, and it would make sitting on his face a *lot* more fun if he whispered some fibs at the same time."

Harper snickered. "Only you, Dev. Only you would think this shit. Ooh, here comes Teague."

Careful not to stand on the people who were sitting on the doorstep, he stepped onto the deck. A beer bottle in hand, the male shouldered his way through the Conga dancers and crossed the gravel pathway that cut through the lawn. He nodded at the other women and then smiled at Khloé. "Hey, gorgeous."

She returned his smile. "Hey, stallion."

He took a swig from his bottle. "What are you ladies talking about?"

"Naughty wooden boys," replied Devon, a twinkle in her eye.

The hellhorse frowned. "I don't know how to contribute to that conversation." He shifted his gaze to Khloé. "How's life at Keenan's lair treating you?"

"Fine," said Khloé. "Honestly, things don't feel much different than they did before."

"Probably because you didn't move out of your house. I like that Keenan didn't ask you to. It shows he knows what you need and, more importantly, *cares* what you need. As mates go, you could have done worse."

Khloé snorted. "Don't think I don't know that you like him." He and Keenan actually got along pretty well these days.

Teague shrugged. "He's not the world's worst guy. I am surprised he's left your side, although we both know he'll follow you out here in about, oh, two minutes." The hellhorse sipped his beer again. "Ciaran looks comfortable."

Khloé glanced at her brother, who'd passed out in the nearby hammock, cuddling a garden gnome. One minute he'd been talking to them. The next thing, he'd been snoring softly.

"I noticed he spent most of the night glaring at you," Teague added.

Khloé sighed. "He's still mad that I nearly died. Like it was my fault."

"It probably eats at him that his attempt to save you didn't work—you know how he is for taking on burdens that aren't his." Raini pushed off the swing. "I need to go pee."

"Me too," said Harper, standing. Her nose wrinkled. "I think my ass is wet. Oh, please tell me I didn't piss my pants."

"You have a wet patch on your butt," said Raini. "But I think it's from the grass. Don't quote me on that, though."

"You all coming back inside?" the sphinx asked.

"Sure thing, pissy pants." Devon stood. "I gotta get more gin."

Harper scowled. "It's not piss."

"It looks like piss," said Devon.

"*You* look like piss."

"How can a person possibly look like piss?"

The two women continued to argue as they made their way up the path—Raini played peacemaker, but it didn't work so well.

Teague helped Khloé off the slide. "I noticed there's still some tension between your incubus and Knox," he said quietly. "Keenan was so pissed at him that day we all thought you'd die—I don't know why, and I'm not asking. But, yeah, I really thought Keenan was going to try to take him out."

Khloé had heard as much from her twin. "He didn't speak to Knox for, like, two weeks. I asked why. He just said he felt that Knox could have done more to save me. I think Keenan just felt guilty for not getting to me earlier and he needed someone else to blame."

"I don't know. Your incubus doesn't seem like the kind of person who'd point the finger at someone else if he knew the guilt belonged to him."

True, but it was the explanation she gave to anyone who questioned her about it. Truly, she wasn't entirely sure why Keenan felt the Prime could have done "more," but she hadn't pushed him on it, sensing there were certain things the sentinels were forbidden to share with anyone—even their mates.

Khloé wasn't mad about it. She understood that some secrets just weren't his to share, and she liked that he had such integrity. His loyalty was still primarily to her, and that was what counted.

Besides, she'd be a damn hypocrite to whine at him for keeping secrets when she, too, was required to keep secrets from people she cared for and trusted. Not from Keenan, though—he knew all about little Asher and what he'd done to Lane. Of course, Harper and Knox had spun the story and claimed to others that *Enoch* had purged Lane of his powers—something people had bought, considering Lazarus demons specialized in death and destruction.

Harper and Knox had been shocked to hear how Asher and his demon had come to Khloé's aid. If she wasn't mistaken, it scared the couple that he was so powerful—especially since people would seek to destroy him while he was young and vulnerable if they considered him enough of a threat.

Understanding why they were so intent on protecting Asher's secrets, Khloé, Ciaran, and Jolene had consented to having the memories of what he'd done erased or adjusted. It hadn't worked on Khloé, though. Probably because it was difficult to manipulate the minds of those who specialized in mind control themselves.

Neither Knox nor Harper had panicked about that, though— they trusted that she'd *never* betray her little dude. They only worried that someone could pluck Asher's secrets from her brain.

At this point, Khloé was pretty sure the kid was *no* sphinx, but she hadn't asked for confirmation of that, just as she hadn't pushed to find out what breed of demon Knox was. There were some things a person was simply better off not knowing.

As for little Lane, Knox's Force had found and returned him to the Prime. Despite that his anger with Thea was still fresh, Keenan had ensured that Lane wouldn't pay for her sins and had placed the boy with a good foster family within their lair, refusing to put him in a home for demonic children.

Lane seemed to be doing as well as could be expected. His gifts hadn't returned, which meant that Asher truly had extinguished Lane's personal stock of power. And that was just damn frightening.

"Careful you don't trip," Teague said to her when her heel sank into the soil.

"Fuck off, Batman," Ciaran muttered, still sleeping.

"Should we wake him?" asked Teague.

She flapped a hand. "Nah, he's fine there."

"What about Beck? I don't know how someone can fall asleep in a sandbox, but it can't be a good thing."

"He'll be okay."

The tall, prickly grass brushed her ankles as they crossed the yard and headed inside. The scents of alcohol, perfume, pizza and other various foods hit her hard. She'd only taken two steps when she noticed Keenan edging his way through the traffic of people near the fridge. His expression softened when he spotted her, and she couldn't help but smile at that.

Stalking toward her, he exchanged a brief greeting with Teague, who then walked away and left them alone. Keenan pulled her close, his mouth twitching. "Are you blitzed?"

"Nope, I'm Khloé. You should know this already."

"Did you know that you have a piece of popcorn stuck to your forehead?"

She blinked. "It's still there? Wow."

He flicked it off and then pressed a kiss to her mouth. "You took too long to come back to me," he complained, tucking her hair behind her ear.

"I was gone for, like, ten minutes."

"You know I miss you when you're not with me."

She snorted. "What I know is that you like to have me in your sight at all times to reassure yourself that I'm fine."

"That, too." He raked his gaze over her, and his eyes grew heated. "Love this dress on you." *And the lacy bra I got a sneak peek at earlier,* he added telepathically. *Do your panties match?*

She lifted a brow. *What panties?*

He groaned. *Little witch.* He skimmed his fingertips over the none-too-subtle brand his demon had put on the side of her neck just last night.

"You like it, don't you?" she asked. "You like that everyone can see it?"

"Yeah, I do. It says that you're spoken for, and that's good. I can't have anyone thinking they can touch my property, can I?"

"Excuse me? Property?"

He chuckled and took her mouth before she could reprimand him, licking and consuming until she was pure goo in his arms. The sound of glass breaking had them both lifting their heads. A bottle of vodka had smashed on the floor. Liquid and fragments of glass were everywhere.

"Come on," said Keenan, tugging her out of the kitchen.

Bopping her head to the music, Khloé let him lead her into the dining room. Many stood around the buffet table, talking and munching on food. Others danced or sang along with Khloé's brother, Robbie, who was singing on the karaoke.

"He has a good voice," commented Larkin as she, Levi, and Knox sidled over.

"Koey!" yelled Asher, balanced on his father's hip.

"Hey, little dude." Khloé blew him a kiss and then smiled at her younger sister, Heidi, who was clinging to Larkin's back. "Having fun?"

"Uh-huh," said Heidi, beaming.

"I found her and some of the other kids jumping up and down on a passed-out imp like he was a damn trampoline," said Larkin. "Jolene rolled the guy under the buffet table. I don't know how he can sleep through all this noise."

"I have a question," Levi said to Khloé. "Why is that guy in the corner wearing a Predator suit?"

Khloé frowned. "You're assuming he needs a reason."

"Yeah, imps don't need reasons for the things they do," Larkin said to the reaper. "Haven't you learned that yet?"

Everyone clapped as Robbie's song came to an end. He took

a bow and then handed the mike to the DJ, almost tripping over the lights he'd wrapped around himself like he was a damn Christmas tree.

A tall figure stalked over and planted his hands on his hips, glaring at Heidi. "Give it back."

The little girl's nose wrinkled as she stared back at the Devil. "What?"

"My wallet," said Lucifer—or Lou, as he preferred to be called. "Give it back."

"I don't have it," Heidi told him.

"Do I look slow to you?"

"Yup."

Lou jerked back. "Well, that's not nice. You imps are all the same."

With her beautiful white-blonde hair and innocent features, the kid looked like butter wouldn't melt in her mouth. Oh, it would. She was a master at pickpocketing, could cry on cue, and was quite the plotter. In that sense, she was pretty much a miniature but perkier version of Jolene, who was currently heading their way.

Standing behind the devil, Jolene folded her arms. "Hello, Lou."

He jumped and mumbled something beneath his breath. Lou crossed his arms and lifted his chin, refusing to acknowledge her.

Sidling up to him, Jolene sighed. "You're sulking because I didn't invite you to the party, aren't you?"

He whirled on her. "Well, would it have *killed* you to give me a call and say, hey, come join us? Friends don't exclude each other like this."

"But we're not friends," Jolene pointed out.

"Don't pick at details." Lou looked at Khloé. "So, you almost died, huh? I heard all about it. Terrible, terrible business."

Harper snorted, appearing at Knox's side. "Like you care what happens to anyone but yourself."

"That's not fair. I care about Asher." Lou smiled at the kid. "And how is my little nephew?"

"Would you stop calling him that," snarked Harper.

"What else would I call him? Ooh, I could have some fun with this. How about . . . the future dark destroyer of all demon-kind? Admit it, it has a nice ring to it. I still think you should have called him Lucifer. He'd have *totally* rocked that name."

Harper sighed. "And I'm done."

Lou eyed Keenan. "So, you went and fell for a Wallis. Ah, such a tragedy. She will cause you only pain and misery, and she will relish every moment of it. In some ways, I can respect that." Lou cut his gaze to Knox. "And now you'll have not only an imp in your lair, but one of Jolene Wallis's granddaughters. Well, good luck with that."

"For someone who dislikes me so much, you sure do turn up at my house often," said Jolene.

Lou's brow creased. "I don't see the connection."

Jolene sighed. "Hmm."

Raini, Tanner, and Devon appeared, all holding fresh drinks. Just then, the song changed to Michael Jackson's "Thriller". Like that, the entire air in the room changed. And suddenly a large number of the guests backed up against the wall.

Keenan stared at them, trying to work out what the issue was. Then they started doing the "Thriller" dance, and he could only sigh.

"They're actually pretty good," said Levi.

"But it disturbs me that they must have practiced this," said Tanner. "I mean, why would you? These are grown-ass people."

Lou tossed him a frown. "No imp is a grown-ass person."

"Says the ultimate man-child," mumbled Jolene. "As for the 'Thriller' dance, it's often done at Martina's parties. I can't remember who started the tradition."

"I think it was Aunt Mildred," said Khloé.

Jolene pursed her lips. "It could have been—she was a wise but strange woman."

Keenan narrowed his eyes. "Wait, Aunt Mildred was a real person?"

"Oh, yes," said Jolene.

"She was *not*," insisted Devon.

Jolene tilted her head. "You don't remember her? She often wore odd shoes. Had a high-pitched laugh. Liked to sing the alphabet backwards. Used to make daisy chains and wrap them around the neck of her three-legged cat."

Devon's cheeks reddened. "You're both full of shit. No such woman ever existed."

Khloé shook her head. "I can't *believe* you don't remember her."

An hour later, Keenan slid an arm around his mate's waist and put his mouth to her ear. "You ready to go home now?" he asked.

"Can I play with sexcalibur when we get there?"

"If you mean my cock, yeah."

"Then let's go, Don Juan."

After they'd said their goodbyes to everyone, they headed out. As they made their way through the tight crowd in the hallway, Keenan stood in front of her, preventing her from being shoved or jostled. An imp was curled up asleep on the high pile of coats near the door. He was also cuddling a skillet.

"I'm not going to ask why he'd do that," said Keenan.

"Good, because I don't have an answer for you," she said.

A few partygoers had trickled out onto the front yard—most simply stood around talking. Others were lying on the grass, laughing and pointing at the sky. Two were brawling while surrounded by a crowd, which he quickly realized had placed bets on who would win.

Keenan led her down the street, passing the many cars that had been parked near Jolene's house. It wasn't long before they arrived at their own home. Stepping inside, he disarmed the alarm. He'd added all kinds of security measures to the place, needing to know she was as safe as possible.

He turned to her. "Dress off. I want to see if you really went without panties."

She gathered the bottom of her dress in her hands and began to ever so slowly drag the material up her thighs. But then she let it go. "You know, I think I'd like a shower first." She whirled and dashed up the stairs, chuckling.

Keenan instantly pursued her. He caught the crazy bitch on the landing, scooped her up, and then stalked into the bedroom. He crossed to the bed and lowered her to her feet. "Take the dress off or I rip it off."

"Okay, okay." An impish smile curving her mouth, she lowered the side zipper and then shimmied out of the dress. Standing there in only her bra and shoes, she said, "Told you."

Jesus, he was getting hard already. Keenan skimmed his fingers over the soft folds of her pussy. "Spread your legs a little. Good girl." He gently flicked her clit while staring at the pretty breasts spilling out of her lacy bra. "Let's see how long it takes for you to get wet."

He drove his fingers into her hair and took her mouth, absolutely ravenous for her. He consumed it. Ravished it. Claimed it for his own all over again.

The air ignited with heat and electricity. Need roared through him, wicked and primal. His body went tight. His head spun. His control began to fray.

He angled her head and thrust his tongue deeper, needing

more. She tasted of her and pink gin and everything he'd ever wanted. He hauled her against him and growled at the feel of her hard nipples stabbing his chest. If he wasn't balls-deep inside her soon, he was going to lose it.

His demon urged him to take her, possess her. It wanted to brand her again. Wanted her to feel so owned she'd never even consider leaving them.

Khloé thrust her fingers through his hair and dragged her nails over his scalp, loving his little growl. His talented tongue pretty much fucked her mouth. There was an intoxicating greed in his kiss that heated her blood and dragged her under his spell. Sexual endorphins swam through her as her body quite simply caught fire.

She pulled at his shirt and tore her mouth from his. "Off."

He reached behind him, fisted the back of his tee, and pulled it over his head, revealing that fabulous rock-hard chest and the tribal-looking brand that her demon had left on his right pectoral.

She smiled. "Rock on."

He shook his head, as if she was beyond help, and then slammed his mouth on hers again.

Even as he devoured her mouth, Khloé tackled his fly and fisted his shaft. It was full and long and hard. *Oh, yeah.* She pumped him with a firm grip while he thrust into her hand.

Her demon wanted to see his self-discipline crumble again. It loved that no other person had had the ability to make him hard against his will. Loved that only Khloé and her entity had ever seen him out of control.

Keenan snarled. "You keep pumping me like that and I'll come all over your hand." He peeled her fingers away from his dick. "Lie down for me."

She did as he asked and watched as he shoved down his jeans, exposing the perfect V of the hips and rock-hard thighs. His cock jerked and tapped his belly as his gaze drifted over her, hot and possessive. That territorial look went right to her damp core.

Keenan raked his gaze over his mate, drinking in her perky breasts, slender body, bald pussy, and the brands his demon put on her neck and navel. He parted her plump folds and almost groaned at all the slickness there. "Nice and wet." He curved his body over hers and rocked his hips, dragging his cock over her clit.

She gasped and gripped his shoulders. "Fuck me."

"Not yet." Filling his hands with her breasts, Keenan latched onto her nipple and suckled. She moaned and dug her nails into his skin. Alternating from one nipple to the other, he licked, sucked, and nipped them over and over; teased them into hard little buds.

She pulled on his hair. "I want you in me."

"I'll give you what you want." He slid down her body and dropped to his knees at the foot of the bed. "Eventually." He pulled her legs apart and nuzzled her glistening folds. "Love going down on you."

Khloé bucked and squirmed as he devastated her pussy with his lips, tongue, and teeth. He lapped, nipped, probed, and flicked her clit until flames of need danced over her skin.

Her body wound so tight it was a wonder her muscles weren't cramping, she arched and moaned and demanded more. Her pussy spasmed, ached to have him deep inside her. A powerful orgasm hovered close, but he was holding it back.

He dipped his tongue inside her pussy and swirled it around. "Ready to be fucked?"

"You know I am." She sucked in a breath as her orgasm crashed into her. Hot waves of pure pleasure tore through Khloé, making her back arch and her pussy contract. He didn't stop there, though. He kept on devastating her with his mouth, and she soon imploded again.

Standing upright, he grabbed her hips, yanked her closer, and hooked her legs over his shoulders. Oh my, this seemed promising. She fisted the bedsheet as he lodged the broad tip of his cock in her pussy.

He licked his glistening lips. "You won't come again until I'm ready for you to come." He slammed home in a rough, aggressive thrust that shocked a gasp out of her, forcing his way past swollen muscles. "Love that you take all of me."

Relishing the feel of her overstretched walls fluttering around him, Keenan reared back. He ground his teeth as her inner muscles tried sucking him back inside. Fuck if he didn't love the sight of his dick all wet and shiny with her slickness.

"Nothing I love better than being inside you." Keenan fucked in and out of her at a ruthless, unrelenting pace. Every thrust was deep, forceful, and savage, exactly how he knew she wanted it. "Your pussy looks even prettier when it has my cock buried inside it."

The sexual energy emanating from her assaulted his senses and filled his lungs. His demon greedily inhaled it, urging Keenan to take her order.

Keenan needed no such urging. He pounded into her, her moans and gasps spurring him on. He soaked in the carnal picture she made—the sex-drunk look in her eyes, the bounce of her breasts, the flush that had swept up her skin, the sight of her pussy stretched tight around his dick.

"Oh God, I need to come," she rasped as the walls of her pussy superheated around him. The sensation made his balls tighten and the base of his spine tingle. He wasn't going to last.

"So do I." Keenan dipped his thumb between her folds and rubbed her clit. "Come." A scream seemed to get trapped in her throat as her pleasure took her, making her back bow and her pussy clamp down on him.

Sheer bliss sizzled its way up Keenan's spine and acted like a lash of lightning to his dick. "*Fuck.*" Digging his fingertips into her thighs, he rammed his cock deep and exploded, spurting jet after jet of come inside her.

His chest burning for air, Keenan let her legs slip from his shoulders. He curved his body over hers and buried his face in her neck. She weakly stroked his back as they waited for the aftershocks to pass.

She let out a shaky breath. "Ever thought of making a living as a porn star?"

He frowned, hoping it wasn't a serious question. With Khloé, you never could tell. "No."

"Really? Because I'd buy the vids."

He lifted his head. "You'd happily watch me fuck other people?"

"Other guys, yeah, I could get behind that."

Unreal. "I'm going to forget we had this conversation."

"How could you ever forget such a conversation?"

"Maybe if you sucked me off and blew the sense right out of me, I wouldn't remember anything but my own name."

She pursed her lips. "I'm willing to try that. In the name of scientific experimentation."

"The world of science will indeed thank you for it." He braced himself on his elbows and smoothed the strands of hair away from her face. Her smoky gray eyes were still a little glazed over, her lips were swollen, and her cheeks were flushed. He loved that post-sex look. Loved that he was the only one who got to see it.

He dropped a kiss on her mouth. "Did you enjoy the party?"

"There was pink gin, food, and lots and lots of shots. What's not to like?"

"Hmm." He left a trail of kisses down her throat and raked

his teeth over her pulse.

And he remembered a time when that pulse had been slow and weak.

Feeling tension bunch each of his muscles, Khloé gave his shoulder a light slap. "Stop thinking about what happened. It's over now. I'm fine."

He brushed his nose against hers. "It's not so easy to forget the sight of you near death's door. If it wasn't for Maddox . . ."

"You know, I'm so grateful for what Raini did for me, but I worry that she agreed to something bad." The succubus had sworn she hadn't, and she'd seemed utterly genuine. But Khloé was still worried.

"I don't think it was something bad. I think it was just something she wouldn't have otherwise agreed to. It could be small and simple, or it could be big and substantial. Either way, it doesn't seem to be stressing her out. She's her usual self."

"True." Khloé licked her lips. "He's just so powerful, Keenan. I felt it." Powerful enough to cause a lot of harm.

"He'd never hurt Raini."

"You can be so positive of that?"

"Would you ever hurt Teague?"

"Never. But I accept him as my anchor. I formed the bond with him." She hoped that Keenan might one day find his own anchor. Until then, she'd do her best to keep his demon on its best behavior.

"Just because Maddox hasn't embraced the bond doesn't mean he wants nothing to do with Raini or that she won't matter to him," said Keenan. "I am surprised he didn't capitalize on the situation by demanding that either me or Jolene agrees to owe him a favor in exchange for healing you."

"Going by how strong and lethal he is, I really don't think he needs favors from other people, no matter what he might say."

Khloé lifted her hand to scratch at a spot just behind her ear. He caught her hand in his and stared at the black diamond ring he'd given her. "No regrets?" she asked.

"Only that we spent so long dancing around each other. The best decision I ever made was to stop that shit and take a chance." He dabbed a kiss on her mouth. "I love you."

"And I love you."

"Never stop."

"I couldn't even if I wanted to."

"Same here. But I'll never want to stop. My world would be a dark place without you. I know that, because I felt it creeping up on me when you were dying right in front of me. I got a taste of what my life would be like if you weren't in it. Empty. Meaningless. Lonely." Just thinking about it made Keenan's stomach harden. "Don't ever make me go there again."

"I can't promise I'll live forever—no one can promise that. But I'd never leave you on purpose."

"I wouldn't let you. I claimed you, and I'm keeping you."

"But not in, like, a dungeon or anything, right?"

He frowned. "Why would I ever keep you in a dungeon?"

"Why would you ever deny you have a mammoth-size cock?"

Keenan ground his teeth. God, she was off her fucking rocker.

She snickered. "Your blood pressure just shot up, didn't it? Will it improve your mood if we play Park the Porpoise again?"

"Park the Porpoise?"

"You know . . . getting a hole in one, having a hot beef injection, burying the sausage, parting the red sea, going to the boneyard, mining with the meat shaft—"

"Enough, enough." He sighed and looked up at the wall. "So this will be my life."

"You're excited, I can tell."

His mouth hitched up. The thing was . . . she was right.

ACKNOWLEDGEMENTS

I want to thank the usual suspects—my family for being so supportive and encouraging; my assistant Melissa for being the best right-hand woman ever; everyone at Piatkus for taking a chance on this series and working so hard to get the book published without too much of a delay; all those who gave *Omens* a whirl, especially the readers who clicked "pre-order" when the book didn't even have a blurb—it's humbling for a writer to know there are people who are so sure they'll enjoy what you've written that they'll auto-click on an upcoming release. Thank you all!

Do you love fiction with a supernatural twist?

Want the chance to hear news about your favourite
authors (and the chance to win free books)?

Keri Arthur
Kristen Callihan
P.C. Cast
Hailey Edwards
Christine Feehan
Larissa Ione
Darynda Jones
Sherrilyn Kenyon
Jayne Ann Krentz
Martin Millar
Tim O'Rourke
Lindsey Piper
Christopher Rice
J. R. Ward
Suzanne Wright

Then visit the Piatkus website
www.yourswithlove.co.uk

And follow us on Facebook and Instagram
www.facebook.com/yourswithlovex | @yourswithlovex

PIATKUS